Take You Away

by

Kira Hillins

Take You Away

Cover Art by *Kristian Norris*

The Wild Rose Press, Inc.
PO Box 708
Adams Basin, NY 14410-0708
Visit us at www.thewildrosepress.com

Publishing History:
Previously published by Loose Id, 2015
First Champagne Rose Edition, 2020
Print ISBN 978-1-5092-2929-1
Digital ISBN 978-1-5092-2952-9

Published in the United States of America

Ben stood at the stove, his midnight strands stuck up in tufts. He dipped the spatula in the pan and flipped over a large pancake with purple speckles. The man was sexy in relaxed jeans, and a dark T-shirt that hugged his upper body.

"Aww…You're making blueberry pancakes."

"Your favorite." Half grin. Right brow arched. She could melt like the butter on the hotcakes.

She leaned back against the counter. "Thought you didn't like pancakes."

"I'm an egg-and-meat kind of guy. But every once in a while I'll crave something sweet." He handed her a plate. His other brow arched. "I must say, you look especially beautiful in yellow."

"Oh. Thanks." She sat at the table and admired the single red rose he'd set out as a centerpiece.

"I picked it for you this morning." He sat beside her. "I hope you're not allergic."

Warmth flooded her face. He'd picked her a flower. No man had ever given her flowers. Except Renji who bought her a bouquet to spruce up her kitchen or the bakery every so often. But Ben had gone out and picked one. Could there be anything more romantic?

"I'm not allergic to flowers."

"Are you sure?" He took a bite of his pancakes. "Your face is the same shade as the rose."

Praise for Kira Hillins

"A suspenseful thriller all wrapped up in real world romance."

~Kimberly Adkins

~*~

"This was a great book that provided me with all the twists and turns that a girl could ask for in a book. The author knows what she is doing when writing her characters and giving them a real life feel. I was able to relate to these characters, enjoy the good times, yell in the bad, and cry at the worst time…the author did a great job navigating the subject matter and bringing it to the light in a respectful way."

~Exquisite Reviews

~*~

"I really enjoyed this story. The characters had a great chemistry and the story flowed with a great speed. I loved the events that happened along the way and the suspense gripped your attention to want to know what happens next. Very well written."

~LLEP Book Blog

Dedication

To all women who have
walked through hell and found salvation,
and to those who are suffering now.
Stay strong.
Be courageous.
Fight back.

Chapter One

Of all days to invade this sector of the world, *they* chose her birthday.

Darned aliens messed up Sonya's plans to sit atop her brand-new lighthouse and flirt with Soljer. It took weeks to work up the courage to ask him to couple. Now with *them* descending from the sky, she wouldn't get the chance.

Zoe Kearny tightened her grip on the Xbox controller. She breathed in deep through her nose, puckered her lips, and then exhaled slowly. No need to get angry. Couldn't stop an inevitable war to celebrate a day *they* had no use for. Preventing aliens from taking over the world was, after all, part of the video game.

"Why now?" she whispered into her headset.

Ben chuckled. "Of all days to attack, huh?"

No doubt about it, great minds thought alike. Or at least, similar minds wishing they weren't spending their days five hundred miles apart.

Zoe focused on the picture on the bottom right corner of her TV screen. Yummy Benjamin Jeremiah Solmer was Soljer in games and in the band he played guitar on weekends. Everyone called him Ben.

Ben was her rock—a cool rock with deep green eyes and bangs sticking up in tufts. Enviable lashes matched short midnight hair perfectly groomed around the sexiest ears she'd ever seen.

The man was hot—melt-to-the-floor kind of hot. So hot she often wondered why he spent his spare time playing video games with her, a woman he'd never met before, when he could be with anyone he wanted.

"Want me to make quick work of this?" he asked.

"No, I got this."

As tempting as it was to let him take over the fight, this was her moment to show off. She was so much better at this game than when they'd met outside the training grounds.

He'd invited her to his chat session two Christmases ago to scold her for carelessly, albeit accidentally, setting his virtual house on fire. She'd cried. He apologized for being a jerk and then invited her to be his acolyte.

"Just don't burn down your lighthouse with a rogue fireball."

She scoffed. "You'll never let me forget that. Will you?"

"Never. It wasn't just my house you burned down. The entire village went up in flames. I had to deal with a lot of pissed-off gamers that day."

"Ah. Poor homeless gamers. You really are a hero."

"Was that sarcasm?" He snickered. "It took two days to reconstruct twenty-five houses and relocate them to another town. Including my own house."

"Five more levels, then I can move there too. I think I'll buy the house next door to yours."

He cleared his throat. "The community's already banned you from the town."

"Are you serious?" She rolled her eyes. "I haven't set anything on fire in months. It'll probably be another year until I'm ready to move anyways. By then, I should be a high level priestess. If I live through this."

Fireballs she could handle. Her problem was taking on too many aliens at a time. Too often she found herself staring up into a pixilated blue sky that turned gray as she died. Dying made for slow character leveling.

"I won't let you die," he said. "But it should be easy for you to take them out wearing the new robe I gave you."

With *+50 willpower*, *+35 endurance*, and *+15 fire magic*, it was the best robe in the game at this level. The dark green garment went well with Sonya's long blonde hair and huge green eyes. Golden streaks woven into the skirt and along the low-cut neckline sparkled in the sun.

If Sonya wore a tiara, she'd look like a queen instead of a fire sorceress. If the dress was pink and this was a fantasy game with dragons and castles and a handsome prince to kiss, then maybe she'd be a princess instead. Defeating aliens, battling to save the world with a big-boobed cartoony character—this was sci-fi meets fantasy at its best.

"I hope you're right," she muttered.

"You'll be fine. I'm right here if you need me."

Zoe screamed inside. *Stupid aliens.* Birthday confessions ruined, Soljer's creator would remain oblivious to how she really felt. Today anyway. No cuddling or coupling would commence. The only fun she'd have was stopping the bad guys from taking over their virtual world.

Clear bubble-shaped spaceships landed on white sands along the endless coastline. Some hovered over the azure sea. Others slowly descended to the car-lined parking lots. Fifteen ships and counting. Twenty by the time they stopped appearing in the blue sky. Red skulls with blinking eyes rotated around each ship, adding a nice touch to the battle theme.

Purple blobs with long, gangling limbs and sharp, pointy teeth emerged from the crafts. Zoe puckered her nose. Disgusting creatures. Oddly cute. She'd keep one as a virtual pet if they were nice, but they were evil, destructive monsters that left trails of purple goo in their wake.

The aliens demolished the lifeguard station on the beach, the kiddie pool near the bathrooms, and the bathrooms too. They'd leveled the ice-cream stand to the ground, which meant no more cotton-candy cones during the summer. When the little monsters headed for the lighthouse, the beloved place she'd bought last week with all her in-game money, Zoe moved Sonya in position.

"Here they come," she sang.

She held down the B button. A giant orange fireball appeared between Sonya's palms. Zoe released the button, sending the ball hurling across the sand. The first wave of aliens charred like purple marshmallows over a bonfire.

"Burn, baby, burn." She released smaller but faster flaming balls. Wicked laughter spilled from Zoe's open mouth as the plum bodies blazed.

They were no match for her kick-ass sorceress. Two more big attacks and she'd rule the beach. Birthday saved. Maybe there was time for coupling after all.

Zoe shoved her thumb down on the B button again.

Nothing happened. She tapped the button faster. The flames wouldn't come. Her gaze slunk to the empty magic meter on the side of the screen.

"Darn it."

"Use a potion," Ben suggested calmly.

"I don't have any more potions."

"What happened to the vials I gave you last weekend?"

She cringed. Drinking a magic-renewal potion created a pretty blue aura around the user. She hadn't the nerve to tell him she'd used them just to watch Sonya glow.

Soljer's tall, muscular frame stepped forward, long black hair waving in the breeze. An arsenal of weapons hung on his back and at his side beneath a dark brown gunslinger's jacket. He was so badass, all decked out in the highest-level legendary gear. Way overpowered for this battle.

"I'll take care of them."

Zoe moved Sonya between Soljer and the approaching aliens. "There's only a few more, babe. I can still do this."

"You don't have any magic left."

"Maybe I can beat them to death with my glowy-stick."

Ben laughed. "You're the only one I know who can make *glowy-stick* sound cute."

If he were sitting beside her now, she was sure he'd see her cheeks turn the same color as her pink pajamas. "Just be quiet. I'm concentrating."

Lips pursed, frazzled, Zoe backed Sonya up the sandy beach toward the lighthouse. Scary aliens followed, laughing, taunting, knowing she'd run out of the good stuff. Her tall, crooked wooden stick with a glowing green ball near the top wouldn't be strong enough to beat them down. But dang it, she'd give it a try.

"Wait a sec," Ben said, raising his voice. "Did you call me *babe*?"

Zoe lifted her hand to her mouth and gasped. With her finger off the trigger, she couldn't block the hopping purple globs. One leaped onto the hem of Sonya's new robe. Another jumped on her arm. If she didn't do something now, her character would lose her clothes and dignity at best. She'd die a horrific, blood-draining death, and then have to run a million miles back to resurrect her naked body.

"Okay, help me." She swallowed hard as Sonya's life meter inched downward. "I'm dying here." *In more ways than one.*

Lump in her throat, she watched her rock coolly unsheathe his gun and sword. *Boom Boom!* The blobs on Sonya's body fell dead to the ground. *Slash!* Purple blood splattered over the sand at her feet. Ten of them gone in seconds, and he hadn't even suffered a scratch.

He was good—too good to be hanging with an epic failure such as her. Even with the pretty new half-eaten robe, she wasn't worthy.

"Thanks, Ben," Zoe sighed.

"Say it, Zoe."

"Thanks, Ben...*Soljer*. Okay, I'll say it. I suck at this game."

"You called me *babe*."

She slapped her forehead. Great. He'd always remember her setting his house on fire. Now he'd never let her live this one down. She didn't mind. It'd been a long time since she was comfortable enough to use a pet name on a guy she liked.

Her stomach growled. She glanced at the clock. 8:30 p.m. Way past dinner time. Time always slipped by so fast when she hung out with Ben. Voicing with him was the highlight of her day, even when he gave her a hard time—especially when he gave her a hard time.

She rose from the couch and headed for the kitchen, controller in hand. "Well, you must have heard me wrong."

"Oh, I didn't hear you wrong."

She stuck a frozen dinner in the microwave. "Heat of the moment?"

"Unlikely."

She punched in two minutes on the timer then pressed start. "Okay, I said it. Did I offend you?"

"You can call me babe anytime you like…*honey*."

Twenty-seven years old today and she laughed like a schoolgirl with a crush. Maybe her birthday wasn't ruined after all.

"*Honey* is a bit old-fashioned, isn't it?"

His deep *hmm* sent a wonderful chill through her body. "I'll call you pumpkin, then."

"I'm flattered." Her face warmed. This talk was way better than playing the game. "Pumpkins are edible in anything," her voice wavered as she continued. "Muffins, breads, soups. Pumpkin pie is tasty."

"Do you taste like pumpkin pie?"

Not knowing how to respond, she swallowed hard. Elbows on the counter, chin against her fists, she watched the numbers count down on the microwave.

"Zoe, did I lose you?"

"Sorry, did you say something? The microwave's blaring loud tonight." She pursed her lips. Such a golden opportunity to flirt with him, and she'd chickened out. *Chicken.*

"What meal are you making for dinner tonight?"

"Lasagna."

"My favorite."

"Mine too."

Thunder growled in the distance. Rain pelted the side of the apartment. These were the woes of living on the end unit. Goosebumps crawled over her skin at the thought of a tornado passing through, or worse, the electricity going out. She hated being alone in the dark.

The microwave beeped. The bamboo chimes hanging from the patio rafters out back chattered as if they'd blow away at any moment. Lightning flashed. Thunder shook the walls. The glassware in the kitchen cabinets rattled.

Zoe shuddered as she lifted her long golden strands off her shoulders. She tied them back with her favorite white tie. She pulled the plastic back from the tray of lasagna, then closed her eyes and breathed in. Sweet basil and tomato sauce.

She set her meal down on the coffee table in her tiny cream-colored living room. Her corduroy love seat wouldn't win awards for the prettiest chair in the world, but it was comfy. Sinking down in the cushions was the best feeling in the world, besides eating a hot meal and talking to Ben.

The lights flickered. Another crack of thunder jangled knickknacks on the shelf beside the front window. She stuck a forkful of noodles in her mouth and watched Sonya stand beside Soljer on the TV

8

screen. If the electricity went out, she was going to be livid.

"Hey, Zoe?"

Her skin tingled. The way he'd said her name, it sounded like he had something important to ask. She hoped this would be the big question, the one she'd waited over a year for, the one where they'd meet for real in a coffee shop, fall desperately in love, get married, and live happily ever after.

Her heart beat a mile a second. "Yes, Ben?"

"I need to head out to the gig."

Blah. Not what she wanted to hear.

It was Friday night. Bars hopped with hot women in skimpy dresses. Gorgeous guitar man Ben could have any woman he wanted. All he had to do was point, and they'd be on him like leeches in a Louisiana swamp. The image ruined the whole *pumpkin-babe* flirt.

Ben had a life in Denver, an exciting, busy life. He probably had a girlfriend or ten, ruining the happily-ever-after thought and making her feel like the dead alien lying in the sand at Sonya's feet.

****

Ben searched his room for his wallet. He'd be late if he didn't wrap up the session. As much as he loved being an active musician, he hated missing another game night with Zoe.

Never one for posting selfies, he'd given Zoe one at her request. She'd complained about the slight blur. The picture was six years old and mostly showed the side of his head. The past six months she'd badgered him to send her a new photo. He'd finally caved in and turned his smartphone's camera on himself.

"I sent you a new photo this morning," he said, finding his wallet in the tan cargo pants he'd worn to work today. He stuffed it in the back pocket of his jeans, and then turned his attention to Zoe's picture on the bottom right-hand corner of his TV screen.

Zoe was a breath of fresh air, an angel compared to the vampires at the bar. Long blonde hair curved around her face. Loose curls hung past her shoulders to her elbows. Bright blue eyes. Perfect smile. She was without a doubt the most beautiful woman he'd ever seen.

Her profile pic was a kick in the pants. She'd posed with a plate of chocolate-chip cookies at a middle-school bake sale. The kids had pinned a ribbon to the collar of her pink button-up shirt for winning best-tasting cookie.

Meeting Zoe in person had zipped to the top of his bucket list. Even if his roommate Sheron had told him to *"get it through his thick skull"* Zoe wasn't the right one.

"Zoe's an innocent bakery manager from a one-horse town," she'd said. *"You're a tortured, guilt-laden city boy who rarely smiles."*

Maybe Sheron was right. His brother's motorcycle accident was his fault. Guilt hung over him like a rain cloud. He shouldn't pursue more than a passing fling, but he couldn't get Zoe out of his head. She made life worth living again.

To think he could get seriously caught up in her scared the hell out of him. He didn't want to admit it, but he kind of already had.

"Make sure your picture's clear this time," Zoe said in her soft, angelic voice.

He chuckled. "I promise, pumpkin."

"Where will I find it?"

"It's the birthday present at the top of the lighthouse. I'd planned on springing it on you late tonight after we talked about…something I've been meaning to talk to you about, but I don't know when I'll be home. We'll have to chat about it later. I'll shoot you a text if I catch a break tonight."

Sheron stood in his bedroom doorway in a tight leather dress, impatiently waiting for him to finish the call. By the way she dug the sharp end of her heeled shoe into the short Berber carpet, she was eager to leave for the bar.

Relentless woman. She was like an evil possessive older sister with horns on her head and a tail to smite him down whenever he got out of line. If she hadn't been married to his late brother, Chase, he would've already kicked her out of his house.

"End the session with doughnut girl," Sheron said.

He covered the microphone with his hand. "Get out of my room, Hateful."

Sheron flipped her long black hair over her petite tanned shoulders. "Jackass."

"Devil woman."

She batted her long lashes once. "Baker's man." One side of her lilac-colored lips curved upward.

"Dammit, Sheron." Ben pursed his lips. "I'll be there in a minute."

"Hope your gig goes well tonight." The sulk worked back into Zoe's voice.

He removed his hand from the microphone, and then sighed. "I'll make it up to you later, okay?"

"Okay."

"Happy birthday, Zoe," he said and then took off his headset.

He ran his fingers through his hair as Zoe's picture disappeared from the TV screen. Would've been a perfect night to ask her if she wanted to meet and pursue some sort of...relationship-type thing if their meeting worked out. Not sure how it'd work since she lived five hundred miles away, but he was ambitious.

Chapter Two

Soljer's wrath lay in purple globs all over the sand. Wouldn't be much longer until the alien bodies disappeared, leaving no more traces of this tragic battle.

Zoe directed Sonya up the winding ladder to the top of the lighthouse. Near the turning light floated a sparkling heart-shaped box with a giant pink bow.

She hesitated. Did she really want to see a picture of someone she couldn't have? She already liked this guy well enough, but it didn't matter. He lived too far away. To fall head over heels for this guy would be disheartening.

She set the controller down on the coffee table next to her unfinished lasagna and leaned back on the couch. The clock on the wall near the stairs read 9:06 p.m. The lids of her eyes drooped as rain pounded the side of the apartment.

"Please, don't storm," she whispered.

Her cell phone rang. She glanced at the name on the screen. *Nicholas Johnson.* An icy claw crept up and down her spine. The creep had called every day and texted several times to let her know the two years he'd spent in prison had rehabilitated him. He wanted to make amends for all the horrifying things he'd done to her, but she'd never forgive him. She'd never respond. The only thing she could do was block his number. Somehow, he always found a way to get through.

Maybe it was time to change her number again.

She'd promised herself she wouldn't let him frighten her. She couldn't, or she would never move on with someone new, someone worthy and sweet. Like Ben.

She picked up the controller and clicked on the box. The photo twirled around. The moment the gorgeous man stopped in the center of the screen, everything in the apartment shut down.

"No." She darted from the couch. "Not now."

Her bare feet slapped against the cool floor on her way through the kitchen. She grabbed the short flashlight and emergency candles from the top drawer beside the refrigerator. With shaky hands, she picked up her dad's old silver smoking lighter, and then hurried through the dark to the kitchen table.

Lightning flashed. Thunder clapped. Her heart thumped harder against her ribs. The kitchen was one big shadow. Someone could easily be hiding in the corner of the room, ready to attack.

Her hands shook as she flipped the switch on the side of the flashlight, illuminating the kitchen with dim yellow light. A breath passed her trembling lips. *Thank God.* There was nobody in the room but her.

She set the three blue candles on the counter, and then lit each one with the silver lighter. She hated the dark. She hated storms like this, when the roar of the wind outside sounded like a train barreling down the tracks. It was perfect weather for a tornado. It reminded her of the stormy night the police dragged Nicholas off to jail.

The doorbell chimed. She swiftly descended the steps to the tiny foyer and peeked out the peephole in the door. She smiled as she twisted the old dead bolt, and the new one she'd had installed last week. She unfastened the chain, slid the bar into the latch, unlocked the handle, and then opened the door wide.

Renji Tanaka, best friend of twenty years and baker at the bakery she managed down the street, stood before her with an LED lantern in hand. He was also her neighbor who always checked in on her during storms, especially when the lights went out.

"Hey, birthday girl." He raked his fingers through his wet brown hair as he entered the apartment. "Brought a deck of cards if you're interested."

Zoe closed the door behind him, locked the dead bolts then hugged him tight. "I'm so glad you're here." She stepped back and drew in a deep, calming breath. "But what if I'd been asleep?"

"During a storm like this?" He kicked off his loafers and parked them along the wall beside her boots. "Nah. Zoe Kearny doesn't sleep on Friday nights anyways. Not when she has *Coastal Universe*. I don't understand why you play. Games kill brain cells and makes people fat."

"I'm not fat. And even if I was, I'd still play. Not everyone's an outdoorsman fitness junkie who loves to hike and camp."

"I'm not a junkie." He followed her to the kitchen and set the lantern on the table. "I sit every once in a while too."

"When you're fishing on the reservoir." She offered him a seat at the breakfast bar. "I figured you'd be out with your new girlfriend."

"That chic was crazy." He took off his coat and draped it over the back of the bar stool. His tousled dark hair was wet below his ears. His bangs mingled with muddy-brown eyes that glistened in the candlelight. "She was obsessed with me. Kept telling me I looked just like the character in her favorite Japanese anime. '*Tall, Asian, and gorgeous*,' she'd said."

Zoe laughed. "A girl knows when she's lucky and doesn't want to let go."

"It's true. I am a very hot guy." His grin twisted and his eyes widened. "But, she made a plushy of me. I like weird women, but she was just too much for me."

"Aw. I think it's sweet." *For a young adult.* But Renji's new ex was thirty-six. He'd always liked women who were older than him. Preference maybe. He'd always said more experience meant better sex. "You broke her heart. I bet she's in bed crying and hugging her toy, the poor thing."

"Says the woman who spends all her time playing video games with some guy she's never met."

Ignoring his tease, she folded her arms across the table and groaned. The photo on the screen had been crystal clear, but she'd only caught a glimpse of him. Short midnight hair and pale skin. Had she seen emerald eyes, or were they the same faded color from the older picture?

She had seen an amazing smile. But why did it matter? They were online friends playing a silly video game. They'd never meet in real life when he had hot girls hanging on him at the bars.

Renji patted her arm. "What's wrong?"

"I was in the middle of something when the electricity went off."

"Was Sonya having sex with an alien?"

"Yuck no." She scoffed. "Characters can't have sex

with aliens, only with other characters."

"Discrimination."

"No, it's not." He always teased to get her flustered. Worked every time, especially when he harped on her about playing a mature video game in which players had sex with each other. In game it was called *coupling* or *popping the virtual cherry* for first-timers like her. She'd wanted Soljer to be the one to pop her cherry.

"You lead an unhealthy life, Zo'. Your blood isn't flowing as well as it should be. It makes your brain all crazy-like." Renji pulled a deck of cards from his coat pocket. "You sit here in your lonely little apartment tapping buttons all night when there's a real world outside to explore."

"I'm not ready to explore the real world yet." She shrugged. "And I don't need a lecture from you. Keep your nose out of my business, or…you're fired."

The corners of his lips rose as he shuffled the cards. He dealt one card face up, one card down. Her face card showed a five of diamonds; his, the king of hearts.

"You need a break." He peeked under his hidden card. "How about you and I go see a movie this weekend?"

She studied her hand. A five and a hidden two were terrible cards. "I need another card."

He turned his card over to reveal the ace of spades. "I've already won."

"Luck," she muttered through a roll of thunder.

"I cheated."

"Ha. Figures."

"Shall we make a friendly wager on our next

round?"

In their history together, they'd made millions of bets. She'd lost ninety-five percent of them. Most of their bets were kind of fun, but she'd paid a good amount of settlements doing dishes at the bakery.

"What kind of bet?"

"If I win this next hand, you go out with me on a date. A real one."

She wrinkled her nose. They'd tried dating once when they were freshmen in high school. After several weeks of movies, holding hands, and sharing a few innocent but awkward kisses, the relationship fizzled.

The decision to break up was a mutual one, but it also came with a pact. If they were both unmarried by her thirtieth birthday, they'd tie the knot and have a ton of children. It was a silly bet she wouldn't hold up until she turned at least forty.

"We are not going on a real date."

"Come on, Zoe. I'm good for you. I am a faithful guy, you know."

"Have you forgotten about Amber, and the night your girlfriend caught you and her in her father's barn...naked?"

"Amber was just...curious how big my muscles were."

"And why wasn't *she* wearing clothes?"

He shrugged. "She's a kickboxer. I wanted to see her muscles too. Anyway, I never cheated on Patty. She and I had broken up a few days before I got naked with Amber."

"So you've sworn all along," Zoe said with a laugh. "Okay, cheater, what do I get if I win?"

"I'll cook dinner for you every night for a week if

you win." He leaned back in the chair, hands behind his head. "If I win, you go on a romantic date with me."

"Romantic now?" She rolled her eyes. A night holding hands with Renji would happen never.

The lights turned on. Zoe tossed her fist upward. *Yes.* Eager to get Ben's picture on the TV screen, she slid off the stool and went straight to the living room.

"Come on. What do you have to lose?"

"My best friend." She picked up the controller. "Dating will ruin our friendship."

"Yeah, I know. All joking aside, we're both single and at an age to bear lots of children. With our looks, can you imagine how gorgeous our offspring will be?"

"Seriously?" She pressed the X button on the controller. The console whirred to life. Happy to see the Power button glow, she went back to the kitchen. "The first pretty girl with muscles to come along, you'll be in the buff in the barn."

"You'll never let me live it down," he said with a sigh. "Deciding hand, Zoe. Bet or no, check your cards."

She picked up her hand. Jack of hearts and queen of diamonds stared back. She could taste the home-cooked meals now. Teriyaki Chicken Monday. Lasagna Tuesday. Beef Stroganoff Wednesday. What other hearty meals could she dream up?

"I'll stay," she said, holding her cards together in one hand.

He drew a five card from the deck and placed it beside his ten. A grin crept across his face as he held the second card up before him. Eyes on her, he stood upright.

"Tomorrow is a good day for an outing."

"No way."

Renji tossed the six of spades down on the table.

"You cheated, didn't you?"

"Fair and square," he replied. "Let me take you to Wichita. We'll have dinner at a fancy restaurant. We can catch a movie. Maybe stroll leisurely in the park like we used to."

She shuddered. Nicholas lived in Wichita. Hell, no was she going there for anything. "Not a good idea."

"Well, fine," he grumbled. "Dinner here and a movie rental like usual?"

It wouldn't be a big deal since he occasionally came over and cooked anyway. Ben had his Saturday-night gig. Microwave meals were getting rather tedious. Even the lasagna was getting boring.

"You cook and rent the movie."

"Yes, ma'am." He gave a short nod. "I suppose I'll head home." He shoved his arms through the sleeves of his coat. "I'll see you in the morning."

She followed him down the stairs. He slipped on his loafers and then opened the front door. The refreshing breeze blowing into the apartment brought a widespread grin across his face.

"Hey, Renji."

He caught her gaze. "Yeah?"

She placed her hand on his arm. "Thanks for coming to check on me."

"Always will, Zoe," he said with a wink. "Sleep well."

"You too."

As he strode down the sidewalk, thunder rumbled in the distance. Thank God no tornado warning sirens went off this time. She so disliked cramming herself in the one underground basement with a crowd of worried tenants.

She locked the door and then hurried to the couch. Sonya stood before the heart. Zoe pressed the A button. The box opened. The photo whirled around and stopped dead center on the screen.

Oh my. There he stood, crystal clear with a brilliant smile on his handsome face. Deep green eyes penetrated her soul. A black T-shirt hugged his tall, toned upper body. He folded his arms across his chest, pale biceps rounded below the hems of his shirt's short sleeves. The stance showed off a tattoo of a gun-toting soldier on his forearm.

Zoe's heart skipped. She was sure this man made beautiful girls fall to their knees and worship the ground he walked on. The kind of man no woman should ever call *babe* in light conversation. He probably had model girlfriends. A lot of them. A player in all aspects of the word meant she'd never meet him and have anything real.

Chapter Three

With the exception of Sundays, and some holidays, Renji knocked on Zoe's door every morning at 4:30 a.m. They walked together to the bakery then went their separate ways to prepare for the day. While dough rose in the giant steel bowl on the west side of the kitchen, Renji started on doughnuts he'd prepared the previous night. Zoe tallied up sales from the day before then took inventory until seven. The rest of the morning was spent tending to customers and cleaning shop until Millie Saunders came in at the usual time of one p.m.

Millie had three rambunctious sons who took all-year-round sports trips, and an outgoing ex-minor-league baseball-player husband. With so much going on with her family, she still had time for a part-time job at the bakery and the house visits she made for makeup and hair products sales with the elderly ladies in their community.

The woman was pulled from one person to another, one job to the next, and still dazzled like a million bucks. Long sleek black hair, big brown cat eyes, and a body that would make a young fitness guru jealous, Millie was a superwoman. She also had a gift to decorate the ugliest thing in the world with frosting and make it look edible.

Millie wrote on the specialty cake the preacher from Main Street Baptist church ordered a week ago.

PS I love you were the words he wanted to add on his wife's birthday cake. Millie, genius cake decorator, somehow managed to fit it in with brilliant gold letters below *Happy Birthday.*

Millie wiped her hands on the dish towel then picked up the yellow tube of frosting. "I hear Renji has special plans for you tonight."

Zoe shrugged as Millie drew tiny flowers around the top layer of the cake. "He's coming over to cook dinner and watch a movie. We do it all the time."

Millie placed the tube on the counter then stepped back. "I think it's great you're taking interest in something else besides video games." She winked her left eye. "Renji's beefy."

"Millie," Zoe whispered. "For the millionth time, I'm not romantically interested in him."

"The man's been head over heels in love with you since you were kids. Isn't it about time you gave him another try?"

Renji was mighty beefy. Huge muscles bulged beneath his short-sleeved baker's shirt. Gorgeous tanned skin was like silk to the touch. He'd make a good cop, especially since he enjoyed going out on patrols with Deputy Fred from the police department. Renji always said he'd rather lend a hand than sit in the boonies all day in a squad car waiting for someone to speed by, which rarely happened.

A blonde woman in a bright yellow coat walked through the door to the counter where Renji stood. She had flirt in her big blue eyes as she pointed at the blueberry doughnuts in the case. She laughed at something Renji said. Knowing him, it was probably some cheesy joke to impress her.

"Who is she?" Zoe asked.

Millie stole a glance at the woman. "Drema Holetzer. She's the owner of the new sports bar going in across from the church. Moved here from South Dakota a few weeks ago. I hear she's hiring a bartender."

"Well, I hope she's not trying to steal Renji."

"Renji wouldn't dare." Millie shrugged. "Anyway, she's supposed to be at church tomorrow. But I wouldn't think a woman of her nature would be so…*holy*."

"What do you mean?"

"Apparently, she started a big uproar in the last town. The waitresses were call girls, and most of the clients were married men." Millie giggled. "She's not going to find any waitresses here when ninety percent of our population is over fifty. Can you imagine old Gertrude Holly in nipple tassels, swinging her droopy boobs around?"

Zoe laughed. Renji tossed her a glance. Drema waved goodbye to Renji then left the building.

Renji meandered Zoe's way, brows shifted upward. "Ready for a home-cooked meal tonight, my darling?" He stopped at the steel counter and inspected the purple dots Millie made in the center of the cake's flowers.

"Yes." Zoe sighed. Here he went on his rant about them falling in love and having kids. He did it all the time to pester her. All in good fun on his part. It drove her crazy when he did it in front of Millie who rooted for it to happen. "Did you rent the movie?"

"I rented *The Notebook*—the perfect date-night movie."

"This isn't a date."

"Yes, it is," Millie said. "Suck it up, deary. You and Renji are going to get married and have a ton of babies."

Renji's smile broadened. It was clear as day the two worked together on this. No matter what Millie said or what Renji believed, Zoe wasn't ready to fall in love, and definitely not with him. However, she did want to explore options with her gaming partner.

"Now." Millie placed her hands on Zoe's shoulders. "You two go on. I'll close up tonight." She turned Zoe around and shoved her toward Renji.

He caught her in his arms. "Do you realize…" He led her by the hand to her office to get her things. "You haven't taken time off in two years?" He picked up her purse from the office desk. He lifted the strap up over her shoulder and then turned her toward the door. "Now, let's go."

Zoe swallowed hard. "Where are we going at this time of afternoon?"

"You'll see."

Zoe followed Renji outside. Although hungry for one of Renji's delicious meals, she'd rather be locked up in her apartment, playing her game tonight with Ben. It sucked. He was always busy Saturday night.

They hopped in Renji's old red Chevy. The truck rumbled to life and purred deeply as he drove it out onto the main road.

Zoe glared. "We're not going to Wichita, are we?"

"Of course not," he replied as he rolled down the windows. "We're going to the grocery store."

"As usual."

A cool breeze blew through the open windows and into the cab of the truck. She breathed in deep as her hair lifted and twisted around her face. With the late-afternoon sun warming her chest and legs, she smiled.

The last few years she'd been cooped up in her apartment, scared to go anywhere by herself. On rare occasions, she'd tagged along with Millie to the store, sometimes the mall. Renji was a persistent man. He dragged her everywhere he went every chance he could get.

Zoe breathed in deep. Maybe it was time to make a change. It was time to set fear aside, put the game controller down, and be alive. With the weather this nice, it'd be easy. With Renji, nothing and nobody would hurt her. With Renji, she was safe.

"You look happy." Renji parked the truck near the store's entrance.

"I have to admit. It feels good to take time off and relax."

"I'm glad." He turned off the engine. He stretched his arm down the length of the bench seat and palmed the back of her head. "You're so lovely in the sunlight."

She narrowed her eyes. "What the heck are you doing?"

"I want to kiss you." He sighed as he wrenched his fingers around the steering wheel. "I've wanted to kiss you forever."

Please Renji. Don't ruin this good moment. "We've kissed before."

"Yeah, but not kissed, kissed. We're getting older. We're still stuck here in this town together. It's like we're supposed to be together or something."

"I don't want to do this with you. Or anyone. I'm not ready yet."

"Yeah. I know." He opened the door and stepped

down on the ground. He helped her out on his side. "But you're safe with me. No matter what. I'll take care of you."

"I know you want to."

He cupped her face. "I'd never hurt you."

"You don't have to say all this, Renji." She cocked her head to the side then smiled. "I know you wouldn't."

"Okay then." He took her hand and led her toward the store's entrance. "Just wanted you to know how I feel."

Renji. Her sweet barbarian always protected her. He was like a safety net, catching her when she fell. Being her guard wasn't a good thing. He shouldn't have to put his life on hold for someone who would never fall in love with him. No doubt, she loved the big lug, but not how he wanted.

****

Ben sat on his gaming chair, rocking back and forth. He'd logged into the game half an hour ago hoping to find Zoe, wishing she'd log in soon so he could talk to her about meeting up next weekend. He'd tried calling her home phone and texting her, but she hadn't answered.

He turned off his console and TV then put on his old torn sneakers. He headed into the living room where Sheron sat watching the local news and filing her nails.

"The baker's not online?" she asked.

Ben sank down in the couch cushion beside her. "No." He took his cell phone from his pocket, debating on whether to call Zoe again.

"Are you meeting her next weekend?"

"Haven't asked her yet."

"Did you call her?"

"What do you think?"

"All right smart ass." She narrowed her eyes then went back to filing. "Last night's gig went pretty well."

"Yeah." Lack of bar fights and no missed chords was always a good thing. The rare mistakes he made never mattered since most of the metalheads who frequented the bar were too smashed out of their minds to care. "You'll never believe who I ran into at the bar."

Sheron's catlike eyes snapped to his. "Please say you two aren't going out for coffee."

He cocked his head to the side. "How'd you know?"

"I saw you guys at the bar." Sheron dropped the file on the cushion then crossed her long, smooth, tanned legs. "I followed her into the bathroom to see what she was up to. Overheard her telling one of the girls you invited her out."

"She asked me out."

"Figures. You're better off meeting the baker chick in the one-horse town."

He often daydreamed about Zoe's gorgeous blue eyes, the perfect pouty pink lips he wanted to kiss. The girl had him feeling strange, not himself at all. "If she'd just answer her damn phone—"

"—text her."

"I did," he muttered.

"Maybe she's out on a date with a hot hunk." Sheron twisted her lips to the side. "She's probably some church-going sweetheart anyway. Doesn't fit your style."

He scowled. "How do you know where she fits?"

"Look at you, Mr. Popular Gorgeous. According to

you, she's Ms. Blonde Sweetie-tooth. Fulfilling a high-maintenance princess's wish when you're a million miles away doesn't quite work."

Zoe did have a certain niceness about her, an innocence he wasn't used to. She wasn't just sexy. She was cute and often said the silliest things to make him laugh. He'd never met anyone quite like her. Something about her drew him in.

He stood. "You don't know her yet."

"Yet?" Sheron cackled. "You're really into this girl, aren't you?"

He stepped over her feet on the way to the kitchen, about to go insane. Didn't matter how many times he had to call he'd get through to her tonight. By the end of next week, they'd be face-to-face, ready to find out if they were in tune with each other.

He dialed her home phone again. It was still early evening. Maybe she'd gone out for a stroll, and hopefully not out on a date as Sheron suggested.

Chapter Four

Renji stood in the kitchen in baggy blue jeans and a formfitting T-shirt, stir-frying vegetables and chicken in his steel wok. A pot of rice sat on the burner, giving off a heavenly popcorn-y scent.

Due to his mother's intense cooking lessons, he was a chef not to be reckoned with. Zoe was quite keen on eating anything he fixed, especially now. Her stomach growled.

"You have nothing but microwave meals in your freezer," Renji said with a shrug of his broad shoulders. "Your skin is paler than it should be. Lack of grains, proteins, carbs—not good for you."

"Some frozen meals are chock-full of proteins and carbs."

"You eat processed meals and pastries."

"I switched to low-fat microwave meals. They're healthy."

"You're eating too much sodium and preservatives."

Zoe rolled her eyes. "Did you come over to cook or lecture me about my diet?"

"You need other kinds of foods too. Buy an apple next time you're at the grocery store."

This coming from a man who could easily be a model in a weight-lifting magazine, she made no effort in continuing their argument. She leaned back against the counter near the sink as he worked his culinary magic. He fluffed the steaming rice with a fork out onto her peach dinner plates. He scraped vegetables and chicken from the wok onto the rice, making it look like a dish on the menu cover at a Chinese restaurant.

Her mouth watered after every bite. Microwave meals had their moments, but this ensemble of unbelievable flavors—chicken so tender, vegetables warm and crisp in a sweet and savory brown sauce—brought tears to her eyes.

"You really enjoyed dinner tonight."

She licked her flavorful lips. "Mmm. I wish there was more."

"I'll give you the recipe."

Recipe or not, she sucked at cooking. He'd known that since the day she'd made a grilled cheese sandwich and almost burned the apartment down.

"You know I'd just screw it up."

"This dish is easy. Just use the proper heat for the chicken. Add ingredients to the sauce a little at a time until you find the right chemistry. It'll come together as long as you pay attention and not wander off while it's cooking."

She set the fork down on her plate and closed her eyes. *Best meal ever.* Something soft and warm touched her lips. She opened her eyes to find Renji kissing her.

"What the hell." She hopped off the bar stool and ducked past him. She leaned back against the counter near the kitchen sink. "Why'd you kiss me?"

He strode toward her. "I don't think you realize how much I care about you."

Oh, please. "I appreciate everything you do for me. But, I don't want to—"

"—I understand." He palmed her cheek. "After what Nicholas did to you."

"Don't talk about him." Her face burned. He knew better than to bring up the devil in the conversation—in any conversation. Not only did it piss her off, it scared her. To know the vicious monster was out there, free to do whatever he wanted, sent chills through her. "I don't ever want to hear you say his name."

"I'm sorry." He shook his head. "It's been two years, Zoe. I just wish you'd let me in. I wish you'd love me. Let me love you. I'll do everything in my power to protect you."

"I do love you, Renji. But not how you want me to." She shuddered. How would she get through to him without hurting his feelings? There was no other way around it. "Right now, I'm happy staying home and playing my game. I like spending my time with Ben."

"Oh." Renji cocked his head to the side. "He's the guy you've been playing games with, isn't it? You like him?"

"Yes. I like him. We've played together for a year and a half. He's sweet and fun, and I think I want to meet him."

"Is he interested in you too?"

"Yeah. I think so." Her phone rang. Renji caught her hand before she could get away. "I need to answer."

"Let it ring so we can finish our conversation."

"Renji." She sighed as she gave his hand a gentle squeeze. "I know you're worried. But don't be. Ben's a good person. He makes me laugh. He makes me forget about all the bad in my life. Please. Don't make this hard on me."

"He may make you feel good, but he's not here to

keep you safe." He loosened his hold on her hand then let go. "He'll just keep you hiding inside your apartment when you need to be out."

"What I want to do with my life is my business." She brushed past him. "We're finished talking about this."

By the time she reached the phone, it stopped ringing. Hands on her hips, she turned around to find Renji leaning back against the counter, arms folded across his chest.

"I'm the one who makes sure you get home safely every night. I make sure your doors and windows are locked. You cried on my shoulder for months. I've been here for you."

"And I'm thankful for everything you've done for me." She made her way to his side. "But, please, stop worrying. I can take care of myself."

"While he's out there planning God knows what? Nah." He shook his head. "I can't leave you alone."

Zoe shuddered. The thought of Nicholas out there plotting revenge sent chills over her body. All the calls and texts she'd received since he was released, there was nothing anyone could do. Not even Deputy Fred could do anything when the phone numbers kept changing.

"I'll be fine."

"You're scared enough to have an extra lock installed on your door." He put his arm around her shoulders. "So what am I supposed to do? Ignore my feelings for you and go on like I have been?"

Zoe's heart sank. As much as she hated to admit it, she needed him. Now more than ever. But she couldn't ask him to put his life on hold any longer.

"I don't know what to say or do, Renji. I can't make it any clearer. I don't have those kinds of feelings for you. But, I don't want you to go anywhere or leave me. Because yes..." Tears welled in her eyes. "Nicholas is out there, and he scares me. I'm tired of sleeping with my blankets over my head at night. Every time I close my eyes, I see him over me. I feel the pain he put me through. I'd give anything to make it stop."

He pulled her into his arms. "I'm so sorry, Zoe. I didn't mean to—"

"—No." She stepped back then wiped her wet cheeks with rigid fingers. "I don't want your sympathy. I'm tired of being scared and depending on someone. I love you, but only as my friend."

"Zoe," he whispered.

"I'm sorry. I don't want to hurt you. But, please, Renji, find someone who makes you happy. Someone who'll be there for you."

The phone rang again. Dammit. Why'd Renji have to look so heartbroken? She pursed her lips. The answering machine picked up on speaker.

"Hey. It's Ben. Sent you a few text messages. I've tried calling you several times now too. I guess I should've left you a voice message earlier, but—"

Zoe lifted the phone off the receiver. "Ben, I'm here."

"Hey. It's good to hear your voice."

Zoe glanced at Renji, who frowned. "It's good to hear yours too."

"Are you busy?"

"I'm not busy," she replied. She returned Renji's glare. "I mean, I was eating dinner with a friend, but we're finished. And we're done talking too."

Renji yanked his jacket from the hanger on the wall then left the kitchen. Zoe listened to his heavy footsteps on the stairs. When the front door slammed shut, she jumped.

If Renji had just kept this a friendly dinner, she would've told Ben she'd call him back after the movie. She glanced at the box on the table. *God.* He'd rented *Man of Steel*—her favorite.

Zoe hurried down the stairs and twisted the lock on the door knob. "I thought you were playing at the bar tonight."

"Doogen hit a high note he rarely reaches and got excited. Fell off the stage."

She laughed as she turned both dead bolts. "Is he okay?"

"Had to take him to the hospital."

"Oh no." She slid the bolt to the side and locked it in place. "Did he break anything?"

"Sprained arm. He'll be fine." He cleared his throat. "So, I've been thinking about you all day."

She latched the chain then leaned back against the door. His image popped into her mind. If only he was here with her, she'd fall into his arms and kiss him.

"I've been thinking about you too."

"Have you, pumpkin?"

She grinned. "I have, baby."

"How about we explore in game tonight? Something different."

"Explore?" She made her way to the living room. "Do you want to quest in another area?"

"I think it's time Soljer and Sonya coupled."

Zoe gasped. He'd spoken so freely, so calmly, like it was no big deal. She was tongue-tied and horrified and yet so excited she couldn't say anything. Not even an *um* or an *oh my* would work past her quivering lips.

"We don't have to," Ben said. "It's just a suggestion."

"Yeah. I'm game. Let's do this."

She pressed the X button on the controller. The console whirred to life. As the game loaded, Zoe sat on the couch.

Sonya stood on the balcony in front of the open box Ben had sent his picture in. When Soljer faded in beside her, gooseflesh swept over Zoe's skin.

A message popped up. *Soljer would like to couple*, with a green *Yes* button and a red *No* button beneath it. She'd seen the same message from other characters before and had always clicked *No*. This time, she placed the pointer over the *Yes*. Holding her breath, she clicked in the green box.

The camera view flew over the ocean toward her lighthouse. Their characters lay naked in bed, his over hers, moving to romantic classical music. The sounds they made, gasping breaths, moans of delight, made her cheeks hot. Sonya cried out in orgasm.

If Ben were sitting in the same room with her, witnessing this wondrous atrocity taking place, she'd pass out from the tension. Until their characters finished doing the deed, which took about thirty seconds, she peeked through spread fingers.

She swallowed hard. "Oh my gosh. What just happened?"

****

It'd been a long while since he'd laughed like this. Felt good. Through their sexual encounter, he kept his eyes on the picture of the gorgeous blonde in the bottom corner of his screen. He wanted to be with her now to see her reaction, to touch her and do the same kind of things to her real body. Imagining her skin on his, hot and wet with sweat, he couldn't help the stir inside him.

A new message popped up on-screen. He read aloud as Zoe read hers. "Congratulations. You've procreated. The human race has advanced by one."

"Wait. What?" She scoffed. "Are you serious?"

"'Grats, pumpkin," he said with a laugh. "Looks like we're having a baby."

"A baby? No, no. This can't happen. Is there a save point we can go back to?" Her soft, sweet voice wavered. He imagined her lips trembling. He'd give anything to be there to calm them down.

"Can't go back," he said.

"Why would anyone want to have children when aliens are taking over the world? I wouldn't have clicked *Yes* if I'd known I was going to get pregnant."

"I'll fix it."

"How will you fix this?"

"I work for the game developer."

"*Oh*," she said, followed by a little sigh of relief. "You'd do that for me?"

"Yeah, Zoe," he said, oddly a little hurt she didn't want to have his virtual children. "So, hey. Are you free next weekend?" He'd meant to ease into the conversation but figured what the hell. It was a good time to find his balls and take a dive. "Thought we could make plans to meet. For real. If you're interested."

"Yes. I'm very interested."

"Great. How about I drive down there on

Thursday? I'll grab a hotel and spend the weekend."

"I'll take the weekend off."

"Good." He gave Soljer a command to blow Sonya a kiss. When she blew a kiss back, he grinned. "Okay, pumpkin. Let's go burn some aliens before your belly's too big to fight."

Chapter Five

Renji gave her the silent treatment all week. Every morning, she'd found him standing outside her door waiting to walk her to work. Like a sad, sorry puppy dog, he'd quietly follow her to the bakery.

She'd apologized for hurting his feelings, but he never said a word unless it was work related. Even then he gave her short answers. He left the second he was off the clock. Although she walked home alone, he always watched from his front steps to make sure she arrived safe and sound. Then the next morning, it started over again.

Thursday morning, Zoe'd had enough. She tugged the hem of her shirt over the top of her khakis. She marched to the counter where Renji transferred beautifully browned croissants to a tray.

"Are you going to stay mad at me forever?"

"I'm not mad."

"Would you stop what you're doing and look at me?"

"Why? So you can tell me again I'm not good enough for you?" He growled. "No, thanks."

He dropped the spatula on the counter, and then picked up the full sheet. He went to the storefront and placed the croissants beside the new loaves of honey-wheat bread.

When he returned to the kitchen, she caught his

forearm. "I'm sorry. But I don't like talking about *him*."

"Yeah, I know. But this isn't about him." He shook his head. "It's about you and me."

The whites of his eyes had a pinkish tint, as if he hadn't slept a wink in days. She wanted to comfort him, put her arms around him and tell him it was okay, but the bell above the entrance door jingled.

Millie walked through the doorway, lips pursed, and eyes narrowed. Zoe had texted her last night to tell her about Ben's upcoming visit. She wasn't thrilled.

"I hear this gamer guy's coming to town for the weekend." Renji snorted a laugh.

Zoe folded her arms over her chest. "Millie. You told Renji before I could."

"Sorry." Millie raised her hands in the air, palms out. "I thought you had already told him. Renji and I are worried about you. You've never met this guy, and suddenly he's coming to town for an entire weekend. What if he's an ax murderer?"

"I've been talking to him for over a year and a half. I'm willing to bet the only ax he's ever touched is his guitar." Zoe smiled. Nice witty comment. "He's way better than the friends your husband's set me up with in the past."

"Eww. Remember the guy Hank introduced her to?" Renji placed the spatula in the sink. "The one with all the long hair."

"Oh yeah. George." Millie snickered. "I think their date lasted thirty whopping minutes."

Zoe rolled her eyes. "He wanted to date someone who likes snowboarding. I mean, where in the heck am I supposed to learn to snowboard in Kansas?"

"How about the yard-maintenance guy from

Maize?" Renji said as he scooped out dough from the mixer.

Zoe palmed her forehead. *Oh please. Not this joke again.*

Millie grabbed the star cookie cutters from the top drawer of the cabinet and set them on the counter. "I think he had something against white flour."

Renji placed his hand on Millie's shoulder. "He told her he was a *wheat-eater*."

They burst into laughter. Zoe hid her grin. "You've told that joke a million times. It's not funny anymore."

Millie elbowed Renji. "Yes, it is."

This happened every week. They'd tell jokes about her past dates and how awful they'd been. No way was she going to let them get away with making fun of her this time.

"In my defense, every man you and Hank have ever set me up with has had some bizarre quirk. I mean, really, where does your husband find these odd friends of his?"

"They were nice men. And Hank was only trying to help." Millie scowled, the mom-face coming out in her. Her scolding tone made Zoe feel like a child who'd done something wrong. "You've fantasized about falling in love and getting married, but nobody's ever good enough for you. Don't you think you should give someone a try? Someone local?"

"Nobody *is* good enough." Renji dropped the dough on the flour-coated counter. "Not after the abusive mother*fuc*—"

"—Renji." Millie's mom face softened. "She'll be ready to try again when the time is right. And I don't blame her for wanting to look elsewhere for a mate, but, mark my words, long distance relationships never work out."

He pursed his lips. "So true."

Zoe rolled her eyes. Was she even in the room anymore? They spoke to each other like they had control of her life and knew what was best. Sure, she'd made a huge mistake by dating Nicholas. But how was she to know he was the devil? A monster she never wanted to see or hear from again. She had only known him for a few weeks when he showed his true colors. By then, it was too late.

She'd known Ben for a long time. A year and a half was plenty of time to see how different he was from any other guy. From the very first moment they met online, she could tell he was trustworthy. Sweet. A gentle man she could fall in love with.

"Ben's not like anyone I've ever met. He's an amazing guy who makes me happy. I'm meeting him tonight whether you like it or not." Her gut churned with excitement. *Oh God.* She was meeting him tonight.

"He's probably some fat ass with greasy hair and pimples." Renji snorted a laugh as he rolled out the sugar-cookie dough. "Plus, five hundred miles is a long way to travel to be with someone. It won't work out."

"He's not fat and greasy. He's exceptionally hot. Millie, just wait until you see him. He's *dreamy*."

"Still won't last." Renji lifted the pin off the dough and pointed it her way. "Care to make a wager on it?"

"Life is nothing but a gamble for you, isn't it? You two are supposed to be supportive, not always trying to prove me wrong."

Zoe hit Renji with her elbow on the way to her

office. "Just…get back to work."

She slammed the door shut. He could keep being a big jerk. Millie could continue condemning her for breaking Renji's heart. This relationship with Ben could work out, even with the distance problem.

Zoe hurried through the morning paperwork, skipping her usual pastry and coffee to get it done. At noon, she retrieved the zippered pouch from the top drawer of her desk. She got down on her hands and knees and unlocked the safe. As she grabbed the money from the previous day's sales, the office door opened.

"Zoe," Renji said as she stood. "You're wanted out in the store."

"Thanks."

On the way out, he caught her forearm. "Okay, listen. I'm an idiot, and I swear I'll never give you the cold shoulder again. I'm just worried about you."

"I'll be fine."

"Just promise…please promise me you'll be careful. If this guy turns out to be bad…if he hurts you in any way, I'm here. Okay?"

"Thanks, Renji."

"Want me to take the money to the bank?"

She handed him the pouch. On her way to the storefront, she drew in a deep breath, happy her friend had come back to his senses.

"Ms. Kearny." The petite woman held her hand out over the store counter.

Zoe accepted her hand and shook. "Please, call me Zoe."

"Drema," the woman said, tossing Renji a glance. "I'm the owner of Holetzer's Sports Bar."

"How can I help you?"

"I'm throwing a grand opening for the bar soon. I'm thinking barbecue, live band, dunking booths." She cocked her head to the side. "The butcher at the grocery store told me you were the person to contact about helping me coordinate the event."

Zoe wasn't the owner of the bakery, but she might as well be. She took care of all the media and special events. I'll see what I can do to get you a spot on the local news."

"Wonderful." Drema smiled. "It's pretty impressive keeping a business running in such a small community."

"The bakery's not a far drive from Wichita. Plus, we've been here for sixty years. The customers are loyal."

"Fair enough," Drema replied.

Zoe couldn't help thinking about the waitresses of Holetzer's being call girls, and Drema moving her business here because the law shut her down. "I've heard things about your last…establishment."

"Oh, they're rumors. Awful ones." Drema shook her head and sighed. "I assure you my workers weren't prostitutes. And I've never run any kind of illegal drug operation. My place caught on fire due to faulty wiring."

"What an awful thing to happen." Zoe wasn't sure what to think. By Drema's watery eyes, it was easy to believe her story. It was definitely more believable than the rumors, since all the old ladies did around this town was gossip. "So, of all places to reopen, why'd you choose this town?"

"My mother lives in Wichita and I wanted to be closer to her." Drema shrugged. "I like small communities. It's cheaper here than in the city. Plus, this is right close to Wichita so I'll get a little of both worlds. I hope anyways. With your help."

Did she really want to help coordinate a party? Yes, she could get word out and organize the event, but did she really want to be involved?

"Stop in this weekend and have a look around," Drema said. "You don't have to give me an answer yet, but it'd be nice to have one soon." She turned to leave but stopped. "Oh. Would you mind telling Renji the blueberry muffins are to die for?"

"I will."

Drema's face turned a shade of pink. The lady had an obvious crush on Renji. By the grin across Renji's face, maybe he had a crush on her too.

Zoe spent lunch hour researching on the Internet. Holetzer's in South Dakota had been a bar with walls of televisions offering sports broadcasts. The popular place had parties during big games and local college homecomings. It sounded like a nice place for the sports fanatic. Had a great family atmosphere too.

Too bad it'd burned down. Funny, a few weeks later another sports bar was getting built across the street. Drema's dreams had been smeared by local rumors ruining her reputation.

At one p.m., Zoe put her research away and left the office. Jittery, she met Millie near the counter. The four-tiered masterpiece Millie decorated was set for a fifty-year wedding anniversary and renewal of vows happening at church on Saturday.

"Wish me luck?"

"You know how I feel about this," Millie said. "But I love you and want to see you happy. If this video-game guy makes you laugh and smile, then you have my blessing."

Zoe laughed. "You mean if he doesn't ax murder me?"

"With your luck…?"

"I know I don't have a good track record with men. And I'm a little scared to jump back into dating, especially with a guy I've never met. But I really like him. We have fun together. I just hope this one works out. If it doesn't, I think I'll join a convent in the mountains of Norway."

Millie stared, lips pursed, tube of frosting held before her like a dagger. She lifted the tip and squeezed a big glob of icing onto the end of Zoe's nose. "You, my friend, are impossible. Think positive, my sweet. And don't you dare let him lift a finger to hurt you."

Zoe stood cross-eyed until the frosting slid off to the floor. "I need to go. I have a dinner to cook."

"Oh gosh. You're cooking?"

"Yes," Zoe muttered.

"Not microwave meals, right?"

"No."

"What are you making?"

Zoe cleared her throat and switched her stance. She was ready to run when Millie told her she couldn't pull it off. "Lasagna."

"Oh, the horror." Millie gasped. "What time is he arriving?"

"Five."

Millie turned her fast and shoved her toward the exit. "Renji and I have the store handled for the weekend. Just get moving, or you won't get your dinner finished on time."

Zoe smiled. "Thanks, Millie."

"Make sure you don't burn the apartment complex down," Renji yelled from the back room.

Zoe rolled her eyes. Nobody would ever forget her poor choice in men. Now they'd never let her forget about the darned grilled cheese sandwich that nearly set her kitchen on fire.

****

The open road. What a rush. Nice sunny day. Not a cloud in the sky. Ben wished he'd rode his motorcycle instead but wasn't sure how Zoe would feel riding on the back of one.

Some day he planned on making the trek on his bike to enjoy the straight stretches at a cool 170 mph. Maybe on a warmer day. Hopefully, the weekend went well enough he'd get to make another trip across the flat Kansas terrain.

He pushed the Jeep Rubicon hard. Ninety-five miles per hour wasn't bad at all, even with the roof back and the cool wind messing with his bangs. It wasn't so much the thrill of driving fast but was the desperation to touch Zoe's silky pale skin, to run his hands over her soft curls. He couldn't wait to kiss her lips and find places on her body to make her sigh.

"*Take it slow*," Sheron had said this morning before he left. "*Being in a real relationship causes emotional stress. Don't get too serious too fast. Treat the baker like glass, but with respect, not like the floozies you've dated in the past.*"

Zoe was real, not made of glass. He'd never treat a woman poorly but putting up a fake front wasn't his style. He'd show her his dark tortured heart if they were to find out if they had any chance of working out.

He couldn't wait to see the gorgeous woman he'd been dying to meet for the past year. This sweet, caring woman made him happy, happier than he'd been in a long time.

He inwardly laughed. She sucked at playing the game, though he was pretty sure it wasn't games drawing her in. She was so damned cute, unable to step a foot off the lighthouse without him. Even then, she followed him closely.

The laser detector beeped. He slowed the Jeep to a crawling fifty-five miles per hour. Half a mile later, he passed a giant sign on the right side of the road with a brown and white police car sitting next to it.

The billboard ad pictured a restaurant in Wichita thirty miles ahead. Only twenty more miles and he'd be standing on the front steps of Zoe's apartment greeting her, holding her warm body in his arms. He hoped she'd forgive him for being a little early, with an argument that, at least he wasn't late.

The police car pulled out onto the road behind him. It followed for a good five minutes before turning left down a long dusty road. Then, Ben sped up.

Chapter Six

Zoe jogged to her apartment, careful not to trip over the horizontal lines across the sidewalk. Her knees were already skinned from the last time she fell, a week ago. Embarrassing. The unsightliness of bandages left her feeling like an unattractive klutz. She didn't need to feel ugly tonight.

Safely locked inside her apartment, she hurried up the steps to the kitchen. As she made the ricotta-cheese mix, she breathed in. The apartment still smelled like the Italian sausage and hamburger she'd fried this morning. It reminded her of her favorite restaurant in the mall.

She hoped Ben liked Italian. Otherwise, she'd take him out to eat instead. Maybe they'd go to Granny's Diner down the road to have a cheeseburger and a piece of Granny's famous pumpkin pie.

She hoped he called her *pumpkin* tonight. It really didn't matter what he called her as long as their first meeting went without a hitch. Hopefully, her alien-fighting partner was as interesting and handsome and nice in person as he was online.

After a quick shower, she blow-dried her hair. She put on her favorite white sundress, applied her makeup, and then positioned her shiny bangs to the side.

It'd been a long while since she'd put on a pretty dress. Getting attention from men was less than desirable. First impressions always stuck, and she didn't want Ben to remember her as some kind of Suzy Homemaker in jeans and a pink button-up shirt.

She hurried to the kitchen, turned on the oven light, and checked the baking dish. The lasagna wasn't bubbling yet—a good sign it would take the hour to cook.

Her cell phone chimed. It was Nicholas. Why the hell was he texting her again? Did he really believe she'd reply? Just the thought of him made her want to vomit.

—I'm out on my hog today. Want to go for a ride?—

Zoe shivered as she set down her phone. *Shake it off. Don't let the creep ruin your day.* She was meeting a nice guy. Ben. Soljer. The gorgeous man from Denver, Colorado.

Determined to forget Nicholas, she pasted on a smile and put on her apron to tackle the dishes in the sink. She twisted the hot-water knob. The faucet coughed and sputtered.

She turned it off. "What the heck?" She turned it on again. Water gurgled from the spout. After several bursts of air, it ran normal again.

She groaned. Of all times for the water company to work on the lines, it had to be today. She positioned the washcloth under the stream. The faucet sputtered again and quit running. A strange sound, like rapidly flowing water through a long, hollow tube, came from beneath the sink.

She cocked her head. No, not beneath it—inside it.

She opened the emergency drawer and retrieved the flashlight. She shined the light inside the drain, hoping to see the problem. A fountain of water bubbled up from the hole.

She screeched and stuffed the stopper in the drain. It did no good. Water came, faster, filling the sink. Bits of black gunk and an upheaval of ripped noodles, and God knew what the white things were, gushed from the garbage disposal.

She turned on the disposal to send the flow back down, but the sink filled, now dangerously close to overflowing.

"This can't be happening." The hallway seemed endless as she ran to the linen closet. Tears sprouted in her eyes, but she wiped them away. There was no time to cry when the kitchen was drowning. She hurried to the kitchen with a handful of soft bath towels. She spread a towel around the wet sink and dropped the rest on the floor.

There had to be a way to unstop this clog. She leaned over, plunging her hand into the muck. Water sprayed upward like a geyser, showering down on her, soaking her hair, her clothes. She dug for the clog and was soaked once more for her efforts.

Hair and body drenched, she tiptoed across the kitchen until her back touched the far wall. The pesky tears welled in her eyes. This wasn't happening. It was just a horrible nightmare. She shut her eyes tight and shook her head. *Wake up, Zoe.*

She opened her eyes. Every muscle in her body weakened. Oh God. Her kitchen floor was a pond. If she didn't call someone soon, the entire apartment would become a lake.

The doorbell rang. It took her a moment, but she managed to pull herself together and walk down the stairs. She unlocked and opened the door to Ben.

The man she adored looked her up and down. His gorgeous smile vanished as he drew a quick step back. She was sure he must be thinking she looked like the monster's bride.

"Oh *no*," she said in a strangled voice. "You're not supposed to be here yet."

She wiped her eyes, smearing mascara on the backs of her hands. Her eyes stung as fat tears blurred her vision of this exceedingly handsome guy standing before her, looking absolutely mortified.

****

Ben glanced at the number on the side of the door, wondering if he'd found the right apartment. Number ten. This was the place. The woman was definitely Zoe, but a scarier version.

"Zoe, what's wrong?"

"I'm so sorry." She fell back on the bottom step and buried her face in her hands. "We weren't supposed to meet like this."

He rushed up the stairs and into the kitchen. Dirty water bubbled from the drain and overflowed into the floor. He wasn't a plumber, but he'd done enough home improvements to know this wasn't a normal clog.

"Where's the plunger?" he asked from the top step.

"Down the hall, first door on the left," she said, palm against her forehead. "Next to the toilet."

He picked up the plunger. At first, he didn't think it would do any good. But after a few hard plunges, the fountain of water died down and then finally stopped.

Okay. This is odd. The water drained normally. "Check the kitchen sink."

"It's draining," she said.

Ben set the plunger in the tub. He made his way to the kitchen, then turned off the stove. Zoe hid her face with the small pile of hand towels and rags. Head hung low, she dropped to her knees. She moved the towels around in slow circles, creating shallow waves over the floor. The poor thing fell back on her rear end and sobbed in her hands, louder than before. Not knowing how she'd feel about him touching her, he stared at the top of her head. What should he do? Hold her? Leave her sitting there brokenhearted?

"I wouldn't blame you if you left." Her voice squeaked a little, like a mouse. "Go home if you want. I'd understand."

He knelt beside her and helped her off the wet floor. He wrapped his arms around her shoulders and pulled her against him. *Damn, this felt good, holding her close.* Even through the thick aroma of garlic and mildew, the scent of roses wafted from her hair.

Her wet body trembled. "I'm so sorry." She sobbed into his shirt.

"Hey now." He swayed her gently back and forth. "Nothing to be sorry for."

"Everything's ruined."

"No, it's not." He leaned back so he could look into those beautiful blue eyes, but she lowered her head. "Look at me, Zoe."

"I'm hideous."

"Come on. Lower your hands so I can see your eyes." When she didn't budge, he sighed. "Just a little peek? Please…*pumpkin*?"

She slowly slid her hands to her cheeks. It was enough to show her blood-shot, mascara-stained eyes. Her wet forefinger had a lasagna noodle stuck to it.

When he picked it off and tossed it into the sink, she cried harder.

****

Oh God, why? Of all times for this to happen, it had to be now. She peeked through spread fingers. The top of her head barely reached his chin. It took effort to keep her trembling arms from giving out.

Dark green eyes accented smooth, pale skin. Midnight hair was cut short behind his ears. His bangs stuck up in front, tousled slightly. Considering the mess she was in, she resisted the urge to touch him.

How could she salvage this moment? What else could she do but stand here crying and melting and feeling like the world was about to end?

"Get your things together." He swiped a lock of soiled hair from her wet eyes. "You can take a shower in my hotel room. We'll come back later and deal with your apartment. Okay?"

She nodded. Not looking at the messy kitchen, she dragged her feet over the carpet to her room. Her reflection in the mirror above her dresser made her stomach churn. She looked bad—like a zombie girl on prom night. No wonder he'd taken a few steps back when she answered the door.

She pulled a sheet of makeup remover from the bin on her dresser, and then wiped the black off her face. She changed into a T-shirt and sweats, brushed her hair, and pulled it back with a tie. After packing her yellow bag with fresh clothes, she tossed her leather jacket over her arm and went out to the living room.

Ben stood on the bottom stair near the open front door. A smile lurched across his face as she descended the stairs to meet him. Perhaps he was happy to see she wasn't the undead wanting a wilted corsage.

He brushed his thumb across her brow. "You smell a little funny, but you clean up nice."

Warmth flooded her cheeks. "Thanks."

He led her to his Jeep. She hopped up in the seat. When he got in beside her, he turned the key. The engine growled to life.

He reached over and cupped her cheek. "You okay?"

She shivered beneath his warm touch. "I'll feel better once I've showered and changed."

He returned his hand to the steering wheel and shifted into gear. "I reserved a room at the hotel a few blocks away."

Sigmund's Hotel was the only hotel in town. Probably the only hotel in the world with drive-through service. When he pulled up to the window, Zoe sank down in the cloth seat. She leaned back hoping Mrs. Sigmund wouldn't see her.

The Sigmunds were an older Baptist couple who visited the bakery every morning to buy doughnuts for their continental breakfast. They were old friends of her dad's. They also badgered her about not attending church anymore…every single time she ran into them.

Mrs. Sigmund slid open the bay window. Dressed in her blue-flower-print dress and with her gray hair up in curlers, she looked like she was getting ready for church.

"Would you like an upstairs or downstairs room?" Mrs. Sigmund asked. Zoe swore she detected a hint of flirt in Mrs. Sigmund's raspy voice.

"Downstairs is fine," Ben said.

"Well, it's not often we get a nice young couple in

town. Where are you traveling from?"

"Denver."

"Oh, one of the elders from our church moved to Denver, North Carolina, not too long ago. I wonder how he's doing these days."

"I'm sure he's fine, ma'am."

Mrs. Sigmund leaned forward to see who he had with him. Zoe sank farther down in the seat. Mrs. Sigmund would find out it was Zoe, even if she had to snoop around the hotel room window.

"Zoe?"

Caught. Zoe flashed a nervous smile. "Hello, Mrs. Sigmund."

"Well, my word, sweetie, I didn't even recognize you. What happened?"

"Plumbing problems," Zoe replied. "My apartment flooded. My friend's letting me use the shower in his room."

"Now isn't that the sweetest thing." Mrs. Sigmund grinned. She leaned over her small cash desk and pulled a key off the hook. Ben took the key from her wrinkled hand.

"Your room is in the back of the building. Number three. It's the nicest room we have, with a kitchenette and cable TV. It also has a coffeemaker and two packets of the finest coffee in Wichita."

"Thank you, ma'am," he said.

"You take good care of our Zoe, now. She's such a dear, even if she doesn't go to church anymore. Talk her into it if you can."

There it was. The beginning of the "*she doesn't go to church*" speech. If Ben didn't start driving now, Zoe was going to get out and walk.

"I'll take good care of her, Mrs. Sigmund."

Ben parked the Jeep in front of room three. He grabbed their bags from the backseat. When he met Zoe at the door, he unlocked it and went in.

He set the bags down on the bed. "Pretty nice for an old place. Clean." He turned on the bathroom light. "Go ahead and take your shower while I bring in my bags."

"Okay."

He lifted a curl resting along her mid-arm and gave it a small tug. "I'm glad I came, Sonya."

After the blubbering mess he'd found her in, she took his gesture as a good sign. Maybe the weekend would make a turn for the better. "I'm glad you're here, Soljer."

"It's funny," he said, gazing into her eyes. "Here we are finally together in real life, and I'm still finding ways to get you out of trouble."

She laughed. "So right. You've saved me many times in the game."

Now he was here, her epic hero, standing before her. Instead of a lighthouse, they were in a hotel room. Alone. No aliens or other players. Just them…in the flesh…beside a king-size bed.

Heart beating at a mad pace, she picked up her yellow overnight bag. Goosebumps spread over her on the way to the bathroom. When she turned to close the door, catching his emeralds still watching her, she lost her breath.

Chapter Seven

Zoe slipped her arms through the short sleeves of her dress then draped her jacket over her arm. After one last check in the mirror, she stepped out of the bathroom. Ben sat on the edge of the bed, plucking the strings on his acoustic guitar. When he met her gaze, her heart quickened.

Damn, he was so good looking. Those eyes could stare a hole right through her and make her melt to the floor like ice cream on a hot day. His black hair was perfect, tousled on top, but slicked back around his ears. And his five o'clock shadow. If she could just run her palms over his face and feel those short hairs tickle her skin, she'd be in heaven.

He pulled his fingers off the fret board. "Very nice." He set the guitar on the floor. "You smell great too."

"I don't always take baths in stinky water, mind you." She sat beside him on the bed. Her cheeks burned as she straightened the wrinkles on her violet dress. "I rarely bawl like a baby either."

"It's understandable. You thought your kitchen would float away. I'm a little disappointed I didn't get to try the dinner you made. You probably worked hard on it."

"I did." She inwardly laughed. If he only knew she'd almost burned down the apartment making a grilled cheese sandwich. "Maybe you should consider yourself lucky. I'm not much of a chef."

"Says the gal who runs a bakery." He traced the scar on her forearm. His gentle touch sent electricity through her. She shivered. "What happened here?"

"I burned myself pulling a loaf of bread from the oven."

"Must've been some loaf of bread."

"They can get pretty big and heavy."

He slid his thumb across the thin slanted scar on her index finger. "And where did you get this from?"

"Electric bread knife."

He snorted a laugh. "You weren't kidding when you said you were accident-prone."

"When I was a little girl, my dad sent me to school with a note telling the teacher not to let me use scissors."

He arched his brows. "No joke?"

"The teacher thought my dad was paranoid. I have several scars on my stomach to prove otherwise."

"Hmm." He combed his eyes over her body. "You'll have to show me the scars sometime."

Face on fire, she nodded. "Sure." This was so much better than earlier. The eagerness in his eyes was nice and a little scary. She swallowed apprehension. Maybe she shouldn't be in this hotel room alone with him.

"Maybe we should head back to my place," she whispered.

His cool, musky scent enchanted her, lured her in. Closer. Just a little further and they'd connect. His nose slid against hers. His lips brushed the top curve of hers. Every inch of her skin buzzed. She wanted a taste. She yearned for it. He cupped her face. Her breath quickened and her shoulders tensed.

His hold on her was a little too confining. She wasn't afraid he'd take her against her will. It was an uncomfortable smothering sensation, as if the walls of the hotel closed in on her.

She inhaled and then exhaled. She fought the urge to rush out the door and get some fresh air, but it was too hard. She stood fast. She stared down into his eyes. By his furrowed brow, he obviously didn't understand her reason to pull away. But she wasn't ready to share the violence in her past with him yet, just as he probably wasn't ready to learn about it.

"My apartment's a mess."

"Yeah." He lowered his hands to his lap. "Okay. I suppose we can't leave it the way it is."

He rose from the bed and held out his hand. She hesitated, but then placed her palm on his. Regret ate her insides as she walked beside him to his Jeep.

She'd liked to have kissed him, but the firm hold he'd had brought back unwanted memories. If he attempted to kiss her again, she'd let him this time. With his hands in hers instead of on her face.

Mrs. Sigmund stood at the lobby window watching as they drove by. The frumpy woman frowned as she waved. She'd probably seen them holding hands and realized their relationship may hold more value than friendship. Zoe hoped so.

The night breeze sent goosebumps over her skin. Though a little cooler than she preferred, clear skies were in the forecast. Even in the town's hazy lights, the stars shined brightly.

She prayed to see a shooting star, ready to make a

wish to let this one relationship work out. The moment her shooting star streaked through the sky, red and blue lights flashed behind them.

Ben glanced in the rear-view mirror. "I wasn't speeding, was I?" He pulled the Jeep over to the curb. "Twenty-five, right?"

"Yeah," she said, curious why Deputy Fred jumped out of his police car with his gun in his hands.

"Hands up." Fred shouted in a gruff tenor voice.

Another police car pulled in front of them. Sheriff Clemens too?

"What the hell is going on?" Ben whispered. He took the words right out of her mouth. His guess was as good as hers.

Pistols cocked in unison. "Hands where I can see them." Fred shouted. Ben lifted his arms, elbows bent, palms open. "Get out of the car."

Fred opened the driver's side door and grabbed hold of Ben's arm. He pulled him out of the vehicle and shoved him hard against the Jeep's side. Zoe cringed. Ben made no attempt to struggle as Fred read him his Miranda Rights and cuffed him.

"Fred. What are you doing?" Zoe shook her head. This had to be a bad dream. "This is a *terrible* misunderstanding."

"Sorry, Zoe," Fred uttered as he led Ben toward the police car. "Got my orders."

Sheriff Clemens holstered his gun at his side. He meandered to Zoe's side of the Jeep. He opened the door and held out his hand.

"You all right, Zoe?" he asked in his deep, monotone voice. His salt and pepper mustache twitched.

"Of course I'm not all right," Zoe snapped. Fred forced Ben into the back of the police car. "You just arrested my date." Fred drove away fast, lights flashing, and siren blaring the entire three blocks to the station. "What in the world is going on?"

"We received a call you'd been forcefully taken from your apartment. When we went by, the door was ajar, so we went in. Good thing Mrs. Sigmund was listening to her scanner tonight, otherwise we might never have rescued you from the kidnapper."

Zoe put her fingers to her temple and massaged. This was like a horrible episode of some bad cop drama on TV. "I'm on a date with the guy who saved me and my apartment from floating away. Those signs of struggle were from faulty plumbing."

"Maybe so." He grumbled as he stroked his gray mustache with his thumb and forefinger. "But we did what we had to."

"Come on, Sheriff. Don't put Ben in jail over a misunderstanding."

"Let's get to the bottom of this then." He gave a short nod. She got in the driver's side of Ben's Jeep and took off for the police station to save him from being booked.

This was ridiculous. The stars were working against her. If this didn't scare Ben away, then nothing would.

Zoe parked near the entrance and hurried inside the station. Millie stood inside glaring at kidnapper Ben.

"Millie," Zoe scolded then rolled her eyes as she walked toward Ben.

"It's all right, Fred," Clemens called out from the entrance door. "Let him go."

Zoe grabbed a fistful of Ben's dark green jacket. "I'm so sorry. Are you okay?"

His brows furrowed. Frustrated. If he left now, there'd be no one to blame but herself, and her plumbing, and Millie of course. She was pretty sure Renji had his big hand in this too.

****

"Another apology," Ben said.

"Would you please take off his cuffs?" Zoe whined, glaring at Deputy Fred who tossed Sheriff Clemens a glance. Clemens nodded and took off the cuffs.

Ben massaged his wrists. He removed Zoe's hold on him then straightened his jacket. This night was not going well. At least he wasn't getting arrested for God knew what. If he didn't know any better, someone in this town was trying to sabotage their weekend. Though he tried not to be put off about it, he couldn't help wondering if he should've stayed home.

"I can't believe this is happening," Zoe muttered, taking the words right out of his mouth.

A dark-haired woman stepped forward. She cleared her throat then pointed her forefinger up toward the ceiling. Her mouth opened. Nothing came out but a quick puff of air.

"Did Renji do this?" Zoe asked. No response. "Come on, Millie. Answer me."

Zoe often talked of this Millie and Renji, her two so-called best friends. They weren't very good friends if they were behind this horrible evening.

Then again, Zoe was sweet. She was also clumsy. Watching her made sense. Being labeled the bad guy when he had no intentions of being one didn't feel so hot, but he understood. Sort of.

Millie sighed. "Renji was worried about you, Zoe. When he went home and found you weren't there and the lights were off, and the door was cracked open, he called me." She cringed. "I'm the one who called Sheriff Clemens and told him you were missing. If it's any consolation, I didn't tell him you were kidnapped."

Zoe shuffled to the lobby couch. She sat and stared at the lime green cinder block wall in front of her. "This was doomed from the start."

Ben too had thought the same thing, but this was obvious sabotage and not fate playing a terrible joke on them. He never believed in fate anyway. He had plenty of experience with psycho exes though. Maybe this Renji guy was hers.

Ben plopped down in the seat beside her. He grasped her hand. She turned her glittering blues on him. My, how just a glimmer of tears in this woman's eyes melted his insides.

"I've never been arrested before." He gave a short snort through his nose. "Well, almost got arrested after I was caught in the middle of one of the fun brawls during a gig at the bar."

"I'm surprised you're not running away," she said lowering her gaze to the floor.

He caught her chin with his curled forefinger then lifted, catching those beautiful eyes again. "It'll take a lot more than a few mishaps to run me away from you, Zoe. We have the entire weekend to explore possibilities."

"I'm so sorry," she whispered.

He draped his arm around her shoulders. "Sounds like your friends just wanted to protect you. A little more than I'd call normal, but I'm not mad about it. You're lucky to have them."

Her pale face turned a slight shade of pink. Taking this slow was going to be difficult, but he was prepared to do whatever it took to make her trust him. If he hadn't promised to be gentle, he'd never have left the hotel after her shower. He'd have leaned her back on the bed and found out just how sweet she really was.

Millie dragged her feet across the floor. She leaned down and kissed Zoe's temple then touched Ben's hand. "Thanks for not being too angry with me. And don't murder Renji for this. He did what he thought was right." She stood straight. "I need to get home before my husband thinks I've left him. Hope your date gets better from here. Love you." She waved once more as she left the building.

"Apologies, Zoe." Sheriff Clemens cleared his throat. "Better safe than sorry, I always say. Millie did the right thing. We'd hate to see anything bad happen to you again."

Again?

Zoe stood fast. "Thanks, Clemens. Are we free to go?"

The sheriff stretched out his arm, offering his hand. Ben stood and shook it once before letting it go. "Sorry about the mix-up. But at least now you know we're watching. Next time, Zoe, tell someone where you're going and save us from having to arrest your…date."

Ben grabbed Zoe's hand and hurried to the Jeep. He drove out on the open empty road and couldn't help wondering if she thought the same thing. Maybe they'd met at the wrong time.

By now a normal guy would've run away, far, far

away, but he had what Sheron called *the patience of Job*. He did contemplate dropping Zoe off then high-tailing it out of here, but one look into those beautiful blue eyes and he couldn't fathom doing such a thing.

Chapter Eight

Zoe drew in a deep breath when they arrived at the apartment. As Ben parked the Jeep, she read the yellow tape across the cracked front door. "*Police Line: Do Not Cross.*"

She closed her eyes and leaned back against the seat. Hyperventilate? No. Never. All those locks wouldn't secure with the door busted. How was she supposed to get through the night? Or tomorrow or the next night?

Landlord Charlie might have an extra door in his storage unit out back. Renji could install it. After what he did to her tonight, he owed her. Big time.

Ben turned off the engine. The keys rattled when he pulled them from the ignition. "I'll help you clean your apartment on one condition."

"An ultimatum?"

"Let me take you away for the weekend." He gave her a mischievous grin. "To my house."

Being kidnapped by Ben wasn't a terrible idea, especially now she didn't have a working front door. It'd been at least twelve years since she'd stepped foot out of Kansas. But to go away with this man? What would Millie and Renji think?

"After everything you went through tonight, you still want to hang out with me?"

"Yes. Very much." He got out of the Jeep. "So how

about it? We'll leave tomorrow morning. I'll show you around my stomping grounds. You can stay at my house."

"I don't know. That's a lot of driving for you."

"It'll be fun." He opened the passenger door then offered her his hand. "The two of us on the open road, top down, wind blowing through our hair."

She slipped her palm onto his. "God knows I need a break from this place." *Especially now. The door's broken.*

He led her by hand up the sidewalk. "Think about it. But make sure you tell everyone you're leaving town." He tore off the yellow tape then opened the door. "I'd rather not get hauled off to jail for kidnapping you again."

He followed her inside the apartment. The strong musty, garlic scent about blew her over. They had their work cut out for them.

She scrubbed the kitchen floors and counters with hot bleach water. Ben cleaned the tub and tossed the soiled towels into the washer.

When the lasagna went into the garbage, reusable pan and all, the heavy garlic scent worsened. Zoe sighed. Even if her kitchen hadn't flooded, dinner would've been a disaster. Eight full cloves of garlic might have been a bit too much. How was she to know? Maybe it was supposed to have a heavy garlic smell. It was an Italian dish, after all.

Ben took the bag out to the large green trash bin at the end of the lot. He returned with wood putty and screws from Charlie's maintenance shed. As he fixed the door, she opened the windows and lit mulberry-scented candles around the room. The odors dissipated.

She breathed in deeply. *Ah. Much better*.

She took another quick shower. While Ben took his, she hopped into her soft lounge pants and tank top.

By the time they sat on the couch, it was twelve-thirty in the morning. Normally she'd sit here alone, turn on the game to meet Soljer, and then play with him for a while. This time he sat here for real, handsome, eyes closed, yawning. The game didn't call to her at all.

She pushed her bare shoulder up tight against his arm. "Thanks for helping me clean."

"You're welcome." He opened his eyes. He slid his hand over hers. "I have to be honest, Zoe. This was a really fucked-up day."

"It *was* a terrible day." She glanced down at her hand, the one he fumbled through his long fingers.

He stroked the back of her thumb with his. His other hand slid gently against her cheek. Goosebumps formed over her skin.

"For such a bad day, it was also one of my best. I finally got to meet fire sorceress Sonya. And she's more than I imagined her to be. Beautiful. Kind. Sexy."

"Sexy?"

"Mm-hmm."

He leaned down and ever so gently kissed her lips. One single kiss. No tongue. The simple press sent Zoe's head spiraling out of control. Her body trembled. She became dizzy, wanting more of him, afraid to confess it.

She touched his face with her free hand, loving the way the short hairs on his shadowed jaw brushed against her palm. His lips parted. His tongue briefly touched hers then he drew back. After another short kiss, he grinned.

"I better go," he said in a low, even tone.

"But we just sat down," she whispered, trying to find the voice he'd stolen from her. *Just stay and kiss me a little longer. Don't go.*

He stood, pulling her with him by the hand. She staggered as he led her to the front door. "I'll pick you up around six. You'll be ready?"

"I'll be ready." She stuck out her bottom lip and batted her lashes. When she smiled, he did too. "See you tomorrow."

He kissed the back of her hand then let go. He gave her a quick wave as he left her standing at the open door. The ache in her heart spread through her as he drove away.

This was a good sign. He wasn't here to hurt her. Leaving town with him was a little scary, but it also felt right. Right and exciting.

How quickly the nice caring feeling Ben instilled in her turned to fury with Renji's presence. Somehow, within his calm demeanor, blazed a jealous fire so hot he'd ruin her life and apartment to get what he wanted.

Renji walked up the sidewalk. A sly grin spread across his face as he shoved his large body in the doorway and leaned against frame. "So how was your date?"

"It was great, except for my kitchen flooded." She shook her head and marched up the stairs. "Then Ben got arrested for kidnapping me. Really, Renji? Why'd you have to call Fred?"

"I found the door pried open with a crow bar. What would you have done?" He followed her inside the apartment and shut the door. "How the hell'd your kitchen flood?"

"I don't know. You tell me."

He scoffed as he followed her to her bedroom. "You think it was me?"

"No, I don't." Renji would never do anything so vicious. She shuddered to think Nicholas had anything to do with tonight. He'd done crazy things in the past. Like throw her dresser through her bedroom window because she was spending the night at Millie's to babysit her kids.

Dummy. Why had she stayed with the creep? Maybe if she hadn't listened to his sappy apology the next day, she wouldn't be living in fear of him now. None of this would've happened.

Goosebumps spread over her like wildfire. Was she setting herself up for another traumatic experience? Maybe she should forget about this trip and stay home. She palmed her forehead. *No.* Ben wasn't a creep. He was a good guy and he'd proved it tonight by taking all this crap in stride.

"I don't know how any of this happened, but I'm glad it didn't scare Ben off." She plucked her dusty suitcase from the closet shelf then tossed it on the bed.

Renji narrowed his eyes. "What are you doing?"

Oh boy. The lectures were about to commence. "I'm leaving town for a few days."

His eyes widened. "You're leaving with him?"

"Tomorrow morning. I'm going to his house in Denver." She opened the top drawer and retrieved several pairs of panties and her favorite white bra. "I'll give you the address before I leave."

He ran his fingers through his slick dark hair. "Are you crazy? You just met him today."

"He's not a stranger."

"He's a charmer, fooling you into going with him."

Her lips trembled when she smiled. *Nice show of confidence*. "I'll be fine."

Renji growled. "What if he overpowers you? What if he gets you to his house and rapes you like Nicholas did?"

"Shut up." She pressed her hands against her ears. "I don't want to hear that word."

"You need to hear it." He pulled her hands down to her sides. "You're walking on a ledge, Zoe. And look at you. You're shaking like a leaf."

"Yes. I'm scared to death about this, but I'm also excited. I promise I'll be okay." She wriggled from his grip. "Ben's a very kind man. I trust him."

"You trusted Nicholas too." Renji leaned back against the wall. "These kind of guys reel in their victims. They're charming at first. Cool. Once they win your trust, they turn on you like a venomous snake."

Renji was right. Nicholas had charmed her with those golden curls and big blue eyes. But even at the beginning, when they'd first met, he'd shown signs of shadiness. There was something evil in his tone of voice. Demanding. Her gut had told her not to go out with him, but he'd practically forced her to.

She didn't feel uncomfortable with Ben. She felt…safe with him.

"I can't be afraid forever." She sat on the bed. "I'm going with him."

"If he turns out like Nicholas, nobody will be there to save you."

"I promise I'll be fine." Zoe glanced down at her hands as if the answer was there. Two years was too long to be cooped up in this apartment. It was time for a change. A drastic change. Fear or not, being with Ben was what she wanted. "It's like I've been asleep all my life. Meeting Ben woke me, let me trust someone again. I'm not afraid of him. It must mean something."

"Fairy tales." He folded his arms over his chest. "He's not the one for you. I don't want you to find out the hard way."

"This one will work out. I know it."

"He lives in Colorado."

"Technicality." She shrugged then smiled. "I've made up my mind. I'm going with him."

He rolled his eyes. "Fine. It's your decision. Just…don't go all bat-shit crazy and elope."

"Get out." She laughed as she picked up her pillow and threw it. It hit his chest and landed at his feet.

Renji tossed the pillow back to her. "If you find yourself in trouble, just call me. I'll come get you."

"Thanks, Renji."

She followed him to the front door. By the frown on his face, he wasn't a happy camper. He'd get over it. He had to.

"Be safe, Zo'." He gave her a quick hug good-bye and then left the apartment.

Zoe breathed a sigh of relief as she locked the dead bolts, twisted the knob, and slid the bolt in place. She and Renji had some whoppers of fights. This one wasn't so bad. He knew how badly she needed a change. To stop being scared to get out of this box and live a little. This was a big step forward, but she was ready.

Excited, she hurried back to her room. She packed her suitcase with all her favorite outfits. It was a little tight, but she managed to zip it up and heave it off the bed.

She strode to the bathroom and opened the medicine cabinet. There they were. Birth-control pills sat on the top shelf. She'd gotten them from her doctor not long ago but never had use for them. Until now.

Maybe.

She studied her reflection in the mirror. Did she really want to do this? Was this the time to overcome her fear of intimacy? Whatever the answer was, she couldn't let the anxiousness she'd experienced at the hotel room happen on this trip. She had to find a way to forget about her past and think about her future. A future with Ben.

Chapter Nine

At six a.m., Zoe waited for Ben to arrive, front door open, sitting on the stairs in her khaki capris, tugging on the hem of her pink T-shirt. She'd stretched so many shirts out this way. It was a nervous quirk, one she'd had since childhood.

As the minutes passed by, excitement fizzled. Six fifteen. Six thirty. She called his cell phone at six thirty-five, but he didn't answer. Didn't even have the guts to call or text her with a reason why he hadn't come. A "good-bye and no-thanks" would've been fine. At least then she'd know.

Figuring he'd left for home, never desiring to look back, Zoe left her luggage sitting inside the front door and headed for the bakery. She greeted Millie in the kitchen. Her sympathetic sad-face made Zoe burst into tears.

Darn it. She hated crying at work. It made the cinnamon rolls taste salty. The tears didn't stop her from eating three rolls, one after another. The buttery goodness of the bread and sugary drizzle made her feel a little better. A chocolate doughnut would've curbed the depression more, but Millie stopped her with a gentle slap on the hand and then a hug.

Zoe wiped tears away. She ventured into her office and fixed her makeup. She leaned back against the wall then closed her eyes. This was ridiculous. No sense in crying over a guy who'd gone through hell last night. She didn't blame him for taking off the first chance he got. She would've run away too.

The bell above the entrance door jingled. Zoe leaned around the corner to see who it was. Ben stalked through the entrance of the store, hands in the front pockets of his dark blue jeans. Her heart pounded against her ribs as she met him near the pastry case.

Thank God he didn't leave.

"Sorry I'm late," he muttered. "It's been a fucked-up…" He pursed his lips. "It's been a crazy morning."

"What happened?"

"Front tire on my Jeep was flat. The spare had a puncture in it too. My cell phone disappeared. Mrs. Sigmund called a tow truck so I rode with them to the shop. I tried calling you from the tire store, but you didn't answer."

"I thought you went home."

"I'm not leaving town without you." He cleared his throat. "Unless…you've changed your mind."

"No, I haven't."

"Glad to hear it."

Ben led her out to his Jeep. He gave the brand-new front tire a light kick before hopping up in the driver's seat. He stopped at her apartment, picked up her suitcase and stuck it in the back seat beside his.

"Nice day for a drive," Zoe said, enjoying the sunshine as he drove out on the main road.

"Got off to an iffy start, but things'll turn around. I—" He clenched his fists around the steering wheel. "Shit."

He slammed his foot down on the brake pedal. Zoe jerked forward. The seat belt kept her from flying through the windshield and out onto the pavement. The Jeep stopped and she fell back against the seat.

Pain shot from her nape to the middle of her back. Shoulders tense, she groaned. A cool breeze winded through the Jeep and crept up her spine and the ache intensified.

What the heck just happened? She followed Ben's gaze to a black cat sitting in the middle of the road. It was like an omen telling them to turn around. *Don't leave town.*

"I'm not a superstitious guy," he said.

"I'm not superstitious either."

The cat arched its back and hissed. It scurried to the sidewalk and then disappeared behind an old dusty trash can.

With all they'd gone through in less than twenty-four hours, they should listen. But she'd be damned if she'd let some cat ruin her weekend.

"Let's go."

He gave Zoe a side-long look. "You okay?"

Determined not to submit to pain, she nodded. "Just drive, babe, drive."

He let his foot off the brake. Slowly, cautiously, he drove the Jeep across the town's border. The sky didn't fall. Hell didn't unleash on earth. Maybe now they could enjoy the rest of this trip. She cringed. It'd be better if this pain would go away.

For the first hour of the drive, neither of them said a word. The engine's hum played a monotone song with the roaring tires. The Jeep's cover tied in the back flapped in the constant wind that blew colder with each passing minute.

Zoe held her mouth closed, fearing she'd swallow a

bug. It wouldn't surprise her if the wheel of the Jeep fell off, or a tornado spawned in front of them and lifted them into the sky like a toy.

Her shoulders ached. The wind blew harder. Her hair lashed her face and stung her eyes. It hurt. Swiping locks away from her mouth and nose became a constant motion. After an hour and a half of Ben driving way above the speed limit, through desolation and dust, through her pain and misery, and silence—lots of cold silence—she couldn't take any more.

"Pull over," she shouted in the howling wind.

He hit the brakes and pulled to the side of the road. She jumped down to the ground and drew in a deep breath.

Ben rounded the Jeep to her side. "What's wrong?"

"My shoulder hurts. It happened when we stopped for the cat."

He took off his sunglasses and placed them on the hood. "You've been in pain this long?" It hurt when she nodded. He positioned his body behind her and gathered her hair in his hands. Lord the goosebumps spread like lightning. "Why didn't you tell me earlier?"

"I thought it'd go away."

He clutched her shoulders and gently squeezed, thumbs working their way up and down the back of her neck. "Is this the spot?"

His touch stirred a fire inside her. "Yeah," she whispered, closing her eyes. Legs weakened, she leaned back against him. *Never stop touching me.* A breathy moan escaped her open mouth.

"Are you more relaxed now?" His warm breath brushed her ear and she shivered.

"Yes."

His mouth found her skin just below her lobe. Heat spread through her arms to her fingertips. Her belly quivered. This couldn't go on much longer or she'd end up on the ground.

His hands slid down her sides to her lower back. Slow, heavy strokes of his thumbs sent a jolt of lightning through her. No man had ever touched her like this before. He was so gentle.

He turned her around to face him. "Better?"

"Much better." She pivoted her shoulders. The pain was still there, but not as bad as it was. "You're quite the masseur."

"Nah." He shrugged. "I dated a woman for about a week a few years back." He leaned back against the door of the Jeep then folded his arms over his chest. "Don't remember much except she taught me pressure points on the upper body."

Zoe stuck her hands in her front pockets. "Well, it worked great."

The corners of his lips curved upward. "Doesn't it bother you?"

She squinted in the sunlight. "Does what bother me?"

"Most women get jealous when their guy talks about an old girlfriend."

"My guy?" Her heart quickened its pace. *Ben's my guy. Ben and Zoe.* Their names just sort of rolled off the tongue. "Well, I'm not like most women."

He chuckled. "I can tell."

She tugged the hem of her shirt. "You've had a lot of girlfriends."

"Never got serious with anyone."

"At least you learned useful techniques with your

hands." Her face warmed. If he could massage a kink from her shoulder in minutes, imagine what other interesting things he could do with those beautiful hands.

He took hold of her elbow and pulled her close. "You're nervous."

She swallowed hard. "Why would you say that?"

"You're fidgeting with your shirt." He scanned her body. "Pink is definitely your color."

He leaned closer. This was the moment she'd waited for. To feel his lips against hers, the warmth of his tongue on her tongue. She anticipated their first passionate kiss with held breath.

Just shy of her mouth, he cocked his head to the side. "Do you hear that?" he whispered. He brushed his lips against hers, teasing, driving her mad. It would be so easy to lean in and get the intense kiss she desired, but she listened for whatever it was he'd heard.

The sound of the plains winds kicked up dust around her feet. Birds chirped. The distant rumble of a jet played with the faint chime coming from the Jeep.

"My cell phone," he said.

He jogged around to the driver's side. He searched between the seats. Under them. When he found the ringing nuisance crammed down in the crevice between the backseat and luggage, he grinned. "There you are."

Disappointed she didn't get the kiss, Zoe hopped up into the passenger seat. She listened to him speak on the phone, agreeing, arguing a little. By the time he ended the call, the calm, sweet man she'd ridden with all morning breathed a disgruntled sigh.

****

"Dammit." Ben placed his cell in the holster

attached to the dashboard vent. He stepped on the accelerator. The tires peeled out onto the road, leaving a huge dust cloud behind them.

This weekend was supposed to be free and clear to spend with Zoe. Doogen knew this, and he still made last-second plans for them to play tonight.

With Doogen's sprained arm in a sling, he couldn't play guitar. The backup guitarist called in sick. Now Ben had to end his vacation and come in to play.

Ben glanced at Zoe. Dressed in pink, fair skinned with beautiful blonde locks, the woman would stand out like an angel at hell's gates. How could he drag her through a cesspool of scummy drunkards at the bar? Every moron there would hit on her. Sheron keeping the dogs off Zoe wouldn't be an easy task.

"What's wrong?"

"There's nobody to play guitar at the gig in Aurora tonight." He groaned. "Looks like I'm cutting my vacation short."

"Oh, yay." Zoe bounced in the seat with her hands together. "How exciting. I get to hear your band play."

She tied up her hair. Her smile beamed, and her blue eyes sparkled in the sunlight. The woman sent him to his knees. Imagine what the scum of the earth would think about her. That settled it. He'd call Doogen back and refuse to play. One missed gig wouldn't hurt the band.

Zoe scooted toward him. She placed her hand on his leg. "Could you slow down a bit?"

He let off the accelerator. He'd pushed the Jeep to ninety-five without noticing. Zoe's hair had partly come out of the tie and lashed her soft, supple cheeks. She massaged above his knee and he slowed to a calmer 60 mph.

"Should I put the top on?"

When she nodded, he pulled to the side of the road. He lifted the top over the Jeep and then worked his way around, snapping it into place. As he zipped up the window on the passenger side, he caught her gaze.

The pink in her cheeks deepened as she pulled the tie from her hair. Blonde strands enveloped her shoulders and fell down her arms. *Damn*. What man in their right mind would not want to be in her company?

He jumped in the Jeep and shut the door. Instead of placing his hands on the steering wheel, he cupped her face. "This might be a corny thing to say, but…I'm going to kiss you now."

Her hands slid over his. "It's about time."

He pressed his lips against hers. He worked his tongue into her mouth. She tasted sweet. Cinnamon and sugar. Delicious. He could stay here for hours kissing her, but they needed to get going.

He leaned back. "I've wanted to kiss you since we met," he whispered against her lips.

"You can kiss me again, if you like," she replied in a breath.

He gave her a gentle peck on the lips then let her go. If he didn't concentrate on getting back on the road, they'd never get to Denver. Not that he cared. He'd rather stay here and kiss her and do other things with her.

He shifted the gear into drive and took off down the road. Now if he could just get a handle on the rise in his pants, the trip home might turn out all right. This was going to be a long trip.

Chapter Ten

Denver offered plenty of traffic, which was overwhelming for Zoe. Though Ben drove like a responsible adult since she'd asked him to slow down, she thanked God they were almost there. According to the sign, there were only eight more miles to the city center.

He ventured off the next exit and turned left at the light. After about three miles down a two-lane highway, he turned right on a short side street lined with tall, leafless trees and big fancy houses. When he pulled into the driveway in front of a long, single-story home in a cul-de-sac, he sighed.

"Home, sweet home," he said, turning off the engine. "I hope you brought warm clothes. Weather's unpredictable here. Might even snow." He got out and grabbed the luggage from the back. She met him in front of the Jeep and walked with him to the front door.

"Nice house," she said, noting the brick exterior.

"It's home," he said, opening the door. She followed him inside the warm house. It only took one look around to feel ashamed of her tiny, poorly decorated apartment. This place was elegant, modern, and much different than how she imagined his house would look.

Houseplants potted in fat, dark brown vases sat in each corner of the room. A large flat-screen TV hung on the far wall near the open-bar kitchen. A leather sectional couch stretched around from the living room window to the entrance where she stood.

"Come on," he said with a quick glance.

She followed him past the kitchen and down the short hall on the right toward double doors. He opened one of the doors and flipped on the light.

He stepped aside. "After you."

Aha. This was more like it. A king-size bed with a headboard bookcase was pushed against the far wall. Two guitars and an amplifier sat in the corner of the room beside another flat-screen TV hanging on the wall. Game consoles were in each slot of a six-tiered shelf, along with hundreds of video games.

"Sorry about the mess." He set the luggage on the floor near the bed. "I normally keep my equipment in the art room, but my roommate needs it for her supplies."

"Her?" A pang of jealousy worked through her. He'd mentioned a roommate before but never said his roommate was female. "All this time talking, and you didn't think it was important to tell me you lived with a woman?"

"I didn't think so at first." He rested his hands on her shoulders. "By the time I felt it did matter, I was afraid you wouldn't want anything to do with me."

"So you kept it from me."

"I'm sorry. I should've told you." He lowered his hands to his sides. "Are you mad at me?"

"A little." Zoe giggled at the expression on his face. Furrowed brows. Pursed lips. He looked so cute, like a puppy getting scolded by his owner.

Those green eyes widened. "Are you laughing at

me?"

"No." She snickered. "I mean yes. You should see your face." She placed her palms against his chest then leaned against him. "I'm kidding. I understand why you didn't say anything. I guess some women would be hesitant to date a guy with a female roommate."

"But you're not like most women." He took hold of her hands. "I swear. Sheron and I are like brother and sister. We hate each other half the time."

"It's okay. You don't have to explain."

He raised her hand to his lips. "We need to get ready."

"I need a shower."

"Me too."

He strode to his duffel bag and unpacked. "I'll take the hallway bathroom and you can have mine."

She heaved her suitcase onto the bed. As she searched for something to wear, he slung clothes he'd packed into the hamper beside the door. He took off his shirt then tossed the garment in the pile of dirty laundry.

Her face burned as she inspected his tall, striking physique. He was strong but not overly muscular. The blue rose tattoo on his shoulder had a name beneath it, but she was too far away to see what it read.

"Come on." He led her through double doors on the far end of the bedroom and into the biggest bathroom she'd ever seen. Bigger than her living room at home. "This is yours while you're here. There's a garden tub, if you'd like to bathe. Might be good for your sore shoulders."

"Nice."

He lifted his dog-tags over his head. He leaned

forward and kissed her temple. "I'll meet you in the bedroom when you're done."

He left her alone in the room. She glanced around. Clear glass surrounded the open shower big enough to fit six people. Her bathroom consisted of a normal, everyday fiberglass tub-and-shower combo enclosed by a non-see-through blue shower curtain. This was lovely. Luxurious. Out of her league.

She took off her clothes and stepped in. She felt more naked than usual. The spray nozzle was so wide, the warm water rained over her like a gentle waterfall.

She picked up the body wash on the stand beneath the knobs then lifted it to her nose. She closed her eyes and breathed in. The light musk fragrance smelled just like him.

This was amazing. Being here in this nice place with a wonderful man. If this was a dream, she never wanted to wake up.

She quickly washed then stepped out. She dressed in her jeans and T-shirt then blow-dried her hair. As she applied her makeup, Ben's tenor voice came from the bedroom. A deep, raspy tone followed—his female roommate.

Zoe pressed her ear against the door, eager to hear what they talked about. The woman scolded him for bringing his new girlfriend home. She said something about the dog following him here, or the girl would follow him around like a dog.

Zoe opened the door and stepped into the room. Ben lay back on his bed in a pair of dark blue jeans, holes in the knees. His T-shirt sported an alien spaceship on the front with an overstuffed purple blob inside. A Coastal Universe shirt. She had to get one of those.

"Nice shirt." Zoe ignored the glare she received from the stunningly attractive woman standing in the bedroom doorway.

"My design," he said proudly.

"Is she going to the bar?" The woman folded her arms over her chest.

Dark complexion, long, sleek hair, and perfect body in a sleeveless curve-hugging dress—breathtaking was an understatement. Metal spikes stuck out around her belt, giving her a heavy-metal look—a taste of what this bar they were going to would be like.

"Of course she's coming," he said. "Zoe, meet Sheron. Sheron—Zoe."

"Hi," Zoe said with a wave of her hand.

"Hello." The woman's nose wrinkled as she ran her gaze up and down Zoe's body. "I'm sorry, honey, but you're not going anywhere in a plain-Jane outfit. Come with me." She took two steps down the hall, and then stopped. "Don't make me wait, doughnut girl. We've got to get you dressed for the ball."

Zoe followed the dark princess through the living room, down the next hallway to a bedroom much darker than Ben's. What had she gotten herself into? Ben lived with a woman who put beauty-pageant contestants to shame. No way could he resist this temptation.

"My name's Sheron. Long *o*. People often mistake the pronunciation and call me Sharon. I hope you won't."

Sher-ohn opened the door to her walk-in closet and went in. She pulled the dangling chain, and the ceiling lightbulb flickered on.

"I have plenty of clothes. Pick out whatever you

like. This is a heavy-metal bar. You'll get laughed at if you show up in your current wear. I'll be damned if you embarrass Ben. Oh," she said on her way out. "If you do anything to rip out his heart, I will kill you."

Overprotective? Understatement of the year. The woman was direct. Hopefully, she didn't mean *kill* in a literal sense. Zoe didn't plan on hurting Ben anyway.

So many choices of clothes hung in this closet, if the person was into the dominatrix thing. She could see Sheron, oddity as she was, with whips and chains and handcuffs. Black skirts, shirts, tank tops, dresses, shoes—they were all gloom and doom, except for the wedding gown hanging in a plastic bag at the end of the closet.

Continuing up the wardrobe, Zoe found a nice spaghetti-strap dress. A really short dress. She pulled it from the hanger, draped it over her arm, then made her way back out into the bedroom.

"Nice choice," Sheron said. She sat on the edge of her bed with a pair of long stockings and knee-high boots.

"You don't own anything with color?" Zoe asked.

"I'm not Perky Pam. I don't wear bright colors or dye my hair blonde like some women."

Zoe glanced down. There was nothing wrong with her yellow shirt. It was plain, but pretty. "My hair is naturally blonde."

Sheron snorted through her nose. "Did you think I was talking about you?"

Zoe opened her mouth but had no comeback.

"Listen, girl. You've got serious looks. Filled out in all the right places. You'll get hit on tonight, so you better stick close to me. I don't want Ben getting in a bar fight."

"I don't either." Zoe squeezed in her words before Sheron continued.

"He likes you, and he'll fight for your honor if he has to." Sheron handed Zoe the stockings and boots. "You are on the pill, right?"

Zoe's jaw dropped. Her mind went to the now opened pills in her bathroom cabinet. "Of course."

"You're a grown woman. I'm sure you know not to play without condoms and shit." Sheron shrugged. "Get dressed, and then come out to get some food. Ben says you guys haven't eaten all day."

Sheron left and closed the door behind her. Zoe stood for a moment, wondering what to do. Though comfortable in her jeans and T, she needed to fit in for Ben, at least for tonight.

The minidress dipped a little lower in front than she liked. It fit snug around her hips. At least the hem covered her rear end. Barely. Once she put on the thigh-high stockings and boots, she looked in the mirror.

Never, *ever* would she dare wear something like this. Anywhere but a metal bar and she'd get propositioned as a hooker. She did look pretty good for spending a wild night with her lover, but not for going out on the town.

She stood, hand on the bedroom doorknob. Why did she want to dress like this when all she was going to do was sit at a table to listen and watch? She didn't want to be propositioned or hit on. If some weirdo laid his hands on her…she shook her head. There was no telling what she'd do.

Nicholas. Her breath quickened. She squeezed her eyes shut then backed away from the door. *Zoe, stop.*

Get a hold of yourself.

"Suck it up," she whispered. "You'll be all right."

A deep breath passed her lips. She opened the door and quietly treaded down the hallway.

Ben and Sheron sat at the kitchen table with a plate of shrimp linguine. A third plate sat in the empty space beside Ben.

"Smells good," Zoe said as she pulled the chair out.

"Oh damn, girl. You're scorching hot." Sheron nodded in approval. "Now you're ready for the bar."

Ben's eyes widened. He dropped his fork. It clanged loudly on the edge of the plate, and then fell against the glass-top table. When he stood, mouth agape, his chair tipped over onto the floor behind him.

"What the hell, Sheron?" he choked, scanning Zoe head to toe. "I didn't bring her here for you to play…dress up with."

"You don't like it?" Zoe hugged her torso which just made the inner curves of her breasts more visible.

Ben picked his chair upright. He grabbed his leather jacket from the floor then hung it around her shoulders. "My God, Zoe," he whispered. "You're the hottest thing in Denver. Anywhere."

The spark ignited. When the corner of Sheron's lips rose, Zoe understood why she'd made her dress this way. Perky Pam no more. Bright was not her color tonight.

"She's going to turn heads," Sheron said, directing her comment to Ben, though she left her startling catlike eyes on Zoe. The wink she gave was in secret. "Don't worry. I'll watch out for your sweet little baker."

Zoe knew then. This was the beginning of a

beautiful, albeit odd, friendship.

Chapter Eleven

No way would Ben let Zoe out of the MINI Cooper looking the way she did. Her beautiful pale thighs showed. The jacket parted, exposing the soft, supple skin of her neckline and the inner curves of her breasts.

He struggled, wrenching his hands around the steering wheel. This was a horrible idea. Men were going to have a field day, eyes feasting on her. Mouths salivating.

"Can we go in now?" Zoe asked in the quiet car. He was sure she enjoyed his misery. "Your jacket covers most of the outfit."

"Most," he replied. "Doogen should go on without me so I can take you back to the house."

"He has a sprained arm. Plus, I want to hear you play."

"This is a rough place full of meatheads who'd love to get their hooks in you." He groaned. He had no choice but to accept the fact they had to go in. She had to be gawked at and hounded by the scum of the earth. "If I see one guy bothering you, I'll—"

"—you'll do nothing. Sheron and I don't want you fighting. Trust me. I can take care of myself."

"Come here." He cupped her face then pulled her close. "Can I kiss you?"

"Ben." She smiled as she placed her hand on his chest. "You never have to ask permission for a kiss."

He pressed his lips against hers. One kiss caused a big stir inside him. If he wanted to play the gig, he'd need to concentrate on something besides her.

"Let me take you home," he whispered into her mouth. "You can wear the outfit for me."

He caught movement in the corner of his eye. He glanced at the back entrance, where Dom, the bar's bouncer, stood waving his arms. Ben ignored him to hopefully get the answer he wanted from Zoe.

"We need to go in, or you'll be late."

"Then promise me." He kissed her lips once more. "Don't accept any drinks unless they're from Sheron or the bartender. And keep your hand over the mouth of your glass."

"Why?"

"Don't want your drink to get roofied."

She laughed a little. "What's *roofied*?"

He arched his brows. "Really?"

Zoe shrugged and then shook her head. "I don't know what it means."

Where was this girl from? Innocent baker from Kansas, that's who. He had no right to be with such a woman. She was too sweet for his world and had no idea what she was in store for tonight with all these ruffians. It wasn't just the men either. There were women who'd want to start a fight just because she didn't fit in.

"Just don't accept drinks from anyone. Stay beside Sheron and everything will be fine."

He got out of the car. Dom shouted for him to hurry as Ben grabbed his guitar from the backseat. He took Zoe's hand and held tight as he led her toward the rear entrance of the bar.

Dom stared at Zoe as she passed, flashing his golden-toothed smirk while massaging his fat, gray-bearded chin. "Well hello…sweetheart."

Ben kept Zoe moving through the kitchen and down the short, chair-cluttered hall until they reached the door to the main room. He retrieved his guitar from its soft case, slipped the dark blue strap over his head, and then positioned it on his shoulder. One more quick kiss on Zoe's lips, then he caught her gaze.

"I know," she said when he opened his mouth to speak. She clasped her hands behind his neck and pulled him down to meet her face-to-face. "I'll stay with Sheron. I won't accept drinks from anyone but her and the bartender. I promise." She nuzzled his ear, sending sparks through his body. "I'll sit in the seat next to her all night and won't move until you come get me."

"Good girl," he said and then kissed her one more time before leaving for the stage.

****

Ben walked down the darkened hall. Those holey jeans were meant to be worn only by him. He had no reason to be concerned when she had all the means to defend herself, courtesy of Deputy Fred's self-defense training.

She peered through the small rectangular window in the door. Sheron sat at a table near a man dressed in leather pants. His long red hair flowed down his shoulders to his morbidly muscular chest showing through a loose tank top.

Zoe drew in a deep breath then opened the door. She went out into the noisy, crowded room. She hurried into the seat next to Sheron and pulled Ben's leather jacket tighter around her.

She'd never frequented the bar scene in college. She'd ventured inside one once during the midafternoon break at a friend's request. Even then she only went in to retrieve a library book she'd lent her.

So here she sat like a virgin. Not dressed like one. Nervous. Stranger in a strange land. Though Sheron acknowledged her with a wink and bump of her elbow, she wished Ben could sit with her.

The band walked through a curtain and took their places on the short stage. Shouts and profanity broke through the roaring chorus of voices. Zoe cringed as several overly tattooed bald men below the stage violently shoved one another around. Nobody cared.

"I wanted to apologize for last weekend." The singer spoke calmly into the microphone. He held up his arm, showing off his bright blue sling. "Doctor says I'm a clumsy son of a bitch."

More shouts of profanity and boos followed. Even Sheron booed then heartily laughed.

So, this was the infamous Doogen, front man of the band and Ben's best friend. Though ruggedly handsome with curled shoulder length hair and slim body, the wrinkles at the corners of his eyes showed his age.

Doogen flipped his hair from his right eye. He tossed Ben a glance. The guitar gave a high pitch ring through the speakers as a deep evil chortle rolled from Doogen's mouth.

Zoe shivered from the excitement.

"All right, fuckheads." Doogen shouted into the microphone. "Let's tear this fucking place down."

The crowded room went wild as the music began loud, fast, and heavy. Zoe pressed her hands tight against her ears. People shoved tables and chairs aside, creating an empty space in the center of the room. They thrashed about, bodies hitting bodies, convulsing, ultimately finding pleasure in hurting one another.

Zoe had never seen anything like this before. Heavy music, lots of people, hateful dancing, lights flickering throughout the entire bar—this was somewhat inspiring and horrifying at the same time. Best thing was, nobody noticed she existed.

Sheron stood. "I'll be right back."

Zoe nodded. Her attention went straight to Ben who played his guitar like a rock star. Damn he was good and quite comfortable on stage. He made it look so easy.

He caught her gaze. The short wave she gave was in secret, but everyone probably saw the great big smile spread across his handsome face.

This wasn't a big deal as long as she stayed here in her seat with the jacket wrapped around her, although it was getting a little warm. Eventually, she'd have to take this heavy thing off.

Sheron returned to the table carrying two tall glasses and a bottle of beer in her hands. She set a glass down in front of Zoe and then sat beside her.

"What's this?" Zoe inspected the full glass of brown liquid, ice chunks bobbing near its surface.

"It's a Long Island Iced Tea," Sheron replied. "Have you ever had one before?" Zoe shook her head. "You'll love it."

Zoe picked up the drink. Last and only time she had alcohol was on her twenty-first birthday. One glass of wine with Millie at her favorite restaurant in Wichita and she was about to fall off her seat.

Zoe placed the straw between her lips. Cool liquid found her tongue. The powerful taste of alcohol swarmed in her mouth. She swallowed hard, trying not to choke as the drink burned down her throat.

Oh God, the taste was awful and oddly good at the same time. She'd expected green or black tea. But this drink packed a different kind of punch.

Her muscles relaxed. Everything relaxed. She drew another sip, a little more than her last. Warmth flowed through her veins. In no time, she'd found the bottom of the glass.

"Wow." Her head swam. Heat rose to her face and neck. Too hot, she slipped the leather jacket from her shoulders and draped it over the back of the chair. Sheron's friend made a point to lean over and look her up and down.

Sheron smiled. "Want another?"

"Sure," Zoe replied, and then leaned in close. "Where's the ladies' room?"

"Come on." Sheron turned to her friend. "Hey, Chug. Go after more drinks and meet us on the dance floor."

"Sure," he replied in a deep, unsettling voice. Chills spread up and down Zoe's spine.

Sheron held Zoe's hand as she whisked her around the convulsing floor. As they pushed through the crowd, the song ended. Bodies didn't move as much. Maneuvering through the gaps became easier as all eyes were now on her and Sheron.

The dance floor was an obstacle course. If the alcohol hadn't worked its awful magic, Zoe would be nervous. It was kind of nice being the center of attention, especially when she had Ben's eye.

As she walked in front of the stage, she waved with her free hand. She wanted to stop and say hi, but Sheron pulled her down a dark hallway and into the women's bathroom.

Zoe glanced at the women at the sink dressed similarly to one another. Boobs half spilled over tops of tight leather. One woman wore a spiked collar around her throat. They were all pretty, in a deathly dark kind of way. With jet-black hair and ghostly skin, black lipstick, and thick eyeliner, they reminded her of vampires.

Zoe turned on the faucet near the far wall. The three vampire women boxed her in at the sink.

"Look at the blonde bimbo," one said, diamond-pierced nose stuck up in the air. "Never seen you here before."

"I'm not from Denver," Zoe said.

The woman laughed. "You don't quite fit in with this crowd, Princess."

Sheron shrugged as she leaned her back against the wall, inspecting her black-painted nails. "How many restraining orders do you have now, Mandy?"

Mandy sneered. "Get lost, Sheron."

"I don't think Ben would appreciate anyone roughing up his new girl, especially you. So why don't you take your pins and needles and go stick yourself, you know, where the sun doesn't shine."

The woman glared. "I'm Ben's girlfriend."

"Ex." Sheron sighed. "Like two years ago. Get a fucking life."

This was Ben's ex-girlfriend? What did Sheron mean by pins and needles? Maybe this was the acupuncturist he'd dated for a week two years ago. The woman was an absolute knock-out, for a vampire.

Mandy shoved Zoe's shoulder. With held breath, Zoe caught the edge of the sink, saving herself from a humiliating fall to the floor. She clenched her fists, angry and ready to defend herself if the stupid ex-girlfriend tried anything else.

Mandy shoved Zoe's shoulder again. "What the hell do you think you're doing with *my* guy?"

Zoe found her balance. "Your guy? What would Ben want with a psycho like you?"

Sheron laughed. "And there you have it, girls," Sheron said in her deep, raspy tone. "Psycho bitch is put in her place."

Mandy turned her wild gaze on Zoe. With clenched teeth, she pulled her arm back and swung.

Zoe saw it coming. It was the easiest punch in the book to avoid. She leaned back and to the side and tried not to fall to the floor.

Mandy's fist missed her face by a mile. The girl hit her hip on the sink's edge and spiraled to the tiled floor.

Her two friends whispered to each other. They gave Mandy a glance and then left for the music-filled hall. Some friends they were.

"You should find trouble elsewhere," Zoe said as Mandy rose to her feet. "I'm not easy to bully."

"Bitch." Mandy sprang forward with both hands, aiming for Zoe's neck.

Zoe ducked in time to avoid the attack. Reflex took over as she grabbed Mandy's right wrist and twisted it around to her back. Mandy cried out as Zoe pulled upward. The music started again as she walked Mandy to the end of the restroom and shoved her into the graffiti-lined wall, ironically, right below the word *crazy.*

"Like I said," Zoe shouted over the loud, muffled song, "find trouble somewhere else. You're pretty. Stop wasting your time on someone who doesn't want you and find someone who does."

Zoe let go of Mandy's arm. Mandy slid down the wall to the floor, mascara streaking her face. Zoe felt a little sorry for the girl, but stalking was stalking, no matter what gender.

"That was so fucking cool," Sheron said.

"Thanks," Zoe replied, chin in the air, smile draped across her face as she followed Sheron out the bathroom door.

Zoe stepped through the crowd. She could take care of herself. Confident she didn't need a babysitter anymore, she went to the front, near the stage where several of those vampire women stood and watched Ben play guitar.

His gaze found hers. Though he kept playing, his brows furrowed. He scanned the room, probably looking for Sheron, who returned to Zoe's side with two full drinks and barbarian Chug.

Ben relaxed as Zoe danced. Two-step was about the only thing going on in small-town Kansas. To let loose and move her body seductively to a heavy tempo was exhilarating.

Sheron danced too, arms in the air, drink in hand, rear rubbing against Zoe's. Not like Zoe at all to dance with a woman in such a provocative manner. With anyone but Sheron, this would be weird.

Zoe laughed, feeling free and beautiful. Nothing in the world mattered but being here with new friends. And Ben. When the song ended, Ben leaned down.

"Where's the jacket?" He spoke fast. "Is that a Long Island Iced Tea?"

Zoe nodded with a smile. She sucked on the straw, letting the cool alcohol flood her mouth. Such a tasty drink, smooth, flavorful, strong, but well worth drinking to relax. Boy, was she relaxed.

"Don't get too drunk before the first set's over." Ben stood as the drummer started the beat.

The music was loud. The party grew louder. Zoe ignored the glares she received from the other women in the room as she danced with Sheron and Chug. She danced with the guy behind her, who smelled like stale beer and exhaust fumes, and another guy who bathed in cologne.

One drink led to another until Zoe had to stop. Too high, vision blurred, balance lost, she stumbled toward the table and plopped down on the chair.

Her feet ached, but it was okay. It felt good to be out, away from her town, away from her boring everyday life. This was the life here with Ben, watching him play guitar, catching his gaze every other second. Loving it.

Sheron leaned against her shoulder. This fun, amazing woman, this dark princess she adored, reminded her of an evil Millie.

Zoe gasped. *Crap*. She hadn't called Millie at all since she left town. Millie had probably called her a dozen times and left a million text messages.

Zoe checked her watch. Midnight. Millie might still be up writing on her memoir, since late at night was the only peace and quiet she got.

"I'll be right back," Zoe told Sheron.

"Where are you going?"

"I need to make a call." Zoe reached in her purse and pulled out her small flip-up cell phone.

"You are from this century, aren't you?"

Zoe stuck her tongue out then stood. Smartphones were the thing these days, but she was happy with the little old cell phone she'd carried around for years. It did its job, though texting was a bit tedious using the number pad.

Zoe stumbled through the door and headed toward the kitchen. She dialed Millie's number, and then pressed the green button. It rang twice. Millie answered. Her hushed tone meant everyone in the house was asleep but her.

"Hey, Millie," Zoe shouted. "I'm here. Ben's taking really good care of me. I'm having the time of my life."

"Zoe, honey, are you drunk?"

"Yes, but don't worry. I feel so happy and alive, Millie. I feel so free, and I want to celebrate everything."

"You've never been drunk before."

"I'm in love, Millie."

Zoe gazed at the fluorescent light on the ceiling in the hallway. She expected Millie to come back with words of wisdom about falling in love and using protection and all the other motherly stuff, but she breathed a sigh.

"Ben seems like a nice guy. So have fun while you can. Make sure you protect your heart and everything else. Be careful."

"I'll be fine," Zoe said. "I love you, Millie."

"I love you too, sweetie," Millie said with a laugh. "Now I need to go, or I'm going to wake someone, and then I'll never get any writing done. Call me before you leave for home so I know you're on your way."

Zoe closed her cell phone. As she leaned against the wall to steady her balance, exhaust-fume guy walked through the door. The creepy short man smiled as he waggled his bushy dark brows.

"You're quite a dancer," he said, stroking his short brown beard.

"Thanks." Zoe maneuvered around him. Chills swept through her as she hurried down the hallway. Hell, no would she get cornered by him or anyone.

"Wait up. I only want to talk."

She ran through the door then sat at the table. Out of breath, woozy, she scooted closer to Sheron. The man strode through the door. He stared as he headed toward the bar.

Zoe shivered. No telling what the guy had planned on doing, but she wasn't afraid. She could defend herself. She'd really hate to have to hurt anyone else tonight.

Nicholas's face flashed in her mind. The night he'd boxed her in, he'd hit her. Repeatedly. She covered her face with her hands determined to quit thinking about him. *Stop, Zoe.*

This was ridiculous. Nicholas was in Kansas somewhere. Here, she was safe. She wasn't alone. Ben wouldn't let anything happen to her.

Another drink would get her back to happy-go-lucky. Not caring if Sheron followed or not, she made her way through the thick crowd to the bar.

"Long Island Iced Tea," she said, leaning forward, elbows on the long wooden countertop.

The bartender grinned and puffed out his hairy,

naked chest. He mixed her drink then set the glass on the counter.

"A pretty lady like you deserves one on the house," he said with a wink.

"Thank you." She picked up the drink. She turned around to make her way back to the table when exhaust-fume man stepped in front of her. Anxiety tore through her. The guy had the same build as Nicholas.

"Can I buy you a drink?"

"I have one." She took a step to the right, but he blocked her path again. *Oh God, don't do this.*

The giant hairy mole on the end of his fat nose became a focal point. His brown moustache and beard covered most of his face. Though his dark eyes were gentle, he wanted more than to buy her a drink.

"Want to dance again?"

"I'm on my way back to my table."

"Mind if I join you?"

"No." He touched her arm, but she stepped back. "I'm already in a party tonight."

"Come on." He pinched her elbow and tried to coax her toward the bar. "Just one drink."

She planted her feet solidly on the floor. No way would she follow this guy anywhere. *Darn it.* Why couldn't people just leave her alone?

His face reddened and jaw tightened. Thick veins in his temple grew prominent as he tightened his grip.

"Get off me." Zoe jerked her arm away. Her drink splashed on her chest. She let out a short scream as the cool liquid streamed to the crevice between her breasts.

A wild grin spread across his pudgy face as he reached for the neckline of her dress. A tall body in a T-shirt and holey jeans stepped in front of her. Her vision blurred, but there was no mistaking who this was.

"Ben." She leaned her forehead against his back. She touched his side with her free hand and his muscles tensed. Thank God he was here to save her.

"You heard the lady," Ben said. "Step back."

"She's with you?"

"Yeah," Ben replied. "Now get lost."

"Hey, man, I didn't know."

Ben turned around. Zoe's temple slid across the green alien spaceship on the front of his shirt. A grin crept across her face as she stared up into those heavenly eyes. His face was distorted. Blurry. Darn this wonderful elixir in her glass for not letting her see the most handsome man on earth.

"Soljer." She playfully smacked his chest. "My sexy guitar hero. Are you done playing?" Her words—she could barely get them out from the slur.

He held her firmly against him. "Just taking a short break."

The man was gorgeous. She raised her hand to touch his smooth face, to run her fingers over every inch of his skin and through his bangs and hair, but he caught her wrist.

"Ah." She puckered her wet lips. "You're mad at me."

"You're wasted."

"I'm not wasted…though I've never been wasted before. I'm all dizzy and happy and woo. I've never felt quite like this before. I feel a little like falling. Maybe flying too. It's so weird." She giggled as she put the straw between her lips. She drew the cool drink into her mouth, swallowing each time she sucked. Her eyes watered. "I'm having fun."

"How many have you had?"

"This is my third, I think. I can't really remember." She hiccupped and then laughed. Wow. Last time she had hiccups was…she couldn't remember, but it was quite rare.

Ben didn't crack a smile.

Party pooper.

"I think you've had enough."

"Ben." Sheron put her arm around Zoe's neck and laughed. "Miss Baker here is awesome. She met your ex-girlfriend in the bathroom and kicked her ass. It was *fan*-tastic."

"I didn't kick her ass." Zoe shrugged. Sheron's excitement was contagious. "I only kept—*hic*—mine from getting kicked."

"Sent Mandy to the floor crying like a baby." Sheron kissed Zoe's cheek. "You're a keeper."

"Great." Ben rubbed his temple. "Bringing you here was a really bad idea."

Zoe rolled her eyes. "Oh, lighten up, Benny baby." *Benny baby* sounded so funny.

He took her by the hand and led her to the table. He grabbed his leather jacket off the chair on the way out the door. Once they reached the hallway, he draped the heavy garment over her shoulders.

Zoe planted her feet solidly in the hall. No way was he about to kick her out of this party. He nudged her toward the exit again, but she leaned back hard.

"Would you stop pushing me?" she said in a hushed voice, careful not to alert the people standing near the kitchen. She put her forefinger to her lips and shushed herself, giggling as she shook off the jacket. "It's hot in here."

"Men are staring."

"No, they're not." She raised her glass to get another sip. He took it from her. "Hey…"

He set the glass down on the small, rickety wooden table along the wall. "You're very drunk."

"And you're uptight." She sighed. How could she get it through his brain? She was fine. This was a new experience. "I live in a small town where the only excitement I find is playing a video game alone in my little apartment and watching—*hic*—tornadoes cross the road. I've never even been to a bar before. Heck, I've never been drunk." Hopefully, her words were making some sort of sense. "Did you know during the town's New Year's party, they serve sparkling cider? I'm tired of sparkling cider."

A half grin broke on his lips. "Is that so bad?"

"I just wanted to try something new." She picked up her drink from the table. "I'm having fun, here with you and your fabulous roommate. Why don't you grab a drink and join me?"

"I haven't touched the heavy stuff in a long time." He sat on one of the chairs along the wall. "My brother drank heavily. Decided to wrap himself around a tree with his motorcycle one night."

"Oh, honey." Her heart dived to the floor. "When?"

"Two years ago."

She sat on his lap and slid her arms around his neck. "I'm so sorry." She leaned her forehead against his cheek. "Why didn't you tell me before?"

"Never wanted to talk about it." His hand slid up her back to her nape. "Sheron's my sister-in-law. When Chase died, she had nowhere to go, so I let her stay in the house."

Tears welled in her eyes. What an awful thing to go through. Losing a brother, a husband. "Oh, now I understand why she has a wedding dress in her closet."

"Oh, man. I didn't mean to make you cry." He thumbed the tears from her cheeks. "I'm such a buzzkill."

She shook her head. "Oh, Ben. I shouldn't have drunk so much."

"I want you to have fun tonight." He kissed her lips. "I promise I'll take care of you."

Her head swam enough. This was the only and last time she'd get drunk again. She leaned her head on his shoulder. Comfortable enough to fall asleep, she closed her eyes. Maybe this was what passing out felt like.

"Can I stay here with you…like this?" she whispered, unsure if she even said the words.

"Stay as long as you want."

His touch was gentle as he massaged her back. His other hand caressed her side. The warmth of his breath brushed the bridge of her cheek and she shivered. By far, this was the safest she'd felt in two years. If she could trap this moment in a bottle, she'd take it with her and uncork it every time she got scared. She'd have it open all the time. Except now. With him.

"Ben," a man's voice called out. "We're back on, man."

Ben palmed her cheek. "One more hour, and we'll go home. Okay?"

It took all her strength and his strong hands to steady her rise to her feet. The room spun. She stumbled back. He caught her before she fell to the floor. He pulled her up to him, corner of his lips curved downward. He didn't like her being drunk.

The alcohol kept hitting her, beating her senses, blurring her vision. *Wow*, she had no idea she'd feel this way. The world turned like a fast-moving merry-go-round.

"I'll be fine," she said, leaning against Ben's side as he helped her to her chair. She leaned her chin on her fists, elbows on the table, fighting her falling eyelids. The music blared, blending together with loud voices and shouts in the chaotic room, until there was no sound at all.

****

Zoe's head smacked against the table. Sheron swiped the golden locks from Zoe's face, and then gave a quick thumbs-up, letting him know she was okay.

The final set took forever to finish. He usually stayed after to drink a beer with Doogen but wouldn't tonight for obvious reasons.

After packing his guitar in the backseat of the MINI, he hurried inside the bar to retrieve Zoe. Her right cheek was pressed against the table.

"Zoe." He scooped her face up and lifted. "It's time to go."

"Hey-y-you." She grinned but wouldn't open her eyes. "Baby aliens…are invading the bakery…eating…doughnuts."

Sheron cackled heartily. Ben scooped Zoe up in his arms and narrowed his eyes. This wasn't funny. If anything, Sheron was the reason Zoe was wasted.

"Wow, Ben." Sheron sat up from the nook of Chug's giant arm. "Glare at me much?"

With Zoe's right side shoved against his chest, her nipple showed. "Put my jacket over her, will you?"

Sheron did what he asked, then held the door open.

He carried Zoe down the hall with Sheron on his heels.

"Are you blaming me for her inability to handle alcohol?" she asked as he stepped through the kitchen toward the back door.

"I blame you for getting her drunk."

"I had no idea she'd get plastered on a few drinks."

Ben shook his head. "I didn't either."

Zoe's eyes fluttered open. "Oh, Ben baby, my...super guitar hero sandwich." Her eyes rolled and then closed again. "Let's go to the lake and...skinny-dip." She snorted a laugh, and then slurred quietly, "You'd look naked holding my goods. I'll have you...bake a cake when we get home. I love you...my...*peep.*"

Sheron tossed her hand to her mouth, but her raspy laugh broke through. Ben tried his best to keep a straight face, but even he couldn't help cracking a grin.

He carefully placed Zoe in the passenger seat of the car. He pulled the seat belt across her lap and shoulder and then latched it as Sheron hovered behind him.

"For what it's worth," Sheron said as he repositioned his jacket over Zoe's exposed chest, "I really do like her. She's sweet and fun. A definite keeper."

Ben shut the car door. Sheron was right. This woman had his undivided attention. It scared him, and yet, he couldn't fathom not having her here.

"We'll see," he said as he rounded the front of the car. "Need a lift home?"

"Taking a cab to Chug's tonight."

"Be safe."

"Always."

When he drove out on the road, Zoe stirred. She

whimpered, hopefully not about to be sick in his car. He'd rather not spend the night cleaning puke off the MINI's floor.

The jacket fell to her lap. He tried not to look at her exposed chest, but it was there, nipple showing again. He swallowed hard, returning his attention to the road.

It'd been a year and a half since he'd dived into a bottle. He didn't want to go back down inside. He didn't want to end up like Chase. And Zoe, though unknowingly, had tempted him to take a drink.

"Stop…" she cried in a soft breath. Tears fell from the inner corners of her closed eyes. "Nic—Stop…"

Her eyes opened, and then slowly closed. She slid her hand under her face and leaned against the door. She whimpered again.

Ben sighed. He had nightmares too. Seeing Chase bloodied and broken on the ground kept him up at night. Maybe Zoe had a past haunting her as well. By the tears falling down her supple cheeks, maybe she was more fragile than he'd thought.

Chapter Twelve

Faint blue light gave Ben's darkened room a soft glow. The distant sound of water swirling kept the room from silence. The relaxing white noise might have put Zoe back to sleep if she didn't need to pee.

She patted the space on the other side of the bed. Ben wasn't there. She hadn't expected him to be since they'd never discussed sleeping arrangements.

She swung her legs over the edge of the bed. *Oh, blech.* Her head ached. Stomach in knots, she rose, and shuffled to the bathroom.

So this was the agony of a hangover. Never again. Forget the booze. From now on she'd stick to sparkling cider.

She caught her reflection in the bathroom mirror. The skimpy dress was wrinkled and her breasts had popped out of the neckline. She pulled the garment over her head and then peeled the tight shorts off her rear end.

After a short sit on the toilet, she grabbed a washcloth and towel off the shelf and hung them inside the shower stall. Zoe stared at the garden tub. She envisioned herself surrounded with bubbles, bathing the headache away. Positive Ben's invitation was still valid, she grabbed her linens and stepped up to the tub.

She twisted the hot-and-cold handle until the water ran warm. As the tub filled, she wrapped the towel around her body and then went to the bedroom. She stuffed her hand down inside her suitcase and pulled out a pair of socks, a fresh pair of panties, and a bra.

She grabbed her yellow gown and toiletries and then headed for the bathroom. She brushed the awful taste of alcohol from her mouth, tied her hair up with her favorite tie, and then took off her remaining clothes. She poured a small amount of cherry-blossom-scented body wash beneath the flow of water, and bubbles formed.

When she sank down in the warm water, she shivered. Soft suds caressed her skin. Water lapped around her neck. It tickled. Slowly, the ache in her stomach and the throb in her head eased.

She closed her eyes and thought of last night. Poor Ben. He'd worried. She'd made it difficult on him. The last thing she remembered was sitting on his lap in the hallway while he told her about his brother. There was also a brief memory of him carrying her in his arms. She had no idea how she got back here.

In the year and a half they'd talked, he'd told her many small things about himself, and yet she was still learning about the deeper troubles he dealt with. This was good. It meant he trusted her. After last night, she trusted him. He was a good man.

She opened her eyes and smiled. Maybe this was love.

Visualizing him next to her in the tub, touching her in all the right places, sent goosebumps over her skin. If he were here, would she let him in? Could she do it without thinking about her past? Without fearing he'd hurt her like Nicholas had?

She shut her eyes tight. *No*. Don't think about

Nicholas now. Not here in this heavenly tub. Not in Ben's house.

She pulled the tie out of her hair and set it on the tiled lip of the tub. With breath held, she ducked down in the water. When she resurfaced, she wiped the suds from her eyes.

She dipped again, this time holding herself underwater for a long while. Her cool face warmed. The soap tickled her skin. All thoughts moved to the back of her mind. The muscles in her body eased.

She was about to come up for air when a pair of hands grabbed her arms. Adrenaline shot through her like a bolt of lightning. Every muscle in her body tightened. Nicholas's hands held her down. She screamed, and water rushed into her mouth. No way would she allow him to get the best of her again.

She turned her body, feet slipping against the tub. She fought as the hands lifted her to her feet. "Get off me." She choked on soap suds as she blindly waved her arms to break loose from the strong grip.

"Whoa. Zoe. Calm down."

Zoe stopped fighting. "Ben?"

"Yeah, baby, it's me."

Zoe flung her arms around his neck. She held tight. Breath labored, she stood on shaky legs. "Thank God it's you."

His hands slid around her waist. "Who else did you think it would be?"

She couldn't answer. Not yet. And especially not now while she was wet, naked, and hugging Ben, whose warm chest felt really good against hers. Being in his arms, although awkward, was safe.

"Don't ever sneak up on me again." She opened

her stinging eyes but wouldn't let go. "You scared the hell out of me."

"I can tell." He tightened his hold on her. "You're shaking."

"I'm going to sit back down in the tub now." She cleared her throat. "If you don't mind, close your eyes."

"Okay," he said. "They're closed."

She loosened her hold on his neck. Using his hand as a guide and careful not to slip, she lowered herself into the warm water.

He stood before her with his eyes shut. Stretchy boxers—the kind leaving nothing to the imagination, hugged his lower body. Her face grew hot. *Holy crap*, he was big under the tight cloth. She shouldn't be checking him out, but how could she not? He wasn't easy to miss.

Her gaze went back to his closed eyelids. "I'm in the tub now."

He caught her gaze. "Are you okay?"

"My eyes are stinging. But, yeah, I'm fine."

"I'm sorry. I knocked." He handed her the wash cloth. "When you didn't answer, I came in and found you underwater."

"I was just trying to relax."

"Underwater?"

Not wanting to explain, she nodded. "You scared me."

"I know." He gave a short laugh through his nose. "I'm sorry, but I thought you were drowning."

"Well, I wasn't." She ran her palms over the top of the water. Her face burned with embarrassment. He'd seen her naked. What thoughts went through his head? "Thanks for saving me, though. It was…nice." *Nice*.

What a cop-out. She'd rather enjoyed being in his arms, body squished up against his.

"You're welcome." He stepped out of the tub. The muscles in his long legs tightened as he strode toward the door. The man could be an underwear model. "So I was thinking if you're up for a short road trip, I'd like to show you my cabin in the mountains."

A cabin? She'd seen pictures in magazine articles but had never visited a real one before. Ben was full of surprises. Good ones. Maybe a romantic getaway like a cabin in the woods would be just what she needed to open up to him. Stop being scared and put her past behind her.

"Sounds lovely. I'll be out as soon as I get ready."

He left the room and shut the door behind him. She pulled the stopper. As the water gurgled down the drain, she got out and then dried her body with the long towel.

After drying her hair and applying makeup, she shimmied into her yellow gown and then followed the sweet scent to the kitchen.

Ben stood at the stove, his midnight strands stuck up in tufts. He dipped the spatula in the pan and flipped over a large pancake with purple speckles. The man was sexy in relaxed jeans, and a dark T-shirt that hugged his upper body.

"Aww…You're making blueberry pancakes."

"Your favorite." Half grin. Right brow arched. She could melt like the butter on the hotcakes.

She leaned back against the counter. "Thought you didn't like pancakes."

"I'm an egg-and-meat kind of guy. But every once in a while I'll crave something sweet." He handed her a plate. His other brow arched. "I must say, you look especially beautiful in yellow."

"Oh. Thanks." She sat at the table and admired the single red rose he'd set out as a centerpiece.

"I picked it for you this morning." He sat beside her. "I hope you're not allergic."

Warmth flooded her face. He'd picked her a flower. No man had ever given her flowers. Except Renji who bought her a bouquet to spruce up her kitchen or the bakery every so often. But Ben had gone out and picked one. Could there be anything more romantic?

"I'm not allergic to flowers."

"Are you sure?" He took a bite of his pancakes. "Your face is the same shade as the rose."

****

He studied her, memorized her hair and the color of her eyes. Blonde, blue eyed angel. Sweet, and quiet. How did he get to be with such a woman? She was stunning, and even more so naked. He'd been forced to turn away or risk her seeing how aroused he'd been.

Maybe if he hadn't scared her like he had, he'd have joined her in the tub. But she was genuinely scared. Not startled but frightened to a point she couldn't stop shaking. What had happened in her life to cause such a strong reaction?

He shoved his empty plate to the side. He folded his arms over the table and watched her eat. "Sheron's taken with you." He grinned when he caught her gaze. This was the first time Sheron had ever liked anyone of the same gender. Hell, maybe even the same species. "She usually hates everyone."

"I'm glad." She set her fork down on the plate. "I

mean, I like her too."

"Doesn't bother you that she lives here, then?"

"Oh, not at all. She's so much fun. I get why you let her stay."

He tapped his fingers lightly on his forearm. What was this sensation? He'd had girlfriends here before. They'd made him feel as though he were trapped in a dark room with no escape. Zoe was real—a light at the end of a tunnel. Though a little troubling, this woman had tipped his world upside down. It felt good having her here.

"Thanks for making pancakes. They were delicious." She picked up their plates and took them to the sink. "I usually eat a cinnamon roll for breakfast," she said as she rinsed off the syrup. "I've been meaning to change my diet. Apparently, I don't eat enough fruits and vegetables to stay healthy."

He opened the dishwasher. She handed him the plates and he stuck them on the bottom rack. "You look healthy to me."

Zoe wasn't skin and bones like a lot of women these days. She had flesh on her body, beautiful pale and perfect flesh with just enough color to make her glow.

"Aw…thanks." She dried her hands on the towel and smiled. "You're sweet to say so."

"And you're just sweet." He brushed his palm across her cheek. "Want to see the rose garden in the backyard?" First time he'd ever asked a woman to see them. He'd never cared about anyone enough to show this intimate side of him.

She flashed a beaming smile. "I'd love to."

He led her through the kitchen and into the dining

room. He unlatched the lock on the back door and then slid it to the side.

Her eyes lit up. "Oh wow," she whispered as she viewed the roses along the fence line. "They're beautiful."

"It was my brother's idea to line heated coils under the dirt. The roses start to bloom in March." He led her across the wooden deck and then stopped at the top of the stairs. "When it frosts, I pull the cover from the fence line and hook it to the ground. It holds in the heat."

"This is Chase's garden?"

Ben shrugged. "The manly guy had a fascination for flowers. Sheron took over the upkeep of the roses when he died."

She let go of his hand and stepped down. Her bare feet sank into the soft grass. For a moment she stood watching her wiggling toes. She glanced back, catching his gaze, and then giggled as she took off down the path.

Stepping stones led down the side of the yard where the pumpkin roses bloomed. Like a young girl playing in the yard, she followed their zigzag pattern, blonde curls bouncing around her shoulders, until she reached the end near the tall wooden fence.

He had to admit, the flowers were gorgeous. But seeing Zoe happily make her way through his big open yard, as if she hadn't a care in the world—she was the most beautiful thing he'd ever seen.

He stepped in the grass and walked toward her. She knelt and closed her eyes, breathing in the sweet flowery scent he knew all too well.

"Ben." She rose to meet him. Her hands slid over

his forearms. "This is absolutely amazing."

"You're amazing." He kissed her pouty lips. His tongue briefly touched hers. "You look like one of the yellow roses, dancing across the yard," he whispered near her lips. "But you taste of blueberries."

"So do you."

He leaned back. "You should see the trees around the property early summer. When their blooms fall, it looks like pink snow. Might even start by the end of next month if this nice weather keeps up."

Her hands slid from his arms. Her smile faded. "I'm sure it's beautiful."

"Hey." He palmed her cheek. "What's wrong?"

The color in her cheeks deepened. "I'd like to be here to see the trees bloom."

He understood. They'd never discussed anything more than meeting each other to see how they got along. He definitely wanted more time with her. Now they'd need to find a way to make the five-hundred-mile trip easier. Since she didn't own a car, it was going to be tough.

He sighed. "We'll figure something out."

"Do you think I should change clothes before we go to the cabin?"

"Yeah. It'll be chilly in the mountains." He motioned with his head to follow. "Let's get ready to go."

Chapter Thirteen

When they reached the summit, Zoe's ears had popped, plugged, and then popped again. Ben veered the Jeep off the road and parked near the edge of what seemed the highest spot in the world.

She gazed out the window. Mountaintops stretched like white pyramids across the horizon. A mass of clouds sat below their snow-covered peaks and then cleared in the valley below.

"Wow," she whispered, leaning forward. "It's so beautiful."

He opened the door and got out. Without pause, she followed and met him in front of the Jeep, near the guardrail. Though warm in her hoodie and the winter coat Sheron had lent her, she shivered.

She wasn't so sure she'd wanted to go anywhere. But now, with this gorgeous scenery, and being with Ben who'd treated her kindly, she was glad she was here. Two years locked inside her apartment, afraid to go on an adventure like this, melted away like the dust of snow beneath her feet.

Right now, at this unbelievable moment, she wasn't afraid.

Ben stood behind her and wrapped his arms around her shoulders. "There's a coffee shop there." She followed the point of his forefinger to the tiny town in the valley. "Thought we could stop and have a cup if you'd like."

"Coffee sounds wonderful." She loved the way he held her. Not confining, just close. "I haven't been out of Kansas in such a long time. I was with my dad on a mountain just like this one. We were on our way home from a vacation at Yellowstone and stopped off at a scenic view for lunch."

"You've mentioned your mom before, but never said much about your dad."

"He passed away about six years ago."

"What happened to him?"

She shook her head. Not a conversation to get into right now. Or ever. "I don't talk about him."

He turned her around to face him. "You don't talk about him? Or won't?"

"I haven't in a long time." Those green eyes stared straight into her soul. He wanted to know, but she wasn't sure she was ready to tell the story. "You really don't want to hear about my nightmare of a life right now."

He swiped a lock of blonde from her eye. "I want to know everything about you, Zoe Kearny. The good. The bad. Tell me about the nightmares that keep you up at night, so I can chase them away."

Uh-oh. Had she talked in her sleep? Screamed too loud? Renji had woken her from a nightmare about Nicholas before. She'd about scared the life out of him with her shrieks.

"Everyone has nightmares."

"I have them too." He leaned his temple against hers. "I can tell something bad happened to you and I want you to know I'm here for you."

What the heck had she said in her sleep? He knew

something had happened, but did he know what? She had to believe *no*. He was fishing for answers she wasn't prepared to give yet. At least, not about Nicholas.

Maybe it was the moment, standing on this mountain overlooking the world's most beautiful scenery. The sexiest guy in the universe stood before her, inviting her to open her heart. She couldn't help being drawn in.

"It's a sad story, and I might cry."

He pulled her tighter against him. "I have a comfortable shoulder with a lot of padding."

She sighed. Where to begin? It'd been a long while since she'd dredged up the memory of her dad. Her heart broke every time she heard his name. It was breaking now—and she hadn't even said a word.

"My dad shot and killed himself on my sixteenth birthday."

"Oh, shit, Zoe." His brows arched. He obviously hadn't expected the conversation to start like that. But, who would? "It must've been difficult for you."

Zoe's throat tightened. She leaned against Ben's chest and blinked back tears. This was harder than she thought.

"Dad promised he'd buy me a car when I turned sixteen. The morning of my birthday, he asked me to wait a little longer because he'd spent part of the money on an engagement ring. I was pretty angry."

"He broke his promise. It's understandable you'd be upset."

"I gave him the silent treatment during the birthday party he'd thrown for me. I wouldn't say a word until everyone had gone home. On the way to my room, I

123

told him I hated him for going back on his promise." She shook her head, remembering the resentment. Guilt swept through her. She shuddered, and then all the pain she'd buried spilled out in a mess of tears. "Those were the last words I said to him." She cried in her hands. "I was a terrible daughter."

"You were a teenager."

"A snobby, spiteful teenager." She sniffled as she dragged her fingers beneath her eyes to wipe off the tears. God, she was such a blubbering baby. "Ever since I was a little girl, I'd always reminded him to check the chamber of his guns before cleaning them. I didn't that day."

"Oh, honey." Ben pressed his lips against her temple. "I'm sorry."

"If I could just see him one last time to apologize." She buried her face in the padding of his coat. "Oh. I'm ruining our fun with my awful story."

"I'm glad you shared your story with me." He curled his finger under her chin then lifted. "You can tell me anything. Okay?"

"Yeah." She drew in a deep breath. *Get a hold of yourself.* "What about you? You've never said anything about your parents. Do they live around here?"

"Nah. They died when I was six. Plane crash near the state park. Chase was sixteen, so he dropped out of school to take care of me. I think taking on too much responsibility drove him over the edge."

"Oh, Ben," she whispered puckering up to cry again. "What an awful thing to go through."

"Ah now, come on, babe. Don't cry." He put his arms around her and gave her a quick squeeze. "Let's put this depressing conversation aside and go get coffee. Then we'll head up to the cabin."

On the way down the mountain, a serious calm swept over her. Ben was alone in the world. So was she. He was easy to talk to, especially when he held her in his arms. It'd be great to continue this every day if they didn't live so far away from each other.

The quaint little coffee shop, charming and aromatic, reminded her of the bakery. The only thing missing was the smell of breads and pastries baking in the oven.

Two older women, gray hair netted and tied up in buns, stood behind the counter. Both were friendly and knew Ben well as they greeted him by name.

Zoe sat at the bar on a round, padded stool made for a fifties diner. Baby-blue top cushions on the stools coordinated well with the pumpkin-colored walls. White swirls of steam rolled above giant posters of coffee cups, giving the place a nice warm touch, perfect for a getaway during the colder seasons.

Ben sat beside her and ordered a caramel macchiato. She chose the dark-chocolate mocha.

Zoe sipped her drink. The wide mouthed lime-green coffee cup looked much like the picturesque cup on the wall. Whipped cream and chocolate drizzle sweetened the drink and warmed her cool lips.

Ben's leg touched hers under the bar. His elbow nudged hers. He leaned close and stole a kiss.

"Come here often?" she said shyly. She'd often seen cute couples sitting in the corner of the bakery, drinking coffee and sharing a doughnut, but never did she imagine she'd join the ranks.

"Several times a month." He pressed his lips above the corner of hers. "Whipped cream," he whispered.

Weak, melting like the cream swirling around the hot liquid in her cup, she set the heavy mug down on the bar. He kissed her lips. Her eyes closed. When his tongue gently touched hers, her heart quickened.

He leaned back. She couldn't open her eyes. She just sat and smiled and prayed she wasn't dreaming.

"You okay?" His whispering breath tickled her ear.

She inhaled deeply and then let it out slowly through parted lips. "I think so."

"Dizzy?"

"In the clouds right now."

He chuckled. "It's the elevation."

When she opened her eyes, she caught his gaze. "Something on your mind, handsome?"

"Besides you and the cute amount of whipped cream on your chin?" He kissed her lips again. "Yeah. I'm working on a solution to our long-distance…problem."

"Any ideas?"

"A few. But I'd love some input from you."

Zoe picked up the napkin and wiped her chin. All the time she'd worried about *if* they'd see each other again, she'd never given much thought on how.

"We could take turns," she said. "You fly to see me. I'll fly to see you."

"We could also meet halfway."

Traveling on weekends, even halfway down a straight stretch road, didn't seem appealing. She didn't own a car. Flights were expensive. But she couldn't stand not seeing Ben for weeks at a time.

Her stomach knotted, just like this morning when he mentioned the blossoms on the tree. "What do you mean by halfway? There aren't many places to stay between here and my house."

"Well." He cleared his throat. "My band plays in Goodland once a month."

"Goodland, Kansas?" She turned to face him, shocked. He'd never said anything about it before. "You've played there and never told me?"

"You're mad at me now, aren't you?" He cringed. "I would've said something before, but I wasn't sure what you'd think about meeting in such a dirty place."

"I wouldn't have come unless you invited me."

"Oh, Zoe, baby." He lifted her hand and pressed his lips to her wrist. "You're invited to everything I do. Anything you want of mine—garden tub. My roses. My blueberry-pancake mix. Just name it, and it's yours."

She laughed. "You're crazy."

He gave her a peck on the lips. "Crazy about you."

Warmth spread through her veins. She felt the same way about him. Perfectly crazy.

She lifted her hand to his face. He leaned his cheek onto her palm. His solemn grin sent her heart fluttering. He was so close. His warm breath on her skin made her shiver. Every fiber in her body relaxed as his lips parted and his tongue swept inside her mouth.

Caramel and dark chocolate mingled as if they were meant to be together. This was by far the best feeling in the world. Right now he could take her to the end of the earth, and she'd jump over the edge with him. It was an unnerving way to feel. She'd paid a heavy price letting her guard down with Nicholas, and promised she'd never do that again. But this—this was too amazing to fight.

After coffee, they headed farther down the mountain. At the end of the small town, he took a right on a dirt road, and then drove up a winding hill to a small log cabin. Tall trees hung over the house. Shadows moved over the snowy ground. As she followed Ben inside the house, a chill shimmied up her spine.

The carved wood decor reminded her of the old log home she'd seen in the magazine. Near the front window sat a wooden rocking chair. A high-back bench stretched along the far wall next to the dark hallway. A unique coffee table made of curved lacquered driftwood stood in the center of the room near a brown couch. It didn't quite fit in with the rest of the furniture.

How she'd love to own a house like this instead of the tiny apartment she called home. Home just didn't appeal to her anymore. After everything she'd seen here with Ben, how could she possibly return to her boring life of microwave meals and pastries? At this moment, she never wanted to go back, but make a life here with him.

This troubled her. She'd never envied anything before in her life. Granted, she'd known Ben for over a year, but why, after just two days' face time, was this man so deep in her heart?

She followed him to the large paned window in the kitchen. A sour, putrid scent wafted into her nostrils. She pinched her nose and peered at the rotting vegetables in the garbage can. Someone had tossed a meat tray full of gristle on top of the peels, and they'd turned green from the time it'd been here.

"Oh, shit." He groaned. "Forgot to take the garbage out last time I was here." He grabbed the bag from the can. "Be right back."

Ben disappeared out the patio door. He passed the

kitchen window to a small square enclosure made of lattice. He stuffed the trash bag into the can. She giggled as he struggled to reattach the lid to the bin.

Except for the clock ticking on the wall in the living room, the house was quiet. It'd be nice if this was her house. Ben was her husband. They owned the coffee shop in town and worked together to make it thrive. Their son slept in his crib in the back bedroom while she made dinner on the old gas stove beside her.

It was a silly daydream. She'd only met Ben two days ago, although she knew a lot about him. His favorite color was blue. He loved Chinese food, working on cars, and playing guitar. He enjoyed video games and sometimes joined his work football team during the fall.

This relationship would work out so much better if they didn't have to part ways. Her gut churned. To go back to Kansas, to lock her apartment up with her inside, to be afraid again, was agonizing to think about.

He passed by the window again, brilliant teeth showing in a smile. Her heart beat so hard it nearly leaped out of her chest. He stopped at the sink and washed his hands. When he finished, she fell into his arms.

The force of her body sent him back a step. "Whoa." He wrapped his arms around her shoulders. "What's wrong?"

This felt right, her cheek against his chest, arms squeezing his torso. She didn't want to let go of the moment or the daydream. To stay here forever in his arms, hiding away from the rest of the world, would be wonderful.

He held her tightly. She didn't know if this was

love, or if it could be so soon. If she had the guts, she'd say it now. She'd tell him she loved him.

"Zoe?" He leaned her back. "Talk to me."

"I'm fine." She placed her hands on his chest. "Better than fine if you kiss me."

He was quick to connect. His tongue swept inside her mouth. He cupped her face as caramel mocha burst through. The kiss deepened.

He leaned back just enough to catch her gaze. "And how are you now?"

"Better than fine," she whispered. She was ready for this. To be with him here in their quiet house would be her ultimate experience. She'd finally know love—be loved by a wonderful, gentle man.

The material of his coat was cool on her fingers. She slid her hands slowly down his chest to the hem of his jacket. She tucked her fingers under his shirt. When she touched his abdomen, his muscles tightened.

He placed his palms on each side of her neck. With his thumb gently tracing her bottom lip, he dragged his other hand down. He slowly unzipped her jacket. The back of his hand grazed her nipple through her shirt. Electricity spread through her veins. Her body jolted and she whimpered.

She'd never allowed anyone to touch her. Sex was just a fantasy that happened in dreams and always turned to nightmares. If she could keep her past from interfering, she'd give in to him now. The heat low in her belly was proof of how much she wanted him.

He lifted his hand to her face and studied her eyes. Maybe he searched for hesitation. Maybe even permission to let him continue touching her. She opened her mouth to tell him to touch her, but he silenced her with a kiss.

She lost her breath as he backed her through the kitchen. Her gut somersaulted. Her back touched the kitchen counter. She tensed.

Don't freak out, Zoe. He'd boxed her in. She had room to move if she needed to. Not that she'd want to leave his touch, but it was good to know she wasn't confined to this spot.

He grasped her sides beneath her shirt. He gently pinched her flesh. Mouth never leaving hers, he enveloped her in his arms and pushed her tighter against the counter.

Nicholas's face flashed in her mind. He'd held her down. His fist hit her cheek, her nose, her eyes. He dragged his fingernails over her skin as he held her to the floor. He ripped her gown from her body. She couldn't get up. Oh God. He wouldn't let her up.

Zoe opened her eyes wide. She leaned back, drawing in deep breaths she couldn't catch. "Get back." She shoved on his chest. "I can't… It's too much."

He released her from the counter. She ran through the living room and opened the front door. She leaned against the banister outside, panting as if she'd just finished running a marathon.

Think about something else—anything. She shut her eyes tight. The scenery from the mountain. High snow-capped peaks stabbed the blue sky. Nicholas still held her down. *Stop, Zoe.*

Another deep breath in through her nose, released through her mouth. There had to be something else to calm her down.

Sonya and Soljer. They stood on the lighthouse balcony. Ben's voice spoke in her ear through the headset. Every time she'd gotten scared, it was his voice that soothed her. His tenor calmed her nightmares.

Ben walked out onto the porch, hands in the pockets of his jacket. "Zoe?"

"I'm so sorry," she whispered. "Just let me catch my breath."

For a moment she'd forgotten about her violent past. She'd bought into the fantasy she'd created with a man she could love. But this whole weekend was nothing but a ruse. A trick in her mind that everything was fine. The daydream had offered her comfort long enough to take down the wall she'd built around her heart. But now, the wall had gone up faster than it'd crumbled.

"Zoe?" Ben clutched her shoulder. "What happened?"

"Nothing. I'm fine."

He turned her around to face him. "I don't think you are."

"I am fine. I just thought I was—" She'd almost said *ready* but shut her mouth. Telling him she was afraid would just lead to questions about her past she didn't want to answer. Nicholas sickened her.

"It's okay. It'll happen when we're both ready." He tucked a stray lock of hair behind her ear. "Up for a little fresh air?"

"Yes." Another deep, calming breath and she felt better. Still a tad shaken, she followed Ben through the house to the back door.

He grabbed a short silver key off the hook on the wall. He led her outside and up to an outdoor garage. Inside the building sat a dark green ATV.

With a swing of his right leg, Ben mounted the vehicle. He turned the key, and the engine sputtered to life.

He gestured with a nod. "Get on."

With held breath, she slid into the space on the seat behind him. She wrapped her arms around his torso, and they immediately took off up the dirt road.

The terrain was smooth through the forest. The sun cast its warm rays across her face, though the brisk air kept her nose cold. Her breath fogged in front of her, and then quickly fell behind as he drove toward the summit.

Leftover winter snow beautifully decorated the ground and some of the short budding trees and brush. The scene reminded her of a Christmas card she'd received once from Millie.

"Hang on," he called back. "Might get a little rough."

She held tight as he swerved off the path, through the tall trees and patches of snow. He steered over sticks and dry leaves until they stopped at a steep clearing on the side of the mountain.

"What is this place?" She scanned the four-legged structure with a tiny wooden house at the top.

"Ranger lookout."

He parked the ATV next to the stepladder and got off, leaving her sitting, staring in awe at the little wraparound walk outside the building. It looked as sturdy as a house on stilts made of sticks. Surely he didn't expect her to climb up there.

He stepped on the ladder. "You coming?"

She dismounted the ATV and trudged through the dry leaves. "I'm not one for heights."

"Go first." He jumped to the ground. "I'll be right behind you."

"All right." She drew in a deep breath, and then stepped slowly up the ladder. She glanced down to find Ben right beneath her. He grinned.

When they made it to the top, Ben unlocked the door to the house. "Haven't been here in a while. Probably a little dusty."

He stuffed the keys in the front pocket of his jeans and went in. Zoe followed on wobbly legs, happy to get off the high balcony.

The inside was clean and bright with windows all the way around the building. It was almost livable with the small cot in the far right corner and a desk along the wall on the left. It needed curtains, a kitchen and bathroom, and a few decorations. By the looks of the lantern and half-melted candles on the table, the place also needed electricity.

The wood floor was surprisingly solid. It barely creaked as she walked across to the scenic side.

"Wow." She scanned the long tree-lined slope down the mountain. Miles of snowy peaks spread across the horizon.

"Inspiring, isn't it?"

"Breathtaking."

"You should see sunset," he said as he stood beside her. "The next time you visit, maybe we'll stay long enough to see it."

The next time you visit. It hit her like a punch in the gut. This amazing, adventurous weekend with Ben would soon end. She wouldn't be here with him anymore. They wouldn't be together again for God knew how long.

Zoe turned to face him. "Do you think this…us will work out?"

"I want us to. Don't you?"

"Of course I do."

He gave her a sidelong look. "We discussed our options at the café. We'll work out visits between us."

"But if you think about it, this is all it'll ever be—just a visit."

"What are you saying? You want to quit before we even get started?"

She bit on her bottom lip and then sighed. "Eight hours is so far away. We can't plan on meeting for dinner after work. Or go see a movie on a Friday night like a normal couple. There will always be distance between us. As much as I want this to work out, I don't know if it can. Maybe we should just call this quits before it gets serious."

Ben straightened his slouch and let go of her arm. "Hm." He strode to the door and went outside. He made his way around the balcony to the front. He stood with his back to her, hands in his pockets and attention on the horizon.

Had she hurt his feelings? Or maybe she'd made him think something he hadn't thought about? A long-distance relationship might be too hard to manage. It'd be expensive. It also meant facing her fear of intimacy.

She met him on the balcony. He caught her gaze but didn't say anything.

"I'm sorry." She looped her arm through his. "I just…don't want to make life complicated."

****

"Complicated?" Ben gave a snort. He leaned his elbows on the banister. "This lookout was my haven when Chase died. If it wasn't for this place, I probably wouldn't be standing here with you." She quickly turned away. She understood what he meant. "Downing a bottle of vodka makes the guilt go away for a little while. But eventually, you have to come down and face reality. So, I stayed drunk."

"You blamed yourself for Chase's accident?"

"Every time I look in the mirror, I see his face."

"How did it happen?"

Ben sighed, wondering why he was talking about this when they apparently had other problems to discuss. Still, this was a proper time to lay what he could on the table. Maybe she'd understand him better.

"One of our many parties got out of hand. I was voted to go on a liquor run, but Chase insisted on going in my place. Said he'd rather not bail his little brother out of jail for a DUI. The man was plastered. More than I was."

He hung his head. Chase's gruff voice still haunted him. The shit-eating grin he'd flashed had widened when Ben tossed him the key to the motorcycle.

Ben pressed his thumbs against his temples. He fought back emotions he'd locked in the back of his mind. The urge to drink away the pain was strong, but he cleared his throat. He couldn't lose his cool now. Not in front of her.

"Spent many nights replaying the last moment I saw him. The stupid grin on his face. Him giving me the finger as he walked out the door." A short laugh rolled from his mouth, but the ache in his gut crawled back. "It should've been me, Zoe. I should've died. Not him."

"Oh, Ben," she whispered near his ear.

Her hands slid over his shoulders. One look in her tear-filled eyes and the world stood still. He could barely breathe. She was so beautiful. To feel her arms around him would ease his pain, but he couldn't do it. Not until she understood exactly how he felt and what she meant to him.

"I was at rock bottom when I met you online. I don't know why, but the moment I heard your voice, something sparked inside me. I didn't need to come up here anymore. I didn't want to get drunk and forget about life. Your voice pulled me out of the hole I was drowning in. You saved me."

"Don't say that," she said, shaking her head.

He lifted his hands to her face. "I've been trying for months to ask if you want to meet. Just wasn't sure I was ready. Now I know I am. I'm ready to get serious about you. I'm already serious about you."

"How can we have a real relationship? I want to see you every day, and I can't." She backed away from his touch. "It won't work out."

"Come on." He reached out to grab her hand. She slid around the wall toward the ladder, and then made her way down to the ground.

"Where are you going?" He followed. No way was she getting away from him. Not like this.

"I'm walking back." She stomped toward the shadowed woods leading to the main trail.

"It's a long walk."

"I'll make it."

By the time she reached the tree line, he'd caught up to her on the ATV. He pulled alongside her and shoved the gear into park.

"Stop."

She kept walking.

He turned off the engine and dismounted. Snow crunched beneath his sneakers as he jogged toward her. He caught her hand and, with a quick jerk of his arm, pulled her around and against his chest.

"I know you're worried. But we can make this work."

She shook her head. "I don't want to borrow Renji's truck every weekend. And I can't afford to fly."

"You could take the MINI Cooper home."

"What?" Her eyes sparkled in the sunlight shining through the trees. The red in her eyes intensified her blue irises. *Beautiful.* "That's ridiculous."

"Just hear me out."

"I'm not taking your car."

He palmed the back of her head. "I care about you. I'll do whatever it takes to make things easier on you. Just please. Give it a chance."

"It makes sense to meet in Goodland. But taking your car just doesn't seem like the right thing to do."

"You have a license, don't you?"

"Yes."

"Then what's the problem?"

She fisted the collar of his jacket and straightened it around his neck. "After one weekend together, you'd trust me with your car?"

"We've known each other for a while. I trust you."

"You do?"

"All the crazy things we've put up with this weekend and look at us now. It all boils down to one simple fact. We like each other. Well…you've already confessed you're in love with me."

She smacked his chest playfully. "I was drunk."

"Excuses," he said, brushing the tip of his nose against hers. "Come on, Zoe. Just say you'll take my car."

"No." She shook her head. "I can buy my own car."

"Until you do, use the MINI. As long as you want. I trust you more than anyone."

****

A squirrel shimmied up a tree. It stopped near the first branch and nodded, staring down as if to tell her everything would be okay.

Just breathe. Let whatever happens happen.

Taking a squirrel's actions as a sign was insane, but Ben's solution didn't seem illogical. Four and a half hours wasn't a bad drive down a straight road. She'd been to Goodland several times with Millie in less time, though, Millie drove like a madwoman.

"What about the weekends you play somewhere else?"

"I'll take an early flight to Wichita on Sunday mornings. We'll spend the day together."

"Flying will get expensive."

He lifted her hand to his lips. "Worth every penny."

She sighed as he kissed her wrist. "Flying to see me would eventually get old."

He groaned. "Let's take this one step at a time. You can also come visit me here. Not just weekends. Anytime you want."

"Where are you playing next weekend?"

"Aurora, I think. I'll have to check with Doogen."

Her heart dived. If they only lived closer. They could meet for dinner tonight. Go to a movie the next night. Have lunch hour together at some tiny restaurant in town. Didn't matter what town, as long as they were both in it.

"Yay. I get one whole day with you in Wichita to last me an entire week."

"You're impossible." He snickered. "Just say yes, Zoe. Say you'll give it a try."

Zoe shivered. How could she say no to those puppy-dog eyes? Who knew? Maybe this could work out. Maybe Millie was wrong about people who lived apart. Maybe the much-assumed phrase, *long-distance relationships don't work out*, might actually have an escape clause.

She loathed Wichita with a passion. Nicholas lived there. She'd avoided the city since he got out of prison. God knew what would happen if they ever came face to face.

"Fine." She sighed when she caught his gaze. "Wichita. Sunday."

He grinned. "Wichita. Sunday."

Chapter Fourteen

Clause A. Long-distance relationships never work *only* if the couple lives more than eight hours apart.

Clause A, part one. Both couples must own a car, or borrow one in Zoe's case, and must be willing to meet each other halfway.

Clause A, part two. If one person from the couple is lent a car by the other, she must first be sure it's okay with her best friends, otherwise suffer their wrath.

Millie gave Zoe "the talk" as they wrapped leftover breads and goodies to send to the homeless mission in Wichita. Hank, Millie's husband and daily driver for the potato-chip company, stopped there every morning to drop them off.

"Rich guy meets small-town girl and sends her off with an expensive gift. While small-town girl sits at home believing she's special, rich guy is messing around with the other woman, who happens to live in the same house with him."

"Ben and Sheron's relationship isn't romantic." Zoe stuffed a loaf of French bread into a bag. "She may be beautiful, but she's his sister-in-law."

"I'm just saying." Millie gave a quick shake of the bag of doughnut holes. "Urges between handsome guy and beautiful girl might become too strong, and then one thing will lead to another."

"They argue too much to be romantically

involved."

"So do Hank and me. And we're married."

Zoe zipped the bag. "They've lived together for three years under the same roof. And sure, it'd make sense for them to turn to each other. But even if they had slept together before, there's no indication they're sleeping together now."

"Loins are loins," Millie said in a loud voice.

"Millie." Zoe pressed her finger against Millie's lips to shush her.

The handful of local women who'd come to the bakery for Monday-night doughnuts stopped their chatter. They whispered, gaze shifting from one another then to Millie. They lifted their purse straps over their shoulders.

"Hank wanted the store-brand loins, but I said no way. Every off-brand we've ever tried turns out tough as jerky." Millie's lips pressed together as the women stood to leave. "So, I bought a name-brand loin instead. Made Hank put it on the grill, and it turned out nice and tender. Juicy."

As the ladies left the bakery, Zoe laughed. "Nice one."

"Yeah, I'll be the talk of the town tomorrow morning." Millie guffawed. "Anyway. Do you and Ben have plans to see each other soon?"

"This weekend." Zoe lifted the last baguette from the tray and dropped it inside a bag. "I'm picking him up at the airport on Sunday." Zoe couldn't wait. It'd been thirty-five hours since she'd left him. He'd kissed her good-bye several dozen times before she drove off in the MINI. That was the weirdest moment she'd ever experienced. It kind of felt like she'd stolen his car.

"Wonderful." Millie set the last few full bags inside the donation box, and then turned to face Zoe. "I wanted to tell you this earlier, but I didn't want to upset you while you were working. You seemed so happy today."

"Uh-oh." Zoe zipped the bag. "Do I want to know what Renji's done now?"

"Not Renji, honey." Millie lowered her voice. "I ran into Nicholas at the grocery store Saturday."

The hairs on the back of Zoe's neck stood. Hands shaking, body weak, she dropped the bag on the floor. She leaned back against the counter and palmed her forehead. *Oh God.* What was he doing this close to town? And Millie? She gasped. What he could've done to her. "Oh, no. Millie. I'm so sorry. He shouldn't have…I should've been here to—"

"—now you stop." Millie picked up the bag and set it inside the donation box. "Don't ever apologize for what the bastard says or does. It's out of your control."

"What'd he say?"

"He wanted me to ask you to forgive him." Millie's brows furrowed. "I told him he must've forgotten about what he did to you."

Zoe shuddered. The grocery store was only a few blocks from her apartment. To think he'd been that close. Nausea crept up her throat.

"What else did he say?"

"Nothing. He just laughed and walked away." Millie placed her hands on Zoe's forearms. "I'm usually not scared of anything, but, I called Hank to come get me."

"Oh, Millie."

"Don't you worry." Millie wrapped her arms

around Zoe. "Hank and I told Sheriff Clemens and Fred. And Renji. You know he'll be at your beck and call."

The bell above the bakery door jingled. After an uneasy glance between them, they walked together toward the dining area. A young man in a ball cap stood near the door with a clear glass vase full of the most beautiful pumpkin-colored roses Zoe had ever seen. *Aw.* Millie was the luckiest woman in the world to have a man who sent her flowers. Hank was so sweet.

"Sorry I'm delivering late. Got stuck in traffic." The kid set the vase on the bistro table beside the door. "These are for a Miss Zoe Kearny."

"Hey, I'm Zoe." Goosebumps spread over her skin. "Hang on."

She went to the back room and picked up a bag of doughnuts from the donation box. She pulled a five-dollar bill from her purse and then went back out to the lobby.

"I hope you like pastries."

"Yes, ma'am." A big grin crept across his boyish face. "Thanks."

"You're welcome."

The bell above the door jingled on his way out. Zoe understood his excitement. The little, positive things in life brought happiness. But this wasn't little. This was the first bunch of roses she'd ever received, and she was overjoyed.

She lifted the small rectangular card from its holder and read the note.

Miss you already. Can't wait to see you Sunday. Ben.

Zoe pressed the card against her chest. She could

just cry. "Oh, Millie. Ben is the sweetest man."

"Indeed he is. These roses are fabulous." Millie stuck her nose against one of the petals and breathed in. "They smell divine. I'm so jealous. Hank rarely sends me flowers anymore."

Hank's truck rumbled to the curb outside. Renji stepped out of the passenger side. This was the first time she'd seen him since she'd left Friday morning with Ben.

Renji walked through the door. "Hey, Zoe."

"Hey," Zoe replied, happy to see him with a smile on his face.

"I'll talk to you tomorrow." Millie gave Zoe a quick hug. "And don't worry. Everything will be all right."

As Millie left with Hank, Renji shoved his hands inside his pockets. "He sent you flowers, huh?"

"Yep." Zoe admired the roses again. So pretty. They were going to look great on the breakfast bar counter. "I had a really good time with him in Denver."

"I heard." Renji picked up the vase. "These are nice."

Zoe gathered her purse and slipped on her jacket. She met Renji at the exit and followed him out on the sidewalk. He stood near the curb as she locked the door.

The weather was nice. Warmer than a typical mid-April night. Something was off though. It was darker than usual. One of the street lights was out.

She shuddered. What if Nicholas stalked around the apartments, watching, waiting for Renji to leave? She looped her arm through Renji's and leaned closer. No way would she let him leave her alone tonight.

Renji transferred the vase to his other arm. "You

okay?"

"Yeah." She swallowed apprehension. "Why?"

"Millie told you about the grocery-store incident, didn't she?" He sighed. "Dammit. She shouldn't have said anything."

Zoe clung tighter to Renji's arm. "She told me a little while ago."

"Well, don't worry. I'm right next door if you need me. Plus, the entire town's got your back now."

Zoe gasped. "The town knows?"

"I don't mean to scare you any more than you already are, but—" Renji held her hand tighter. "I found out how your apartment flooded."

Zoe stopped, forcing Renji to a halt. It felt like a million eyes watched her from the shadows, but she had to know now. "How?"

"The door to the crawl space behind your apartment was broken. Someone had strung a hose from the spigot to the pipes beneath your kitchen. Whoever it was left the hose there. I told Fred, who told everyone to report any suspicious activity or vehicles."

"Oh God." Zoe took off for the apartment. She glanced back. Renji was right behind her, holding the vase in his arms like a football.

The tip of her toe caught in a crack on the sidewalk. She sailed forward, arms waving. The concrete sped toward her face. Renji caught her arm and pulled her back to her feet.

She swallowed hard, throat clenched, body shaking. "I've got to get home and lock my doors."

"Slow down. We're almost there." Renji slid his arm around her shoulders and held her against his side as they walked. "It's okay, Zo'. I won't let anything happen to you. I promise."

They reached her apartment door. Breath rampant she lifted the keys from her pants pocket. "Is the crawl space fixed?"

"I boarded it up. Chained it and added a padlock."

Zoe's hands shook too much. Renji took the keys from her and unlocked the door.

Once they were inside, she flipped all the locks back into place and then breathed a sigh of relief. This was so stupid. Being here. Living in fear again. How would she get through this without dying of heart failure?

Renji followed her up the stairs. When she turned on the light, he set the vase down on the breakfast bar. "Should I go home?"

"No." The thought of being left alone was unnerving. "Sorry. I mean, you're free to go home. It's just…could you stay with me for a little while? I'll make us some hot cocoa."

A grin crept across his face. "With marshmallows?" The man never ate sweets. It was an obvious attempt to make her feel better. It helped.

"Let's sit on the couch and listen to music and talk like we used to."

"Okay." He turned on the radio beside the TV. "So, let me tell you what happened with Drema over the weekend."

"Drema?"

He shrugged. "I spent time with her Saturday night."

"Oh, really?" What a wonderful change of pace. To hear about his adventures would be refreshing. "Well, then, Mr. Tanaka. Let me change into my jammies.

Then I want to hear all about it."

Zoe put on a pair of sweatpants and a tank top. She met Renji in the kitchen who'd started heating water in the teapot on the stove. He'd set out her two favorite coffee mugs and had emptied a packet of hot-cocoa mix inside each.

Zoe grabbed the bag of marshmallows from the cabinet. "So, I'm dying to find out about Drema."

Renji folded his arms across his chest. "I went to Holetzer's Saturday night, sulking because you went out of town. Drema sat beside me. We talked all night."

Zoe waited for more, but he turned his attention to the screaming pot. "About…?"

"A lot of things," he said, pouring the boiling water into the cups. "Mainly about sports. Oh, and she wanted to know if you'd meet her this Thursday at eight. She wants to ask if you mind helping her with some marketing for the grand opening barbecue."

Zoe palmed her temple. She'd completely forgotten about helping Drema. Maybe working on a new project was just what she needed to fill in the lonely times of the week until she saw Ben again.

Zoe dropped a few marshmallows in her cup. "I guess I could meet with her."

"Good. So hey, I'm sorry I scared you." He handed her a spoon. "I shouldn't have told you about the crawl space."

"I'm a little spooked." Understatement of the year. "Just the thought of the creep out there running free, able to come into my town, my life, whenever he wants—it's just downright scary."

"I can't believe he had the nerve to talk to Millie. How she must've felt. I'll kill him if I ever see him around here."

"You'd go to prison longer than he ever did." She stirred the cocoa with the spoon. "Who'll be here to make doughnuts for the bakery then?"

"It'd be worth it as long as you and everyone else are safe."

She sat at the breakfast bar and took a sip of her hot drink. Her house phone rang.

"Don't go storming off if it's Ben," she said in a laugh.

"I promise this moron will never run off mad again." He stepped toward the living room, cup in hand. "I'll be right in here waiting for you."

She picked up the phone. "Hello?"

"Hey, Zoe." Ben's voice sent a rush through her.

"Hey." Her heart pounded against her ribs. "You'll never guess what I received today."

"Hm. Nope. No clue. What'd you get?"

"The most beautiful roses I've ever seen," she said swirling a melting marshmallow around in her cup. She gazed at the roses. "I think I have a secret admirer."

"I'm jealous." He snickered. "I may have to come down there and steal you away."

"Oh, promise?" She set her cup down and leaned her elbows on the table. "It's so good to hear your voice. I really, really miss you."

"Everything okay?"

No chance would she tell him anything about Nicholas. "I'm all right. Just sitting here with my friend Renji, drinking hot cocoa."

"The guy who ruined your apartment?"

"Oh, Renji didn't…" A tap on the window startled her. She peered out into the dark. A shadow crept across the bush near the back patio. Icy fingers crawled up her neck.

Zoe squeezed her eyes shut. Don't panic. It was the branch of the bush scratching against the window. Or maybe it was just her imagination. No way was Nicholas lurking around her apartment.

"Ben, I—" She opened her eyes and stared out the window. Those fingers crept down her spine and then up again.

"Hey. You want to play our game to—"

Loud static on the phone made her jump. She exploded from the chair. It tipped over and crashed on the floor. She screamed.

"Zoe?" Renji ran through the doorway. "What's wrong?"

"Someone's outside. They're tapping on my window. My phone—" She dropped it from her trembling hand. "It's not working." Two more loud raps on the window startled her. "Renji." She fell into his arms and huddled against him.

His fingers closed around her upper arms. "Stay here."

"No, wait." She caught Renji's arm before he could leave. "Where are you going?"

"To check it out."

Zoe's gut churned. "You're not leaving me here alone."

"You'll be okay, Zoe. Just lock the door behind me."

"Renji, please." She hugged his neck. "Be careful."

"I will." He lowered her hands to her sides. After giving her a peck on her forehead, he left the kitchen. He descended the stairs to the front door. Zoe followed.

The moment he left the apartment, she twisted all the locks and hung the chain. She leaned back against the door and stared up at the wall between the hall and kitchen.

Nicholas was doing this. It had to be him. He'd done this before, back when she'd learned the hard way he was a violent drunk. She'd locked him out of her apartment—the old place on the other side of town. He'd busted through the kitchen window to get in. What was stopping him now?

Renji could take care of himself, but this was Nicholas. He'd always been out to get Renji. The thought of something bad happening to him outside, in the dark, motivated her to step away from the door.

On shaky legs, Zoe hurried to the kitchen. She retrieved her cell phone from her purse. She was about to dial 911 when it rang. Renji's name lit the screen.

"Hey," Zoe answered. "Are you all right?"

"Yeah. You can unlock the door and let me in now."

"Did you see anything?" She made her way down the steps.

"I found an empty bottle of tequila behind your apartment."

Zoe twisted the locks. Her skin tingled as she unlatched the chain and opened the door. When Renji walked in, bottle in hand, she shut the door again and locked it.

"You can use your phone now." He turned to face her. "The wire connected to the main box was loose. I just had to push it back in."

"Oh God," she said, staring at the empty bottle of tequila. An ocean of chills swept through her. Wave after wave, they crashed over her. A cold sweat formed on her temple. Nicholas would never leave her alone. He'd keep terrorizing her until he got what he wanted. She wasn't even sure what that was. Revenge?

Renji shook his head. "I called Fred."

"Is Fred going to arrest him?" she asked in a strangled voice.

"He's sending someone to patrol the apartments."

Zoe sat on the step and put her head in her hands. "What am I going to do, Renji? This can't go on. I can't keep living in fear. How am I supposed to move forward with anyone if I can't walk out my own front door?"

"You'll keep doing what you always do." Renji sat beside her and shoved his arm up against her shoulder. "Don't let the bastard control your life. Go to work. Play games with your boyfriend. Let Ben come visit you."

"I don't want him to come here." Zoe shook her head. "Not with Nicholas around." If anything happened to Ben, she'd die. Just bury her in the ground beside him. It was a morbid way to think, but she couldn't help the way she felt.

Renji set the empty bottle on the floor. "Does Ben know about him?"

"No way. I don't want him to know either."

"Why not?"

"I don't want him to feel sorry for me." She shrugged. "I'm afraid he'll decide it's too much for him to deal with."

"Nah. I don't believe that for a second." Renji leaned his elbows on his knees. "He lent you his car. I don't know about him, but I would never have given anything unless I really cared about the woman. He must care a lot about you."

Zoe bit her bottom lip and then smiled. "I hope you're right."

He grabbed the bottle and stood up straight. "I'm always right."

"Wait. Where are you going?" Zoe rose before him. "Will you stay with me tonight? I don't want to be alone."

Her cell phone rang. Ben's name lit the screen.

"I'm going to sit with the patrol tonight." He brushed his palm across her cheek. "If you get scared, I'm like twenty feet away. Right?"

Zoe nodded as he unlocked the door. "Keep your phone next to you."

"Promise."

He strode toward his apartment. She scanned the parking lot and spotted the patrol car Fred had sent sitting at the curb near the main road.

After a short breath of relief, she shut the door. She locked the locks and then answered her phone like nothing was wrong.

Chapter Fifteen

With the effort of Millie's family, and Renji's uplifting words everything would be fine, Zoe felt safe again. The police patrolled the area every night. Sometimes Fred stopped by to see how she was doing. Work was...well, same old work, but it just meant life was getting back to normal.

Though scared Nicholas would eventually show his ugly self, she focused on the good things. Her nights were spent playing games with Ben online or talking on the phone until she fell asleep. For the past three weeks, they'd met every Sunday in Wichita. They'd only had four hours to hang out until he had to fly home, but they'd had enough time to get in a stroll through the park and have an early dinner.

This Saturday night, his band was playing in Goodland. He'd taken Thursday and Friday off of work to spend the weekend with her and was on his way down on his motorcycle.

With the town on alert, there'd been no more incidents with Nicholas. She was sure he'd finally given up on his obsession with her. Everything would be just fine.

At eight p.m., Zoe parked at her apartment. She'd just finished meeting with Drema Holetzer about the grand opening of Holetzer's bar. They were to have a barbecue on July fourth. Drema needed a band to play.

Zoe told her she'd ask Ben. Drema thanked her profusely, offered her one night of free drinks, and then talked about her crush on Renji for fifteen minutes straight.

Zoe hurried into her apartment and shut the door. As she locked herself in, her cell phone beeped.

She read the message.

—Zoe. It's Nicholas. Some bullshit cop came to my door a few weeks ago asking where I was the other night. What the fuck's that about?—

Zoe tossed her phone down on the table. It slid to the edge and stopped. Her pulse quickened. The silence of the apartment deafened her. She stared at the phone, hoping it wouldn't chime again.

Not now. She'd finally stopped being scared. Ben was on his way here. Why did Nicholas have to start this all over again?

She picked up the phone. A mist of perspiration formed on her upper lip. Clammy hands made it difficult to dial Renji's number. It chimed again.

—I was at my house all night with my girlfriend. If I find out you're telling lies to get me in trouble, I'll press charges for harassment.—

What the heck? *He'll* press charges for harassment? Her cheeks burned. Fire spread through her veins to her fingertips and toes. She hated being scared. She hated him for making her feel like she couldn't be happy. This wasn't how she wanted to live life—in fear of what he'd do next.

Maybe it was because Ben was on his way here, but she couldn't stand this anymore. It was time to take charge of this situation. Enough was enough.

If she had any chance of alleviating the fear and

anger Nicholas instilled in her, she'd need to tell him to go away. She'd send him one message. After, she'd change her phone number. *Again*. Maybe she'd also change her name and rent an apartment in Denver.

She typed the message out.

—*NEVER EVER come see me. Don't ever call or text me. I don't want anything to do with you. Worry about getting your life together and leave me alone.*—

She pressed Send. *There*. It was done. If he didn't figure out she wanted nothing to do with him, then he was sick in the head. But he was sick in the head. The creep needed mental help.

She cringed. Maybe she shouldn't have sent a message.

Her cell phone chimed.

—*Holy shit, Zoe. You've grown a pair, haven't you? Don't you believe in rehabilitation? I'm not the guy I used to be. I've never even set foot in your town. Whatever. Stop blaming shit on me. Bye.*—

Just like him to turn things around and make *him* look like the victim.

Her home phone rang this time. Caller ID read *Unknown*. She debated on whether to answer, but with Ben on his motorcycle and on his way here, she couldn't take the chance that it could be an emergency.

"Hello."

The line was silent.

She glanced at the screen. The call was still in session.

"Who is this?"

She hung up. How quickly the anger fled, and fear crept in its place. She stood in the center of the kitchen, unable to move or breathe. Heart beating at a mad pace, she hugged her torso.

Ben was on his way here. It wouldn't be long until she found comfort in his arms. She wouldn't be alone.

Imagining him beside her, caressing her, telling her everything was all right, calmed her down enough to draw in a deep breath.

The cell phone rang, loud in the quiet kitchen. Ben's name lit up the screen. Thank God. Eager to hear his voice and tell him she wanted him here now, she answered.

"Ben."

"Hey babe."

"Please tell me you're almost here."

He sighed. "Ran into a bit of a snag."

"Snag?" She swallowed hard. One deep, calming breath turned into a pant. "You okay?"

"Some truck ran me off the road about ten miles outside of town."

Oh no. She palmed her forehead. Nicholas owned a truck. A big black one. No way was he stupid enough to run Ben down and make him wreck. But how would he know Ben was even coming?

"You're not hurt, are you?"

"A little scraped up, but I'm fine. The bike's in the ditch with a bent rim. Can you come get me?"

"Yes." She grabbed her purse and keys off the counter. "I'm on my way out the door now." She slipped on her shoes then hurried down the steps, breath in her throat. She unlocked the door, opened it wide, and then stopped.

Chills crawled across her shoulders, down her back, and over her scalp. The streetlight on the other side of the parking lot was out. Ben's car was cast in shadow. She couldn't go out there alone. What if Nicholas was out there watching and waiting for this very moment? What if he'd planned this entire thing to get her outside and attack her?

No. She bit her bottom lip. Ben was stuck out there in the dark on the side of the road waiting on her. No matter how scary this was, she had to do this.

"Ben. Are you still there?"

"Yeah. I'm here."

She stepped onto the sidewalk. She shut and locked the door. Heart in her throat, she briskly walked through the parking lot.

"Just stay on the phone with me, okay?" she whispered.

"Why are you whispering? Is something wrong?"

"No." She pressed the remote to unlock the door. It gave a short, loud honk. Startled, she broke out into a quick jog. The last thing she wanted to do was draw attention to her location. If Nicholas was here, he'd have heard the car disarm. "I'm getting in the car now. Hang on."

She hurried into the driver's seat. She slammed the door shut and shoved her thumb down on the auto-lock. Safe inside, she set the phone on the passenger-side seat and started the car.

Thank God she'd made it. She drew in several deep breaths. She shoved the car in gear and took off down the road.

This was insane. Three entire weeks without a word from Nicholas. Now with Ben coming to town, he'd shown himself. Everything had gone wrong since she met Ben. With her luck, a tornado would set down on top of her and blow her into oblivion.

Her cell phone rang. *Crap*. She'd still had Ben on the line. She glanced at the screen as she drove closer to the edge of town. *Unknown*. It was just like the call she'd received at the apartment.

Hair stood on her entire body. Nicholas was toying with her. Scaring her. Trying to hurt Ben. She regretted sending the text, but what else could she do? Keep letting him harass her? She had to find a way to get him to stop.

Her cell phone chimed. She read the message on the screen. —*Hey, Zoe. I'm a jerk. Aren't I?*—

What the heck did he mean? She tossed her phone on the seat again. Why did she have to go through this? Tears welled in her eyes. This was ridiculous.

High beams glared in the side-view mirror. "Oh, what now?" She sniffled. A vehicle sped up fast behind her in the other lane. Zoe let off the accelerator so whoever this idiot was would hurry and pass.

The lights dimmed as it reached her side. With her gaze on the road, she waited for the vehicle to pull up, but it slowed down to match her speed. A white truck sitting on four very large tires rolled beside her on the left, so close she could almost reach out and touch its body.

The truck drifted closer. She inhaled a sharp breath as the right tires of the Mini hit the gravel shoulder and slid. She gripped the steering wheel tight and slammed both feet on the brake and clutch. The car stopped abruptly as the truck sped ahead.

"Jerk." She pulled the car back on the pavement. Any closer and he'd have sideswiped Ben's car and ran her off the road. Way too close. Her face and neck burned. It didn't matter what happened from here, she had to keep going. If Nicholas was in the truck ahead, who knew what he'd do when he reached Ben.

She rolled down the window and filled her lungs with fresh air. The fire on her cheeks and forehead cooled. But her heart—it wouldn't stop pounding like the drums in Ben's band.

The brake lights on the truck glowed in the distance ahead.

"Please, please, don't turn around. Don't turn around."

The vehicle whipped around. A dust cloud spiraled through the air in the headlights. The bright lights were blinding.

"Oh no." Zoe shrank in the seat. She clenched her jaw tight. Was he really going to play chicken? Oh, heck no was she going to do anything of the sort. The truck's high beams got closer. Bigger. Brighter. The engine's loud roar vibrated as it headed straight toward her.

Palms slick with sweat, she cranked the steering wheel to the right. Her legs shook so hard she could barely lift them to stop the car. She couldn't see for the high beams in her eyes. A shrill scream broke from her mouth as the truck barreled by her within an inch of hitting her. The MINI sideswiped the guardrail. The piercing screech of metal against metal deafened her.

She swerved toward the left lane. The car lifted on its right tires and slowly rolled down the road. Adrenaline pumped through her veins as she held her breath. She squeezed her eyes shut.

Please don't flip. Please don't flip. Just let one thing go right tonight. After a few more feet of wobbling, the car slammed to the ground on all four tires and then stopped in the middle of the road.

Every muscle in her body weakened. She breathed as if she'd held her breath underwater until she'd reached her limit then finally resurfaced. The air smelled like Renji's truck when it overheated. It burned her nose.

Steam rose from the hood of the car. *Oh God. No.* This couldn't be happening. This was just a horrible, vivid nightmare she was about to wake up from. Nobody had run her off the road. She was still in her apartment waiting on Ben.

"Deep calm breaths, Zoe." She breathed in then out several times, but it didn't help. She checked the rear-view mirror. No brake lights. No high beams. At least the truck was gone.

She let off the brake. She popped the clutch and pressed the accelerator. The car lurched forward. It clinked and clanked up the darkened road at a cool twenty miles per hour. Wouldn't go any faster. At least one of the headlights worked.

The engine squealed. A loud pop and wheeze came from underneath the car. The scrape of metal on asphalt was loud in her ears. "Oh, man, this isn't good at all." The steering wheel wouldn't turn with ease. She leaned her body into it and held tight as the car wobbled toward the shoulder.

The engine coughed and sputtered then finally gave out on the gravel shoulder. The one working headlight went out leaving her in pitch black.

Tears sprouted in her eyes. Now she was stuck out here in the dark on the lonely road where nobody ever drove at this hour. She leaned over the center dash. She slid her palm along the floor and found her phone. Ben was going to be so mad. She wiped her eyes then drew in a deep breath. Calm down. Get a grip.

She dialed 9-1-1.

The dispatcher picked up. "Nine-one-one. What's your emergency?"

"Someone ran me off the road. My car's broke down, and now I'm stuck out here in the dark by myself." Goosebumps spread over her skin. She tried not to cry, but how could she not? Nicholas was out there preparing to terrorize her again. "I need help," she cried. "I don't know where he went."

"Where are you located?"

"East of Mount Hope. On 96."

"I have a unit on route now. Are you injured?"

"No, I'm fine." At least she had her health. "Just shaken up." Understatement. She could barely hold her phone to her ear.

"All right. Take deep breaths. And stay on the line until help arrives."

She drew in a breath then exhaled with a whimper. It wasn't working. Nothing worked. Her phone was the only light she had and wasn't much. It just made the shadows outside more frightening.

Headlights beamed behind her, bright, blinding. So wrapped up in tears, she hadn't noticed it coming. Or maybe it had been there all along. The engine revved and kicked up dust around the vehicle. The lights went off and on in the right lane. Every hair on her body stood as the truck, the same one that'd run her off the road, slowly rolled by on her left.

"Oh. Please hurry. The truck is right beside me."

Zoe's hand shook so much she dropped her phone on the floor. The light went out. *Dammit.* She'd hung up on the dispatcher.

She cried out as she turned the key in the ignition. The engine sounded like a jackhammer pounding into concrete. "Come on." She tried again. Nothing happened this time. No lights. No sound. The car was completely dead.

The truck swerved off the road and then whipped around just like the last time. As it rolled by slowly, she covered her mouth with her hands and stifled the shriek forming in the back of her throat.

For a long moment she stared in the rearview mirror, watching as the truck's brake lights fell farther away. Whoever it was—Nicholas headed back toward town.

Her cell phone rang. The lump she'd kept under wraps exploded into a scream. Her throat clenched. She found her phone on the floor near her feet. She pressed the green button then held her phone steady against her ear.

"Who is this?"

Nobody responded.

"I've called the police. They're going to find you. You'll go back to prison. So stop harassing me. Stay away from me."

The call ended.

A shadow crept across the front of the car toward the passenger side. The handle jimmied. She covered her mouth with her hand but couldn't silence the short, abrupt screech. What was she to do? Jump out and run? Stay inside the locked car? Whoever was out there could shatter the glass and take what he wanted anyway.

The police were on their way. She just had to hang

tight until they arrived. If he found his way in, she'd have to do what she could to stop him.

She balled her fists. Stop being afraid and remember Fred's training. If Nicholas or whoever got in, she'd give him one hell of a fight.

The phone rang again. Her heart galloped as she glanced down. Ben's name flashed on the screen. She answered fast.

"Oh my God, Ben, help!" She couldn't catch her breath to tell him how much trouble she was in. "I'm up the road. The truck...Nicholas. He—"

"—Zoe. Honey. Calm down. I'm right outside the car. Let me in."

She leaned over the center console and peered out the window. *Oh thank God.* She pressed the lock. Relief swept through her as Ben sat down and shut the door.

"Oh, Ben." She hugged his neck and held on tight. "Thank God you're here." No lock on her apartment could compare to being in his arms.

"I saw what happened." His thick jacket crinkled as he held her. "You okay?"

"No." She closed her eyes and whimpered. "Scared to death."

"I know." He tightened his hold on her. "It's okay, baby. I've got you."

"Don't let go."

"I won't." He pressed his lips against her ear. "I promise."

His woodsy cologne was like incense that soothed her cries. As she leaned back, her body relaxed. She inhaled deeply then let it out slowly through her mouth. "Oh, I'm a mess." She sniffled.

Ben opened the glove compartment. He yanked

several tissues from the small box and handed it to her.

"Thanks." She pressed the soft cloth to her nose. "I can't believe this is happening," she whispered. Her heart dived to the floor. "I'm so sorry about your car."

"I don't care about the car," he said in a soothing tenor. He pushed her hair behind her shoulders and she shivered. "I was afraid for you, Zoe. I was afraid you were hurt, and I couldn't get here fast enough."

Great. The tears were coming again. "I don't know what to say."

"For starters, you could tell me what's going on. Who was in the truck?"

It wouldn't be a lie if she told him she didn't know. It could've been some psycho in a giant white truck. Nothing like this had ever happened. But there was no sense in covering this up. Nicholas was the driver. Nobody else was stupid enough to do this. Ben would want her to explain. She just couldn't. Not now. Not yet.

"Zoe." His abrupt, cold voice startled her. "Tell me who was driving the truck."

She buried her face in her hands. She couldn't respond. Not until the shock wore off. Not until she was safely locked in her apartment. It was too soon to tell him anything about her past. He'd just leave because she was damaged goods. After this, he'd probably high-tail it out of here anyways.

He gave a heavy sigh then groaned. Irritated. It was an awful sound. She didn't want Ben to be upset, but how could he not be? His car was totaled. His girlfriend wouldn't tell him what was wrong. Some psychopath was out there running people off the road. All Ben wanted was one answer, and she couldn't give it to him.

Red and blue lights flashed blindingly as the police car pulled in behind them. Another vehicle parked on Zoe's left. Renji's truck.

Without a word, she opened the car door and got out. She met Renji in front of his truck and tossed her arms around his torso.

"Holy shit, Zoe. What happened?" Renji hugged her then let go to inspect Ben's car.

"Somebody ran me off the road. I hit the guardrail."

"Yeah, I heard. I was riding with Fred tonight when he got the report. I stopped off to get my truck in case someone needed a tow." Renji placed his palms on her shoulders. "What are you doing out here alone? With Nicholas out there—"

"—you can tow us back to town," she said as Ben rounded the front of the car.

Renji searched her eyes. "I didn't know he was with you."

"His motorcycle's in the ditch up ahead. The truck ran him off the road first. I was coming to get him."

Renji pursed his lips. By his furrowed brows, he too suspected Nicholas. "Okay. Get in the warm truck while I hook up the car."

Zoe hopped up in the passenger seat of Renji's truck. She scooted to the center of the bench seat, giving Ben enough room to climb in, but Ben shut the door behind her. He wasn't happy.

Watching the two men work together in the headlights was awkward. Best friend and new boyfriend didn't speak a word or even acknowledge each other.

Ben leaned inside his car. He cleaned out the glove compartment, while Renji picked car parts up from the ground and tossed them in the back of the truck.

Zoe sighed. She should be out there helping. Not sitting here feeling sorry for herself.

Fred opened the passenger door. "You all right, Zoe?"

She gave a short nod. "I'm still a little shaken, but I'm better now you guys are here."

"Want to tell me what happened?"

She cleared her throat. "Ben called to tell me a truck ran him off the road. On my way to pick him up, the truck did the same to me. Whoever it was kept turning around and coming back." She shuddered from the chill. "At one point, he headed straight for me."

"Head-on?"

"Yes." She lowered her voice so Ben wouldn't hear. "I think it was Nicholas."

"Why do you think it was him?"

"He's been texting me and calling."

Fred cocked his head to the side. "Mind if I see those texts?"

"I left my phone in the car."

She scooted toward the door, but Fred held up his hand. "Just stay here and keep warm. I'll find it for you. I'm going to call this in and get someone out to Nicholas's house." He gave a reassuring smile. "I'll meet you back at your apartment."

Zoe smiled. "Thanks, Fred."

"It's my pleasure," he replied then shut the door.

Renji hopped inside the driver's seat. He shifted into gear then pulled ahead of the car. With Ben's guidance, he backed in. As Ben hooked the chain to the Mini's chassis, Renji sighed.

"Nicholas did this. Didn't he?"

"I'm pretty sure it was him," Zoe said over the hum of the truck. "Ben will find out about him now, but please don't say anything about what he did to me. I don't want him to know."

"You're going to have to tell him eventually. The asshole's stalking you again. No telling what he'll do with Ben around. It's best you give Ben a heads up."

Zoe shut her eyes tight. Her internal prayer turned to begging. *God. Please. Let this hit-and-run be a random idiot. Let the tequila bottle outside my apartment be from kids partying.*

Zoe sighed. "I'm waiting for the right time to tell him."

"When is the right time, Zoe?"

"I don't know. But I'm sure it'll be soon." She caught Renji's gaze. "Nicholas texted me tonight, right before this happened."

Renji lowered his brows. "What?"

"He said the cops questioned him about being at my apartment Monday night. I texted him back. I told him to go away and never bother me again."

"Dammit, Zoe." He pursed his lips. "After what he did to you, I thought you were smart enough not to respond. You shouldn't have sent him anything."

"I just want him to leave me alone."

"The violent bastard's obsessed with you. Now he's pissed." Renji took hold of her hand. "I don't want anything to happen to you."

The passenger door opened. Zoe pulled her hand from Renji's as Ben stepped up into the truck. When he shut the door, he tossed her a glance.

"Tailpipe's broken. Had to pull it off and stick it in the back of the truck."

She hunched over, hands covering her face. "I'm so sorry."

"Hey." Ben leaned against her. "This isn't your fault."

"Yes, it is," she said. "I shouldn't have sent him a message."

"Sent who a message?" Ben asked.

She leaned her head against his arm. If Nicholas did this, Ben needed to know. He deserved to know what he was getting himself into by being involved with her.

"His name's Nicholas."

Renji shifted the truck in gear and pulled onto the highway. "Her asshole ex-boyfriend." He slapped his palm against the top of the steering wheel. "He's fucking with her again."

"Come on, Zoe." Ben shrugged her off his arm, forcing her to sit up. "What's going on?"

"I dated Nicholas a few years ago—he was a little…possessive."

"Possessive?" Renji let out a deep growl. "This guy's a major creep who likes to beat on women. Especially Zoe."

She elbowed Renji's side. He'd divulged too much information.

Ben arched his brows. "He hit you?"

"Yep." Renji leaned forward as he slowed the truck. The wrecked motorcycle appeared in the headlights. "Ah, man. You're lucky you weren't killed."

Zoe felt the heat of Ben's stare, but she stayed focused on the motorcycle lying in the ditch on the side of the road. Feeling like the bent rim, having put Ben's life in danger, she covered her face with her hands and cried. Again.

Renji shoved the gear stick into park. He heaved a grunt as he got out and slammed the door behind him.

"Zoe," Ben said. "Look at me."

"I can't."

"It's okay."

"No. It's not okay." She shook her head. "I'm sorry you got mixed up in this. I didn't want you to know my past, but it looks like it's out in the open now." Thanks to Renji. *The jerk*. Now she'd have to tell Ben all the embarrassing details of what she went through.

His hand pressed against her back. "We'll get this sorted out later. Okay?"

"Yeah," she whispered. All the explaining she had to do now—this wasn't how she wanted to spend their first weekend together as a real couple.

Ben opened the door and got out. When the door shut, Zoe fell back against the seat, palm on her burning temple. The stress was too much.

What if it wasn't Nicholas who did this? She never saw his face. The guy owned a black truck, not a white one. What if it was just some dumb teenagers out wreaking havoc on everyone on the road? She thought of her prayer. Miracles could happen.

She might as well face the facts. Nicholas had contacted her. He'd stalked outside her apartment for God knew how long. The proof was the empty tequila bottle. To think he could've broken in anytime made her stomach churn. She never would've known until he'd beaten and raped her again. Or worse—killed her.

Chapter Sixteen

Deputy Fred stuffed his left hand in the pocket of his gray jacket. The short, sandy-blond man stood between Renji and Ben, who both towered over him, waiting for an answer.

Fred was a fearless man—a man Zoe respected. He'd been her dad's friend and had watched over her after her father died. He'd given her lessons in self-defense, which helped her work through the tough time she'd had after the incident with Nicholas. He'd helped her get her self-esteem back and made her believe she was in control of her life again.

"Nicholas was home all evening with his girlfriend who vouched for him," Fred said.

Renji gave a short angry grunt. "They're both lying."

"He doesn't own a white truck. Whoever ran you guys off the road wasn't him."

"Bullshit." Renji folded his arms across his chest. "He probably stole the truck from a dealership, and then used it to terrorize her before dumping it down some dirt road."

"There's an APB out on the truck now. Unfortunately, there's nothing we can do about Nicholas when he has an alibi, and we don't have a license plate number." Fred placed his hat on his head. "Don't worry, Zoe. I'll do whatever I can to find whoever's responsible for running you two off the road."

"Go to Nicholas's house." Renji clenched his jaw. Zoe had only seen him this angry once before—the time he found out what Nicholas had done to her. "You know it was him."

"Nothing would give me more pleasure than to put him back in prison. But I can't arrest him on speculation. I need proof."

Ben cocked his head to the side. "Back in prison?" Zoe shrank in her seat. This was too much to deal with. Maybe he'd be okay, as long as Renji and Fred didn't reveal everything.

Renji hissed through his teeth. "Nicholas called and texted her. Should be enough to arrest the creep for harassment."

"There was no hostility toward her. No threats made." Fred turned his attention to Zoe. "Now if he contacts you in person, let me know the second it happens. *If* it happens. I certainly hope it doesn't." He sighed. "In the meantime, I'm sorry I can't do anything more. If you don't want him contacting you, best thing for you to do is get a restraining order. You can also change your phone number."

"Well, you're no help, Fred," Renji said. "She's already changed her number a dozen times."

"Thanks, Fred." Zoe walked him to the front door. "Don't mind Renji. I know you're doing what you can."

"I'll keep a patrol outside your apartment for now." Fred tipped the brow of his hat. "Once we find the truck, I'll let you know."

Fred left. She shut the door and leaned back against it. Not knowing who terrorized her left a sick feeling in her gut. Did Nicholas do this? Or was he really at home like Fred said? It just didn't seem right to believe some random stranger did this.

Exhausted—physically and mentally—Zoe shivered. She went to the kitchen and leaned back against the counter. She folded her arms across her chest and waited for someone to talk. Everyone remained silent.

Renji stood in the kitchen doorway, eyes on the floor. It wasn't like him to stay quiet. Maybe he didn't know what to say in front of Ben.

Ben sat on the bar stool. Who knew what went through his mind? He'd barely said a word after he'd told Fred the truck had run him into the ditch. He just sat there and listened to her talk about her scary encounter.

"You know what. I'm out of here too," Renji said. "Are you gonna be all right?"

"I'll be fine." She drew in a deep breath. Her stomach churned. With Renji gone, she'd be left alone with Ben who wanted answers. She had no choice but to give them to him.

Renji gently kissed her temple. "I'm worried about you."

"Don't be." She gazed up into his eyes. "I'll be all right."

"It doesn't mean I'm turning a blind eye." He glanced at Ben. "I don't care who's around. I'm still going to watch over you."

She hugged his torso tight, cheek against his shoulder. "Thanks for saving us."

"Anytime," he said with a quiet laugh and then lightly patted Zoe on the head. "See you later."

"See you."

"Take good care of her," Renji warned Ben on the way out of the kitchen. "Or I'll kick your fucking ass."

Ben's eyes narrowed, but he said nothing. Maybe he wanted to leave too. She wouldn't blame him if he did. Tonight's drama had been one big messy nightmare.

She followed Renji down the stairs. He gave her a wink before he stepped outside in the dark. She locked the door and then made her way to the kitchen.

Ben still sat on the stool. He scrubbed his face.

"I guess you're pretty freaked out about all this."

He dropped his hands to his lap. "A little bit, yeah."

"How do you feel now..." She paused to find the right words to say. Even after all this time, saying she'd been abused out loud was difficult. "Now you know about my past?"

His hand enveloped hers, and he pulled her close. "I already knew someone hurt you. I wasn't one hundred percent. But you say things in your sleep. You whimper. You have nightmares." He loosened his hold on her hand. "The day at the cabin, when we got close, you were scared. You were scared of me."

"I wasn't scared of you."

"Yes. You were." He shook his head. "I would never in a million years hurt you. Zoe, I swear, I—"

"—Ben, stop." She cupped his face. It felt good to touch him. Console him. To look into his eyes and reassure him of her faith in him. "I know you wouldn't hurt me. I trust you."

A kiss would lighten the mood. She leaned forward, but he turned his head. Her mouth caught the

174

corner of his, and her heart sank.

He peeled her hands from his face and lowered them to her sides. "Trust is earned. And I don't feel like I've done that yet." His eyes were tired. "I want to know what he did to you."

She leaned back on her heels. "Not exactly something I'm proud to talk about. But I'll tell you what I can."

"He…hit you." His voice was strained.

A flashback of Nicholas's fist against her cheek, her nose, her body went through her mind. "Repeatedly."

"How long were you with him?"

"Two months."

"He hit you when you broke up? Or did he do this throughout?"

She swallowed apprehension. "Throughout."

He averted his gaze. If only she could read his mind, find out what he was thinking. Had she lost his respect? Was he not willing to stay with someone who had suffered through months of abuse?

He looked at her again. If she could relieve him of the question in his eyes without answering anything, she'd do it in a heartbeat.

"Were you too scared to leave him?"

He spoke in a softer voice. It was a higher pitch than before. Maybe he was trying to understand why she'd stay with a monster. She'd spent hours thinking of answers to this same question, but all she could ever come up with was how truly afraid she'd really been.

"The first time he hit me, he was drunk. I mean, he always had a drink in his hand or smelled like liquor, but it never occurred to me he was an alcoholic. Not until I told him he should lay off the tequila." She touched her cheek. Nicholas had raised his hand, brows low against his brown eyes. "He smacked me across the cheek with the back of his hand. Not hard. Just enough to get my attention."

"Why'd you stay with him?"

She shook her head. "I guess I thought maybe I could help him, but I learned the hard way. You can't help someone who's that sick."

How could she be so stupid to stay with him? All those bruises she'd received—they were her fault.

"Things were fine when he was sober. But when he got drunk—which was more often than not—then look out. Duck and cover."

"When did you finally say enough was enough?"

Humiliation swarmed through her. She palmed her temple, trying to keep the memories of the night Nicholas raped her from moving to the front of her mind. If only she'd left him after the first time he'd hit her, it never would've happened.

"I finally told him—" She cleared her throat, choosing her words carefully. "I didn't want to be with someone who wants to hurt me. And he left—at first. I think a week went by before I started getting hang-up calls."

"He began stalking you."

She nodded. "He'd leave me nasty texts on my phone. The hedge I'd planted outside my bedroom window was cut down and left on my doorstep. One morning, I found the bakery door shattered and an empty tequila bottle on the floor in my office. He'd spray-painted profane words on my desk."

"Is that why he went to jail?"

Chills crept up and down her spine. Time to tell the dreaded story. She hadn't said it aloud in two years. Not wanting to look Ben in the eyes, she lowered her gaze to his chest.

"I'd seen him drunk before, but not like the night he forced his way into my apartment. He held me down. He hit me over and over until I could barely see or feel anything anymore. I thought I was going to die."

"Oh shit," he whispered. His hands had balled into tight fists on his lap.

Her heart hammered. God knew she wanted to tell him the entire story but couldn't find the words. They were stuck in the back of her throat, just as the images lingered in the back of her mind.

"Maybe you should go home. Knowing I'm damaged is obviously upsetting to you."

"Well, yeah, I'm fucking upset." He pulled her close. He curled his forefinger under her chin and lifted, catching her gaze. "Someone hurt the woman I care about. He's still hurting her. That doesn't sit well with me."

Worried and tired as she was, she couldn't help the smile forming on her face. "You care about me?"

"Of course I do." When his palm touched her cheek, she leaned against it. "We all have scars, Zoe. Your scars run deeper than most, but you're not damaged."

"Then what would you call me?"

"Beautiful. Kind. The best person I know."

She slid her arms around his neck and pressed her lips to his, indulging in a long, simple kiss. His tongue gently massaged hers as his fingers stroked her back.

He pulled away and breathed a short sigh. "It's

been a long night," he said in a soft tone. "You're probably tired."

"Exhausted."

"Me too. I need to get up early and rent a truck and trailer so I can haul the car and bike home." He draped his jacket over the back of the bar stool. With his arms exposed, she could get a good look at the tattoo on his forearm.

"What's your tattoo mean?"

He picked up his duffel bag. As he followed her down the hall toward the bedroom, he glanced at the gun-toting soldier. "Had plans to join the army when I was eighteen. Me and a few friends went to the parlor and got inked."

"You joined the army?"

"Nah." He shook his head. "Things didn't quite work out the way I'd wanted."

"What happened?"

"Chase talked me out of it." He shrugged. "Actually, he forbade me to join. Said he'd never speak to me again if I left him."

"Well, that's not very nice."

"Brothers." He dropped his bag beside the bed and took off his shoes. "I tried to join anyway, but they wouldn't let me enlist."

She pulled a gown from the top dresser drawer. Anxiety crept through her. They'd never talked about sleeping arrangements. Was he staying in here with her? In her bed?

She cleared her throat. "Why wouldn't they let you?"

"Juvenile record." He shrugged. "I was a bit of a hellion when I was young. Basically, I have lots of regrets."

He grabbed his toothbrush from his bag and left the room. She sat on the edge of the bed and clutched the soft material of her peach gown. Should she change in here? He'd already seen her naked. It wouldn't be a big deal if he saw her in her panties and bra.

She set the gown beside her on the bed. She fisted the hem of her shirt. Holding her breath, she pulled it over her head and tossed it to the floor. She released the air in her lungs as she lifted the garment.

He stepped into the room. Zoe jumped to her feet and hid behind her pajamas.

Ben pulled his shirt over his head. Electricity spread through her. Though she'd seen his toned upper body before, it'd always been just a glance. This time, she wanted to look—to see all of him.

His arms were well built. There were a few thin patches of hair on his rounded pecs, just above his nipples. Thicker hair stretched from his navel down below the waistline of his dark jeans. Then there was the rose on his shoulder.

"What about the blue rose?"

He unbuckled his belt and glanced at the rose. "Got inked after Chase died. The sissy loved his blue roses. But yeah. His name's beneath it."

"Oh." She swallowed hard.

He took off his pants. Butterflies danced in her belly. She admired his long legs as he lay back and folded his arms behind his head. The thick bulge beneath his boxers was prominent. She turned away.

She went to the bathroom. She put on her nightgown, brushed her teeth, and then caught her reflection in the mirror. Her horrible night had turned into a longing to be touched. Was she ready for this?

Her bloodshot eyes drooped. The skin was dark beneath her lashes. It was too stressful to even think of being intimate now. Her anxiety was already through the roof. Right now, she needed sleep. So, *no*. Nothing would happen tonight. But, she might sleep better if he held her in his arms.

She snuggled under the covers on her back and lifted the comforter to her chin. "I'm glad you're here."

"Me too." He leaned over her. "You okay?"

"Yeah." She smiled and tucked the blanket tighter around her. "Just tired."

"Well then." He kissed her lips once. "Good night, Sonya."

"Good night, Soljer."

He reached over her and turned off the light. He pulled the covers over him. As he lay on his back, he drew a heavy sigh, as if he'd been up for days and was finally able to sleep.

It was twelve-thirty a.m. Shadows. Too many lined the walls. Nothing to worry about. It was just the street lamps outside, shining light through the blinds over her window. Nothing to be afraid of.

Zoe closed her eyes and snuggled down a little more. The soft patter of rain on the roof relaxed her mind. Eased her tension. As long as it didn't storm, she'd be asleep in no time.

****

The rain sounded nice on the metal roof. Noisy but relaxing. Ben folded his arms behind his head and stared at the dim light along the shadowed wall.

This town was cursed. There was no other explanation for all the bad luck he'd had here. Or maybe Zoe was cursed. She'd had more bad luck than anyone he'd ever met.

Poor thing. He wanted to hold her in his arms, let her know he was here if she needed him, but figured she was ready for some much-needed sleep.

Understandable. It'd been a long night. A long life. The girl had been through the wringer from the moment she was born. She'd lost her mother at birth and her father when she was sixteen. She'd been beaten and taken advantage of. She'd lived in fear in this apartment for who knew how long. Damn. It'd been one horrible thing after another.

Anyone else would feel sorry for her, but he could relate. Almost. He'd been through some tough times too. Not as bad as her, but heart wrenching enough. Maybe it's why they got along so well.

Why would a guy hit a woman, especially one as wonderful as Zoe? She was amazing. Sweet. He loved her smile. The way she laughed. She hadn't even said one curse word since he'd known her.

Was there a side of her he hadn't seen yet? Had she pissed this guy off so much he'd take a swing at her and keep on swinging?

Didn't matter how pissed Ben got at a woman. He'd never do anything to hurt her. Even if she hit him first, he'd just walk away and cool off.

A faint flash lit the room. A rumble of thunder in the distance sounded nice. The rain pounded harder as another roll of thunder shook the walls.

"Ben?"

He rose up on his elbows. "You okay?"

"No." She turned on her side to face him. "Could you hold me for a while?"

"Come here."

He pulled her into his arms and held her close. Her warm cheek pressed against his bare chest. Her fingers raked his abdomen and caused a big stir inside him.

"I can't sleep," she whispered.

"Thinking about what happened tonight?"

"Can't stop thinking about it." She huddled closer. "Could you hold me until I fall asleep?"

"As long as you want me to."

With her body this close, his breath quickened. The flowery scent of her hair enticed him. Soft skin against his aroused him. If she lowered her arm just a little, she'd touch his erection.

He was helpless. Hopeless. One touch from this woman, and he wanted her in a terrible way. After the horrifying night she'd had, sex was probably furthest from her mind. Or maybe asking him to hold her in bed was her way of telling him she wanted to be with him.

"Zoe," he whispered, gently gliding his fingers up and down her arm.

No response. A deep inhale and exhale told him she'd fallen asleep.

He held her tighter. He pressed his lips against the top of her head then grinned. Who needed sex? Just holding her like this felt right.

Chapter Seventeen

Incessant pounding and chiming drove Zoe to open her eyes to the clock. 4:36 a.m. *Crap*. Renji was here to walk her to work.

Careful not to wake Ben, she pulled from his arms. He rustled slightly but went back to sleep. She tossed her legs over the edge of the bed and then rose.

Pain shot down her neck and shoulders. The wreck had taken its toll on her body. She'd pop an ibuprofen and go back to bed if it weren't for the insufferable pounding on the door.

Her head ached as she shuffled down the dark hall to the kitchen. She felt for the switch and flipped on the light. It blinded her.

Careful not to trip, she took the stairs to the front door. She turned the outside light on and then glanced out the peephole to see Renji's face.

She unlocked the knob, unchained the silver chain, turned both dead bolts, and then opened the door. "Why are you here so early?"

Renji leaned against the door frame. "You're not ready for work?"

"Not today." She groaned. "Not after last night."

"Are you sore?"

"And groggy."

"Well. Since I'm here, can I come in?" he asked. "I'd like to talk for a minute."

She stood aside. As he walked by, she noticed his bloodshot eyes. Didn't look like he got much sleep either.

She shut and locked her door. "You look tired too."

"Didn't sleep a wink." He followed her to the kitchen. He sat at the breakfast bar and leaned forward against folded arms. "I like your new guy. He seems to really care about you."

She placed her hand on his forearm. "I really like him too. He's been a perfect gentleman. Even in bed."

"Too much information," he said with a quiet laugh. "So, I wanted to tell you about my date last night."

"With Fred?" She stuck out her tongue.

"Good to see lack of sleep hasn't ruined your sense of humor." Renji's eyes narrowed. "The date was before I went on patrol with Fred. I took Drema out to dinner."

"Okay, lover boy. Tell me all about it."

"It was amazing." He beamed, a hint of red in his olive-toned cheeks. "She's incredible. Beautiful. Funny. Sexy. We ended up back at her place. I totally got some."

"Talk about too much information." Zoe laughed. "Well, good for you. Are you going to see her again?"

"I hope so."

Ben appeared in the doorway. His stretchy boxers hugged his body as he strode to the kitchen sink, muscles flexing.

"Sorry," Ben grumbled as he grabbed a glass from the cabinet. "Didn't mean to interrupt."

Renji stood. "Hey, man. No hard feelings about last night."

"No problem." Ben turned on the faucet and filled his glass. "We were all under a lot of stress."

"You're welcome to use my truck today." Renji tossed his keys on the counter. "There's a motorcycle shop near the interstate. They'd hook you up with a new wheel."

Zoe's heart sank. Renji was being awfully nice, especially after he threatened Ben with a warning last night. He must've had a lot of fun with Drema.

"Thanks." Ben leaned back against the kitchen sink. "I'll probably rent a truck and trailer and haul both vehicles home. Fix them myself."

"You work on cars?" Renji arched his brows. *Oh boy*. She could see the excitement in his eyes. If they got into a big conversation about mechanics, she was going back to bed.

"Ever since I can remember." Ben folded his arms across his bare chest. "Thought about opening up a shop but haven't decided yet."

"Dude. Awesome. You'll have to let me know when so I can bring up my truck. It needs some work."

"Sure," Ben said with a half grin.

Renji cleared his throat. "Well. I better get to work. Take good care of our Zoe."

"Always."

Gooseflesh spread over her body. *Always*. What a great response.

She followed Renji to the door. He stepped out on the darkened walkway, and then turned around.

"Text me updates." He gave her a wink. "Relax today. Have some fun with your guy. Millie and I have the bakery under control."

"Thanks, Renji." She palmed his cheek. "You're

the best."

"Yeah, I know."

Renji took off down the sidewalk. Best friend ever. What would she do without him in her life? She never wanted to find out.

She closed the door and locked it up tight. She made her way up the steps and into the kitchen where Ben still leaned against the counter, a grin on his shadowed face.

"Should I be jealous?" He set down his glass. "Should I leave?"

She wrapped her arms around his torso. "You're not going anywhere."

He clutched her shoulders. "You love him, don't you?"

"Like an obnoxious brother." She pressed her lips to his chest. "He's my best friend. We grew up together."

He brushed her hair back behind her shoulders. "I understand."

"Good." She cocked her head to the side. "It's still pretty early. What should we do?"

He grinned. "Breakfast?"

"I usually eat at the bakery, but nothing will be done until around six." She opened the refrigerator to empty space. Maybe she should start buying real food for these occasions. "I'm not a very good cook, so all my meals come from either the bakery or the freezer."

"We could go out to eat in Wichita while the bike's being fixed."

Zoe closed the fridge. *Wichita. Nicholas lives there.* With all that had gone on in the past week, maybe going to the city wasn't such a good idea.

Of course, she'd be with Ben. He wouldn't let anything happen to her. As long as she stuck beside him like glue, everything would be all right.

She turned around to meet him face to face. Dog tags around his neck. Bare chest and tight boxers, he was so beautiful. None of her decorations compared to this man. Nothing and nobody did. She wished he could stay with her. Live here with her. They could wake up every morning together.

"I should probably make coffee then."

"Coffee." He placed his palms against the refrigerator on each side of her head. "Sounds good."

She opened her mouth to speak. Nothing came out but a puff of air. What should she say or do?

He leaned down and kissed her lips. The kiss deepened. Her legs grew weak. She closed her eyes. As his tongue licked hers, fire spread through her body. If she could just get past her fear, she'd drag him to her bed and show him just how much she wanted him.

He leaned back and smiled. "Good morning, Ms. Kearny."

"Good morning, Mr. Solmer," she whispered, knot in her throat.

"We have a busy day today." His nose glided against hers. "Shower." He kissed her top lip. "Breakfast." He brushed both lips. "Motorcycle ride." His tongue swept inside her mouth. Her belly quivered as he traced her jawline with his forefinger. He dragged his fingertips slowly, delicately down her neck to the soft flesh above the neckline of her gown.

The heat between her legs intensified. As much as she wanted his touch, she wasn't ready. Not yet. Their first time had to be special, not some early morning thing. She didn't want to be scared of being with him or afraid of flashbacks of Nicholas.

He leaned back. Her entire body trembled. He pressed his palm back against the refrigerator and gazed into her eyes.

"What are you thinking?"

"Um," she whispered. "I've never been on a motorcycle before."

He stood upright. "Then you're in for a treat."

She ducked by him. "Mind if I grab a shower first?"

"Sure."

He followed her down the hallway to the bedroom. She searched her drawer for undergarments, grabbed a sundress from the closet, and without a word or glance, hurried to the bathroom.

She breathed hard. This was unbearable. Her insides ached for his touch. Why'd she have to be so scared? Why couldn't she just give in and make love to him? Why couldn't she jump in bed with him like a normal person would?

"Not yet, Zoe," she whispered to her reflection in the mirror.

Shaking off the desire, she hopped in the shower.

****

Ben closed his eyes. When the shower turned on, he groaned. Damn this hard on. If it were any other woman, he'd have pushed a little harder to get what he wanted, but this was Zoe. He respected her. He wanted to win her heart. Her trust. The woman had trembled so much she could barely stand. He had to back off.

This bastard who'd beaten her had her scared to death. Maybe he did more to her than she was willing to admit. Maybe he didn't let her make decisions on whether to be touched or not.

Ben ran his fingers through his hair. Did Zoe really have him dangling from a string ready to do her will? The answer was evident. Here he lay in her bed, waiting on her in more ways than one. He'd wait as long as she wanted him to. Even if it meant he had to wait forever.

Chapter Eighteen

Ben rented a truck and trailer, and then dropped his motorcycle off at the shop. After breakfast at some little joint near the mall, Zoe suggested they take a short trip through the shops while they waited for his wheel to be fixed.

Ben wasn't into malls. But with Zoe, it didn't matter. He enjoyed her company. Her laugh. Her beautiful smile. After she told him it'd been two years since she'd been here, always shopping for new clothes online or just wearing the clothes she already had, he was all for it.

As they strolled past the shops, she held his hand. He never cared for public displays of affection either. Kissing in public was something he'd never done. He hadn't even held a woman's hand since he was a teenager in high school. But with Zoe, he enjoyed her touch. If she wanted a big wet kiss right here in the middle of the mall, he'd do it in a heartbeat.

Not many people were out shopping on Friday, though, it was only eleven a.m. The theater was empty, but Zoe showed no interest in a movie. She had other things in mind.

They took the escalator to the second floor and stopped in front of the lingerie shop. Skimpy silk and lace hung on all the mannequins in the window. No big deal. He'd seen it all before.

"You don't have to come in with me," she said. "I'm just going to see if they still have those pajama shorts I like. All mine are pretty worn now."

Ben was hesitant to follow her in, but he stuck his hands in the front pockets of his jeans and grinned. "I'll go with you."

This was nothing new. Sheron had dragged him through a lingerie shop not too long ago. He'd followed her blindly as she shopped for bras and panties, aiding her in her fascination for see-through teddies.

It was quite a predicament coming in here with Zoe. Imagining her in any of these tiny cloth seductions could cause a stir he couldn't contain. He had to think of something else.

The vanilla scent of the store was nice. Was it perfume or lotion? Maybe it was an air freshener sprayed by one of the customer associates. Or possibly the scent squirted from an electronic gadget on the wall that went off every ten minutes or so.

Zoe lifted a pale pink lacy ensemble and held it up in front of her. "Who in the world would want to wear this? And how would you get it on?"

Such a tiny outfit. "No idea," he muttered. Pink was her color. Any color was her color.

"Yeah," she said hanging it on the rack. "I wouldn't even know where to begin."

He pursed his lips. If only she understood how difficult this was. Maybe he should've stayed outside.

He followed her to the back of the store where the lounge pants hung. Not as many fun outfits on this rack. Good. He could handle looking at these.

She plucked a pair of dark blue shorts with tiny white cloud prints from the rack. She happily draped the garment over her arm with a matching tank top and headed toward the cashier standing behind the long wooden counter.

Thank God. Almost out of temptation alley. First and last time he'd come into this store with her, at least until they were intimate. Then he'd bring her back to try on the pink outfit and maybe a few others.

He walked past a long pink gown with a low cut back then stopped. He caught her arm before she could get away then pulled her back with him. "Check this out." He lifted the garment off the rack and held it up before her. "This is classy."

She inspected the soft, silky garment, briefly playing with the tiny spaghetti strap shoulders. "It's beautiful."

This was probably overstepping his bounds, but what the hell. "Try it on."

A grin played on her luscious lips. She puckered her nose and shook her head. "That's not a very good idea."

"It's just a gown. Tasteful," Ben said with a sidelong look. "Nothing slinky or demoralizing." Her grin faded. Damn. He'd pushed too much. "Sorry." He hung the garment back on the rack. "Just thought it'd look stunning on you."

Zoe gazed up into his eyes. Her smile returned as she lifted the gown off the hanger. "Okay, I'll try it on for you." She handed him the shorts and tank and headed for the fitting room.

Ben sat on the recliner as she headed for a stall. What was he thinking asking her to model lingerie? Granted the outfit wasn't a teddy or ridiculously provocative, this was still a bad idea. Not only for her sake, but for his as well.

She disappeared in the dressing room. He balanced his right ankle on his left knee and shoved his shades over his eyes. After a moment of waiting, the door opened, and her soft voice called out.

"Ben."

He went to the door and leaned against it. "Zoe?"

"Could you come in here for a second?" she whispered.

The door opened. *Ah shit.* This was a very bad idea.

He glanced around to make sure nobody was watching, and then quickly slipped inside the fitting room. "What's wrong?"

She turned her back to him. "My zipper's stuck."

He grasped the zipper on her flower-print sundress between his fingers. As he pulled down, the straps on her shoulders loosened. The dress fell to her ankles. With her green panties and white bra exposed, he couldn't help but stare.

Her skin was soft, supple. Blonde curls stretched down her arms and around her back. Her panties were bikini style and revealing quite a bit of perfect, rounded flesh beneath the material.

Vanilla scent. Electronic devices on the wall. Pink lace. *Shit.*

"This is very dangerous," he whispered in her ear.

"Control yourself," she scolded. "Thanks for the help, but you can go now. I got this."

"Oh, no fair," he replied, twisting his lips to the side.

He turned the knob on the door. If he stayed any longer, he'd lose control. Walking around the mall with a boner wasn't his idea of fun, though that was already unavoidable.

He sat back down on the recliner. This was unbearable. Heavenly vanilla scent. Spraying devices on the wall. Associates walking through the store spritz-ing the air.

A short, stocky man in a black leather vest and blue jeans strode into the fitting area. He stopped near the entrance, and rolled his long white sleeves to his elbows. His eyes narrowed as they shifted from Ben to the fitting room stalls then back to Ben. He gave a short nod of his shaved head then turned and left.

Ben inwardly laughed. The guy was probably having the same issues with his girlfriend. Why else would he be in the lingerie shop looking like misery followed?

Zoe stepped out of the stall. Ben inhaled a quick breath then held it as she gave a slow twirl in front of him. Damn. The woman was absolutely stunning. The gown hugged her curvaceous body and showed off her perfect, voluptuous breasts. Her erect nipples showed through the thin silky fabric. This garment was tailored just for her.

"Holy shit, Zoe. I'm…at a loss for words."

She folded her arms across her chest, hiding. "I feel very exposed."

"But absolutely beautiful."

She smiled as she gave him another slow turn. The back of the lingerie dipped close to her tail bone and showed off her smooth back. "It's a little cold in here."

He shook his head. "Not where I'm sitting."

"Enough." Her cheeks turned a shade of pink. "I'm going to change now." She hurried back into the stall.

Ben swallowed hard, squirming to keep the stir in his jeans under control. This wasn't the time or place for such calamities. They still had things to do. Outdoors stuff. Motorcycle rides. Nothing else sounded better than jumping in bed with her, or in a fitting room stall if luck would have it.

Zoe emerged clothed in her simple sundress and no gown in her hands. She grabbed her lounge pants and tank from the recliner then waited until he joined her.

"Aren't you buying the gown?"

"No," she replied then lowered her voice. "A hundred-sixty dollars is a little pricey for sleep-wear. Don't you think?"

"I'll buy it for you." He reached into the stall and pulled it off the hook.

"No you won't." She attempted to grab it, but he held it behind his back. "I'll buy it next week." She reached around his torso, but he lifted the gown above his head.

"Nope. I'm buying it now."

"I don't need charity."

"Charity?" He scoffed. "Is that what you think this is?"

He strode to the register and laid it down on the counter. Why the hell would she say such a thing? Hadn't the woman received a gift before?

She huffed. "Ben, please. Don't."

"I'm buying the gown. End of discussion."

"Why?" she whispered.

He pulled his wallet out of his back pocket and took out his credit card. "Come on, Zoe. Do I have to have a reason to buy my stunning girlfriend a gift that makes her look and feel beautiful?"

"Aw…" the cashier butted in. "That is the sweetest thing I've ever heard."

Ben blinked, suddenly aware the few women in the store were staring. If he didn't know better, they were all doing the, '*aw…how sweet*' chant.

He turned his attention back to the cashier. The lazy-eyed woman rang up the gown. "One hundred thirty-five dollars and thirty-five cents."

"See," he said without looking at Zoe. "It's on sale."

He swiped his credit card through the machine. Once he signed the display, Zoe tossed the garments down on the belt. She headed for the exit and kept on going. *Fuck*. Why was she so pissed about this?

He grabbed up the bag and took off after her. "Zoe. Stop." She picked up the pace, staying ahead of him. He followed close behind, into the department store and down the clothing aisle toward the mall exit. What was he to do?

When they were close to the mall exit, she stopped. All he could see was her in the gown, nipples showing, and skin blushing a shade of pink. Before she could speak, he grabbed her hand and quickly ushered her through the store and into an empty stall.

He closed the door. "Why are you running from me?" he whispered.

"I'm not," she replied. "I'm just not used to getting gifts. Especially expensive ones."

"Well, if you're going to stick with me, you'll have to."

He couldn't deny the thrill of this moment, in the fitting room, alone with her. The stir in his jeans was too hard to fight.

He quickly kissed her. Lips gently moving against hers, his hands grasped her back.

Zoe pulled away. Her eyes glimmered in the light. Her body trembled beneath his touch.

Take a step back. Calm the fire inside. Stop pushing her into something she's not ready for.

"I'm sorry," she whispered, body stiff as a board. "I want to be with you, but I can't…we can't do this. Not here."

"I'm sorry, baby." He released his hold on her. "I guess I got carried away."

"No." She laughed nervously. "It's just…my stomach's growling. Plus, I don't want us to get arrested for vandalizing a fitting room."

He gently pressed his lips to hers. "Nobody's in here but you and me."

"Well," an elderly lady's voice said from the stall next door. "I'm in here trying on pants. But I promise I won't tell a soul what you're doing."

Zoe stood slack-jawed and eyes wide. Her palm covered part of her mouth.

"Should I knock if I see someone coming?" the little voice continued. "Oh, now, what a silly thing for me to say when you're obviously trying to be alone. I'll just be quiet now."

Zoe exploded into laughter. He too broke out in a quiet chortle. When the elderly lady joined in with her raspy cackle, he grasped Zoe's hand and pulled her out of the stall, eager to get her out before someone else caught them.

Chapter Nineteen

By the time the wheel was fixed on Ben's motorcycle, it was 3 p.m. As he unloaded his bike from the back of the rental truck, Zoe went inside to use the bathroom. She dropped the bag with her gown on the counter, changed into jeans and a T-shirt, and then slipped on her jacket and boots.

She inspected her reflection in the bedroom mirror. This was it. After the motorcycle ride, she was going to have sex with Ben. Here. In her bed. Maybe even wear the new gown he'd bought at the lingerie shop.

Since the intense kiss this morning and the moment they'd shared in the fitting room, she'd thought about it—decided to do it, not to do it, then decided again it was time. So, her mind was made up. Tonight, she'd be ready to forget all the bad in her life, her past, and concentrate on how good it'd feel to be with him.

"Hey." Ben's voice startled her. He stood in the bedroom doorway with a tooth-baring grin. "Ready to go?"

"More than ever." She closed the distance between them. She slid her arms around his neck and then pulled him down to meet her in a kiss.

His arms slid around her waist. Tongue massaging hers, he lifted her off the floor. He carried her down the hall to the top of the living room stairs then set her on her feet. "Come on."

He led her down the stairs. She shut and locked the door then followed him to the bike at the end of the sidewalk.

"Is there a special way to sit?"

"Nah. Just keep your arms around my waist. Lean when I lean, and we'll be fine."

He shoved the helmet down on her head. It was loose but fit better after he tightened the strap. A grin spread across his face as he snapped the buckle under her chin.

"Is something funny?"

"No," he replied. "You just look cute."

"Well, I'm sure you're cute in a helmet too. Shouldn't you be wearing one?"

"This is the only one I have," he said with a shrug. She opened her mouth, but he shushed her. "We'll be fine, pumpkin."

"All right," she said, not wanting to argue. "Just…don't go too fast."

Ben straddled the seat of his blue street bike. He zipped his jacket to his neck, kicked the kickstand back, and then started the engine. The growl was loud in her ears. He revved it several times before offering his hand to help her get on behind him.

Zoe tossed her leg over the seat. Her heart raced as she scooted tight against him. She wrapped her arms around his torso and locked her fingers together.

The motorcycle lurched forward. She let out a short, breathy scream.

"You okay?" he called back.

"Yeah."

"Hang on."

He pulled out on the main road. Her stomach

churned with excitement and fear. As they zipped off toward the reservoir, she pressed her head against his back, shut her eyes, and held tight.

Soaring down the road kind of felt like flying. She glanced down. The ground moved swiftly below her boots. It was dizzying and yet satisfying in some weird way.

She tightened her legs around Ben. Her heart pounded as she inhaled deeply. His helmet carried his musk scent. Not too strong. Just enough to make the anxiety go away.

The motorcycle leaned. She squeezed him tighter as she leaned with him. Any further over and her knee would scrape the ground. She closed her eyes. Maybe this wasn't such a great idea. She'd never liked roller coasters. With all their loops and sharp turns, she'd always come off the rides sick. She half expected the motorcycle to jet down a steep hill at Mach four, but it kept pushing forward. Steady. Fast.

She gazed out at the familiar scenery. The flat landscape panned by. Green trees lined the blue horizon. Daffodils bloomed in patches of sunlight on green and brown grass. Old farmhouses sat among dirt fields.

She'd been down this route a million times, but never like this. She was outside, exposed to the elements. She was free. Alive. Happy. Nothing could wipe the smile from her face, not even as he turned down the road leading to the reservoir.

It usually took twenty-five minutes by car to get here. Ben must've gone above and beyond speeding to get here in ten. Too bad. She could've ridden for hours, hands in the air like some young kid on the roller coaster.

He carefully drove over the dirt road and parked near the water by a group of short budding trees. He shut off the engine then kicked the stand into place. Hand out, he helped her off the bike.

She unbuckled the helmet and removed it from her head. "Woo! That was so awesome."

His grin widened as he rose to his feet. "You enjoyed the ride?"

"Absolutely." She handed him the helmet. "It was refreshing. Breathtaking. I wish we could've kept going."

He locked the helmet around the handlebar. "We could keep going. I'd like to see the reservoir first."

"Yeah. Of course." She swallowed hard. It'd been a while since she'd been to the reservoir. She had a lot of memories here. Some good. Some bad. Others nightmarish. "How about we hike down to the beach?" Away from the spot Nicholas had taken her way back when.

"Sure."

"I haven't been here in a long time. It doesn't look like much has changed." As they started down the trail, she held his hand. "I used to come out here with Renji all the time. He has a camper and boat on the south side."

She stepped over the root of a tree showing on the dirt-covered path. Maybe the place had changed a little. The weeds had overgrown the bank and covered the hillside. Hopefully, the park had finally fixed the erosion leading down to the east side beach. If not, they'd have to walk on the right side of the path.

"Ah. Renji."

She laughed. "You're not jealous are you?"

"Jealous? Not of him. No."

"You don't have anything to worry about." She kicked a small rock with the toe of her boot. It fell down the incline on her left and splashed in the water. "He and I have been friends since grade school. He's a lot to me like Sheron is to you."

The path narrowed. She let go of his hand and took the lead.

"I just think the guy's got a thing for you."

Zoe watched her feet as she walked. "How do you figure?"

"His eyes light up when he sees you." He shrugged. "I imagine I have the same crazy-about-you look."

"Aw." She glanced back. "You're crazy about me?"

"You know I am."

Her heart leapt to her throat. "Well, I'm crazy about you too."

As they trod down the narrow path shadowed by brush blocking the late afternoon sun, she kept her gaze on her feet. Good thing she'd worn her boots and changed into thicker clothes. It was getting a little chilly.

"We're almost there," she called back to him. "The path on the left side is eroding, so stay near the wall so you don't sink into the—" Zoe's foot landed on a wobbly rock and twisted. Sharp pain sliced along her ankle. She stepped to her left. The hillside gave way and she slid toward the water.

She lurched to the right and scrabbled at rocks, twigs—anything that might keep her from plunging into the reservoir. Her heel snagged on a bend of root protruding from the dirt. It stopped her short, with breath trapped in her throat.

With her hands digging into the ground, she drew in several quick, panicky breaths. *Darn it.* Now she was stuck.

Ben stood on the edge of the hill. He reached out but couldn't get close enough to catch her. "Grab my hand."

"I can't." She swallowed hard. "I'll slide if I let go."

"You have to try." He leaned closer to the edge. The dirt crumbled under his feet, and he quickly stepped back to the solid ground. "Fuck!"

Zoe cringed. The word summed her situation up perfectly. She was *fucked*—destined to fall into the water and swim to shore. She'd be riding on the back of the motorcycle soaking wet.

The muscles in her legs weakened and shook. The only option she had was to start climbing. Fifty percent chance she'd make it to the top. Problem solved. Crisis averted.

She gave a short nod. "Okay, I'm going to try to grab your hand."

He extended his arm as far as he could. "You can do it."

"If I don't make it, tell my friends I loved them."

"You'll make it." He gave a short nervous laugh. "Come on, baby. You can do this."

She drew in a deep breath. "Okay. Here I go." She shifted all her weight to the right foot and pushed upward. She reached for Ben. Her fingers curled against his. Adrenaline spiked through her veins as she climbed, but the dirt continually gave way.

Ben gave a short grunt. "Hang on."

Ben reached with his other hand. As he did, the ground beneath him collapsed. A string of F-words flew from his open mouth as he slid past her and plummeted into the water.

Accepting her fate, she shut her eyes tight and let the landslide take her away. She held her breath as water engulfed her body.

The frigid temperature knocked the wind from her lungs. Her feet found the bottom fast. When she stood upright, the waterline nipped at her neck.

She wiped her eyes and glanced around. "Ben."

Ben laughed behind her. Her teeth chattered as she turned to face him. Thank God he was close.

"Best date ever." His voice was strong, but his lips trembled. "I'm freezing my ass off."

She swallowed apprehension. "Are you mad at me?"

"No, baby. Why would I be mad at you?"

"You fell in the water trying to save me."

He scooped her into his arms. His gaze stayed on her as he carried her to the shore. He set her down on the beach. As he knelt over her, he stroked her wet hair from her face.

"I'd swim across the ocean to save you," he said, water dripping from his hair.

"What about the Arctic?"

"I'd bring fire to melt the ice."

Her heart fluttered as she stared into his eyes. "Maybe you can warm me up now."

He brushed his lips against hers. "And how should I do that?"

She meant to say, *with a kiss*, but couldn't get the words to come out. They were stuck in the back of her throat.

"Touch me," she whispered.

Gooseflesh spread over her skin. The birds chirping in the surrounding trees offered her encouragement. She placed his hands on her sides.

His mouth found hers. He gently pinched her flesh under her shirt. He worked his fingers inside her pants to her clit. Heat surged through her entire body. She fell against him.

Warm was an understatement. Her cheeks and neck burned. Her heart beat a fast tempo. She shook so much she could barely stand it.

This was so very wrong. Her toes were numb from the cold. Her clothes and hair were drenched. The wet, heavy feeling reminded her of the last time she was here with Nicholas.

She shut her eyes tight. *No*. She couldn't think about Nicholas now. Not while Ben touched her.

Nicholas had dug his fingernails into her sides. He'd lifted her off the ground. Pain had shot down her back as he squeezed her flesh. When she'd cried out for him to let go, he threw her into the reservoir.

She opened her eyes. "Stop!" Her voice echoed around them.

Ben pulled his hand from her slacks. She clambered to her feet and backed away. Breathing hard, she climbed the hill toward the path.

****

"Zoe. Wait." Ben followed close behind. What the hell? Had he hurt her? Had he taken her plea to touch her wrong? Maybe she'd just meant a kiss, and now she was angry.

With long strides, he caught up, but made no attempt to stop her. When they reached the end of the path, she tripped on a tree root. He caught her arm and pulled her up. Her body was rigid and trembling, but she didn't struggle against his hold on her.

She lowered her gaze to his chest. "I told you I was accident-prone."

"Yeah. I totally see that." He let go of her arm and palmed her cheek. "What happened, Zoe? Did I hurt you?"

"No."

"Did you want me to touch you?"

"No." Her eyes snapped to his. "Yes, and no. I don't know." She covered her face with her hands. "I don't know what I'm doing here. Could you just take me home now?"

"I'm sorry if I scared you." When she didn't respond, he sighed. He took her by the hand and led her across the parking lot. "Something happened here— with Nicholas. Didn't it?"

She yanked her hand from his. Without saying a word, she walked back to the motorcycle, hugging her torso the entire way. Something terrible must have happened, but he wouldn't push anymore. When she was ready, she'd tell him the story.

The ride into town wasn't as nice as the ride out. The sun had sunk below the horizon, offering the sky an orange-and-purple glow. It was fucking cold. Too cold for a wet motorcycle ride.

Zoe's body trembled against his back. He shook too. The heavy clothes made it difficult to drive. His hands were so stiff he could barely keep them curled around the grips.

When they were inside the apartment locked-up, she went straight to the bedroom. She pulled fresh clothes from her drawer. Without acknowledging him, she hurried to the bathroom and locked the door.

"Zoe." He knocked. "Will you please talk to me? Tell me what you want me to do."

She didn't answer. *Dammit.* He'd fucked up. Maybe he should go to Goodland and stay the night there. Give her space to recuperate from whatever the hell he did to her.

"Do you want me to leave?"

"Yeah. Okay. Could you lock the door on your way out?"

"Sure." He shook his head, disappointed she didn't ask him to stay. He should stay and hash this out with her, but it was obvious she needed space. "I'll see you in Goodland tomorrow night, okay?"

"I'll try."

Try? Ben swallowed hard. Whatever was wrong, he would do anything in his power to make things right.

When she turned on the shower, he went to the bedroom. After a quick change of clothes, he grabbed his bag and headed for the door. He locked the handle and pulled the door tight against the frame.

After a moment of standing on the outside step, debating whether to leave things like this or stay, the dead bolts clicked. The chain rattled against the door, and then the last lock slid into place. *Yep.* That was his cue to leave.

Chapter Twenty

Ben was too exhausted to drive all the way to Goodland, so he spent the night at Sigmund's Hotel. He also wanted to wait, in case Zoe changed her mind and decided to ride with him.

On his way out of town, he stopped at the bakery to talk her into coming with him. When Renji told him she didn't want to see anyone, Ben took that as his answer and left.

It was a perfect Saturday. Though the gentle breeze blew cool, the sun shone warm through the window of the rental truck.

It would've been a perfect day for a drive, moonroof slid back, music blaring, but his poor car sat wrecked on the trailer behind him. At least it wasn't totaled.

Wouldn't be difficult to fix the damage when he got it home, just time-consuming. Doogen was more than happy to lend his expertise to get it back into shape. That brought up the old dream he and Doogen had of opening a body shop together. Though the dream had died with Chase, Ben gave it serious thought on the way to Goodland.

Ben pulled the truck onto the hotel lot beside Doogen's van and parked. Hopefully Doogen remembered his guitar; otherwise Ben would have to use the bartender's crappy ax. The thing wouldn't stay tuned longer than five minutes.

Chipped paint and stucco made the single-story hotel look like a broken-down place on the bad side of Denver. Windows were cracked. The roof missed shingles. Judging by the crumbled wall on the end unit, maybe the building had seen a tornado or two. Regardless, he liked this hotel. It was a fun bar to play at. The usual biker crowd gathered here. They were like family.

Ben hopped out of the truck and stretched. He inspected the building on the other side of the parking lot. The doors were open. Sounds of a ball game played on the TV and a country song on the jukebox in the background. A strong aroma of beer and hot wings hung in the air. Smelled like Doogen's house.

Ben walked up the short set of steps. An older woman dressed in a red shirt and faded jeans met him in the doorway. Her salt-and-pepper hair, usually curled beneath a pink cowboy hat, was tied up in a bun.

"Sassy," he said, giving Sheron's mother a quick hug. "Looking hot as ever, ma'am."

"Oh, flattery will get you everywhere." She laughed her raspy laugh. "Look at you. All mighty fine and in snazzy clothes."

He glanced down at his loose-fitting jeans and T. "New outfit." He grinned. "Buy you a beer?"

"You're talking my talk now, cutie."

Ben chuckled as he followed Sassy to the bar. He sat down and ordered two beers.

He loved the afternoon atmosphere here. Kind of felt like a saloon from the John Wayne movies he'd seen on TV. On nice days like today, the doors were open, letting in plenty of fresh air.

"Heard you've been seeing some hottie from the country," Sassy said with a wink. "Same gal you play games with?"

"Yeah."

Great. Sheron told Sassy about Zoe. Now twenty questions would fly. Sassy would analyze his feelings. Hell. She'd probably get her tea leaves out and read his future. Knowing her, she'd hear wedding bells going off in her head.

"Sheron says you're serious about her."

He shrugged as he set his beer bottle down on the brown square coaster. "Maybe. I don't know."

"You don't know?" She snorted a laugh. "Either you are or you aren't."

"We only met a month ago."

"But you've been playing and talking for how long?"

"A year and a half."

"That's plenty of time to get to know someone well enough." She shook her head. "A woman likes to be told straight-out she's cared about. She doesn't want any in-betweens."

He took off his jacket and draped it over the back of the wooden stool. "I've already told her."

"Told her what?" She took a swig of beer.

"I told her I cared about her."

She glanced around the room. "Then where the hell is she?"

"Home."

"Didn't you just come from her place?"

Funny how her voice got higher with every question. "Yeah, Sassy. I did."

"Then why didn't you bring her with you, son?"

"Long story." He didn't want to explain why, when he really didn't know. Whatever happened at the reservoir definitely had something to do with her ex. She'd refused to talk to him about it. So, what was he supposed to do? Get down on his knees and beg?

"All I'm saying is if you really care about the woman, nothing else matters. You make her feel special. Wanted. I'll bet the poor girl's at home crying her eyes out because you left her."

He drew in a large mouthful of beer, and then swallowed it down. "I didn't leave her."

"Oh." Sassy's eyes widened. "She kicked *your* ass out? Well, shit, Ben. That changes all the questions I had lined up. What'd you do to the poor thing?"

Like mother, like daughter. Sassy was just as pushy and outspoken as Sheron. But unlike Sheron, Sassy gave great advice. She had a knack for showing the truth when it didn't want to be seen.

"She has issues."

"Who doesn't have issues?" Sassy set her beer bottle down and turned to face him. "Is she ugly and mean?"

"No." He sighed. "She's incredibly beautiful and kind."

"Then what's the problem?"

"The abusive, stalker ex-boyfriend. She's scared and won't let me touch her." That was the problem at the reservoir. He'd scared her, just like he'd frightened her at the cabin. Even if she did come around, he'd be afraid to break her. Like glass, she was fragile. As much as he cared about her, he wasn't so sure he could handle this anymore.

"Oh goodness." Sassy cupped the bottle. "You

pushed her into something she wasn't ready for."

"I didn't push her into anything. Our lines of communication got crossed."

He downed the last of his beer. The things Zoe had told him. She'd endured so much pain. She'd lost trust in men. If only he'd kept his hands to himself, he'd never have lost the trust she had in him. She'd be here with him now.

"Well, give her some time," Sassy said in a low voice. "Sounds like she's got some problems to work out on her own. When she's ready, I'm sure she'll let you know."

"I know." He groaned. "What am I supposed to do in the meantime? Should I give up?"

"It's up to you, cutie pie." She motioned for the bartender to bring her another drink. "If you care about her, tell her to meet you here. Show her a good time. Let her know you're not like the asshole she dated before. Let her know she's safe with you."

Sassy was right. She was always right when it came to love and advice. "You should get back into psychology, Sass."

"Ah, no." She gave a hefty harrumph. "I'm tired of dealing with everyone else's problems. I'm happy right where I am—selling beauty products from the trunk of my car."

"Have you seen Doogen around?"

"Last I saw, he was in his room sitting on his lazy ass, smoking a damned cigarette." She shook her head. "Sheron has a thing for him lately. Not sure if it's a good thing or not. Just wish your handsome brother was still around to keep her in line. Chase was a good man."

Ben's heart sank. Nobody ever talked about his

brother when he was around. Sassy never held her tongue, always spoke her mind about everything. She'd been like a mother to Chase, to him.

"You listen to me, honey." She laid her hand on his forearm. "You stop feeling guilty. It was not your fault he died. It was the booze he couldn't get away from."

"I know," he said, grabbing his jacket off the stool. "Still hurts."

"You're a better man than he was," she said as he slid his jacket up over his shoulders. "The woman is lucky to have you. Don't forget that."

He leaned down and kissed her cheek. "It's great to see you, Sassy."

"Likewise, sugar." She blushed. "Play me a fast-moving song later, and I'll see you on the dance floor."

"Sure thing."

As he left the bar, his head ached. He crossed the parking lot to his room. Lucky number five. Once inside, he lay down on the bed and closed his eyes. Rest would do him some good. Maybe later, he could focus on playing this gig instead of worrying about what he was going to do about Zoe.

Chapter Twenty-One

It was nine thirty p.m. when Zoe arrived at the bar. She parked Renji's truck beside the first motorcycle in a string of them lined along the front. The scene reminded her of an old western she'd watched on TV, where cowboys tied their horses in front of a saloon. The only things missing were the gunslingers, though the night wasn't over yet.

She wasn't going to come, but she owed Ben an explanation. He deserved to know the truth of why it was so difficult to let anyone cross the line. She needed to apologize for pushing him away without giving him a reason. And thank him for giving her the space she needed to work it out.

Zoe passed two huge bouncers near the door and into the noisy bar. Goodland was such a tiny town, but their band really packed them in. People must have come from all over to see them.

She scanned the crowded room. The band played on a stage near the back wall. Her heart leapt to her throat. There Ben was, handsome in holey jeans and plain black T. He'd kept the scruff on his face, which was nice. It'd be nicer if he smiled a little.

He played guitar as Doogen sang with a calm country twang. Sheron danced below him in a pretty green sundress and a short shawl that covered her petite shoulders. Another woman in a red rhinestone cowgirl hat danced with her.

There was an abundance of flannel-clad people with cowboy hats on, dancing in various places throughout the building. At least twenty women, all between forty and seventy years old, wore vests with the words *Fire Women Chapter, Denver, Colorado* printed in a circle on the back. They must be the ladies who own the motorcycles out front. *Pretty cool.*

Zoe drew in a deep breath. She straightened her short black skirt, tugged the hem of her white long sleeve, and then headed for the bar.

Relax. She'd come to make amends, but also to have a little fun.

She stopped at the counter and glanced at the woman beside her. The drink parked on the bar looked like soda.

"What'll you have?" the bartender with rings through her nose shouted over the music.

Zoe pointed at the woman's drink. "One of those."

"Rum and Coke?"

Zoe nodded. As the bartender made her drink, Zoe glanced in the mirror above the shelf. She should've touched up her makeup before coming in. Maybe she should let her hair down from the ponytail.

The bartender set the glass in front of her and gave her a wink. "First drink's on the house."

"Thanks." Zoe sucked two mouthfuls in through the straw. Her muscles relaxed. She smiled and maneuvered through the crowded room toward Sheron who still danced on the dance floor.

Goosebumps spread over her skin. After the reservoir incident, maybe Ben didn't want to see her again. Maybe he'd be so mad he'd tell her to leave. Not that she'd blame him.

She wove her way around tables, ignoring stares from some of the scariest-looking men and women she'd ever seen. Bikers in leather vests and jeans sat around a large table, drinking beer while they listened to the music. They reminded her of exhaust fume guy at the heavy metal bar.

Ben's band attracted all kinds of people. She'd be sure not to drink too much and dance with creepy guys tonight.

"Zoe," Sheron yelled over the deafening music.

"Hey," Zoe replied.

"It's so good to see you, lady." Sheron hugged her neck then turned to the lady with the cowboy hat. "Hey, Mom. Meet Zoe. Zoe…This is Sassy. My mom."

The dark-haired woman had on a Fire Women vest too. Her grin reminded Zoe of Sheron's. Very beautiful. Young. Vibrant.

"You're Ben's leading lady." Sassy raised her glass. "He wasn't wrong. You are a beauty."

Zoe didn't know how to respond. Ben had told Sassy about her. Or someone had. Ben was standing right there on the stage, in her peripheral vision, but she was afraid to look him in the eyes, afraid she'd see disappointment.

The song ended. The room went wild with applause and shouts. When Zoe found the courage to look at the stage, Ben was taking position in front of the microphone. Doogen stepped down off the podium, grabbed Sheron's hand, and whisked her toward the bar.

With no one to get in her way, it was easy to see Ben's handsome face. Those emerald eyes shimmered under the lights. A smile crept across his face.

"This one's for you, babe."

Her heart sank. She wanted to talk to him, hold him in her arms, and tell him she was a fool for letting him leave last night, but the song began. Slow. Beautiful. A heavier ballad than the country they'd been playing.

As Ben sang, the crowded room melted away. A daydream played in Zoe's mind. It was only her and Ben now, standing in the room together. Dancing. Kissing. His song was about being with the one he loved. He'd go to the ends of the earth and die for her. It was the most beautiful and haunting song she'd ever heard.

When the music ended, the crowd went wild. The entire firewomen's chapter hooted and hollered. "You're the hottest guy in the world, Ben," one of the women shouted. "Man of the night," another called out. "Sexy boy." Laughter filled the room.

Zoe laughed too. She'd have to remember to use *Sexy boy* to tease. Ben rolled his eyes, but he couldn't hide the grin on his face as a faster, harder song started.

Damn, the man had a set of vocal cords. Wonderful chills crept over her skin. He sang various songs from bands she'd heard before. Some songs were new. Most were hard but melodic. He screamed a little, but even that was perfect.

After forty minutes of standing near the stage, Zoe had an overwhelming thirst for water. She gave Ben a short wave then purposely avoided the large group of leather-clad ladies that filled up the back tables.

Zoe sat on a bar stool and got the bartender's attention. "Can I get water?"

The bartender nodded. She set a tall glass of ice

217

water in front of Zoe, and then gave her another wink.

Zoe lifted the glass to her lips and sipped. Refreshing. She drew in a few long gulps and then set her glass down on the counter.

"Well, I'll be damned," a man shouted over the music. "Zoe?"

Every hair on her body stood on end. *No, no, no.* This couldn't be happening. It couldn't be Nicholas's voice. He wasn't here. *Don't acknowledge. Leave the bar and never look back. Lock yourself in Renji's truck and drive straight home.*

She took a step toward freedom, but the man grabbed her wrist. "Zoe. It's me. Nick."

She wriggled her hand to break loose, but he wouldn't let go. The only way to get out of this was to face her nightmare. Head on. No fear. Easier said than done.

She drew in a deep breath then turned around to look the demon square in the eyes. It was indeed Nicholas. He sat knees wide apart and heels on the bar below the stool. He had a crooked grin on his face which reminded her of when they first met.

He wasn't a bad-looking guy back then with curled locks he'd streaked with blond dye. He'd had a charming smile and a nice body from his frequent trips to the gym. Now he was pudgy. His head was shaved. Those muddy-brown eyes she used to like drooped. Wrinkles over his brows made him look forty, maybe older.

The devil yanked her toward him. She stumbled into his arms, but quickly backed away. Icy fingers crawled across her shoulders, up and down her back and through her veins. Her chest hurt as her breath turned erratic. If she could only get her legs to move, she would run. Run as far from here as she could.

"Let me go."

Brows arched, mouth popped open in a vicious grin, he laughed. "I can't believe Zoe Kearny's in a bar. Never thought I'd live to see the day."

Her stomach churned. Her reply sat at the tip of her tongue. *I hate you.* Her body trembled as images of that night played like a movie in her mind.

He'd hit her over and over, bloodying her nose and lips. Her eyes had swelled shut. It had stung like hell when she'd cried for him to stop, but he wouldn't.

A scream formed on her lips, but nothing came out. The bar was too packed. The music was too loud. The only way to get out of this was to fight him.

She balled her free hand in a tight fist. He deserved to feel the pain he'd made her endure, but a million times worse. She glanced at the brunette woman sitting on the other side of him. The woman had masked her split lip with bright red lipstick, just how Zoe had once hidden her bruised left eye with a thick layer of eye shadow. No amount of makeup could cover up the evil this man dished out.

Zoe jerked her hand free. "I was just leaving."

"Come on. Haven't seen you in a long while. Stay here and have one drink with me. I insist. Let me apologize to you in person."

His jaw clenched and unclenched as he stared. It was the same look he'd carried right before he'd slap her. In the short time they'd dated, she'd been knocked down and bruised. He'd forced her to do things she wasn't ready to do. *Remorse* wasn't in his vocabulary. Neither was the word *no.*

She swallowed back tears. No way in hell would she allow him the satisfaction of seeing her cry ever again.

Breath in her throat, she sat on the stool. This was exactly how it was before. He told her what to do. She'd do it. A fist to the face didn't feel so good.

God, had she not learned anything? She was still weak. Her legs shook. Her upper lip perspired. It was so hot in here, and yet she couldn't stop the chills overtaking her body.

As long as she stayed here in public, she'd be okay. He couldn't hurt her in front of all these people. Ben was right on stage if she had to scream.

The music ended. She stole a glance at Ben, who held his guitar over his head. The firewomen's chapter crowded around him as he stepped off the podium. Frowning, he hurried out the side exit.

Oh shit. Ben left the building. He left her here, scared to death that her ex, the man she'd sent to prison, the jerk she'd taken weeks of Fred's self-defense classes for, would lash out. Sober, Nicholas wasn't so bad. Drunk—the guy was a nightmare. Right now, with a glass of tequila in his hand, he was drunk.

Nicholas raised his glass and indulged in a sip. "I just finished a cross-state charity run on my motorcycle. Part of my rehabilitation."

Zoe swiveled her stool, bravely returning his gaze. It was a little too coincidental meeting him here, especially after he'd run her and Ben off the road.

He turned to show her his back. "Check out the chapter I joined."

Zoe read the words on his leather vest. "Knight Hogs Club?"

"My probation officer set it up."

"Charity, huh?"

He narrowed his eyes. "St. Rosetta's Church. They run a homeless shelter. I've been working there since I got out of jail."

Zoe shrugged. "I've never heard of it."

"If you don't fucking believe me, I'll show you the god damned pamphlets in my house." He slammed his empty glass down on the bar. "Take a ride with me to the fucking church now and I'll show you."

Zoe jumped off her stool. Okay. *That* was scary. She wasn't here to socialize with him. She wasn't even sure why she was here talking to him when she hated his guts. She'd hoped the time in prison had made him see the error in his ways, but she could tell by the lady sitting next to him, he was still an evil bastard.

She backed away from the bar, away from Nicholas. She turned to leave, but he took hold of her wrist again.

"Where the hell are you going?" His lips parted in a sneer. "I didn't say you could leave."

"Get off me."

"You heard the lady." The bartender leaned forward and grabbed his arm. She pulled hard, but he wouldn't budge. "Let her go, asshole."

"Mind your own fucking business, bitch." His fingers splayed over the bartender's face. He shoved hard and the woman fell back against the sink.

Her eyes widened. "You are so out of here, motherfucker." She waved her arms, motioning for the two burly men at the door.

Nicholas tightened his grip on Zoe's wrist. She yelped in pain as he dragged her toward the rear exit.

She leaned back, tugging and pulling, but there wasn't enough traction in her shoes to stop. He was too strong and determined to get her out the door.

"Let go." She grabbed an empty chair with her free hand, but it fell over onto the floor.

A tall man with a bushy gray beard stepped in front of them. Nicholas turned away. Zoe's arm twisted. Pain shot down her shoulder to her elbow. Her wrist burned from the friction. She cried out.

"Listen to me." Nicholas leaned close to her face. "I'm not trying to hurt you. I just want to take you somewhere quiet so we can talk. You understand?"

Fred's lessons ran through her mind. He'd taught her how to get out of someone's hold on her wrist. She just had to calm down to remember.

She drew in a deep breath. *Find your inner strength. Don't think about who's holding you, but about how to get out of it.*

She flattened her hand and held it rigid. With a quick, hard jab, she struck his throat. His head snapped back. He coughed and stumbled then let go of her wrist.

Oh my God. It actually worked. She was free.

Adrenaline singing through her veins, Zoe took off into the crowd. As she wove around tables and chairs, she threw a glance over her shoulder. Nicholas wasn't following. Hopefully, the bouncers would detain him long enough for her to get away.

A thin sheen of sweat covered her skin. She needed to get out of this bar. Get some air. Run to Renji's truck and get the hell out of this town before Nicholas caught up to her again.

Another man stood at the side entrance Ben had slipped out through earlier. Eyes wide and blurring from tears, she stopped before him. Her body shook as he stared.

Would he let her out? Had they locked this place down until Nicholas was dealt with? God, she didn't want to be stuck in here with him.

He nodded as he stepped to the side. "Go. Hurry up."

"Thanks." Zoe shoved her way through the door. The night air cooled her hot skin. As she drew closer to Renji's truck, she glanced around her. There was nobody in the parking lot. No devils followed. The truck was right there. Just a little farther and she'd be locked inside and heading home.

Voices near the hotel startled her. Her skin crawled. A man laughed heartily. Then a familiar raspy voice caught her attention.

Across the lot, Doogen and Sheron strolled hand in hand toward the far end of the hotel. Ben disappeared inside room number five. Zoe's heart raced. She sprinted across the dark parking lot then stepped up on the walkway.

She made a hard fist and pounded on the door. "Ben, help! Let me in."

Zoe glanced over her shoulder. Three men stood in the bar's doorway, glaring at Nicholas, who stumbled drunkenly down the steps. He staggered toward her and all the hairs on her body rose.

"Come on. Ben, let me in." She drummed harder on the door. "Hurry."

****

"Hang on, Zoe. I'm coming."

Ben's heart rapped against his chest. Whatever Zoe shouted about, it sounded urgent. She was going to beat the flimsy hotel door down if he didn't open up.

He opened the door. Zoe ducked under his arm and hightailed it inside the room. She shut the door, locked the knob, and hung the chain. Breathing as if she'd run a 5k in record time, she leaned back against the door.

"Zoe, what's wrong?"

Tears fell down her cheeks. "He's out there."

"Who's out there?"

"Nicholas."

Ben's muscles tensed. *Holy shit.* The violent ex was here?

A loud knock on the wall made Zoe jump. Another heavier thud sounded on the door. A short scream escaped her mouth as she hurled into Ben with such force it nearly knocked him over.

As she held tight around his torso, he swiped the curtain to the side. Nobody was at the door. There were a few men standing at the bar's entrance. A couple kissed close to the parked motorcycles. But that was it.

"I don't see anyone." He stroked her arms with his hands and gazed into her watery eyes. "Let me go talk to him. I'll get him to leave."

"No." Zoe shuddered as she squeezed him tighter. "You can't reason with him when he's drunk."

What was he supposed to do? Keep quiet and hope Nicholas went away? Call the cops? He sure as hell wasn't letting Nicholas terrorize her anymore.

He caressed her face between his hands. "Did he hurt you?"

"No." Her body trembled like yesterday when she fell into the reservoir. "I mean, he grabbed my wrist. He wanted me to leave with him."

"When?"

"About ten minutes ago. At the bar. The bartender tried to help me, but he shoved her away. They kicked him out."

"I saw you talking to a guy at the bar, but I didn't think anything of it. That was Nicholas?"

"Yes." She whimpered. "He's stalking me again."

The guy had looked vaguely familiar. Ben scrubbed his face. Where had he seen him before? *Wait.* The mall. That was the same guy who'd stuck his head into the fitting room at the lingerie shop. *Holy fucking shit.*

Ben bit back profanities as he lowered her arms to her sides. He placed his hands on his head and paced. *Dammit.* He couldn't tell her about the incident. She was already freaked out enough.

"If I'd known he was here, I wouldn't have come to the room to change my jeans."

Zoe glanced down at his pants. "You had to change?"

"One of the ladies spilled her drink on me. I was going to change and come find you. I wanted to apologize for what happened at the reservoir."

"I don't want an apology." She wrapped her arms around his torso and pressed her cheek to his chest. "I want you to stay in this room with your arms tight around me."

More than anything, he'd love to stay here and hold her. But enough was enough. He leaned her back. "If I don't handle this, he's just going to keep coming back."

"He won't stop. He'll never stop."

"I know you're scared." Ben palmed her cheek. He kissed her temple. "Just stay in the room and lock the

225

door. Call the police. Maybe I can keep him talking until the cops get here."

"Please, Ben." She grabbed his arm as he strode to the door. "Stay with me."

He unlocked the door and opened it. "I'll be right back." When he pulled it shut, he waited. Once Zoe twisted the lock and hung the chain, he turned around to get rid of the nuisance. If he was even here.

Ben folded his arms over his chest and scanned his surroundings. The bouncers were at the door. The kissing couple was gone. Loud music echoed around him. Shit. Doogen was probably pissed Ben hadn't shown up for the last set. Oh well. He'd get over it.

Whoever had knocked on the door was long gone. Hell, Doogen was the most likely suspect, trying to get Ben's attention to go back onstage.

Ben turned to the door. Zoe stood in the window—part of her, anyway. Her fingers showed as she held the curtains slightly open.

He shook his head and shrugged. The lock rattled. She opened the door and let him in.

"I didn't see anyone," Ben said as she performed her routine of locking the door.

"Good." She sat on the bed. She gave a heavy sigh as she covered her face with her hands.

He sat beside her and leaned his elbows on his knees. "You've been through a lot tonight. Why don't you stay here with me? Get some rest."

"Thanks. I'd like that." She lowered her hands to her lap. "Yesterday at the reservoir…I didn't mean to push you away. I just…got scared."

"It's okay."

"No. It's not okay. I told you to touch me and then

ran away like a frightened little girl." Tears welled in her eyes. "I don't know what's wrong with me."

"You don't have to explain." He put his arms around her and held her close. God, he hated to see her cry. No woman had ever made him feel like this—like the weight of the world wasn't heavy at all, like he didn't need anyone else in his life. All he needed was her. No doubt about it. He was falling for her. And beyond words, that scared him shitless.

Zoe didn't belong around these drunken miscreants. She deserved much more than spending her weekends in bars, getting preyed on by assholes while he was busy onstage. It was a good thing he'd come to the room; otherwise he wouldn't have been here to help her.

Chapter Twenty-Two

Zoe lay on her back, arms folded over her chest. She stared at the door. The ceiling. The walls. The clock had read 2:06 a.m. the last two times she'd read it. Either time stood still, or the clock was broken.

The strip between the curtains let in just enough light to see, which was good. At least the room wasn't veiled in black.

She couldn't sleep. Not in this hotel with a door with only two locks. Not with all the motorcycles revving their heavy engines. Every time one motor started, she'd smack her noggin on the headboard.

Ben slept close beside her, chest tight against her shoulder. The man slept so peaceful. Handsome.

If anyone should be mad about the reservoir incident, it should be him. She'd punished him for touching her when she'd asked him to. It wasn't his fault. It wasn't hers either.

It was Nicholas. He'd left scars. They were deep in her body and heart. She never thought she'd trust anyone again. But she had found Ben.

Ben was the most wonderful man in the world. Caring. Trustworthy. More importantly—patient. Any other guy would've told her to take a hike by now. But he'd put up with her problems, and there were a lot of them.

The daydream she'd had at the cabin played in her

mind. Her husband snored lightly beside her. She'd touch his chest to wake him. He'd kiss her lips and move over her body. They'd make love until morning.

Ben's eyes opened. "Hey," he said in a low voice. "Having trouble sleeping?"

"Yeah."

"Are you cold?"

His warm breath on her ear sent gooseflesh over her skin. "A little."

He reached across her mid-section and placed his hand on her upper arm. He gave her a gentle squeeze. "Snuggle closer."

He closed his eyes. Her cheeks and ears burned. Heat spread through her neck to her fingertips. Fantasizing about him had turned into a longing to be touched.

"Ben."

"Yeah."

"Will you—" She cleared her throat. The words *make love to me* were on the tip of her tongue, but she couldn't get them out. "There's a barbecue at Holetzer's next month. Do you think your band could play the event?"

"Sure." His eyes remained closed. "Just let me know when, and I'll tell Doogen."

"Okay."

Zoe stared at the ceiling. *Chicken.* It was so hot under these covers. If she could just take off her bra and the T-shirt Ben lent her to sleep in, she could cool off. Then she'd be naked. He'd be touching her skin. His body would join with hers.

Air quickly left her lungs. This had to be what she wanted. She ached all over.

She looked at Ben again. He was so perfect. There wasn't any doubt. She wanted him to be her first. Her *real* first.

"Ben," she whispered.

"Yeah, Zoe." His voice was just as soft as his breath.

"Will you—" Her throat clenched. Did she want to ask? She had to be really sure this was what she wanted. She definitely couldn't allow awful memories to surface like at the reservoir. If she changed her mind once the decision was made, Ben might lose faith in her. She'd lose faith in herself.

She swallowed the lump in her throat. "Will you make love to me?"

His eyes stayed closed. No more motorcycle engines rumbled. No voices talked in the parking lot or in the room next door. There was just silence. And heat—lots of heat beneath these sheets.

Heart beating against her ribs, Zoe sat up. With Ben's arm draped across her lap, she took off her shirt. She unlatched her bra then tossed it to the floor. When she lay back, she repositioned his arm over her belly and pulled the blankets up to her waist.

She looked at him. His eyes were open. Stomach in knots, she turned on her side to face him.

"Zoe. I didn't bring protection."

"It's okay." She scooted against him. "I'm on the pill now."

He wrapped his arms around her shoulders. "Are you sure you want to—"

She silenced him with a kiss. Butterflies danced in her stomach as he tightened his hold on her. His skin was warm against hers. The hair on his chest tickled her chest. As he moved over her, the thin silver chain around his neck slid down. And the dog tags at the end lay cool in the crevice between her breasts.

She dragged her fingers down his sides. The muscles in his stomach tensed. He shuddered as she slipped her hand inside his boxers.

His groaning voice vibrated on her tongue. It felt good on her lips and throat. When she wrapped her hand around his cock, he broke from her mouth.

For a long moment he stared into her eyes. What was he was thinking? Did he like the way she stroked him? She'd never done this to a man before. It felt awkward but satisfying as his skin tightened. His deeper groan sent a shiver down her body. The ache between her thighs became unbearable.

"I'm afraid to touch you." His nose glided alongside hers. "I lost your trust once. I don't want to lose it again."

She brushed her lips against his. "You never lost my trust."

She placed his hand on her breast. As his thumb massaged her erect nipple, electricity soared through her body. His hand slid down her side. Her breath quickened as he lowered her panties over her hips to her knees. As she kicked them the rest of the way down, he took off his boxers.

He nibbled his way down her neck then enclosed his mouth over her nipple. As his tongue swirled around her flesh, she ran her hands through his soft hair. She'd lose control if he kept doing this. She'd have an orgasm right now. It was too much.

His palmed her breast and lifted. He licked from one nipple to the other, lashing at them with his tongue.

She shuddered and leaned farther back, wanting more.

His finger caught her clit and she jolted. "Oh." Her voice was loud in the quiet room. As he massaged, heat resonated from her quaking belly and shot out through her limbs.

She caught his hand. "Oh, God, Ben. Please..."

"You want me to stop?"

"No." She let go. "Don't stop. It feels so good."

"I'm glad you're enjoying this." The muscles in his arms tensed as he swirled his finger around her clit. He pushed his finger inside her channel. Another shock spread through her and erupted from her mouth in a short, breathy *ungh.*

He pulled out and slid against her clit again. She was warm and wet between her thighs. Every cell in her body tingled as his finger dived inside her again. If he kept this up, she'd be done before it even started.

She enclosed her palm around his shaft. "I want to feel you inside me."

He kissed her lips. His tongue was warm in her mouth. The groan coming from his throat sent a shiver up her spine and poured over her body. With his finger still playing against her flesh, it was inevitable. No matter how hard she struggled against him; she would lose the fight.

He pulled her knee to his hip. His hard tip pressed against her opening. Her breath quickened.

This was it. This was the moment she'd allow someone inside her heart—her body. She'd been okay to this point. But now that she could feel him between her legs, now that he was about to take her to the next step of passion, she was scared.

He entered her slow and gentle. Years of

abstinence parted. She pursed her lips to muffle her cry, but a whimper escaped. She wrapped her arms tight around his neck as he delved deeper into the part of her she'd protected until now.

She shut her eyes. That horrible night, Nicholas had stolen her choice to save herself for the right man. He'd taken her safe world and destroyed her dreams of finding love. He'd beaten her to within an inch of her life.

Zoe clutched Ben's shoulders. What was she doing? Being touched felt wrong and frightening. She wanted to break free from his hold on her, but she couldn't.

Tears crept into her eyes as she studied his lips. His hair. His face. *Breathe. Don't think about the past*. This wonderful man wasn't going to hurt her. This was Ben. Soljer. Her hero who'd saved her so many times. He was the man she wanted to be with more than anything.

His smile eased her mind. With him, she didn't need to be scared. With him, she was safe.

He touched her cheek and kissed her. More tears streamed down her face. It wasn't from being afraid. It wasn't from the pain or the pleasure taking over. The fear she'd held on to for so long melted away. She'd let Ben in and embraced him. Loved him. And now she wanted to be loved by him.

****

Ben barely moved. He could tell by her whimper that he'd hurt her. He almost pulled out of her tight walls, but she clutched his shoulders to keep him close.

He pushed further inside her. She let out another whimpering breath, a little louder than the last. If he didn't know better, this was her first time having sex.

233

He gazed into her eyes. "Want to stop?"

"No." She hugged his neck. "Stay inside me."

He thrust a little deeper. It took all his will not to grind into her until she'd taken him all the way. He didn't want to hurt her any more than he had.

Her luscious lips parted. Peppermint from her mouthwash lingered on her breath. He kissed her, tasting it on his tongue.

She scraped her fingernails gently down his back. He shuddered from the chill. She squeezed his backside then lifted her hips. He plunged deeper. Her whimper turned to a breathy moan.

Holy shit. He was so fucking hot for her. It'd be so easy to slide in and out of her and come in record time. He wanted to take this slow but wasn't sure he could.

He rocked his hips. He kissed her temple, her cheek, her mouth. With her fingers gliding up and down his back, his balls tightened. Adrenaline shot through his veins as he dove harder, faster into her. She lifted her hands above her head and held on to the bars on the headboard. Her breasts bounced with every thrust. Damn if he wasn't close to erupting from that move alone.

He drew her nipple into his mouth. It was soft on his tongue but grew erect as he sucked her sweet flesh. He sucked the other nipple in. Her breathy moan sent sparks deep in his gut and gyrated down through his shaft.

He lifted from her breast and crushed her beneath his body. With his hand on her hip, he ground his pelvis into hers until he was so deep there was no space between them. Just heat from their friction.

She relaxed her legs. He strained harder against

her. Faster. His cock throbbed. This was like nothing he'd ever experienced before. This was making love. He didn't care what happened as long as he pleased her.

He didn't look away from her gaze. He panted and groaned in her mouth, feeling her breath against his. The eruption was coming. He tried his best to stop it, but he couldn't. His cock pulsed too hard against her taut walls.

"I'm coming, baby."

"Me too." She held his backside, pulling on him as she lifted her hips. She cried out in soft breaths. The feeling of her walls tightening and releasing sent him beyond return.

Temple on hers, he released his tension inside her. He gave several more pumps of his hips then held tight against her to catch his labored breath.

Damn. Best sex he'd had in…ever. Not the longest run, or the wildest, but better than any he'd ever experienced. It was skin against skin. No protection. He'd never been with a woman without it.

He lifted his gaze to hers. This was where he was meant to be. In her arms. Her bed. Her life. How had this woman snagged his heart so easily, especially when he wasn't looking?

Tears ran down her cheeks to the pillow beneath her head. *Fuck*. Had he been too rough?

"Baby, why are you crying?"

She shook her head. "I don't know."

Maybe this *was* her first time. "Did I hurt you?"

"No." She swept her fingers across the skin below her eyes. "I've just never felt this way before."

"How do you feel?"

"Safe. Cared about." She took his face in her

hands. "I never thought being with someone could be so wonderful."

He wasn't sure what she meant. It didn't matter. There was nothing in the world he wouldn't do for her.

"I would never hurt you," he said against her lips. "I swear you'll always be safe with me."

He lay on his side and pulled her into his arms. For a long while, he held her. Caressed her. Kissed her. This woman clutched his soul. His heart. He'd do anything to protect her from her nightmares.

"Come home with me. Spend the week at my house to recuperate from the accident. Stay longer, if you want."

"As much as I want to run away…" She folded her arms over his chest. "I can't. I have to get back to work."

He gathered her hair behind her shoulders. "I don't want to leave you."

"I don't want you to go." She shuddered as her eyes closed. "You could come home with me."

"I wish I could, Zoe, but I have a lot of work to do." He had too many responsibilities. His car needed fixed. He had to work on the new characters for the upcoming expansion of the game.

"So what about next weekend?" She nestled beside him. "Are we meeting in Wichita? Goodland? Or how about some exotic beach with white sands and tropical winds?"

"That'd be nice." What he'd give to see her walking down the beach in a bikini. "We're not playing anywhere next weekend. How about you come to Denver?" He nestled down in the bed then wrapped his arms around her. "Fly up on Thursday or Friday. We'll go to the cabin. Maybe stay the night at the station, if you're up for it."

"I can't wait." She placed her palm on his chest. "Thanks, Ben."

"For what?"

"For being gentle and patient with me. You know, during my first time. I'm sure it wasn't easy."

He swallowed hard. Just as he suspected. To hear her say it aloud made him feel like a selfish jerk. Like he'd stolen something he should've left sitting on the shelf. How was he supposed to respond? *You're welcome? No problem taking something you've saved all these years for someone worthy enough to take it?* He wasn't worthy, but he couldn't fathom being anywhere else.

Chapter Twenty-Three

After Nick attacked Zoe in Goodland last weekend, Renji was thrilled she was getting out of town. He demanded she visit Ben to recuperate and stay gone as long as she needed to.

Ben picked her up from the Denver airport Thursday evening. They ate dinner at some lovely Chinese restaurant then went to his house. With Sheron gone for the weekend, it didn't take long for them to continue where they left off last Saturday night in Goodland—in bed, all night until they fell asleep.

A flash of light lit the room and Zoe's moment of peaceful slumber ended with a jolt. Then everything turned black again.

The roll of thunder reminded her of home, but she was at Ben's house. Safe. Secure. No need to worry.

She glanced at the clock. Six a.m. It was too early to be awake, but she dreaded storms. But here, she didn't need to worry about the creep showing up on her doorstep or running her off the road. Here, she could sleep soundly beside her protective angel who snored lightly.

She snuggled closer against Ben, resting her cheek on his warm bare back. Rain pattered on the roof as thunder rolled. It'd be okay if she could see. It'd be better if Ben turned over and wrapped his arms around her.

She shivered once. His snore faded.

"For someone who lives in Tornado Alley, storms sure frighten you easily," he muttered.

"I didn't mean to wake you," she whispered.

"You didn't." He turned on the light and rolled over. When he enveloped her in his arms, it felt right. Comfortable. Perfect. Exactly where she belonged.

"I love sleeping next to you." She rested her palm on his shadowed cheek.

He grinned. "I could definitely get used to this."

Her stomach growled. That was mildly embarrassing. She was sure Ben heard the rumble. The neighbors next door probably heard it too.

"Would you like some breakfast before we leave for the cabin, or do you want to stop off for a doughnut? I know how much you like those things."

"Mm…blueberry pancakes and bacon." She moaned as she stretched her arms around his neck. "I should probably take a shower before we go."

"We could get in the tub together. If you'd like."

"Hot damn," she whispered against his lips. "Breakfast can wait."

A sly grin crept across his face. His hand slid over her backside and down her leg. He raised her knee against his hip then turned her on her back.

"Not yet, Mr. Solmer." She shoved on his chest, forcing him to the side. "Bath first."

"While the tub fills?"

"Nope." She rolled off the bed and stood. Brows arched, grin on his full lips, he liked what he saw. It still felt awkward to stand naked in front of him. She grabbed up the sheet and wrapped it around her body. "I need to check my messages. Let everyone know I made it here all right."

"Do you have to now?" He swung his legs over the side of the bed. Half grin on his face, he leaned back on his palms. His boxers were tented. "You're enjoying my misery. Aren't you?"

Her cheeks burned as she picked up her purse from the floor and set it on the nightstand. She shoved her fingers into the opening and stirred them around to find her cell phone.

Not wanting to be bothered, she'd put her phone on silent. There were five missed calls and several texts.

She read Renji's first. —*Mrs. Thatcher called. She's finally doing it. She said if we're still interested in buying the bakery, she's ready to sell to us for really cheap. It's just like we always talked about. Want to ditch the new jerk and come buy it with me?*—

"Oh wow," she whispered. This was a big, exciting deal. She and Renji had planned to buy the place since they'd started working there. With Ben in her life, did she really want to set permanent roots in her home town? If things worked out with him, maybe she'd want to move here.

She rolled her eyes. It was a bit too soon to be having such ideas. But still—the daydream at the cabin—she couldn't stop thinking about it and how amazing it'd be.

She pressed reply.

—*Let you know about the bakery later. Fat chance on ditching the guy. Like him too much.*—

—*Bah. Have fun. See you Sunday.*—

She deleted Renji's text and then read Millie's messages.

—*Zoe, let me know you got there okay.* —

—You're probably sleeping. —

—Let me know when you wake up so I'll stop pacing a rut in the bakery's floor, worrying about you. —

—Do I need to call Fred—?

Zoe tittered. She replied.

—We made it to Denver. Stop worrying. Love you. —

Millie answered immediately. *—Thank the Lord. Have a wonderful time. When you get home, we'll celebrate the sale of the bakery.—*

Great. Millie and Renji had planned out her life. Buy the bakery and stay there forever. She shuddered. Putting up with Nicholas stalking her for the rest of her life wasn't the life she desired.

While Ben rummaged through his dresser drawer, Zoe checked the other message.

—I can't believe you're dating some asshole behind my back. Don't get too cozy up there.—

Zoe's spine tingled. She dropped her phone inside her purse and drew a step back. What if Nicholas had followed her here? Chills spread over her skin. *No. He wouldn't be that stupid. Would he?*

"Everything okay?" Ben's voice startled her.

"Fine," she said, not wanting to worry him. "Just Millie and Renji making sure I got here okay."

Ben wrapped his arms around her shoulders. "Maybe you should call them back."

"I will later." She gazed up into those beautiful eyes. Determined not to let fear ruin her moment with Ben, she placed her palms on his bare chest and gave a gentle push. "You. Me. Garden tub."

He arched his brows. "Finally." He squeezed her

backside. His kiss was playful, tongue touching hers as he backed her into the bathroom.

"We should leave by ten," he said against her lips. "Go to the store for supplies."

"M-hm." She dropped the sheet onto the floor.

Their mouths met again in a deep, passionate kiss.

His fingers glided up her sides and down her back to her backside. "You're so soft," he spoke into her mouth.

She leaned away from his kiss. "You think I'm soft?"

He scoffed. "I meant perfect."

"And soft." She should probably lay off the pastries a little. Maybe then she wouldn't feel so awkward being naked in front of him. Maybe then, he wouldn't call her soft, which was just another word for plump.

He glanced at the ceiling then back into her eyes. Searching for an explanation for his comment, she was sure. "Soft is perfect. You're smooth and voluptuous in all the right places. You're sexy. Soft and perfect."

Good answer. Though, she was still going on a diet to lose a few pounds. After breakfast.

She stepped close to the tub. "Let's just get in."

She bent forward and turned on the faucet. He growled. His hands glided down her back to her hips. "Temptress," he said as he rubbed the tip of his cock against her clit.

Heat in her cheeks, she turned fast. Doing it like that felt dirty. Naughty. Maybe even painful. She was intrigued, but maybe later, when she was more open to trying new things with him. Right now, she just wanted to make love.

As the water filled, she stepped inside the tub and sat down. He followed her in and settled in on the other side of her.

"This is so nice," she said. "I wish I had one of these in my apartment. I don't think I'd ever leave."

He picked up the bar of soap from the dish on the tub's lip. "I've never been in here."

"Never?"

"Never." He pulled a bottle of shampoo from the tiled bin. "Come here."

He guided her between his legs. His chest brushed her back as he sprayed warm water over her head. Electricity sprouted through her veins as his fingertips gently massaged shampoo on her scalp. By his short laugh, she was sure he felt her shudder.

"Are you laughing at my goosebumps?" she asked, putty in his arms.

"Yes. I'm also trying to keep myself in check until I'm finished with your hair." He grumbled. "I wish I would've started somewhere else."

"Well, I'm not making love to you with my hair all sudsy. So, until you're done, we should talk about something."

He gently pulled the soap through her strands, top to end. Endorphins spread through her like wildfire. She closed her eyes and relaxed. This was the life. No fear. No worries. Just happy thoughts and his soothing voice whispering in her ear.

"So tell me, pumpkin," his breath tickled her ear and she shivered. "What would you like to talk about?"

"How about we have a picnic in the woods?"

He leaned around and caught her gaze. "Seriously? Might be bears or cougars. Wolves, even."

"Well, I have you to protect me."

He twisted the knob on the faucet. He brushed her hair back from her temple as water sprayed over her head. "Do I look like Thor?"

She giggled. "Way sexier than Thor."

He scrunched up her hair as he rinsed out the soap. "What about the fellow with the English accent? Loki."

Loki was a pretty handsome guy, but Ben was much hotter. "Oh. Way sexier."

He whispered in her ear, "You are an amazing woman, Ms. Kearny. Maybe during our picnic, we could have a spot of Asgardian tea."

His attempt to sport an English accent made her laugh. She covered her mouth with her hands, careful not to further enflame his libido until he was done. The bubbles tickled as they slid down her neck and shoulders until all the soap rinsed away.

He replaced the nozzle and then shut off the water. "Come here." He turned her around to face him. She clutched his shoulders as she straddled his lap. He held the tip of his cock against her opening then lifted his hips.

It hurt a little as she slid down on his erection. A gasp escaped her parted lips, but he silenced her with his mouth. His tongue licked hers as he scooted to the center of the tub. He pulled her legs around his waist and she locked them behind him.

"You feel so good inside me," she whispered, gazing into his eyes. Heat spread through her body. This was by far the best place to have sex. The warmth of the water around her body, his breath against hers and skin sliding easily on her skin, nothing could compare to making love in the tub.

He pulled an erect nipple into his mouth and massaged with his tongue. Her belly quivered. She moaned as she rocked slowly back and forth.

He kissed up her neck, over her chin to her mouth. "We could stay here and play all day." He kissed her lips, and then brushed his mouth back down her chest.

"Mm…you like playing?"

"With you, yes."

She grasped his head as he lashed at the other nipple. If he kept this up, she'd fall back in the water. "Oh…I'll go wherever you want to go."

"Come on." He gave the other nipple a quick lick. A bolt of lightning spread down her body to the ache between her legs. "Tell me what's rolling around in your beautiful head."

"We can stay. Go. I don't care as long as I'm with you. I'm just…happy." For the first time ever. She wrapped her arms around his neck and held tight. She'd never been this happy before. Like nothing in the world mattered but being with Ben, making love to him. "Last time I was in here, you thought you were saving my life."

"That was the first time I saw you naked."

She tightened her hold on his neck. "You were looking all sexy in your stretchy boxers. I wanted to pull you in."

He cocked his head to the side. "Why didn't you?"

"I wasn't ready." She gave him a peck on the lips. "If only I'd known then how wonderful you are."

Ben inspected her face. He lowered his hand inside the water and rubbed his thumb over her clit.

The tickle in her belly hit hard and fast. She slumped against him. "Oh, you're going to make me come before you."

"Good."

She squeezed her walls as tight as she could around his cock. "I need to help you along."

"Damn. I don't need help, baby." He licked her tongue. "Just watching you enjoy the way I touch you makes me hot."

Her body begged for release as he held her against him. His warm hands squeezed her backside. He thrust upward. A breath escaped her open mouth as he moved his hips side to side.

Her belly quivered. She brushed her lips over his chin, down his neck. She ran her tongue across his nipple. Soap tingled in her mouth. Hearing his voice hum in delight made it worth the sudsy taste.

That was his spot. Or one of them she knew of so far. She wondered if his balls were as sensitive as her clit. She aimed to find out next time they were in bed.

He pulled hard. She inhaled a sharp breath. Water swelled over the side of the tub and onto the floor. He thrust again. More water sloshed. He leaned forward, holding the lip for balance as she tightened her arms around his neck.

She slipped on his wet skin as he penetrated her deeply, quickly. Warm water gushed around her. She concentrated on her breath. On him. Veins popped out on his temple, and she could see he was ready to burst inside her.

"Baby," he said between labored breaths. "Come with me."

Maybe it was the sound of his voice. Or the way he stared with those emerald eyes. He pleaded for her to come. And her body responded. The orgasm hit fast.

She bit her lip to muffle her cry, but it was no use. She cried out as her walls squeezed against his throbbing cock.

He pressed his temple to her shoulder. She shuddered as his warmth filled her. Breathing hard, he held her close.

She ran her fingers through his wet midnight hair. She kissed his neck. His ear. It'd be so easy to whisper how much she loved him, to never want to leave him. But now wasn't the time. Maybe soon, she'd work up the courage to tell him how much he meant to her.

****

Ben pushed her wet hair off her shoulders. "Damn, honey."

"I think this is my favorite place to do it."

He snickered. "Well, we'll have to find somewhere better or we'll constantly be walking around like this." He held up his hands. She laughed as she inspected the wrinkles on his skin.

She checked her hands. The same wavy lines marked her hands, but slightly worse. "I suppose we should get out."

Though he didn't want to separate from her, he rose from the tub. He held tight to her hand to make sure she didn't slip and fall. They stepped down onto the wet bathroom floor. She shivered as he led her to the sink.

"Here," he said, handing her a folded towel. He grabbed one off the shelf and rubbed the soft cloth over his wet body. "I don't know about you, but I'm hungry."

"Chocolate cheesecake sounds good."

"For breakfast?" He laughed. "How about apple

pie?"

She giggled and wrapped the towel around her. "Double-chocolate-chunk cookies."

"Are you serious?" he said as she followed him into the bedroom. "Is there really such a cookie?"

"Yeah." She unzipped her duffel bag. She pulled out a blue gown and slipped it over her head. He hated to see her pale flesh covered. "They're the same cookies I made for the school."

"The cookies you modeled with?" He pulled on his boxers and a dark blue shirt. "Let's go to the store on our way home from the cabin. You can bake some for me."

By the look in her eye, she'd caught his slip. *Home.* Funny. It didn't feel awkward to say it. With Zoe, anywhere was home, but he was glad she was here.

"We could bake them at the cabin, couldn't we?"

"Sure. If you want to." He glanced at the clock. 7 a.m. "Still craving blueberry pancakes?"

She placed her warm hands on his chest. He could definitely get used to this, seeing her every morning before work. Making love to her whenever and wherever they wanted. They'd spent a morning in a perfect world. Maybe that was what scared him most. Nothing was ever perfect. Somehow, he'd find a way to screw it up.

"I'm game for whatever you want," she said, palming his cheek.

"More of you." He kissed the tip of her nose. "But I suppose I'll make pancakes first."

The cabin was over an hour away and another twenty minutes to the lookout. He couldn't wait to get there. To hold her in his arms. To make love to her again. Maybe while they were there, he'd confess his feelings. He wasn't exactly sure what they were yet, but one way or another, he'd figure it out by the end of this weekend.

Chapter Twenty-Four

The ride to his cabin was dreary beneath tall trees and rain clouds. Though the roads were wet, the drive was pleasant. With it still daylight and Ben's hand holding hers, nothing could go wrong. Everything was perfect.

"Did I tell you about the ghost in the cabin?" He raised her hand to his lips. "If I didn't, I probably should."

Chills shimmied up her spine. She couldn't handle ghost stories right now. "No. I don't want to hear it."

"It's not scary."

"All ghosts are scary."

He chuckled. "Well, have you met one before?"

"Maybe." Zoe had several nightmares of her dad standing at the end of her bed, bullet wound still fresh in his skull. She'd always wake in a pool of sweat staring at the empty space where he had stood. "I think my dad visited me a few times to show me what the gun did to his head."

"Oh. Damn." He turned up the gravel road leading to the cabin. "Yeah, I guess I wouldn't like ghost stories either. But this one's not scary. It's actually pretty sad."

She'd rather not hear his story, but he was adamant to tell her. "Fine. Just don't make it spooky."

He pulled up in the driveway and parked. "An older couple used to live here about sixty years ago.

Her husband died in a mining accident. A few months later, the woman was found sitting in her husband's old rocking chair. They say she died from a lonely heart. Anyway, the chair in the window sometimes rocks, and the floor often creaks as if someone's walking across it. The footsteps go toward the window where she used to stand waiting for her husband to come home."

Zoe stared at the cabin and shivered. If some entity showed up in the window, she was high-tailing it home. No way would he get her to step foot in the place. Even now she didn't want to go in.

"Thanks a lot." She groaned. "I think I'll stay out here."

"It'll be fine. I stay up here alone all the time and I've never seen or heard anything but wolves howl and the wind blow."

"There are wolves out here too?"

He rolled his eyes as he opened the door. "Just come on, babe. You're with me. I won't let anything happen to you."

They were going deep into the forest, surrounded by wild things. She wasn't sure what was worse, a ghost or a rabid wolf. It was frightening to think that cougars, bears, and whatever else lurked in the woods might be just a bush or tree away. So, forget the picnic. Forget spending the night inside the cabin. She'd much rather have stayed at Ben's house.

Ben hopped out of the Jeep. He made a straight line to the ATV. He hooked up the trailer, packed their bags on the back, and then he was ready to go.

On the ATV, she scooted so close to Ben her entire front was squished against his back. He started the engine then they took off up the mountainside.

At least the rain had subsided. The sun peeked through the clouds, lighting the trail ahead. It was dim evening sun. Not perfect, but better than the dark dreary woods they'd set out in.

"Spooked?" he called back.

"No," she lied, refusing to give in to the truth.

He placed his hand over hers at his waist then gently squeezed. "Relax, honey," he said. "We're almost there."

She loosened her hold on his torso, trying not to think about spending the scary night in the woods. She leaned her cheek on his arm, not wanting to look. Dreading the coming dark, she watched the sunlight skim the stretch of dirt road. When they finally made it to the tall wooden structure, twilight had arrived.

Spooked was an understatement. But once Ben unlocked the door and let her inside, she breathed a sigh of relief.

The wooden room glowed orange from the sunset. Zoe couldn't tear her eyes away from the rainbow on the black horizon to the right. It was beautiful, but the dark mass meant more rain was coming their way.

"I brought the portable heater up a few days ago," he said as he set the last of their camping gear down on the floor. "Not sure if it'll be cold enough to use it, but if we do need it, it'll keep us warm."

"Good." She nodded and waved him over. "Now come here and hold me."

A grin crept across his face. He slid his arms around her waist and rested his chin on her shoulder.

She closed her eyes. The ghostly rocking chair, the coming rainy night—how could she not feel like she'd just stepped into a horror movie? It would've been a fine night without the stories.

"You're trembling." He held her tighter. "Was it the ghost story?" he asked with a snort. "Sorry. I was trying to get you to snuggle closer to me."

"Charming." Zoe caught his gaze.

"It's a true story though." He gave her a peck on the lips. "Probably should unpack before the sun goes down."

He pulled a lantern from the duffel bag and set it up on the desk in the room. As he unrolled a sleeping bag over the cot, she unzipped her case and dug around for the pink gown he'd bought her. Her hand caught the soft cloth. She held the garment up before her then smiled. Finally, she'd be able to wear it.

Ben arched his brows. "You think you'll have time to put on your gown?"

"Yes. You're going to let me wear this for you while we watch the sunset."

"Okay." He shrugged. "But it's just going to come right back off."

She twirled her forefinger in a circle. "No peeking."

"Seriously? You're not going to let me watch?"

"Nope."

He shook his head then turned his back on her. She hurried out of her shirt and bra. Pants and panties followed. She pulled the gown up her hips and slid the straps over her shoulders.

The gown hugged her body. It fit a little tighter than it did in the store. She definitely had to lay off the pancakes. She pulled her blonde locks forward on one side then cleared her throat.

"Okay. You can look."

Ben turned around, a smirk playing on his face. He strode toward her. "Classy and sexy as hell. Stunning."

She hugged his torso. "Now we can finish watching the sunset together."

"You're killing me." He put his arm around her shoulders. "But this is one of the reasons I brought you up here."

"It's beautiful scenery."

She leaned her head against his chest. They stood in silence until all the orange from the sun transitioned to black. Raindrops covered the window. Lightning streaked across the sky in the distance. She shivered. Maybe the storm would shift away from them.

"The weather's not cooperating with my plans to sweep you off your feet."

She laughed. "You don't need scenery to entice me."

He kissed her lips as he backed her to the cot. "Good to know."

He sat her down on the soft sleeping bag then got on his knees before her. His hands slid up her legs. He lifted the gown up her waist, her sides, and then over her head.

"You were right," she said.

He spread her legs apart. "About what?"

Her breath quickened. "The gown didn't stay on very long."

His lips touched her neck. "Would you like to put it back on?"

"No," she replied as he nibbled her flesh down her chest to her navel. "Oh, that tickles." She grasped his head as he continued down. "What are you doing?"

"You mean, where am I going?"

His warm tongue flicked against her clit. Electricity shot through her body. "*Ungh*. Oh my," she said in a breath as he kept on licking. "Whoa, that's…" She raked her fingers through his hair. If he kept this up, she wouldn't last long enough for them to have sex.

He slid his tongue fast against her and wouldn't let up. Her body jolted. She squirmed wanting him to stop, but also wanting more. It was weird and pleasurable and…she whimpered. No way could she last another second of this.

"I'm coming," she whispered as her walls clenched. The ache was unbearable. As she leaned back to catch her breath in orgasm, he lifted off her mound and shoved his finger inside her.

"Damn, Zoe." He leaned over her.

"Yeah." She stretched her arms out along the cot. She sighed in relief as she gazed at the wooden ceiling. A smile crept across her face and she laughed. "Oh, wow. That was…" Her brain quit. "I'm speechless."

He grinned as he brushed his finger against her clit again. "Let's see if I can get you to come twice."

She caught his gaze. "Please, do," she said in a breath.

She closed her eyes as he drew her nipple into his mouth. The man worked wonders with his tongue as he licked and sucked relentlessly. When he lifted off, her nipple jutted, the cool air made it ache as if it begged for more time in his warm mouth.

She helped him take off his shirt. His dog tags jingled as he tossed his jeans and boxers to the floor. He leaned her back on the bed. As he climbed over her, the ache in her lower belly grew.

He lay between her legs, tongue lashing from one

nipple to the other. He was hard against her abdomen. Ready to take her into ecstasy. It didn't matter if she came or not. As long as she pleased him this time.

His lips brushed the curve of her breast on the way up her body. He grabbed her wrists and raised them above her head. He locked them in his left hand and held her down as he rubbed his cock against her wet clit.

His lips met hers in a playful kiss. A bright flash of light lit the room. Thunder boomed and rolled across the mountains. Zoe shut her eyes tight, desperate to block out the memory. Nicholas had held her down this same way, wrists locked above her head. Lightning had constantly flashed in the room. Thunder shook the walls as he'd slapped her. *God, no.* She couldn't let him haunt her now.

"Ben. Wait." She wriggled her arms to break loose of his hold. He wouldn't let go. "Ben stop. Stop." She cried out. "Let me go."

Ben immediately released her and sat back on his heels. Out of breath, Zoe rose from the cot. She staggered across the floor to the table and covered her face with her hands.

Ben touched her shoulder, but she shrank away. Her skin crawled with chills.

"Baby, what's wrong?"

"I'm sorry." She shook her head. Now she had to explain why she'd just ruined their night. "I just…need to catch my breath."

Rain pelted the roof of the building. Thunder sounded in the distance. Nicholas's face flashed in a streak of lightning. Her short, breathy scream reverberated through the tiny room.

Coming up to the middle of nowhere was a terrible idea.

Another crack of thunder made her jump. It felt like it hit the roof of the building and spread down through her shivering spine. Zoe fell into Ben's arms and held tight.

"Why'd it have to storm?" she whispered against his chest.

He guided her back to the cot. He pulled her into the sleeping bag and wrapped his arms around her. As he held her close against his warm, naked body, she squeezed her eyes shut.

He pressed his lips against her temple. "Do you trust me?"

She raised her gaze to his. "You know I do."

"Then talk to me." He palmed her cheek. "He did more than hit you, didn't he?"

She couldn't tell him the truth. He already didn't understand how she'd stayed with the guy who beat on her. He'd think less of her if he found out what Nicholas had really done.

"You know how much I hate storms."

"Yeah, you've made that clear." He cupped her face. He lowered his brows as he stared into her eyes. "Why'd you jump off the cot as if someone were chasing you? As if you thought I'd hurt you."

"I don't know," she whispered.

"Yes, Zoe. You do." He sighed. "Just tell me what he did. Make me understand."

She shook her head. "I don't want you to look down on me."

"Why the hell would I do that?" He ran his palm over the back of her head. "I care about you. More than anything."

Tears, a big well of them, blurred her vision. She couldn't stop them. *Dammit*. She didn't want to break down into a sob. Not now. Not like this.

She bowed her head. "Storms make awful memories come back. I try not to think about them, but I can't stop them. They're so vivid." Maybe if she told him the truth, this anxiety would go away. Maybe the night would get better. She loved Ben. If he loved her too, then nothing would make him run away, not even her horrible secret.

"Is that what happened at the reservoir?"

"Yes. I'm so sorry." She wiped her tears with the back of her hand. "I bring up this wall to keep all the bad things he's done in the back of my mind, but sometimes they just pop up. After a while it starts to get better, but then I hear from him. I remember he's out there, God knows where, waiting to get me alone."

"What do you mean, '*hear from him*'?"

"Nicholas won't stop texting me. He calls me sometimes to let me know he's watching." She sniffled. "The last text was this morning."

Ben gritted his teeth. "What'd he say?"

She drew in a deep breath. "It's nothing. Forget it."

"You can't keep going on like this," he said. "Holding the fear inside, not talking to me about it. I want to know what's going on."

"I'm embarrassed."

"Have faith." He kissed her lips. "Confide in me. I'm not going anywhere."

Faith? It'd been a long time since she'd had faith. Nicholas's short reign of terror had left a lasting mark, a few of them. The only way Ben could ever understand what Nicholas had done was to show him.

She sat on her heels between his legs. Swallowing hard, she lifted her arm then turned to the side. Ben gently traced the four short scars under her armpit with his fingertips. Her skin rose with gooseflesh.

"He did this to you?"

"He'd had a few too many shots of tequila at a party we went to at the reservoir. He'd splashed me with water. When I splashed him back, he shoved me down."

She hugged her torso. Her stomach churned. Maybe she should shut up before she made herself sick. The storm grumbled in the distance. She'd rather be making love to him again, not confessing her awful past.

"Go on." Ben leaned back on the pillow.

"I thought he was playing, so I shoved back. He fell in the water. When he rose, his clothes and hair were soaked. I laughed. I mean…I was soaked too. We were playing."

She turned and showed him the four scars on the other side. "When he got up, he was furious. He literally dug his fingernails into my sides then lifted me up. The pain was immense. I mean, I've never felt anything like it before. It was awful." She shuddered. "I screamed for him to let me go. He threw me in the water."

Ben's jaw clenched and unclenched. "You sent him to prison then. Right?"

"No. That was the first time he'd ever laid a hand on me. I thought it was a onetime thing." She gave a short laugh through her nose. "I was an idiot to give him another chance. Every time he hit me, he'd show up at my door the next morning and apologize. He had tears in his eyes, swearing he'd never hurt me again."

"He wanted you to feel sorry for him."

"And I did," she whispered. "Nicholas was...*is* a violent drunk. I just wanted to help him get better. I guess that's partly why I stayed. I had faith he'd change, but he just got worse."

Ben scrubbed his shadowed face. "A guy like him is unpredictable. Even with all the locks on your door, you're not safe there."

"With Renji living close by, he won't come over."

"If Nicholas got drunk enough, nothing would stop him from doing what he wants." Ben sat up. "Fucking bastard. If I ever catch him near you, I'll—"

"—please calm down." She trembled. "I don't like seeing you angry."

"I can't help it. I'm worried about you." He cupped her face. "We're going to be separated. I don't want you to go."

Her heart was breaking. Shattering. She didn't want to say good-bye. Not now. Not ever.

A crack of thunder sent her into his arms. Ben quickly turned her over and pinned her beneath him. He stroked her hair from her face as he stared down into her eyes. "It's just you and me here, Zoe. Concentrate on us and the fact that I'll never let anyone hurt you."

Tears streamed her cheeks. "I love you," she whispered. She'd said it, feelings blurted out in the open. Now what would he do? What would he say?

He brushed her lips in a soft, gentle kiss. When he leaned back, he smiled. "I love you too."

Chapter Twenty-Five

When they got back to his house, they slept. Had sex. Showered. Had sex in the shower. They played video games. Had sex while playing video games. Who knew sex and games went together like doughnuts and coffee?

This was the best weekend Zoe ever had. Though the sex was amazing, the best part was when Ben said he loved her too. He even initiated the words now, letting her say it back.

As they walked toward the entrance of Agate Beach Bar, Ben held Zoe's hand. He looked happy. Relaxed. Confident. Unbelievably handsome. His hand tightened around hers as he pulled her through the open door.

The bar was noisy but not over-crowded. Not in the main room. The back, however, had twenty people sitting around a large table. Beer bottles and shot glasses covered the surface. Sheron and Doogen were there with a few people she'd seen in Goodland, including the rest of the band.

Ben had warned her on the way here that these people knew how to party. She'd have a good time. He told her if she drank too much, he'd take care of her. She'd promised not to get too drunk.

"There he is," Doogen shouted. "It's about time you got here, man."

The entire room exploded with laughter and welcomes. Overwhelming. Several people left their comfy seats to shake his hand or give him a hug. According to one woman who wouldn't let go of his arm, it'd been several months since he'd hung out here with them.

"Zoe." Sheron pranced around the table and hugged her tight. "I'm so happy to see you."

"It's great to see you too, Sheron. How are you?"

"Never been better." Sheron glanced at Doogen who smiled back. The love was obvious there. Zoe wondered how obvious she and Ben were. "I see you and Ben have gotten closer," she continued in a low voice. "I'm so happy for you both."

"Thanks. I'm happy for you and Doogen."

"Oh girl. I'm having the time of my life with him."

Ben butted in. "Hey. I'm going to the bar to get drinks. Coming?"

"Yeah." Zoe slipped her palm on his hand.

"I'll introduce you to the clan when you get back."

"Okay."

Ben took Zoe's hand and led her to the long wooden bar. The bartender batted charcoal lashes as she leaned over the counter and kissed Ben's cheek. She set a beer down in front of him.

"I can't believe you're here. It's really great to see you, Ben," she said in a sweet, high-pitched voice.

"Good to see you too, Brie," Ben replied.

A pang of jealousy worked through Zoe as she inspected the stunningly beautiful woman. Long brunette hair, big brown eyes, gorgeous tanned skin— the woman could be a model.

Brie tossed a glance at Zoe. "How 'bout you, hon'?

What's your poison?"

Zoe never liked beer. It tasted awful. Bitter. Millie had served her a glass of red wine when she turned twenty-one. *What was the name of it?* "Merlot."

"You got it. Want your usual hot wings, Ben?" Brie's perky bosom bounced inside her ripped shirt when she popped the cork off the bottle of wine. "Got a two-for-one special today."

"Not tonight, thanks," he replied as Brie poured the red liquid into a long-stemmed wineglass.

Ben handed the glass of wine to Zoe then led her to two empty stools at the end of the table. Sheron stood fast. She placed her hands on Zoe's shoulders.

"Hey, listen up," Sheron said gathering everyone's attention. "This is Ben's new gal Zoe."

Everyone said *hello* in unison. Then one by one, they introduced themselves. No way would Zoe remember all their names. But she'd do her best.

Ben lifted his beer to his lips and swallowed down a drink. Everyone started talking to him about work and whatever else he'd been into. Zoe didn't know what to say, so she sat, sipped her wine, and listened.

This was his family—a large family who loved and respected him. They knew what he'd gone through with his brother and the hardship that followed. Chase had been a part of this group too.

They talked about the shop he and Doogen wanted to open. Zoe was quite interested in hearing about it. Not only because she'd planned on taking over the bakery at home. Both establishments could limit how much they'd be able to visit each other.

"Ben and I are really serious about this," Doogen told everyone. "We've thought about it for a long time.

It'd been Chase's dream, our dream, to open a shop together, but he died before we got the chance. I think we owe it to him."

The pain in Ben's eyes was prominent. He hid it well from the others, but he couldn't hide from her. The solemn look made her realize how much he'd shared his emotions with her.

Ben whispered in her ear. "Want to play a game of pool?"

This was his way of leaving the disheartening conversation. "Sure." Zoe had never played the game in her life. "I don't know how."

"I'll teach you."

He whisked her through the archway to the pool tables in the back room. He set his beer bottle on the table next to the oak-stained pillar. He took off his leather jacket and draped it over the back of the stool.

"Chase and I used to play at the bowling alley after school," he said, grabbing two long sticks off the nearby wall. He rubbed a chalky cube on the end of one pole, and then handed it to her. "He won every time. Except once. I don't know if he let me win or not, but it was one of my greatest achievements."

As he placed the colorful balls inside the triangle on the green table, Zoe sat on a high stool. She sipped her merlot. It didn't take but a few swallows for the alcohol to work through her veins, relaxing her.

He downed the last of his beer and then leaned the cue stick against the table. "Come here. I'll teach you how to break."

Zoe hopped off the stool and made her way to the end of the table. Brie strode into the room, another beer in hand. The giant rips down the front of the girl's whitewashed jeans showed off tan legs. She leaned over to get Ben's empty bottle. The hem of her shirt rose enough to see the G-string above her silver-studded belt.

"Brought you another beer."

"Thanks," Ben replied, half grin on his lips as she left.

Zoe rolled her eyes. "Flirt a little more?"

"Flirt?" He stepped behind her. A lump formed in her throat as he held her sides. "Now, why would I want her when I have the most beautiful woman in the world right here in my arms?" he whispered in her ear.

"Oh, flattery will get you everywhere."

"Everywhere huh?"

She shivered. "Are you going to teach me this game or not?"

His palm slid down her right arm to the stick in her hand. Her pulse quickened as he wrapped his left arm around her waist, and then grasped the thin end of the stick.

His right leg went between her legs. "One step up. Spread your feet apart." He nudged her left foot with his right until she stepped up and to the side. "Bend your knees a little, and then lean."

He leaned with her, arms around her shoulders, stick between his middle and forefinger in front, palm on the thicker side. The warmth of his body against her back sent goosebumps over her skin. When her chest almost touched the table, he stopped.

"Take it," he said, warm breath on her ear. "Hold it like this."

His right hand held hers on the thick part of the stick. He slid the pole slowly back and forth through her curled forefinger in front. His arms tightened around her.

"You feel that?" he whispered. "Good strong hold on the right. Nice easy slide in front. Then…" He quickly shoved the stick forward, hitting the chalked end against the cue ball. It rolled fast across the table and clacked against the colorful balls, scattering them in all directions. A striped ball sank into the right corner pocket.

Ben swept her hair back behind her shoulder. His lips touched her neck. As he nibbled her skin, she trembled. Oh God, how would she get through this party without stealing him away into a dark closet?

He pulled her up to him. His gaze found hers. Zoe wrapped her arms around his torso. As he held her close, she relaxed against his body.

"Thought we were going to play pool," she said as he backed her toward their table.

He handed her the glass of wine. "I'd rather stay like this."

She scanned the party. All eyes were on them. "You know, we're being watched."

"Let them."

Two mouthfuls of smooth red liquid slid down her throat. He picked up his bottle and downed a few gulps. Inspired, she finished off her wine.

"Want another?" he asked.

"Probably shouldn't. Not much of a drinker."

"I know. But…" A grin crept across his face. "We're celebrating."

"Oh," she said. "Exactly what are we celebrating?"

He pressed his lips against hers. "Us. Together."

"Hey, you two," Doogen shouted, but Ben kept his

mouth over hers. "Get a fucking room."

Laughter filled the bar. Ben cracked a grin. Brows arched, he leaned back and drew in a deep breath. "You're just jealous, D."

"She's too good for you, man."

"I know, dumbass." Ben chuckled as he gazed into her eyes.

An old heavy-metal song from the eighties played on the jukebox, "Talk Dirty to Me."

Ben rolled his eyes. "Sheron always starts the party with this song."

The party was definitely starting. The guys stood close to one another while Sheron and the blonde named Jill counted down. Once they hit the number one, all the men tossed back a shot of liquor.

"Looks like things are picking up," Zoe said, curious of the game. "They're doing shots."

"Yep." He took her by the hand. "Let's go watch."

"Hang on a minute." Brie waltzed into the room with another bottle of beer. "On the house," she said. Those puffy dark lips pouted. "We haven't played pool together in ages. Care to make a gal's day and shoot a game? I mean, if your girlfriend doesn't mind."

Ben shrugged. Zoe caught his gaze. She could see his plea to let him play. "I don't mind."

He slid his palm over Zoe's cheek. "Ten minutes."

"Confident, huh?" Brie said with a laugh.

"Hell yeah." Ben racked the balls. "Learned from the best."

The party was still going on in the other room. The women were doing shots now. Sheron laughed heartily and waved her over.

"Come play with us."

Zoe wasn't so sure she should. She didn't want to make a fool of herself like the last time she got drunk. As long as she only had a few shots then stopped, she should be okay.

Ben gave Zoe a wink. "Go ahead, pumpkin. I'll be over there in a minute."

"There's that confidence again," Brie said.

Zoe strode toward the party. The balls clacked behind her. Brie scoffed. "Oh, you've got to be fucking kidding me."

Zoe smiled. Brie was about to get her ass handed to her.

Zoe stopped at the end of the table. Sheron tiptoed around everyone and then slung her arm around Zoe's shoulder. "Ready for a shot?"

Zoe glanced back at Ben, who was still taking his turn at the pool table. "Sure. But just one."

"All right."

Zoe set her shawl and purse on a seat and then joined Sheron and three other women in a semicircle. Doogen placed a shot glass in front of her then poured the drink.

"Vodka," Sheron said.

Zoe lifted her glass. She'd never tried vodka before. Hopefully, it didn't pack a punch like the drink Sheron gave her at the bar a few weeks ago. It wouldn't be right to get smashed again and miss her and Ben's last night together for another week.

"Ready?" Doogen said. "Three. Two. One."

Everyone shouted, "*Drink!*"

Zoe lifted the glass to her lips. As Sheron downed her shot, Zoe slammed hers. The liquid burned her throat. Heat worked into her nostrils and she leaned over and coughed. *Oh God*. It tasted awful.

Sheron's raspy laugh was contagious. Zoe giggled as warmth spread through her body. Everyone around the table laughed and talked. They were all so full of life, and happy. It was refreshing.

"Let's do another." Sheron poured another shot in Zoe's glass.

"All right. One more." Zoe picked up the glass.

Sheron and Zoe downed their shots at the same time. Sheron gave a loud *woo* and then laughed again as she clung to Zoe's shoulder. "I love you, girl."

Zoe smiled. "I love you too, Sheron."

Ben sat on a chair at the end of the table. A smile dangled at the corner of his lips. God, the man was sexy. As much as she loved hanging out with all these people, she'd rather be alone with him. Dancing close. Kissing. Making love.

"Another." Sheron poured more into Zoe's glass. "This one's for us, Zoe. We're going to drink to…" Sheron pursed her lips. "What shall we drink to?"

Zoe gazed at Ben. He was the best part of her life. She couldn't fathom being without him.

"To love."

Sheron lifted her shot glass toward Doogen. "To love."

Zoe downed the liquor. Her tongue burned, and she swallowed hard. When she set her glass on the table, Sheron poured her another.

Zoe pursed her lips. "Are you trying to get me drunk?"

"Yes. But if you start talking about Ben naked and holding your alien doughnuts or something, I'm cutting you off."

Everyone at the table burst into laughter.

****

Zoe's flushed cheeks had quite a glow and went well with her personality. She'd become the life of the party—the center that'd been missing from this group for a long time. Her laugh made everyone in the room feel good. Their laughter proved it.

In a way, he was jealous. They got to drink with her. Let loose and act crazy. Now he'd found happiness. He was tempted to join in on the games. Having a few drinks with the woman he loved wouldn't be so bad.

He glanced down at his third beer. To get drunk with Zoe, to laugh with her and enjoy hanging with his drunken friends for old times' sake would be worth it. Wouldn't it?

Ben set his beer on the table. "Pour me a shot."

Everyone hushed. Sheron stared, eyes wide, lips parted, ready to grill him for even suggesting he wanted a drink.

"Come on, Sheron." He shrugged. "I'm not the same guy I used to be."

Sheron glanced at everyone around the table. "You're right, Ben." She gave a short nod. She set a shot glass in front of him then filled it with vodka. "You're entitled to let loose like everyone else."

He lifted the glass. "Thanks."

Zoe slid her hand over his shoulder. "Are you sure you should do this?"

"I'll be fine," he said. "We'll have fun tonight."

Her glassy eyes were blue as the sky. Tipsy. He hoped to join her in inebriated fun. Laugh with her. Hold her in his arms on the dance floor.

Ben lifted the shot glass. The gals counted down,

Zoe's voice loudest in his ears. Once they yelled, "*Drink*," the first shot of vodka he'd had in two years burned down his throat.

Chapter Twenty-Six

Sheron and Doogen sat across the table from Ben and Zoe. By midnight, everyone had way too much to drink. The others went home, and it was only the four of them left talking about Chase. Ben usually ran from conversations about him, but this time, Zoe was surprised he'd stayed and joined in.

"I visit his grave often." Sheron slurred her words. "I leave fresh flowers once a week and burn candles on the hearth beneath the tombstone." She whimpered. "I'll do that for the rest of my life."

Doogen stroked the back of Sheron's head. "You're a good woman. Chase loved you more than anything." She leaned against his chest.

Ben set his glass of vodka and ice on the table. He was lit. Everyone was, except Zoe who'd stopped drinking an hour ago. Fortunately, Ben wasn't a violent drunk. But he sure got depressed every time someone spoke Chase's name.

"Chase Magnum Solmer. Beloved brother. Husband. Friend." He pressed his forefinger against the table to make his point. "You had those words chiseled above his name." He threw a glance at Zoe and then leaned back in his chair. "He was only thirty-seven when he died. Too fucking young."

Doogen nodded. "Amen, brother."

"He always hated his middle name." Sheron

laughed as she cried. "He said it made him sound like a mean old fart."

Ben snorted a laugh. "When I was seven, there was this twelve-year-old kid who lived in the apartment next door. Every day he'd chase me home from school, threatening to kick my ass. One day, he caught up with me. Clocked me in the eye. I went home bawling."

"The little jerk," Zoe whispered.

He turned his blurring gaze on her. Her heart sank. Light from the bar made the tears in his eyes glitter. He draped his right arm over her shoulders then pulled her close against his side.

"Chase said, *'Man up, soldier. Real men don't cry. They suck it up and fight back.'* The next day, the same kid punched me in the arm. I shoved him down on the ground and started wailing on him. It took three kids to get me off him. I remember how good it felt to see him cry like a fucking baby."

Zoe placed her hand on his leg. "What happened afterwards?"

"Yeah," he said with a laugh. "Got in big trouble with the law. They threatened to put us in foster homes, but my mom's friend who had kind of watched over us since our parents died, stepped in as our guardian. She got me out of juvie several times. Since Chase was still a minor, we had to move in with her. Then, he started rebelling. Drinking and partying." Ben pressed his forefinger and thumb against his watering eyes. "It's my fault. He's dead because of me."

"Bullshit." Doogen growled. "Chase made the decision to go out."

"But I should've stopped him." Ben sniffled. "I knew he was drunk, and I did nothing about it. I tossed

273

him the fucking keys."

Zoe swallowed back tears. "Stop blaming yourself."

"I know," he said with a half grin. "Real men don't cry, right?"

Zoe palmed his cheek, but he caught her hand and lowered it. When he let go, he lifted his glass and stood. He stumbled back a few steps but caught his balance.

Doogen stuck a cigarette between his lips. "Where are you going, man?"

"I'm stepping outside for some air."

"Leave the keys to your Jeep."

Ben chuckled. "I'm not gonna drive."

"Come on, Ben," Sheron said, standing next to Doogen. "Hand them over."

Zoe rose from the table. Her balance was off, but she could still focus. Ben, however, had one too many. All the things he'd talked about at the lookout their first weekend together had come to light. The pain inside his heart was unbearable.

Ben pulled his keys from his pocket. "All right, Hateful," he said to Sheron. "I'll give my keys to the best lady in the room."

He jiggled them in front of Zoe. She held out her hand and he dropped them on her palm. His eyes shimmered as slow music played on the speakers.

"You know what?" He held out his hand. "I suddenly have an overwhelming desire to hold you on the dance floor."

Zoe set the car keys down on the table. She led him to the dance floor. He wrapped his arms around her shoulders. Holding her tightly, he swayed with the music.

"You fit in well with my people," he said, nose gliding alongside hers. "I've given it a lot of thought and think you should move to Denver, with me."

Ben was pretty drunk. His emotions were high because of the vodka. It was the only explanation for his invitation.

She smiled and shook her head. "I can't just pick up my life and leave town."

"Sure you can." The alcohol was strong on his breath. "It's better than staying in Kansas. Living in fear of the fucking bastard." He gritted his teeth. "I can't let you go back there. If anything happened to you—"

"Ben stop," she whispered. She slid her fingers through his dark mane. "Nothing's going to happen to me."

He growled. "Just stay here with me. At least for the week."

As tempting as his offer was, she had to get home. She had a big decision to make about the bakery, one she hadn't told Ben about yet. That was a conversation for a more sober moment together.

"You know I have responsibilities at home." She sighed. "Plus, my plane ticket's nonrefundable."

For a moment he searched her eyes, frown on his face, brows low. Did he think she was making excuses? She'd give anything to live in the same town with him. To be with him all the time. She loved him, but it was too soon to be making these kinds of decisions.

He let her go and shook his head. "I need some air."

A loud bang made Zoe jump. Her heart raced as everyone turned toward the door. Another bang went off. She grabbed Ben's arm and held it tightly.

It was the same sound she'd heard when her dad practiced shooting his gun in the backyard. She was always inside the house. But every time she heard the pop, it startled her.

"What the hell?" Ben's eyes narrowed. "Sounded like gunshots."

Zoe followed him through the room. As they made their way toward the exit, she picked up the keys and her purse. It was a bad idea to go outside, especially if someone was out there shooting up the place.

Sheron and Doogen stood near the metal picnic table in a gated-off area. Ben stuck his hands in his pockets as he approached them. "What happened?"

"Someone shot a gun, I guess." Doogen lit up a cigarette and inhaled deeply. "I heard something hiss but can't figure out what the bullets hit. Shit man, we were standing right here when it went off. Scared the hell out of us. It's a good thing nobody got hurt."

Zoe glanced around. A black truck was parked on the other side of the lot under a street light. Painful chills prickled her skin. Nicholas had owned the same kind of truck back when they were dating.

The engine roared to life then hummed like a growling beast as it rolled lights off, slowly off the lot. Nobody paid attention—no one but her. They were all looking the other way.

Ben leaped off the step and jogged through the parking lot, Doogen right behind him. Sheron and Zoe followed them to the Jeep.

"What the hell?" Ben inspected the front tires. The passenger and driver's side were flat.

Doogen ran his fingers over the hole on the

driver's-side tire. "Been coming here for years. Never had any random shootings in this neighborhood. First time for everything, I suppose."

This wasn't random. Her stalker was here. *Nicholas* was here in his truck, and he had a gun. He'd followed her to make life living hell, and she'd let down her guard.

Tears welled in her eyes. He knew where Ben lived. He'd followed them here. No telling how many opportunities he had had to do God knew what.

Adrenaline pumped through her veins. Her face felt cold and clammy. Her lips tingled as dizziness swept through her. She had to get out of here before someone got hurt.

Breath shallow, she clutched her purse. Her legs shook as she ran down the front steps toward the taxi parked in front of the bar. Someone must have called for it, but she needed it more.

"Zoe." Ben followed close behind her. He wedged his body between her and the taxi's door. "Where are you going?"

"Get out of my way," she said.

"What's wrong?"

"I need to go home."

"If someone's shooting up the neighborhood, I don't want you out here."

"That's why I'm leaving. I saw his truck." Her body trembled so much she could barely stand.

"Who's truck?"

"Nicholas's truck. *He* did this."

Ben clutched her shoulders. "There are a lot of trucks like his."

"No. It was him. He followed me here. And

now…someone could get hurt because of me. I can't do this anymore." She dropped her purse. "Why me? Why is this happening to me? I just want it to stop."

"Calm down." Ben picked up her purse. "It wasn't Nicholas," he said as he pulled her in his arms.

"Don't tell me to calm down." She wriggled out of his hold on her. He had the nerve to tell her she was wrong when she knew damn well she was right. "Nicholas flattened your tires." The words came out like a train wreck. "He's terrorizing you now because I'm here with you. I can't be here anymore."

****

Ben leaned back on his heels. Her crying voice echoed through the lot. The poor thing was seriously stressed out and he was making it worse. There had to be some way to reach her to calm her down.

Maybe Nicholas was in Denver. It was possible the bastard had buried bullets in the tires of the Jeep. The guy was a complete psycho who needed to be locked up for the rest of his life. But he didn't want Zoe to worry. She deserved to enjoy the last few moments of her vacation without looking over her shoulder.

"Zoe." He took hold of her hand. "If Nicholas did this, we'll deal with it together. I'll protect you."

"You can't protect me all the time."

"I can while you're here." He sighed. "I'll do anything to make sure nobody ever hurts you again. I'll keep you safe if you just stay with me."

Zoe bit the end of her fingernail. "Please. I need to get out of here."

"Fine." He opened the taxi's door. Zoe slid into the seat and scooted to the center. He got in and slammed the door. He told the driver his address, and then leaned back against the headrest. As the car rolled down the street, Zoe huddled close to him.

"You shouldn't be alone at your apartment."

"I know you're worried," she said in a soft voice. "Renji's picking me up from the airport tomorrow. So I'll be in good hands."

"Renji's hands." Ben shook his head. Imagining her in Renji's arms sent fire through his veins. She didn't belong there. "Stay with me here."

Zoe held her lips tightly together. The city lights skimmed across her face. All she had to do was say yes. He'd move heaven and earth if it'd make her happy enough to say it.

"I'm sorry." She clasped her hand in his. "I can't."

He leaned back in the seat and sighed. As much as he hated letting her go, he couldn't change the reality of their relationship. He would always be here. And she would always be somewhere else.

Chapter Twenty-Seven

Ben spent the entire week staring out his office window. Usually focused on drawing up plans on the new character in development, he couldn't think straight.

It'd been a lethargic week and a half since he'd seen Zoe. They'd talked on the phone and texted almost every night. They'd played their game here and there, but she'd often get tired. Tomorrow he was flying down to spend the weekend with her.

He'd met her in Wichita the Sunday after their weekend at the ranger station. They'd had dinner and strolled in the park. The following Saturday, they met in Goodland for the night, but she got sick on Sunday morning and had to cut their visit short. He was supposed to meet her in Kansas last Sunday but had to cancel due to a mandatory meeting with the graphics department in San Francisco.

Now it was Thursday. He had deadlines to meet. Coastal Universe's expansion was almost ready for release. His team had been waiting on him to finish the updated graphics on the characters for several weeks. All he had left to do was apply them and his work would be done. But it was going to take several hours of uploading, and then possibly another week of testing.

He was taking tomorrow off to fly to Zoe's for the gig at Holetzer's this weekend. If he didn't show his boss something soon, he was going to get fired.

Ben wasn't sure he wanted to continue working here anyways. He'd lost the ambition to spend hours and hours designing. It was exhausting and took up too much of his time. Maybe after this project was finished, he'd resign.

Midlife crisis at thirty.

He'd researched his symptoms.

It wasn't uncommon to want a career change at his age. The auto body shop would take care of that. Then there was Zoe. Having her in his life changed him in other ways, ways he'd never given any thought about before.

Marriage and commitment was scary, but maybe it was time to think seriously about it. Maybe he should give his two weeks' notice today and tell Doogen he was ready to open the shop. After the shop was on its feet, he'd ask Zoe to marry him. Then maybe she'd agree to move here.

Yeah. Right. How could he think he was ready for marriage? Or even if she was ready. She'd spent the last few months in hell while trying to love him. How could she plan a life while the freak was out there chasing her?

Thoughts in turmoil, he signed out of his computer system. He changed into sweats and T-shirt with the alien logo on the front. He zipped up his Windbreaker and then headed to the park for a run.

It was a nice afternoon. Sunny. Warm. Joggers and bicyclists were out enjoying the weather. Kids played at the nearby playground. He hoped the fresh air cleared his head, but everything reminded him of Zoe.

If he could grab on to her now, he'd never let go.

He'd earned her trust and love. *Love* wasn't a word he used lightly. He'd never used it with anyone. Now all he thought about was how much he loved her.

Women just didn't affect him like this. Zoe was different. She had a contagious smile and soft, sweet voice. He loved her body. Damn. Her beautiful, voluptuous body—no one else compared.

Zoe had his brain all messed up, not thinking straight. Or at least not thinking about anything but her. He stopped on the short wooden bridge overlooking a small creek bed. He inhaled deeply as he unzipped the inside pocket of his jacket. He pulled out his cell phone and dialed Zoe's number. It rang several times then went straight to voicemail.

Fuck. He needed to hear her voice.

He shoved his phone back inside his pocket and took off toward the parking lot. By the time he reached his Jeep, he'd run a good three miles. Not bad for someone who hadn't jogged in months. He used to go back to his garage and lift weights, but it'd been a while since he'd had time to do that.

Maybe a little jam session with Doogen might clear his mind. He also wanted to check in on the car to see how the bodywork was coming along.

Doogen's small one-story house needed a new coat of paint to cover up the blemishes. Another pole was needed to straighten and support the warped front-porch roof. His two-tone green-and-brown front lawn was trampled with tire marks from parking in the yard to change the oil or tweak some part of his car. And the large gray barn in back of his house was starting to deteriorate.

The guy took pride in restoring old vehicles, more

so than his yard and house. It showed. There wasn't a dent or speck of dirt on his sparkling red 1973 convertible.

Doogen stepped out on the front porch, beer in hand, shirt off. His shoulder-length hair was pulled back with a tie. Grease stained his face. "Hey, man," Doogen said, burning cigarette hanging from his mouth. "Day off?"

"Left early. Just finished blowing off a little steam at the park."

"The car should be done in a few days. Paint's curing now."

"Thanks a lot for helping me work on it."

"No problem."

He followed Doogen into the house, bracing for the usual mess of dirty clothes, empty pizza boxes, and beer bottles on the living room furniture. Doogen had cleaned. There was actually enough space on the old couch to sit down.

"What happened here?" Ben picked up the acoustic guitar leaning against the side of the coffee table.

"Spring cleaning," Doogen said with a proud grin. He doused his cigarette in the ashtray on the shiny glass coffee table. "Not like me at all to do shit like this."

"Hire a maid?"

Doogen belted out a laugh. "No, man. I invited Sheron over last night. She took one step in my house and then went straight back out the door. Said she wouldn't come back until the place was spotless."

"You did all this for Sheron?" Ben was surprised Sheron and Doogen had become close. She'd always said she would never get seriously involved with any band members. They were all jackasses.

"What a guy will do for love, eh?" Doogen plopped down on the couch and let out a long grunt. "How about you, man? You and blondie baker from Kansas are hitting it off." Doogen lit another cigarette. "I'll bet the gal's ass tastes pretty damn sweet. Mmm…finger-licking good."

Doogen never had tact when it came to talking about women. Didn't surprise Ben a bit he'd talk shit. But that was Doogen.

Ben plucked the strings, tuning the guitar. "I actually like her."

"I noticed. Everyone noticed." Doogen sighed heavily. "Can't get enough of her, huh?"

"Can't get her out of my head."

"I understand your pain. Seems I'm going through the same thing with Sheron. Never gave her much thought, other than how smoking hot she is. She was always Chase's girl. Off-limits."

Ben set the guitar back down beside the coffee table. "What happened to change your mind?"

"We hooked up in the motel after the gig in Goodland last month. It was just a one night fling, ya know? But, it turns out we like each other."

"No shit?" Ben said, though not surprised to hear this news. He actually thought they'd already slept together.

Doogen leaned back in the chair. He inhaled a long draw off his cigarette. Smoke rolled from his parted lips, and then floated up in a ring until it disappeared. "Then last Sunday morning, I saw her at the grocery store getting ready to check out. I joined the line to invite her over for a little fun. She took one look at the food in my cart and started taking everything out."

Ben knew all too well what he talked about. Sheron was a stickler for health foods. Doogen was notorious for loving junk.

"She dragged me back through the store, filling my cart with crap like yogurt and fruit and all these vegetables I don't even know the names of. I swear, man, I felt like a child getting reamed in the middle of the fucking produce department by his mom. She's all up in my face, saying, *'You won't live very long on potato chips and frozen hamburgers.'*"

His imitation of Sheron's raspy voice was almost dead-on. The image of her scolding Doogen made him laugh. Finally, someone else got a taste of what life with her was like.

"When I told her to go home and bug you, she started crying. She said you didn't need her anymore. What the hell was I supposed to do?" Doogen's face grew serious as he doused his cigarette in the ashtray. "Always thought Sheron was one fine woman. When I saw her crying, my heart couldn't take it. I figured, what the fuck. Invited her to move in with me and teach me how to make those shitty salads she made me buy. Guess my grubby house was too much for her to handle."

"So you cleaned," Ben said with a nod.

"Hell yeah, I cleaned. I'm thirty-nine, and I ain't getting any younger. Time to make something besides music, you know?"

"Like what?"

"Babies." Doogen chuckled. "I'm going to marry Sheron after we open the shop. Maybe I'll make enough money to fix this place up so I can keep my wife and kids happy."

"Seriously?"

"Yeah," Doogen said. "Can you see me with kids climbing on my back?"

"No."

"Well, that's my plan. It'll be the new me. Maybe even have some little rug rats by the end of the year."

Ben widened his eyes. "You want kids so soon?"

"The sooner the better."

Ben hadn't thought about Sheron moving out of his house until now. It hurt a little. He'd grown used to her being around, taking care of him, conversing when there was nothing else to do. She reminded him of Chase and how fun things used to be when the three of them lived together.

Doogen and Chase had been best friends since childhood. They had always been the life of the party, drinking and carrying on until Chase's fateful night. Sheron tried her best to keep them all together like a family, but nothing was ever the same.

Ben couldn't see Sheron moving here with Doogen, but he'd understand. Maybe being with each other filled the void they'd both carried for so long. That was what Zoe meant to him, why he couldn't get her out of his head. She'd mended his heart, and his world was empty without her.

"I was thinking," Doogen said as he crushed his cigarette in the ashtray. "Why don't we open the shop now?"

"I've been thinking about it too."

"Yeah, man. We're both ready. Got the tools in the barn and bankers lined up for loans. I've got a huge chunk in savings now."

"Same here." Ben nodded. "I could use a change."

"Hell yes." Doogen slammed his fist on the couch. "Chase would be proud of us right now."

"Yeah," Ben said, a pang of guilt inside him. "If it wasn't for me, he'd be here to open it with us."

Chase would be living his dream if he hadn't let him ride off. There'd be no hole in his chest that needed filled.

"Dammit, Ben." Doogen's eyes narrowed. "When are you going to get it through that thick noggin of yours? Chase's wreck wasn't your fault. Once the man made a decision, he was gonna do it no matter what. The guy was unstoppable."

"Until he wrapped himself around a tree," Ben said calmly. After a moment of silence, he stood. "I'm flying to Zoe's tomorrow. See you guys Saturday."

"Ah, now. Don't get depressed." Doogen followed him out the front door. "Think about your life, baby brother. Look forward, not behind you. Marry your lady friend and make babies too. Chase would want to see you happy."

Ben pulled his keys from his pocket. Once inside the Jeep, he breathed deeply. *Fuck it*. Doogen was right about one thing. It was time to make a change. With that thought, he headed for the mall to look at engagement rings.

Chapter Twenty-Eight

All week, Millie had begged Zoe to be her guinea pig for the new makeup sales job she'd taken on last week. It was one of those brand name commission based kits she'd seen on TV. The facial included hair products and a new hairdo too. Zoe figured what the heck as long as she didn't cake the makeup on thick. Ben was flying in at noon. She might as well look pretty.

Millie already had quite a Friday lined up with all the elderly ladies in town, so Zoe was her first stop. Zoe let Millie and her many green totes inside the apartment. As Zoe sat at the breakfast bar, Millie tucked the bottom of her hair in curlers.

"This argon oil blend smells really good." Millie sniffed the air. "Not too potent. It also won't leave a greasy residue once it dries. Plus, it brings out all your lovely blonde strands."

The hint of vanilla did smell nice. Reminded Zoe of the pastries Renji made yesterday. Vanilla scones. She'd eaten two which did nothing for her diet to lose the three pounds she'd gained in the last two weeks.

"You're good at this Millie. Maybe you should market weddings too."

"Oh, dear. Yes. I've already been working on a brochure." Millie lifted a cleansing pad covered in some kind of white cream to Zoe's face. "This is a face wash. Kind of minty and tingly but refreshing. It opens the pores and lets your skin breathe."

She scrubbed Zoe's face with gentle circular strokes. It did feel nice. A little stingy. "Is it supposed to burn?"

"Just means it's working." She wiped a warm wet towel over Zoe's face. "How's that feel? Better?"

The sting dissipated and left a nice cool sensation on her skin. "Yeah. It feels nice. Clean."

"Good." Millie picked up another pad full of green goop. "This is an avocado mask. It'll work deep into those pores."

"Oh, I definitely need a mask." Zoe inwardly laughed. Nothing like a little positive interaction to keep Millie happy. "Is it edible?"

"No, Zoe. You can't eat my beauty products." Millie smeared the thick green mud onto Zoe's cheeks and chin and forehead. "I've been working on a dress lately. A wedding dress. I think I have a knack for it."

"You're very creative. Maybe you should become a wedding designer. I mean, design the entire wedding."

"I thought so too, but it'd just take up all my time. With my job at the bakery and the boys starting high school and all those upcoming sports trips, I wouldn't get any work done." She set the pad down. "Okay, we'll let it dry for about fifteen minutes then peel it off."

"The boys would understand if you missed their away games." Zoe caught her gaze. "And you know Renji's turning the bakery into a coffee shop. There won't be any need for a cake decorator."

"So I heard." Millie leaned back against the

counter with her arms folded across her chest. "I don't know, Zoe. I'm seriously thinking about opening my own place. Not just planning weddings but making them. Dresses. Flower arrangements. Hair styles and makeup. Cakes." Millie giggled in excitement. "Oh, I like it. It'd be a one stop shopping experience for couples."

"There you go." Zoe grinned. Some of the crusted green mud fell off on the cape. "You should do it, Millie."

"Yeah. I wish." Millie inspected Zoe's face. "This stuff isn't drying right." She glanced at the clock. "When do you need to pick up Ben?"

"His plane lands at twelve." Zoe glanced at the clock. It was already eleven o'clock. She still had to put on makeup and change.

"Okay, let's get this stuff off." She picked off the remaining mud then wrapped a warm wet towel around Zoe's face. "I can't wait to hear Ben's band play at the barbecue tomorrow." She unrolled a curler then leaned down to look Zoe in the eye. She opened her mouth to say something, but then returned to Zoe's hair.

"What is it?" Zoe asked.

"Well," Millie said. "Have you decided what you're going to do? Are you buying the shop with Renji?"

"I'd planned on it." What a weird thing to ask since they'd already discussed it several times in the last month. "Why?"

"I'm just wondering how it'll affect your relationship with Ben. You're going to be too busy to visit him every weekend. Do you think he'd ever move here?"

"Probably not." Zoe's heart sank. That would never happen. It was also the reason why she hadn't signed the papers yet. "He's opening an auto shop in Denver with his friend. Honestly, I don't know how this is going to work out."

Millie turned the mirror to show Zoe. The strands were soft and shiny. All the product she'd worked into her hair had paid off.

"You were right, Millie."

"About what?"

"Long-distance relationships." Zoe's face grew hot. It happened every time she thought about Ben. It'd been too long since she'd felt his arms around her. She couldn't wait to see him. "He asked me to move to Denver."

Millie's mouth popped open. "What did you tell him?"

"Nothing." Tears welled in Zoe's eyes. "I love him, Millie. With all my heart. But...I don't know what to do."

"Oh, honey. Don't cry." Millie yanked a tissue from the box on the counter then dabbed below Zoe's eyes. "You're not obligated to buy the bakery. Renji's more than capable to do this himself. He'll understand."

Zoe had been fine with buying the place before. She'd dreamed she'd meet a nice man and settle down. They'd run the shop together. But now she'd found love somewhere else, staying here wasn't attractive anymore.

"The bakery's only part of the problem. I don't even know if I want it now." She gazed at Millie. "I feel bad because Renji's counting on me. This was his dream too."

"The plans we make are never set in stone." Millie rested her hand on Zoe's shoulder. "Life is full of twists and turns that lead us in new directions. Renji will be all right."

"Then there's Nicholas." Zoe leaned back against the counter, her warm palm against her clammy temple. "He'll just keep stalking me no matter where I am."

"You just have to have faith."

"Faith? How can I have faith with Nicholas running around? I can't move my problems in with Ben and put him in danger. The asshole shot up Ben's Jeep last time I was there." Zoe's stomach churned. A wave of nausea crept up her throat and she became dizzy. She drew in several deep breaths. "I'm sorry I'm ruining all the hard work you've done on my face. My stomach's been in knots for the past week."

"I've noticed." Millie poured Zoe a glass of water. "Maybe you should go see the doctor."

"It's just stress." Zoe downed several gulps. She pressed the cool glass to her burning forehead. "I'll feel much better once Nicholas is back in jail."

"Hopefully Fred gets the creep soon and puts him away for the rest of his life."

"Yeah, me too."

Fred and his army were on standby during the party this weekend. The entire town had kept their eye out for Nicholas, and they made sure to tell her every time she ran into them. It was embarrassing, but also comforting to know she was being looked after.

"Well, I need to get to my next appointment." Millie squeezed Zoe's hand. "You better get ready, or you'll be late picking up Ben from the airport."

"Yeah. Thanks, Millie."

"You're welcome." Millie packed up her bags. "I'll see you tomorrow."

Once Millie left the apartment, Zoe changed into her skirt and tank top. She applied her makeup then tossed her fingers through her hair to spread out the thick, shiny curls. *Much better*.

She couldn't wait to see Ben—to kiss his lips and make mad, passionate love to him. She smiled as she grabbed her purse off the bedroom floor.

After one glance in the mirror, she left the apartment. She hopped in the dark green sedan she'd rented yesterday, and then sped down the highway toward Wichita.

****

Ben walked through the airport, duffel bag over one shoulder, guitar case over the other. When he reached the main terminal, he scanned the crowded room.

There she was, beautiful blonde showing off soft, pale legs in her short skirt. She jogged toward him, arm raised, hand waving. Her breasts bounced under her tank top, just enough to turn heads on the men passing by.

Damn, she was hot. Silky hair rested in soft curls over her shoulders. A bright smile formed on her rounded face as he set his stuff on the floor and caught her in his arms.

"Hey, handsome," she said, arms tight around his neck. He picked her up off her feet and kissed her strawberry-flavored lips. "I feel like I haven't seen you in months."

"Tell me about it." He set her down on her feet. "Mm…beautiful as always."

"Come home with me?" she whispered.

"Yes, ma'am." He picked up his guitar and bag. "Frisky already?"

"I haven't seen you in two weeks." She walked beside him through the terminal. "Of course I can't wait to get you in bed."

Being with her made all the stress he'd been under melt away. "I like the way you think."

"Hungry?" She gave a short shrug. "We could stop off for lunch first if you are. Or…get this. I went to the grocery store yesterday. There's actual food in my fridge."

"No kidding." His voice echoed as they strode through the parking garage. "What'd you buy?"

"Turkey and cheese slices and bread. Lettuce. Tomato. Pickles. Mayo."

"Sandwiches for lunch then." He gave short nod. "Sounds good to me."

She unlocked the door on a green sedan. Must be the rental car she'd told him about on the phone.

"I also bought eggs and bacon," she said as they got in the car. "I hope you don't mind cooking me breakfast."

"I'm at your disposal." He leaned back and caught her gaze. The woman had him under her thumb, especially in her tight tank top. He was going to enjoy taking it off her body.

She drove straight to her apartment. The moment she shut and locked the door, he was in trouble—the good kind.

"I've missed you so much," she said, following him up the stairs.

He set his stuff down on the floor. "I missed you

too, babe."

"Come here." She fisted his T-shirt and pulled him down the hall to her room. Clothes went to the floor fast. He grabbed her wrist and yanked her to him. Her body hit his harder than he'd planned, but a wicked laugh rolled past her curved lips.

His mouth parted over hers. He wrapped his arms around her and lifted. She locked her legs around his waist. With her arms around his neck, he carried her to the edge of the bed. Her kiss was furious, intense, a contrast from the softness she usually wanted.

His body fell over hers on the bed. In no time, his cock was sliding inside her tight walls. Flesh against flesh, moving in perfect motion. He lifted his body and held her wrists on each side of her head. Her rounded breasts bounced with his quick thrusts.

"Ben, stop," she gasped.

He let go of her wrists. "Sorry, honey," he said against her cheek. "Too rough?"

"No." She turned her body beneath him, legs apart, ass up. "Do it this way."

Damn. Fire spread through his veins. Who was this feisty woman and what had she done with Zoe? This wasn't going to last very long.

He entered her, pumping fast. He watched her body envelop his cock as he penetrated her, sending him closer to the edge of climax.

He reached around her waist and rubbed her clit with his forefinger. She let out short, breathy screams.

He grinned. "You like that?"

"*Ungh*…I'm about to…"

He shoved his cock in as far as it would go. Hips tight against hers, he thrust until he couldn't hold on anymore. "Fuck."

Her walls throbbed around his pulsing cock. He breathed into her shoulder as he released his tension inside her. She fell on her stomach beneath him then laughed between noisy breaths.

"Damn, honey." He kissed her shoulder. "You're naughty today."

"I couldn't help it." She turned on her back and slid her hands through his hair. "I'm just so happy to see you."

"I can tell." A satisfied sigh passed his lips. "You should be bad more often."

He pressed his mouth against hers. He licked her tongue, enjoying the way her fingers massaged his head. "You and I are good together." He gazed into her eyes. "I wish you'd reconsider moving in with me."

"I have something to tell you," she whispered. "I wanted to wait to say anything, because I wasn't sure what I was going to do. But I think I'm going to do it."

He moved to her side. "Do what?"

Her brows furrowed. "I'm thinking about buying the bakery. With Renji. We've wanted to do this for a long time and now we finally have the chance. The owner said she'd sell it to us for a good price."

"Shit, Zoe. Are you serious?" He lay back on the bed and groaned. If she bought the bakery with Renji, she'd be too busy to visit. With Ben opening the shop, he couldn't meet her as often either. They'd never have time to see each other anymore. Maybe it's what she wanted. Maybe Renji meant more to her than she let on. "Is there something going on between you and Renji?"

"God no. Why would you say that?" She scoffed. "Don't ruin our discussion by starting an argument about my relationship with Renji."

"If there is something between you two, we might as well just end things now."

Her eyes widened. "I can't believe you." She rose from the bed. "I can't believe you'd even suggest that right after we had sex."

"I'm sorry." He sighed. *Yeah. Idiotic thing to say at a moment like this*. "I'm just trying to figure this out."

She stomped to the dresser and opened the top drawer. She pulled out a pair of panties and a bra then turned to face him. "Why don't *you* forget about the shop and move in with me?"

"Not going to happen." He'd never given any thought to moving here. It was a terrible idea. "I've already promised Doogen we'd meet with the loan officer next week."

"But you haven't signed anything yet." She propped her knee on the bed. "If you moved here, we could buy the bakery together and turn it into a coffee shop. Like the one near the cabin."

"Babe, I love you, but I don't want to move to this town." She frowned as she backed away. His heart dived to the floor. She might as well just kick it while it's down there, because it was breaking. "I can't back out on Doogen. I don't want to."

"And I don't want to back out on my plans to buy the bakery with Renji."

"We're going to be too busy to see each other then."

Tears welled in her eyes. "Maybe you should just leave now, since you think our future is so fucking bleak."

"Whoa. Wait a second," he said as she disappeared into the hallway. He followed her into the bathroom. She turned on the shower. "I didn't mean to upset you."

She stepped in and shut the curtain. "Well, you did."

"I'm sorry. I just don't know what to do." He shook his head. She was right. Their future looked pretty damn bleak right now.

****

When Zoe stepped out of the shower, Ben stepped in. She slipped her hoodie over her head and put on a pair of sweats.

He had no idea how hard it was to say no to move in with him. His house was beautiful. To be with him all the time and kiss him in the beautiful garden would be amazing. But so would owning the bakery. One second, she wanted it. The next second, she didn't. If only she had a crystal ball to see her future.

Someone knocked on the front door. Zoe finished brushing her wet hair then hurried down the steps. She peered through the peephole. No one was there. She turned the locks but left the chain connected. She drew in a breath then opened the door and peeked out.

A small brown box sat at the end of the walkway close to the rental car. It'd only take a second to get the package and bring it in. Ben had just turned off the shower anyways.

She unchained the last lock and peered outside. Barefoot, she carefully stepped down the sidewalk. Why would the UPS guy leave it out here instead of on her doorstep?

She smiled and leaned down to inspect the box. Her name was written in bright letters on top. The return label had the name of a jewelry shop stamped on it.

Had Ben shipped a gift? Or maybe Renji had sent her a present to celebrate their chance to buy the bakery. Kind of weird leaving it way out here though.

She picked up the package. The box was light. The contents rolled around. Whatever it was, it was small. A bracelet or necklace? Maybe Ben had sent her a ring. No. That'd be a silly thing to do. The only way to find out what was inside was to open it.

She tore the paper and opened the pretty blue box to a copper bullet.

The cool breeze kicked around her legs. Icy hands clawed her back. She was frozen in place. She shook so much she couldn't hold the box. It dropped to her feet.

"Zoe."

A scream worked its way up her throat. Before it could escape, a hand clamped over her mouth.

Zoe turned quickly. Nicholas released her from his grasp. "Get away from me." She pulled her knee up and kicked out. Her foot caught between his legs and he buckled over. "Don't you dare touch me again."

"Fucking bitch."

His arm reared back. Images of that night flashed in her mind as his fist soared toward her face and made contact with her left eye. Immense pain tore through her skull and down her cheek. She screamed loud.

Balance lost, she stumbled toward her apartment. Her head slammed with a crunch into the side-view mirror of the rental. Her vision blurred. She twisted her ankle and fell toward the ground. The curb of the sidewalk came fast—too fast to do anything about.

"Zoe." Ben's voice rang in her ears, but she

couldn't open her eyes. It hurt too much. She couldn't find her voice to call back. She just lay on the sidewalk, helpless. Face and head throbbing.

The engine of a truck revved and then quickly faded. The pounding in her head worsened as Ben turned her over. She stared up into the blue sky, powerless, stomach turning. Nauseated, she turned to her side and heaved.

Chapter Twenty-Nine

Zoe sat on the hospital bed in the ER with her eyes closed. *What a mess*. Elevated blood pressure. Slight fever. Nauseated. She had a gash on her temple and a bruise forming over her swollen eye.

Ben had to pull over once on the way to the hospital so she could vomit. Then a second time when Fred stopped him for going way over the speed limit. At least he didn't get a ticket. Once Fred found out what Nicholas had done, the police escorted them the rest of the way to the emergency entrance of the hospital.

Zoe sighed as she lay back. The protective paper crinkled as she rested her head on the pillow and stared up at the ceiling.

Nicholas had shown his ugly self again. At least she had proof of the attack this time. The cops could put him in jail for hitting her if they could find out where he went.

Could life get any worse?

"Ms. Kearny," the doctor said as he appeared from behind the long curtains, a pretty nurse on his heels. He positioned his glasses on his thin, slanted nose and then tucked his hair back behind his ears. "I'm Dr. Shin. Looks like you have a few bumps on your head."

"Yeah," Zoe replied in an exhale. "I hit my head on the side-view mirror of my car."

He tapped out a note on his tablet, and then set it on the small stand beside the curtain. "Deputy Jenkins says you were also punched."

She shuddered. Fred had already told the doctor everything.

"He hit my eye."

Doctor Shin curled his forefinger under her chin and lifted to inspect her eye. "Any flashes of light?"

"No," she replied.

"What about vomiting?"

"I did on the way here." She gazed into his light blue eyes. "I'm still a little nauseated, but I have been on and off for over a week."

He palmed her temple then swept her bangs up away from her face. She leaned her head back as he shined his penlight into her sore eye.

"I don't see any immediate damage to the retina, but I suggest you make an appointment with an ophthalmologist. Just to be on the safe side."

"Okay," she said as he set his tool down on the tray.

He pressed his fingers close to the gash on her head. Pain resonated down her cheek to her right ear. "Ah. It hurts."

"You've got quite a wound there." He massaged down the sides of her head then under her jaw. "Any dizziness?"

"I fainted after it happened. But besides the headache, I'm fine now."

He lowered the sheet to her waist. "You said you've been feeling sick for a week." He pressed his hands against her abdomen then pushed down with rigid fingers.

"Off and on." She held her breath. She tightened the muscles in her stomach as he massaged in a circular motion close to her navel. This was uncomfortable. Her bladder was full. Any more of this and she'd need to run to the bathroom to pee.

"When was your last menstrual cycle?"

"Um…May…*ish*, I think." *Sheesh*. Why was he asking these questions?

"Is it normal for you to miss your period?"

"I'm late sometimes."

"You're also a little tender." As he applied pressure on each side of her navel, he spoke in a low tone to the nurse. "Get a blood and urine sample."

"Wait." Zoe raised her head off the pillow. Chills spread up and down her body. "You're ordering tests?"

"It's just procedure," he said in a calm, even tone. "I just want to rule out infection and pregnancy."

"Pregnancy?" She gasped. "Oh no, I am not pregnant, Dr. Shin."

"Relax, Ms. Kearny." A grin crept across his face. "Let's just run the tests to make sure."

Zoe's stomach twisted into a knot. No way was she pregnant. She'd taken her birth control pills like a champ. Except for the one night she wasn't feeling well. But that was just once, and she didn't even have sex that night.

The nurse led her to the bathroom. She handed her a clear container and then shut the door.

The overhead light buzzed. Zoe stared in the mirror, cup in hand. This was ridiculous. *Bandage my eye. Give me a prescription for pain. But don't assume I'm pregnant.*

Zoe sat down on the toilet. *Ugh.* She hated peeing

in a cup. There was no sense in this. It was all the sex she and Ben were having. It was the only reason her belly was tender. Her period was late because of the stress she was under.

On her way back to the curtained area, she swallowed hard. Infection? What kind of infection could she have? A stomach flu? Food poisoning? That didn't make any sense. She hadn't eaten anything out of the ordinary.

She sat on the edge of the bed. Her eye ached. She gently touched her eyelid then sucked in a quick breath. *Ugh*. That hurt.

Nicholas had hit her again. It was pretty shocking and scary to think he was out there waiting for her to be alone.

What did he want? What the hell did the bullet mean? Was he planning on shooting her? Was he out for revenge? Or maybe he was just having fun terrorizing her.

Her stomach ached. She could go pee again, but not enough to make another trip down the hall. She lay back on the bed and shivered. Chills. Maybe that's all this was, just an infection. A cold virus. She should get dressed and go home to her comfy bed. A bowl of chicken soup and crackers sounded good. She'd be sure to drink plenty of fluids and let Ben take care of her.

The doctor stepped in. He grabbed the short stool near the curtain side and rolled it close to her. While he tapped out a few more notes on his tablet, his glasses slid down to the end of his nose.

"What's wrong with me?"

"The urinalysis came back negative for infection. But your pregnancy test came back positive."

Sourness stuck in her throat. "No. I can't be…*pregnant*."

"We tested twice with the same results. You'll need to take good care of yourself in the coming months. Limit your daily stress. Do light exercises and get plenty of rest. Eat small portions five or six times a day and drink plenty of fluids. I'll send in a prescription for prenatal vitamins."

"Prenatal…vitamins?"

He tapped out more notes. "Prenatal vitamins have extra ingredients your body needs for a healthy fetus."

Zoe stared at his pasty forehead. This couldn't be happening. "But I'm on the pill," she whispered.

He arched his bushy black brows. "Contraceptives aren't always one hundred percent, especially if they're not taken properly. Now, I'm going to put you at about four weeks, though we won't know for sure until you've had an exam."

She shook her head. *This can't be happening.* Things were worse. Much worse. This was not how she wanted this day to end.

"Is the father the same person who hit you?" the doctor asked in a serious tone.

"No." Her right eye burned from the tears forming. "Oh God, what am I going to do?"

"There are options." He cocked his head to the side. "Set up an appointment with your obstetrician and talk it over with her. Or if you'd like, I can have the nurse set you up an appointment."

"Okay." Zoe couldn't catch her breath. She slid to the side of the bed then stood on shaky legs. Vision blurred, head pounding, she sat back down. "Oh…"

The doctor steadied her with his arm. "Lie down

and rest a few more minutes before you go."

"I'll be fine," she said, finding the strength to release her death grip on his lab coat.

Zoe put on her clothes. Muscles tense, body trembling, she stepped toward the lobby. Now close enough, she looked through the small rectangular window on the door.

"You didn't protect her," Renji shouted.

Sheriff Clemens held Renji back by his thick arms. Fred restrained Ben.

Ben growled. "I didn't know she'd left the apartment."

Renji wriggled free from Sheriff Clemens's hold on him. Renji threw his fist, clocking Ben in the stomach. The hit forced Fred to let go of Ben, who buckled over. He drew in several quick breaths then punched Renji in the face.

Zoe shoved her way through the lobby doors. "Stop it now."

Ben and Renji turned their attention on her, out of breath. Renji strode toward her. "Oh, Zoe. Your eye."

She stepped back, palm out. "Don't touch me," she said as calmly as she could. He stopped within an arm's length. "We're in a hospital. You're both acting like children."

"Are you all right, Zoe?" Fred asked. "Want me to lock these clowns up in a cell?"

"That won't be necessary," Zoe said purposely avoiding Ben's stare. She'd break down into a sob if she found it. Or maybe she'd run away. Or into his arms. She wasn't sure. This was all so surreal. "I'm fine. Just a little sore."

"You're not fine, Zoe." Renji growled. "Look at

what he did to your face. It's because Ben wasn't there protecting you. He's worthless."

"Fuck off, Renji." The muscles tightened in Ben's arms. Renji balled his fists and lunged toward him.

Fred stepped between them, arms out to his sides to keep them separated. "Knock it off. Or I will arrest you both."

"Zoe's been through enough today. She doesn't need you two fighting." Clemens grumbled, stroking his mustache between his forefinger and thumb. "Don't worry, young lady. I've got everyone out there searching now. We'll get him."

"Thanks, Sherriff," she said, Nicholas the least of her worries at the moment. "I'd like to go home now."

"Sure." Fred gave a short nod. "If you need a ride home…"

"Thanks, Fred. But, I have a ride."

She glanced at Ben. He'd wandered toward the window, hands pinching his sides. The man wasn't happy. She didn't blame him for being angry after Renji sucker punched him. She'd give Renji a good scolding for starting a fight. But later. Now she had to let Ben know he was going to be a dad. *Oh my God. No.* She palmed her forehead. She was having a baby. She wasn't ready for this.

This surreal situation put a new perspective on her relationship with Ben. She needed time to think about what she was going to do about this pregnancy, and about her ownership of the bakery. How could she buy it now? She'd need the money for furniture and clothes and diapers.

She squeezed her eyes shut. *Ugh.* The pain brought tears to her eyes. *Stop, Zoe.* Don't think about it right now. Concentrate on what you're going to say to Ben.

Sheriff Clemens's pat on her shoulder startled her. "If there's anything we can do for you, darling, just let us know."

"I'll protect her like I always do," Renji said.

She eyed Ben, who paced the floor along the window. His muscles had relaxed. He caught her gaze and goosebumps spread over her skin.

"Please." She hated the tears in Renji's eyes. "I need you to go home."

He shook his head. "I just want to keep you safe."

"I'll be fine." She placed her hand on his forearm. "I promise we'll talk later. I'll tell you about everything."

"Come on, son," Sheriff Clemens said, near the exit door.

"You heard the sheriff," Ben said, coming to her side.

"Fine." Renji glared as he backed toward the door. "I'll be waiting for you to get home." He sneered as he left with Fred and Clemens.

Zoe sighed. This was awkward. Ben stood behind her, hands gently massaging her shoulders. What was she to do now? How would she tell him their lives were about to go belly-up? Literally.

"Renji's right. I should've been there."

"No. Don't listen to Renji. It's not your fault."

He stepped in front of her. He lifted his hand to her cheek as he inspected her eye. "Oh fuck. Baby, he clocked you pretty good." He gritted his teeth. "What did the doctor say?"

"Nothing much," she said with a huff. "He doesn't think there's damage to my eye, but he wants me to see an ophthalmologist just in case."

He held her head between his hands. "I'm so sorry I wasn't there."

"Don't be sorry." She pressed her cheek to his chest. "None of this is anyone's fault but Nicholas's."

Ben wrapped his arms around her. This felt so good. Once he found out she was pregnant, no telling what he'd do. Leave her stranded here in the hospital lobby. Fly off the handle. Maybe it was best she tell him the news at home.

Zoe leaned back on her heels. "We need to talk."

"Okay."

Her college friend had dated a guy for five years. He'd taken off faster than she could say *baby*. Would Ben do the same thing?

"Oh boy," Zoe whispered. Her gaze went to the dog tags resting against his T-shirt. "I…I don't know how to say this."

The doctor's words rolled through her head. How could she possibly say she was pregnant after everything they'd been through?

He palmed her arms and gently squeezed. "Out with it."

She drew in a deep breath. This would be it. No more fun in bed. No more sexual tension. Worse yet, no more Ben. "The doctor says I'm…pregnant."

For a long moment he stood with a blank stare. His dark brows lifted as her words sank in. "I'm sorry, what?" He gave her a sidelong look. "Did I hear you right?"

"Depends on what you heard."

He lowered his hands to his sides. "You're pregnant? As in…having a baby?"

"No, Ben," she muttered, with a roll of her eyes. "I'm having kittens."

She brushed past him and went out into the evening air. His reaction rubbed her the wrong way. She wasn't sure why other than she was too exhausted to deal with this right now. She breathed deep as she walked across the darkened parking lot.

"Where's the car?"

"At the end of the lot on the right." He followed close behind. "How'd this happen?"

She belted out a laugh. "How do you think it happened?"

"I thought you were on the pill."

"I was. Am." She stopped at the car and waited for him to unlock it. "They weren't effective."

"What do you mean, *weren't effective*?"

"I don't know," she said, wishing he'd quit grilling her. "I just want to go home and forget this day ever happened."

****

Ben stood beside her, hands on top of his head, keys dangling before his left eye. *Holy shit. What the hell?* This was un-fucking-believable. He had plans for his near future, but this wasn't part of them.

Zoe reached up and yanked the keys from his hand. "Just get in the car."

He grabbed the keys back, and then opened the passenger-side door. "I'm driving. In case you need to vomit again."

"Can you sound any meaner?" She sat, and then slammed the door shut.

"I'm not trying to be mean." He sighed as he got in the car. "I'm just stating that you threw up. I guess we now know why."

He started the engine and pulled out of the hospital parking lot. His gut churned too. Not enough to get physically ill, but close to it. He rubbed his chin with his hand. Nothing they could do now but deal with this problem. Maybe he could look at this in another light. He'd wanted kids someday. Someday just happened to be now while he was about to start up a business, and she fought off the stalker.

"You should just go home," she said. "Forget about me."

He arched his brows, shocked she'd suggest such a thing. "No way in hell am I leaving you here now. You're coming to Denver."

"Really? You're going to tell me what to do?"

He threw her a glance. "What am I supposed to say, Zoe? That I don't give a shit? You want me to tell you to stay here and get beat up by your stalker con of an ex-boyfriend? *Fuck* that."

"Pull over." She opened the door.

"What the hell…?" Ben quickly applied the brakes and stopped the car. She stepped out and slammed the door shut. As she walked down the middle of the road, he shifted into park.

"Get back in the car, Zoe," he called out as he took off after her.

"I'm not ready for this," she said, walking faster. "Everything's so messed up. Your life. My life. I can't do this anymore."

He caught up to her. He stopped her with his hands on her shoulders. "Come on. We'll discuss this when we get home."

"Home?" She covered her face and sobbed. "Just

go away. Leave me alone."

"I'm not leaving you." He pulled her hands down to her sides and then cupped her wet cheeks. "Look at me."

Her glittering gaze lifted to his. "I didn't mean for this to happen."

"Yeah, not all your fault, right?" He kissed her temple. "We'll figure this out. Okay? It'll be okay."

He put his arm around her shoulders and led her back to the car. He wasn't sure what to do. *Shit.* He had a kid on the way.

A stiff drink sounded really good right now. Hell. A bottle'd be even better.

Ben parked at her apartment. Zoe bit the end of her thumbnail. She stared out the passenger-side window at Renji, who stood watching from the sidewalk. Renji folded his arms over his chest, frown on his face.

Ben tried not to think the worst, but how could he not? Renji was always there, sticking his nose in her business. He let her use his truck all the time. He made her dinner. He walked her to and from work. The way Zoe and Renji stared at each other. It was as if they had history—current history.

He understood why Zoe and Renji were close friends. But she didn't want to move to Denver. She'd rather stay here and run a business with him.

Ben clenched his jaw, hating the horrible thoughts swirling through his brain. Maybe she was carrying Renji's baby.

"Are you ready to go in?" Ben asked with a clearing of his throat. "We really need to talk about what we're going to do."

"I don't want to talk about it right now." Her gaze

was still on Renji. "I'm tired. My eye hurts. I just want to go get some sleep."

"Or maybe you'd rather discuss this with Renji," he snapped. He tried not to say anything more, but the words spilled from his mouth. "Maybe he's the father."

Her mouth popped open. He could almost feel the heat emanating off her body. Her lips pursed as she got out. She swung the car door back. It shut with a slam.

Renji put his arm around her shoulders. *Fuck this shit.* Ben backed the car out. He shifted hard into drive and sped off as Renji followed Zoe inside the apartment. Just the thought of her being with someone else set something off inside him, something he hadn't felt since Chase died.

Misery.

Chapter Thirty

This was a terrible place to be.

Here he sat in the car in front of Holetzer's, engine off. Good battling evil. Beer versus vodka. Which one would win tonight? The answer was to drive away and never look back, but he got out of the car, locked the doors, and went inside.

Not many people were here. Two women in the corner booth. A man at the other end of the bar. Not that anyone would actually recognize Ben, but word traveled fast in small towns. He wouldn't want anyone to alert Zoe he was here looking for a drink when he desperately needed one.

The bartender's smug, leathery face brightened when Ben sat down at the bar. The letters on the front pocket of his gray shirt read, *Chauncey.*

Palms against the wooden counter, Chauncey gave him a nod. "What'll you have, man?"

"Shot of vodka."

"Hitting the hard stuff, huh?" Chauncey grabbed a shot glass from the shelf. "Must've been something pretty shitty."

"Yeah," Ben said, wishing the guy would mind his own business.

Clear liquid sloshed a bit from the bottle as Chauncey poured it in the glass, filling it to the rim. "Only been here three weeks. This town is...something else. Much different from South Dakota."

He shoved the shot glass forward. It slid across the counter until it stopped in front of Ben. Ben stared at it, feeling like a schmuck, wondering what to do. Not like he was an alcoholic. Drinking was just an attitude adjustment. He didn't think about things that bothered him when he was drunk. Right now, things bothered him.

Ben lifted the shot glass to his lips. The cool liquid flooded his mouth and burned down his throat. Eyes watering, he tightened his grip on the glass and slammed it down on the counter. Guilt spread through him like the alcohol in his veins. Vodka never tasted so good.

"Another?" Chauncey asked.

Ben nodded. One more wouldn't hurt. Tension was already fading. Another shot slid down, much easier than the first.

"You're not from around here." Chauncey poured Ben another.

Ben lifted the glass and tossed the drink back. He swallowed hard. "Denver."

"Skier?"

Ben shook his head. Though he'd gone snowboarding several times as a young kid, he'd never had the desire to plow through the frigid stuff as an adult.

"Dakota's got some nice snowfields." Chauncey refilled Ben's glass. "Used to go cross-country skiing with the owner of this bar. Been working for her for years. Thought about asking her to marry me, but...I don't know."

"What's holding you back?" Ben asked, curious to

hear someone else's problems for a change. He downed the shot. This would be the last one, and then he'd quit. He'd had enough. Better not get too drunk, or he'd never get out of this town.

The second he set the glass on the bar, Chauncey poured another.

One more. Shouldn't waste good liquor. He'd make sure to stop Chauncey after this one.

"I'm not a coward when it comes to women. But Drema Holetzer? She's one intimidating dame." He chuckled as he poured Ben another shot and then grabbed another glass off the shelf. "What about you?"

"What about me?" Ben swallowed down the shot. He wasn't interested in telling his story.

"Got any gals at home?"

"Got one here. Had one. I don't know."

Chauncey's brows arched. "Anyone I know?"

"Maybe." Seeing Chauncey staring, waiting for her name, he sighed. "Her name's Zoe."

"Zoe from the bakery?" Chauncey said with an excited laugh. "Damn man. You are one lucky SOB. She's fucking hot."

Ben pinched the crease between his eyes. "She won't move to Denver."

"Women don't want to move in." He poured another shot in his glass, then one in Ben's. "They want a ring on their finger."

"I'm not ready for marriage yet." Even though he'd already bought the ring. He was only going to ask if she said yes to moving in with him. Now, who knew what the fuck was going to happen.

"I don't think any man is ready for marriage." Chauncey let out a snorting laugh. "I hear she has baggage anyways. Ex-boyfriend issues."

"The bastard's stalking her."

Ben tossed back his drink and swallowed. Here he was drinking himself into depression when he should've stayed with Zoe. In the chaos, he'd completely forgotten about Nicholas, and what he'd done to her earlier.

Then again, Renji had escorted her into her apartment. So, why should he bother going back?

"Zoe has a stalker?"

Ben growled. "You know, I came to relax for the night."

"Yeah, man, sure. Drink to forget your troubles." Chauncey poured him another shot. "I see you play guitar."

"How'd you know?"

"Calluses on your fingers." Chauncey drank two shots in a row. A third went down before the guy finally continued. "Women dig musicians."

Ben shook his head. "Nah, man. It's the hair."

Chauncey's hearty laugh grabbed the attention of the two women sitting at the booth along the far wall. They smiled and waved. Chauncey raised his hand and then scratched the side of his blond head with his middle finger.

"What do they call that?" Chauncey said as he lifted a rubber band from his shirt pocket. He pulled his shoulder-length hair back and then tied it loosely. "*Googly* eyes."

Ben tossed back his drink. If he didn't quit now, he was going to pass out in the bar. He was already pretty damned buzzed. Just like old times. One night only, then he'd quit.

Sigmund's Hotel was right down the road. He could sleep it off there, and nobody would ever know. Right. With Mrs. Sigmund's hawk eyes, the entire town would know. Maybe he'd sleep it off in the car down some dusty road instead. It wasn't even his car. It was Zoe's rental. He'd eventually have to get it back to her. That meant facing her again.

"Another?" Chauncey asked, lip of the bottle hovering over the glass.

"What the hell," Ben said. He downed it fast. "One more."

"You can sure hold your liquor."

Ben would've taken what he'd said as a compliment before. Now it was wrong. He didn't care. The drink took away frustration. Confusion. His pain.

"Mind if we join you?"

The two women from the booth sat on each side of him. Great. Company. This was his cue to leave. After one more shot.

"You from around here?" the pretty redhead with charcoal eyelids asked. Her hazel eyes dazzled in the light.

"No."

She tugged on her short, sparkling dress. "Just passing through?"

"Sort of," he muttered.

Somehow another drink landed in his glass. Didn't matter. More was better. Another shot went down. The women whispered to each other. Chauncey spoke. Laughter broke out. Ben didn't pay attention to any of it. Just concentrated on his drink, until Chauncey announced the bottle was empty.

Chauncey took interest in the soused brown-haired

girl. The woman returned the favor, leaning over the bar. Her breasts practically hung out of her tank top.

"You gals want more Sex on the Beach?" Chauncey asked. A sheepish grin crept across his mouth. "I suppose that's a yes. My treat, ladies. But I need to grab another bottle from the back."

The redhead placed her hand on Ben's arm. Her pale pink fingernails reminded him of Zoe's favorite shirt. Her other hand slid up his back.

"I'm Mags," she said. "This is Terri. We're from Wichita."

"Heard on TV this is the place to come for the party tomorrow," Terri said. She flipped her long brown hair over her shoulder and then laughed. "Thought we'd check it out."

"It was so worth it," Mags whispered in Ben's ear. Her eyelashes fluttered, and her pouty red lips curved into a smile. "So, you want to party with us?"

Ben tapped his shot glass on the bar. Chauncey turned the bottle over. The last few drips fell into his glass.

"Be right back," Chauncey said.

"Can I come?" Terri hopped off the bar stool. "I've never been in a bar kitchen before."

"Well, ma'am, let me give you the grand tour." He tucked her arm under his and led her toward the back room.

Ben sat alone with Mags, relaxed, not caring about much right now. She seemed pleased sitting next to him, hand sliding up his leg. She was attractive, tempting the devil in him. He could take her in the back room and she'd let him have his way with her. She'd be an easy fuck.

Then he'd probably get her pregnant too.

Mags's hand touched his groin. *Fuck this.* He rose to his feet. He stumbled into the stool beside him. *Damn.* Drunker than he thought. Mags caught his arm, but he wriggled from her grasp.

"Gonna take a piss," he muttered.

Didn't matter if she heard or not; he'd said it. Maybe he slurred his words. Maybe the sentence didn't come out right. He needed to get to the bathroom. At least in there, he'd be alone. That was all he'd wanted from this trip to the bar—to be drunk and alone. To forget about Zoe and Renji.

He stopped at the bathroom mirror and stared at his reflection. His face distorted, and Chase stared back.

Idiot. You're fucked up. You're screwing up the best thing that's ever happened to you because you're too fucking scared.

He gritted his teeth. "Shut the hell up, Chase."

He hated this. He'd made promises to Chase. He'd never touch the stuff again. Not like this. Now he was drunk because he knocked up his girlfriend after a few months of dating. He was wasted because of his insecurities. *Pathetic.*

Worthless piece of shit, Chase continued. *After the hell she's been through, why would she stay with a fucking drunk like you? You accused her of cheating. She won't move in with you now.*

He turned away from the mirror, from Chase's haunting stare. If Chase were truly here, he'd speak those exact words. He'd be disappointed. Chase would tell Ben to call Zoe to come pick him up. Beg for her forgiveness. She'd yell at Ben and then take away his car keys.

Ben pulled his cell phone from his jacket pocket. It fell in the sink. Zoe's image popped up on the display. Blue eyes stared into his. Her smile set his insides on fire.

What an idiot he'd been. He picked up his phone. If this buzz would go away, he'd go back to her apartment and demand she forget about the bakery. Forget about Renji. Didn't matter if she'd fucked the guy; he couldn't have her.

She only lived a mile down the road. This late at night, there'd be nobody out. He could make it. He'd be there in no time, insisting she come home with him. If she wanted to get married, they'd do it tonight.

Ben slid down the wall to the floor next to the sink. He closed his tired eyes and laughed.

Marriage. What a joke. Completely out of the question. Why would she leave this place when she had Renji and their fucking bread shop? The baby was his anyway.

Miserable depressed drunk. That's all you'll ever amount to.

Chase's words lay heavy on his heart. Even though Zoe had healed his wounds, made him feel worthy of love for a while, he couldn't make her happy. It was obvious with the contingency plan she'd made with Renji.

"Ben?"

Ben opened his eyes to a pale blur. A soft female voice spoke, but he couldn't move to see who'd called out. He tried to focus on his hand lying on the floor, palm open. His cell phone had slipped from his hand and lay turned over on the cool gray tile. He closed his eyes.

"Ben. Are you in here?"

He lifted his chin off his chest. "Zoe?"

Shit. He didn't want her here seeing him like this. "Fucking idiot," he mumbled, picking up his phone. He dropped it again. It clattered across the floor and stopped in front of a pair of white slip-on shoes.

Zoe *was* here. Crying. He'd hurt her. God, he never wanted to hurt her.

"This is all my fault," she cried as she fell to her knees beside him. Her hands cupped his face. This was wrong—so very wrong. She shouldn't see him this way.

"Baby, no," he said, shoving her hands away. He stood and leaned against the wall. "You deserve...way better than me."

Ben fisted the car keys. He stumbled toward the door. *Drunk* was an understatement. His bearings were way off. He bumped into chairs and tables to get to the exit.

In the parking lot, he drew in a deep breath. The open road called his name. When he pressed the remote to unlock the car, Zoe grabbed the keys.

"What the fuck are you doing?" he said. "Give me the keys."

"No."

She backed toward the car. He followed, hand out until she was against the driver's-side door. With nowhere for her to go, he reached for the keys.

Zoe drew her arm back, and then punched the air. The keys left her hand. They landed in the tall grass lining the ditch.

"Why the hell'd you do that?" He grabbed her arms and held her tight against the car. "How the fuck am I supposed to get out of this town now? Away from you?"

She whimpered. "I'm not letting you drive."

"Because you love me so fucking much?"

"Yes. I love you."

"Then why won't you come home with me?" He tightened his grip and shook her once. "It's Renji's baby, isn't it? He told you to stay here."

"My arms, Ben." She whimpered. "You're hurting me."

He immediately let go. Heart in his throat, he scanned her face. Her swollen eye looked black in the low light of the street lamp. Tears streamed her face. She was scared to death. Scared of him. Frightened of what he might do. Like a punch to the gut, it hurt.

"Oh God, Zoe." He fell to his knees. "I'm so sorry."

Her fingers gently raked through his hair. "It's okay."

"It's not okay."

He pressed his cheek against her abdomen and her body shuddered. The coolness of her shirt felt good on his burning face.

"I'll take care of you," she said.

"No, baby. I was supposed to take care of you. I can't even do that right."

It wasn't often tears worked into his eyes. First time was at Chase's funeral. He had been drunk then too. Pissed off at the world, he'd caused a scene.

This time, his heart stung. Alcohol drowned his sorrow. He'd make a terrible husband and father. Better to say good-bye than put her through any more of his shit.

****

323

Zoe searched through the grass. Stepping down in the ditch was a little scary, especially with creatures possibly hanging about in July's heat. Not to mention there were bats swooping down at her every so often.

The keys were here somewhere. Too many tears in her eyes to see them, she patted the ground until her hand touched the ring. She grabbed them up and hurried back to the car.

Ben sat on the ground, eyes shut. He leaned against the driver's-side door. Passed out. She pulled on his arm, but he wouldn't budge.

"Come on, Ben," she said, tapping his face with her palm. "I need you to help me get you up."

He groaned. "Just leave me here."

"No. Now come on. Let's get you in the car."

She tugged on him again and he stood. With his arm around her shoulders, heavy weight against her, they stumbled to the passenger side. Once she finally got him in the seat, she blew a quick breath over her parted lips.

All the stress she'd been under today, it was a wonder how she'd made it without heart failure. Hopefully by morning, he'd sleep this off. Hopefully tomorrow they could work this crazy mess out without having to say good-bye.

Chapter Thirty-One

Zoe woke at six a.m. to the sound of rain pelting the side of the apartment. It was a nice sound. Homey. Cozy. Made her want to stay in bed tucked comfortably under the covers with Ben, but she had to get up. She was meeting the girls at the bar to help set up for the barbecue today.

She rolled to her side. The light of her alarm clock gave Ben's form an orange glow. She gently dragged her thumb over his dark brow. He was so handsome.

Last night's chaos flooded her mind, washing away the snug feeling. If the doctor was right about the time, then they'd conceived the first night they'd made love. What were they going to do now?

She didn't blame Ben for alleviating stress with alcohol, but it hurt. It hurt that he thought she'd ever cheat on him. He'd suggested this child was Renji's. After everything they'd gone through, he'd spiraled down the bottle where he shouldn't be.

Her gut churned. Nausea crept up her throat. She moaned as she rolled off the bed then headed for the bathroom. She fell to her knees in front of the toilet and waited. Nothing came up. She drew in several deep breaths. The queasiness subsided just as fast as it began.

She washed her hands in the sink and looked in the mirror. The left side of her face was swollen, and her eye almost glued shut. Her vision blurred from tears.

She couldn't go out looking like a monster. Everyone would want an explanation, and she wouldn't know what to say. She tripped and fell into the car mirror. Not a lie. Not the truth either. But it'd be too embarrassing letting anyone know Nicholas had done this.

She wiped her tears. *Calm down.* She went to the bedroom closet to find something to wear. Today was supposed to be sunny and seventy-five degrees. Not too hot for a July afternoon.

She didn't feel very sociable. Nothing mattered. Not the outfit, her hair, or the lack of makeup on her face. To go meet with cackling, happy-go-lucky women while Ben lay here passed out, face down on the pillow, left arm and leg dangling over the edge of the bed, just didn't seem right.

She nudged him to see if he'd wake, but no such luck. The man was out.

Going with an ankle-length sundress and a jean vest, she slipped her feet inside her tennis shoes and went outside.

She breathed in deep. The air was refreshing on her skin as she strolled down the walkway toward the bakery. The place sat quiet against the lightening sky. It was a lonely scene but would soon be bustling with townsfolk getting their morning fix.

The bell jingled when she walked in. She turned on the neon OPEN sign as she normally did in the mornings, and then strode to the kitchen.

"Good morning." Renji beamed, holding a large cookie sheet in his gloved hand. He tipped the pan, and twenty chocolate doughnuts slid down on the counter. A brilliant smile stretched across his face as he turned his attention on her. "You ready for the party?"

"No." She grabbed up a doughnut and stuffed the warm pastry in her mouth. *Oh, man that's delicious.* "Everyone's going to be asking me about my eye."

"Just tell them to mind their own business."

"Easier said than done." She took another bite. "I'm not as mean as you."

"Ha ha." He stuck out his tongue. "So listen. Drema recruited me to help stack crates in the back room, so looks like I'll be joining you during setup today."

"Drema, huh?"

"Yeah," he replied with a shrug. "I think I'm in love with her."

"Really? I'm so happy for you." Zoe popped the rest of the doughnut in her mouth. It wasn't right to be envious of his relationship with Drema. They lived in the same town. They could see each other any time they wanted. Neither of them had some psycho stalking them either. "You're still closing for me at ten?"

"Of course." He placed his palms on her shoulders. "I'll lock the doors and head over there about fifteen after." He leaned down and kissed her cheek.

"What was that for?"

"After you kicked me out of your apartment, you went to Holetzer's. Drema told me you were there for Ben."

"Yeah." *Can't people keep their mouths shut around here?* "It's not a big deal."

He frowned. "He went out and got drunk."

"Yeah. Drema called me last night to let me know he'd passed out in the bathroom at the bar. He's sleeping it off now."

He took hold of her wrist and lifted her arm. "What

happened? Did he hurt you?"

There were two faint bruises on each side of her left arm. "It's nothing." She stepped back from his touch and covered the bruise with her hand. "Ben would never hurt me."

He growled. "But he did. Didn't he?"

"After what I went through with Nicholas, do you really think I'd stay with anyone who'd intentionally hurt me?" She swallowed apprehension. "No. Ben didn't do this."

"Fine. Whatever." Renji shook his head and sighed. "Well, then tell me what happened at the hospital?"

Zoe shrugged. How would she tell Renji about her situation? He was going to throw a flipping fit. He'd better not pick a fight with Ben or she'd never speak to him again.

The clock above the table ticked and then tocked. The room spun. She stumbled back a few steps, breathless, stomach in knots.

"Whoa there." Renji caught her in his arms. He guided her to the chair and sat her down. With his hands holding hers, he knelt before. "We've known each other since we were kids. I can tell when something's wrong. Something's very, very wrong here. Just please, talk to me. I just want to help."

She breathed in and then out. She breathed again and again, desperately wishing this was a nightmare she could wake up from. But it wasn't. This was a big fat reality check she would have to face for the rest of her life.

She leaned back and covered her eyes with her palm. Renji peeled her hand from her face and gazed intently, awaiting her explanation.

"Renji," she whispered, staring through watering eyes. "I'm pregnant."

He swallowed hard. "What?"

"I found out at the hospital that I'm pregnant."

"Holy shit, Zoe." He stood tall. He stuffed his right hand in the pocket of his apron. His other hand scrubbed the stubble on his face. "What are you going to do? How is this going to affect your decision to buy this place? You can't afford to invest in anything when you have a baby on the way."

"I can still buy the bakery with you," she said.

"No you can't. That's a lot of money." Renji leaned back on his heels. "I mean, I'll do whatever it takes to help you, but you should really think seriously about doing something else. What does Ben think?"

"He wants me to move to Denver."

He sighed. "Then maybe you should."

"I need to go help Drema." She stood to leave.

"Wait." He pulled her into his arms and held her close. "Whatever you decide, I'm here for you. No matter what. I'm behind you one hundred percent. Okay?"

"Thanks, Renji." She pulled from his arms and then waved as she left the bakery.

****

Ben opened his eyes. He lay on his stomach, arm dangling over the edge of the bed. With his face in the pillow, he glanced at the alarm clock on the nightstand.

Eleven fifty-five a.m. He was at Zoe's. How the hell did he get here?

He rolled onto his back. The thunder in his head exploded into a painful throb. *Oh God. Vodka. Too much vodka.*

Last thing he remembered was Zoe tossing car keys in the ditch. Even then, everything was fuzzy.

He shoved the blankets down to his feet. A rip in his gray T-shirt stretched across his chest. The knees of his jeans had dust on them. His sneakers were off. And somehow, he only had on one sock.

He swung his legs over the side of the bed and sat, elbows on his knees. What the hell happened last night? He rubbed his unshaven face with his palms. He vaguely remembered Zoe crying.

What had he done to her?

He rose. He found his one sock and his shoes placed neatly beside the bedroom door. He quietly stepped down the hallway to the kitchen. Warm, blinding sunshine streamed through the window as he searched the cabinet for something to dull the pain.

He sat on the couch, glass of tap water in one hand, medicine in the other. It'd been a long time since he'd had a hangover this bad. The front door opened. The door clicked shut. Zoe walked up the steps.

His heart sank. He was tired. Worn. In too much pain to get into any big discussions with her. All he wanted was to hold her in his arms and tell her everything was all right. He downed the medicine with several gulps of water.

"Hey," she said as she made her way to him.

He cleared his throat. "You found the keys to the car."

She reached into her vest's front pocket and pulled them out.

"Can I have them?"

"Oh, I don't think so."

"Damn. You're really pissed." Gaze fixed on her, he sighed. "I can drop the car off at the rental place on my way to the airport."

She pulled the water from his hand then set it on the coffee table. Her eyes narrowed as she stood before him, arms folded over her chest, lips pursed.

"I don't blame you for getting drunk last night," she said. "But don't you ever, *ever* accuse me of cheating."

"I'm sorry." He reached out to touch her, but she stepped back. He'd really screwed up. After last night, he was surprised she was even speaking to him. "I'm an idiot. There's no excuse for the way I acted. You deserve better than me."

"Don't say things like that." She sat beside him. "We were both emotional last night and not thinking straight."

He inspected the wound on her eye. The circle had darkened since yesterday. The white around her iris was red. If only he'd been patient with her, this wouldn't have happened.

He was undeserving of her forgiveness. Of her. She was so beautiful. And now, with a child growing inside her, she was more precious.

"I don't know how to do this, Zoe." He blinked back tears. "I don't know how we'll stay together if we can't compromise. Now you're pregnant with my baby..." He gave a short laugh through his nose. "Wow. That's so weird to say. *My* baby. My Wee one. Junior."

"Not Junior." She laughed. "I like *wee one*, though."

He clasped her hand in his. "How are we going to

make this work?"

"I don't know." She leaned against his arm. "Maybe we should just keep doing what we're doing until we figure it out."

"Guess that's about all we can do then."

Chapter Thirty-Two

Zoe stayed beside Ben through the barbecue. She officially introduced him to Millie's husband, who introduced him to all his baseball buddies. Ex-pro players. Coaches. College-ball fans. Turned out Ben was also a baseball fan and fit in with Hank's crowd.

They respectfully butted heads about their choices of teams, but Ben enjoyed the friendly banter. Though he barely blinked an eye her way, it was the first sign of life in him since they'd left the apartment.

The festivity went into full swing. The band played country music. People danced. Laughter was aplenty. Grilled burgers and barbecue chicken were set at the ends of four long tables filled with the best-looking party foods Zoe had ever seen.

Zoe piled her plate. Potato salad. Fried chicken. Cheeseburger with lettuce, tomato, pickles, and avocado. It took a second trip for the macaroni salad, and a third for two slices of Gertrude's Razzle berry Pie.

Zoe went back through the food line with Ben during the band's break, telling him who made what. The women in the town were amazing cooks. By his reaction, he agreed.

When he finished his last bite, she was happy to get a moment with him. With his hand on her leg, he chatted with Hank, who sat across the table beside

Millie.

Zoe was proud to be sitting beside her man and ever so glad his mood had changed. Their problems didn't exist right now. Nothing mattered except being here with him—and the need to use the restroom.

"I'm going inside for a few minutes. I won't be long."

"Want me to come with you?"

"I'll be fine," she said, nodding at the band gathering on the podium. "Doogen's waiting for you anyway."

He palmed her cheek. "Are you sick?"

"No." She giggled. "I just need to use the bathroom."

"Take Millie with you. You shouldn't be alone."

"Stop worrying." She stood from the table then kissed his lips. "There are other people inside. I'll be right back."

She headed for the bar's entrance around the corner, out of sight of the party and away from Ben's view. She opened the door and stepped inside. The cool air felt wonderful on her warm skin as she made her way across the bar to the restroom.

Nobody was in here. She stepped into the stall and fastened the lock. As she peed, the door to the restroom opened. A gush of cool air winded around her ankles and crept up her spine.

There were no footsteps moving across the tiled floor. Nobody shut and locked a stall door. It was like the door had opened by itself. Maybe someone changed their mind about using the bathroom.

She flushed the toilet and stepped out of the stall. She washed her hands and inspected her reflection. All the foundation in the world couldn't cover up these bruises. The corner of her eye had turned a deep red and stung like crazy. People must've thought she'd gotten in a fight with a vicious monster, and they'd be right. Nicholas was the worst.

Movement in the mirror caught her attention. Her gaze turned to the reflection of the man standing in the dark corner by the door.

Nicholas.

The temperature dropped twenty degrees. She shuddered as she turned quickly and leaned back against the sink. With nowhere to go, she was trapped.

He made his way out of the shadows. His head was shaved, and a skull had been tattooed on the side of his reddened scalp. His legs bulged below khaki shorts. And his arms were overly inked and larger than she remembered.

Bottle of tequila in hand, he chugged down several swallows. The same cocky grin he'd always carried stretched across his face.

"What do you want?" Her voice trembled.

"You and I have unfinished business."

As he continued toward her, she eyed the door. She prayed someone would walk in, but everyone was outside listening to the band. She couldn't remember seeing anyone at the bar, but there had to be people out there. Maybe they'd hear her scream. Maybe they'd arrive too late.

The only option she had right now was to try to get away from Nicholas before he caught her. He'd been drinking. His reflexes weren't as good as hers.

She darted for the exit. He tossed the bottle to the floor and lunged for her. He caught her arm. And with a quick jerk, he pulled her into his arms. "Where do you think you're going?"

Face-to-face with the demon that gave her nightmares, she screamed. He covered her mouth.

"Thought I'd come see if you liked my gift," he said holding her tight. "Damn. Did I do that to your eye? I'm sorry. I'm just having a hard time dealing with you. You've been a really bad girl lately."

She wriggled out of his grasp. "Don't ever touch me."

"Hey," he said. "I'm not the same guy I used to be, Zoe."

"You're worse." She backed toward the exit.

He chuckled. "How do you figure?"

"You ran me off the road and nearly killed me. You followed me to Denver. You came to my home and hit me. I don't understand why you're like this," she said, out of breath. "You're not right in the head, Nicholas. You need help."

He shrugged. "I'm in therapy. I'm getting better."

"Good for you. Now, I need to go." She continued stepping back toward the door. Just a little further and she'd be free.

He followed her. "Aren't you going to say something about the gift?"

She wasn't sure what to think about a bullet. She didn't really want to know. All she needed was to get out of here before he hit her or did something worse.

"I don't want any gifts from you. You're not supposed to be near me." She pointed her forefinger at his chest. "I'll never forgive you for what you did. You should still be in prison."

He grabbed her middle finger and bent it back.

Sharp pain spread through her hand and up her arm. She yelped as he forced her to her knees.

"You're the same whiny bitch you've always been."

Tears sprouted to her eyes. "Let me go."

He let go. "Just like old times, huh? Why don't we go back to your place and make this an official date?" He grabbed her arm and jerked her to her feet. "Or better yet, nobody's in here. We've got some making up to do."

"Go to hell!" She shrieked as he shoved her into the counter.

He bent her forward over the sink and pressed his body against her back.

"Already spent two years there because of you. Time for some payback." He growled in her ear. "So I guess you're not as innocent as the night I fucked you. Got pretty-boy eating out of the palm of your hand. Slut. You know the gift I sent?" He laughed heartily. "It wasn't for you. It's for your boyfriend."

"God no." She gritted her teeth. *If anything happens to Ben*— "Don't you dare hurt him."

He loosened his belt buckle. "What the fuck are you going to do about it?"

He unzipped his pants then lifted her skirt. Zoe drew in a deep breath. Hell no would this happen again. If it took every breath she had left in her, she'd fight him off.

She reached back. She grabbed his cock and squeezed as hard as she could. Her nails dug into his skin.

Nicholas let out a sharp cry and stumbled back. Zoe let go and quickly turned around. He hunched over and cringed as he held his groin.

"You'll regret doing that," he said, his voice raspy.

"I regret nothing." Nothing would ever be enough to make up for what he'd done. Right now, she felt strong, and capable of beating him to the ground. He deserved to pay for his sins, and to suffer through pain and misery. But right now, she had to get out of here before he recuperated.

He lunged toward her. Too late. She tensed the muscles in her arm. Holding her fingers rigid, she slammed her flattened palm against the tip of his nose. His head tilted back, and he cried out again.

Protecting her face with her fists, she raised her leg and kicked out. The bottom of her foot hit his chest. Nicholas fell on his backside. His loud grunt echoed through the room.

"You'll never touch me again," she said, out of breath. *Time to get the hell out of here.* She hustled toward the exit.

"Stupid...*bitch*!"

Zoe pulled open the door and raced through the empty bar. She threw a glance over her shoulder. *Oh shit!* Nicholas staggered out of the restroom holding his nose with one hand and his crotch with the other.

Zoe ran like hell. Tears blurred her vision as she burst through the exit door. Breath labored, heart in her throat, she sprinted down the sidewalk in front of the building.

Nicholas's heavy footsteps were right behind her. Damn. The asshole was fast. She rounded the corner. The party was right there in full swing. Just a few more steps, and she'd be safe.

Nicholas caught her hair. He clenched his fist tight

against her scalp. Strands of hair tore from her skin. Pain resonated through her head and down her neck. She screamed.

He dragged her back toward the entrance. She wriggled and kicked. With all her strength, she tried to break loose, but he was too strong. His hold on her was too confining. If he got her around the corner, no one would see her.

She shrieked louder, hoping someone at the party would hear, but the music blared. Renji sat at the table with Drema. Millie and Hank had their backs turned. Fred and the other policemen watched the band play. Nobody was looking.

Enduring the pain on her scalp, she tightened the muscles in her neck and tilted her head forward. "Get off me."

"You hurt me, bitch. After you give me what I want, I'm going to hurt you."

"Ben!" she screamed as loud as she could. "Help me."

Nicholas slid his arm around her waist and lifted. "You're coming with me."

The music suddenly sounded hollow. A piercing screech blared from the speakers. Doogen's twang voice lowered to a whisper as everyone turned to see what was going on.

Nicholas released her. She lost her balance and fell to her hands and knees. The impact vibrated up her limbs.

Nicholas's gaze lifted as he backed away. "I'll get you for this, Zoe."

He took off running through the parking lot. Renji sprinted past, followed by Fred and a few other policemen. When Ben reached her side, he helped her to her feet.

Massaging her sore finger, she jogged around the corner in time to see Nicholas speed down the highway in a black truck. The same one she'd seen at the bar in Denver.

Renji ran behind it spouting curse words he rarely used. Fred's police car zoomed off the lot, siren blaring. Three other cop cars followed close behind.

"You okay?" Ben asked, out of breath. "Did he hurt you?"

He reached out to touch her, but she drew a step back. Nicholas had gotten the best of her again. At least this time, she'd hurt him back.

She brushed the dirt off her dress. Stupid tears. Dumb skinned knees. Idiot Nicholas.

"Zoe?" Ben haltingly lifted his hands to her face.

Not wanting to be touched, she leaned away. "I…I'm fine."

As people from the party gathered closer, she could barely keep from breaking down into a blubbering mess. They were all staring as if waiting for an explanation of what happened. Her breath quickened. There were too many people.

"Are you okay?" Millie placed a gentle hand on Zoe's arm.

Zoe flinched. "I wish everyone would stop asking me that."

"I'm sorry." Millie leaned against Hank.

Zoe's legs wobbled. She couldn't stand here much longer, or she was going to fall to the ground.

"Me too. But really. I'm just in need of a chair." She glanced down. Her knees were skinned. Blood dripped down the front of her right leg. "And a bandage."

"Hey, man," Ben said to Chauncey, who stood on the sidewalk. "We need a first-aid kit."

"Follow me."

Zoe folded her arms over her chest. She followed Ben up the steps of Holetzer's. The chill wouldn't go away. Nicholas had attempted to rape her again.

"You okay, Zoe?" Chauncey said as he led them through the entrance. "He needs to be taught a lesson. If I ever see him in town, I'll make sure he goes down and doesn't get up."

Zoe ambled on wobbly legs through the bar and into Drema's office. As Chauncey pulled the first-aid kit from the bottom drawer, Zoe rounded the desk and waited.

"I'll leave you two alone," Chauncey said on his way out of the room.

Ben shut the door behind him. "What can I do, Zoe?"

She swallowed back tears. She set a yellow tube of antiseptic and a bandage on the desk. "Nothing."

"Do you want me to stay?"

"Yes." Her throat clenched. "Don't leave me alone, okay?"

"Okay."

She rested her foot on the office chair and wiped her knee with an alcohol sheet. The sting made the tears she'd fought come fast. Her nose burned. She applied a clear layer of antiseptic and then blew a few times.

"What happened?" Ben asked, brows low against his eyes.

She tossed him a glance. It took all her strength not

to have a meltdown in his arms. Her hands trembled as she peeled the paper apart, exposing the bandage. It slipped from her fingers and onto the chair. He reached to get it, but she grabbed it up faster.

"I got this," she said. "I've done this a million times. I'm fine."

Unable to see, she wiped her wet eyes with the back of her hand. She didn't want to feel weak in front of him, but she couldn't stop shaking.

"No you're not," he said, taking the bandage from her hand. He tossed the paper into the trash can next to the desk and then taped the sticker to her knee. "Zoe." He sighed. "What happened?"

She pressed her palm against the bandage. Once it was stuck to her skin, she rested her temple on her propped-up knee.

"He followed me into the bathroom."

He shook his head. "No way am I letting you out of my sight again."

Her eyes snapped to his. "There's nothing you can do. You're leaving for Denver tomorrow. So, you shouldn't even be here consoling me."

"Honey." He cupped her face. "Please. Please. Come with me. I promise I'll keep you safe."

"You can't. Nobody can."

"Why would you say that?"

"I was foolish to think I was ready to have a life again," she said in a shaky voice. "I may as well just lock myself in my apartment and play games for the rest of my life, because he's always going to be out there waiting for me to let down my guard. He won't give up until he gets what he wants."

It was time to tell him the entire story. This was the

only way he'd ever understand the pain Nicholas had caused.

She gathered her hair to the side. She leaned down to show him the scar near the hairline on the back of her neck. Her skin rose with a chill as he brushed his finger over her skin.

She let her strands fall down her back. "Renji and I had decided to take a night off and go out to dinner. Nicholas confronted me while I was getting ready. He said I shouldn't be making myself look pretty for a best friend. When I told him it was just dinner, he pressed the hot curling iron against my neck. It happened so out of the blue. I didn't have a chance to defend myself. I just remember the fire on my skin. My hair burning. I screamed for him to stop, but he wouldn't."

Ben sat down on the desk, eyes wide. "Fuck."

"I asked him why he wanted to hurt me." She swallowed apprehension. It was time to reveal the worst part of the story. She hadn't said it aloud since the day she'd testified against him in court. "He said I'd lied when I told him I was…saving myself for the right man, and that I'd never slept with anyone before."

She glanced down at the calendar on Drema's desk and then closed her eyes. Nicholas's face had been so close to hers. Tequila was strong on his breath as he choked her. "His hands twisted around my neck as he held me against the wall. I couldn't breathe. I pleaded with him to stop, but he wouldn't let go. I just kept thinking I was going to die."

She opened her blurring eyes. "He knocked me to the floor. He grabbed me by my arm then dragged me down the hall to the living room. I struggled to get away, but he held me down by my throat. He hit me over and over until I didn't have the strength to fight him anymore."

Ben stood and paced the length of the desk.

She could see the truth was clearly sinking in. "Then…he was inside me."

Ben squeezed his fist and punched the wall. He raked his fingers through his hair, brows low, eyes narrowed and wet. "Why didn't you tell me before?" he shouted, face blood red. "I would've fucking killed him when I'd had the chance."

"I wanted to forget what he'd taken from me." She whimpered. "I wanted to believe in my heart that you were the man…the man I'd saved myself for. If I'd told you, then it wouldn't be true. You wouldn't have wanted me."

"How can you say that?" He pulled her into his arms and held her tight against him. "I love you."

"He's after me, and I'm scared to death," she said, letting her tears fall. "I'm supposed to be strong, but I'm not."

He cupped her face. "You are strong." He thumbed the tears from her cheeks. "You've overcome so much pain in your life. You're going to get through this. I'm right here with you. Do you understand?"

"You can't be with me." She covered her eyes with her palm. "He has a gun. The bullet he sent in the package…he told me it was meant for you."

Renji burst through the door. His wild eyes fixed on Zoe. Breathing hard, he made his way to her. "Are you okay?"

"I'm fine now."

"Fred and I searched the area but couldn't find him. There are police everywhere, so he won't get far."

Zoe shivered as Renji turned his glaring eyes on Ben. "You let her go off alone again? Asshole. You think you'd learn from your mistakes."

"Stop it, Renji," Zoe cried.

"It's okay." Ben palmed her back. "He's right. I should've gone inside the bar with you."

"Okay." Renji gave a nervous clearing of his throat. "As long as we're clear that you should've gone with her."

This was such a disaster. She didn't know what to do or where to go. The only thing that mattered was Ben was in her life, regardless if he was here or there.

Still. She wasn't so sure she should leave town anymore. There'd be no one at his house to protect her. But here, she had the safety of her town. The police. Renji. Millie and Hank. Nobody would let anything happen to her here. Until Nicholas was caught, this was where she'd stay. And Ben, he'd just have to find time to come visit when he could.

Chapter Thirty-Three

A large hand shook Zoe's arm.

"Get up, stupid," Renji said. He draped her arm around his neck, lifted her out of a shallow pool of water, and then carried her to the shore.

Water spilled from her open mouth as she spoke. "I'm fine."

"You could've died," Renji said as he stood straight, glaring. "This is real life, Zoe. Not one of your stupid video games. You're pregnant, and now I don't want you. Nobody wants you. You're going to die all alone."

Renji's face morphed into Nicholas, who sported a maniacal grin. The shadow of his boot covered her face. He shoved her back down underwater. Her shriek turned to a gurgle as water rushed into her mouth. Her lungs filled and she couldn't breathe.

Zoe rose in bed, gasping for air. She palmed her face, her round stomach. Her gown was dry.

It was just another bad dream. This one had felt so real, unlike the nightmares she'd had in the past several months.

A dull pain in her side forced her to her feet. She moaned, hand against her abdomen until the ache subsided. Her cell phone rang as she waddled down the hallway toward the kitchen.

"Zoe." Renji spoke loud when she answered. "You

ready to go yet? We're supposed to meet Millie and the gang for breakfast in an hour."

"I just woke up."

"What?" he said. "I'm coming over."

"No, wait. I—" The phone clicked. "…don't want to go to church." She set her phone on the counter.

Renji started pounding before she even made it down the stairs.

"Hold your horses." She unlocked the door and opened it wide. "I said I don't want to go to church."

"You *are* going to church whether you feel like it or not." Renji shoved his way through the door and up the steps. "You've promised for the past three months you would," he continued from the hallway.

Zoe followed him to her bedroom. When Renji slid her maternity dresses across the closet bar, she sighed.

"All right," she said. "Only if we go to Granny's for breakfast. My stomach's growling."

"When is it not?" He tossed her pink dress on the bed. "After months of puking, I imagine you're a bottomless pit. Really. How does Ben put up with you?"

"I feel good this morning. Considering I'm…*ungh*…"

"You're eight months pregnant. Having a baby. With child. Knocked up."

"I was going to say a *blimp*."

The great big smile on his face was hard to resist. "Okay, then, how about these? Sexy soon-to-be mom. Adorable MILF."

"*Pregnant* is just fine." Another sharp pain hit her abdomen. She breathed in and out several times before the ache finally subsided. "And what the heck's a

MILF?"

He cocked his head to the side and laughed. "Never mind. Let's stick with sexy soon-to-be. Does Ben know you're having pains?"

"Of course he does. He'll be here in a few days to take care of me."

She smiled as she rested her hands on her huge stomach. It'd been two weeks since they'd spooned. She enjoyed the way he rubbed her belly. He was so gentle and loving. When the baby kicked, he'd grin and then hold her tighter. She hoped they'd get a chance to have sex one more time before the baby arrived. Sex felt pretty amazing during pregnancy.

"You know I love taking care of you." Renji gently kissed her cheek. "You'll always be my number one girl."

"Don't let Drema hear you say that."

"She understands." He shrugged. "By the way, we're picking her up on the way to the restaurant. She wants to show off her diamond ring."

"Oh, you finally bought her a real one."

"Yes. A big one that almost cost my half of the bakery." Renji gave a crooked grin. "Anyway, I told her she can eat the ring pop I bought her as a temporary."

Zoe held her belly when she laughed. Renji was so happy. He'd proposed to Drema on Thanksgiving, but they hadn't set a date yet. Today was supposed to be the big reveal at church.

"Speaking of food, can we go eat breakfast now?"

"You're a glutton, young lady." He chuckled. "Get dressed. I'll let everyone else know we're meeting at Granny's."

When they were in the car, Zoe gazed out the

window. The sun shone beautifully through the trees. Shadows moved across the road like an old film reel.

She rubbed her belly. Three more weeks and she'd be a mom. It'd been a long journey of mood swings and vomiting. Lots of vomiting. She'd been sick through the entire pregnancy. Almost eight months of tossing breakfast down the morning chute.

It'd gotten so bad in the second trimester that she couldn't stand car rides to Denver. Plane rides were worse. Either Ben flew on a plane to see her, or they met halfway. And sometimes, that didn't even work, but somehow they'd hung in there.

They'd decided once the baby was born, they'd discuss living arrangements. Zoe still wasn't sure about anything. She loved owning the bakery, but lately it'd lost its allure.

The good thing was, she'd hadn't heard a word from Nicholas. Fred and Sheriff Clemens had contacted the state police. Warrants for his arrest circulated throughout the entire state of Kansas.

Renji had installed security cameras around the apartments and at Millie's house. With the police constantly patrolling the town at night, Zoe breathed a lot better.

Once word got out into the community that she was pregnant, nobody would leave her alone. Renji told the reverend how ill she'd been, which led to calls and pleas for her to join them for Sunday worship. They enticed her by telling her about the potlucks on the first Sunday of every month.

Renji picked up Drema in front of her house. Zoe stole a glance at Renji. A cheerful aura surrounded him. He smiled as he held Drema's hand.

God, she missed Ben. It'd felt like months since she'd seen him. Touched him. Spoken to him face-to-face. She hated the times they couldn't be together. Gaming had been the only connection she'd had with him lately. They coupled all the time, but that just made her miss him all the more.

He'd bought her a new smartphone so they could stay in touch. She couldn't resist sending him texts and pictures—many of them to let him know she and the baby were fine.

He'd sent her gifts. Roses. Candies. When she found out they were having a boy, he started sending outfits. Once the holiday season began, the clothes and gifts were wrapped in Christmas paper with colorful bows.

She'd often thought about giving in and moving. But with Nicholas off the grid, a warrant out for his arrest, she couldn't risk leaving the safe net the community had made. Until then, the touch-and-go meetings and text messages would have to do.

When they walked into the fifties-style diner, Zoe breathed in the heavenly aromas. The visuals on the *Deals of the Day* board were the loveliest things she'd seen since sunrise.

There were so many options. Hotcakes and sausage. Eggs and bacon with toast. Thick slices of French toast topped with cream cheese and juicy blueberries. It was going to be difficult to choose which mouthwatering ensemble she'd order.

Millie and Hank sat together in the back of the restaurant. Her stomach growling, Zoe followed Renji and Drema to the table.

"I'm so glad you came, Zoe." Millie bounced in the

seat, making it squeak. Her open hand slid to the center of the table.

Zoe squeezed into the tight space then placed her palm on Millie's. "I'm here."

"You're simply glowing this morning."

Warmth spread to Zoe's cheeks. "It's Renji's fault. He's been calling me names all morning."

"Again?" Millie's eyes narrowed. "Don't stress our girl out."

"Just called her a MILF," he said in a low voice. "She should take it as a compliment."

Drema punched his arm. "I can't believe you'd say such a thing to her."

"It's not like I meant it." He kissed her. "She doesn't even know what it means."

Drema ho-hummed. She held up her left hand to show off the large diamond rock on her ring finger. "Check out the engagement ring Renji bought for me."

Millie's eyes widened. "Ah. He finally found the balls to buy the expensive one."

"Congrats." Hank shook Renji's hand. "When's the big day?"

"We discussed Vegas. Drema wants Valentine nuptials."

"Valentine's in Vegas?" Zoe's jaw dropped. She'd known Ben longer and was pregnant. They hadn't even discussed marriage yet. Renji getting married in February was just crazy soon. "Why not have the wedding here?"

"The reverend's free that day, but—" Drema sighed. "It would be so much fun, the six of us, living it up at Caesars Palace."

"I'll have the baby then." Zoe gazed at Renji. "I

think it's too soon for me to be taking trips anywhere. And Vegas isn't family-friendly."

"Ever been to Vegas?" Drema asked.

"Can't say I have," Zoe said, staring at the menu. "A friend of mine went once. Said she partied for three days straight and couldn't remember what she'd done."

Drema laughed. "Yep. Been there. Done that."

"Really?" Renji arched his brows. "You'll have to tell me the story sometime."

"The reverend preached a sermon about Vegas back when I went to church with my dad." Zoe scanned the tempting photos of eggs and bacon. And *mm...waffles.* "He said the place packed in evil souls. Gambling. Drinking. Orgies. Secrets of the nightlife nobody dared reveal when they returned home to their families. I kind of think it'd be a terrible place to get married."

"What's your deal this morning?" Renji said. "Can't you just be happy for us?"

"I am happy for you. Just hungry, Pa."

"It's okay, Renji." Drema leaned back in her seat. "We figured you'd be too busy with the baby to go to Vegas. So, we decided to get married here and just honeymoon in Vegas."

"Aww." Zoe's heart leaped. She felt bad for snapping at Drema and making Renji mad. "I am happy for you both."

"You guys ready to order?" the pretty young waitress wearing a green bow tie and vest asked.

"I'd like an orange juice with the French toast of the day," Zoe blurted. Everything sounded so good. "I also want a side of scrambled eggs and bacon with a slice of toast. Oh, and hash browns. Can you add cheddar cheese to the eggs and potatoes?"

The waitress smiled. "Yeah, we can add cheese."

Zoe searched the menu one more time. The sliced cinnamon apples sounded good too, but she'd already made herself look like a glutton—or a pregnant woman starving to death. Millie even looked up from her menu, hopefully not about to lay in on her about her diet again. She was not in the mood.

"I'm eating for two," Zoe said handing her the menu.

"I can tell." The waitress tucked it under her arm. A shade of rose blended through the girl's pale cheeks when she turned to Renji. Her slightly crooked teeth showed as she swayed her tall, thin frame.

"How about you, sir?"

"Eggs and bacon, hold the toast," he said. Zoe slugged his arm. "Oww…I meant…with toast?"

Zoe nodded. "Add a side of cinnamon apples too."

"Hungry some?" Hank laughed. "Hotcakes and sausage for me," he added and then handed his menu to the young woman.

"I'll have the same thing he's having," Millie said. She turned her attention on Zoe. "When's Ben coming to town?"

"Tuesday." Zoe smiled. She couldn't wait to feel his chest against her back and his hand on her tummy. "He sent this cute white teddy bear. It has a soft rainbow LED light that changes colors in its belly. It's so adorable."

"Still asking you to move in with him?" Renji asked.

"He always asks." A dull ache hit Zoe's side. "I can't move up there yet."

"Why not?" Millie puckered her lips. She pointed at herself with her thumbs. "The bakery's doing just fine after you hired the beautiful, fabulous, intelligent manager who can run the place blindfolded."

Zoe laughed. The dull ache in her abdomen turned to a stabbing pain that crawled across her abdomen. She drew in a deep breath and then another. "Oh my. If I go into labor before I get breakfast, I'm going to be pissed."

"Ben's waiting on our call." Renji whipped out his cell phone. "Should I let him know the baby's on its way?"

"It's just Braxton-Hicks. Give me a second, and it'll pass." When the pain subsided, she leaned back in the seat. Heat rushed to her face. Her belly grumbled. If she didn't eat something soon, she was going to be ill. "I hope this baby doesn't come before Ben gets here, but God. I can't wait until this is over."

The waitress served their food. Zoe took her hunger out on the two giant pieces of steaming Texas French toast doused in cream cheese, plump blueberries, and loads of syrup. She dug into the large plate of bright yellow scrambled eggs topped with cheddar cheese, two slices of crisp bacon, and crispy, greasy hash browns.

Zoe stuffed her mouth full. Everything tasted divine. Sweet. The taste almost brought her to tears. Forkfuls of egg and cheese melted in her mouth. More French toast landed on her tongue before she realized everyone watched her.

Renji shook his head. "Wow. I am so disappointed in you, Zoe."

Zoe's mouth was full. Syrup covered her lips as the

smiles on the other side of the table grew wider.

She quickly stabbed the hash browns with her fork and then reeled it to her lips. Cheese stretched from the plate, creating a long string that broke when she shoved the bite inside her mouth.

Hank's eyes widened. "You sure you can handle all that, Zoe?"

"Absolutely." Zoe set her fork on the edge of the syrupy plate. She wiped her mouth with her cloth napkin. Her cell phone rang. She leaned down and pulled it from the side pocket of her purse. A heavy cramp hit below her navel. "Ohhhh…" She hunched over. "Oh, this one's…strong." Her stomach churned. "I'm going to be sick."

She waddled toward the bathroom, squeezing between tables and around chairs, hand over mouth. Eyes watering, she found an empty stall in the bathroom. It took some doing, but she finally lowered herself to the greasy floor.

Everything she'd eaten came up and out fast. Sweat beaded her brow. Groaning, she leaned back against the stall, palm on her burning temple.

Her cell phone rang again. Zoe pressed the Answer icon on the touch screen. "Hello."

"Zoe."

Her clammy skin rose with a chill. "Nicholas?"

"Pretty Miss Zoe stepped into the restaurant for breakfast with all her lovely friends." His laugh sent horrible chills down her spine. "She went off and left her apartment unlocked. Didn't think she'd mind me hanging out until she got home."

Tears welled in Zoe's eyes. "I'm calling the police."

"I can't figure out why people keep all their personal info out in the open. I mean, really…bank passwords, credit card numbers…*doctor's receipts*." He growled. "I go in hiding for a few months to come home and find out you're pregnant. You didn't tell me I was going to be a dad. I am not happy about this."

She shivered, the ill sensation working its way up again. "What do you want from me?"

"I want you to pay for ruining my life."

"You brought it on yourself."

"Well, then…" He chortled. "Guess you won't mind me putting a bullet in Miss Millie's skull. I'm looking at her right now. She's getting up from the table. Hank. Renji. Drema. They all look worried for some reason. Maybe it's because you're not there."

"Please." She whimpered. "Don't do this."

"You owe me everything. Now stop being a bitch and get back to your apartment. And don't bother calling Fred. Wouldn't want pretty Millie to have an accident. Those poor little boys need their mother."

The phone beeped. Zoe set her phone down on the floor. It chimed. Text message. She opened the attachment to find a photo of Millie sitting at the table inside the restaurant.

"Zoe?" Millie's voice echoed from the other side of the stall door. "You okay, honey?"

"I'm so sick," Zoe replied, hands shaking. What was she going to do?

"Just a few more weeks, sweetie."

"I know." Zoe flushed the toilet then stepped out of the stall.

Millie touched her arm. "Want us to take you home?" Zoe cried as she ran cool water into the palms of her shaking hands. "Oh, honey. You don't look so good."

Zoe gazed in the mirror that stretched across the entire wall. Her reflection looked terrible next to beautiful Millie, who stared. The dimples in Millie's tanned cheeks showed when she pursed her lips.

"I'm so scared, Millie," Zoe whispered. "Nicholas just called me."

Her eyes widened. "What?"

"He said if I don't go to him now, he'll kill you."

Millie lifted her cell phone from her pocket.

"What are you doing?"

"I'm calling Fred."

Zoe placed her hand over Millie's. "You can't call the police."

"Why not?"

"He's watching us."

Zoe lifted her cell phone. When she showed Millie the picture he'd sent, Millie dialed Fred's number.

As Millie talked to Fred, Zoe shivered. She couldn't stop shaking, worried Nicholas would do what he said. Nicholas had never threatened her friends before. This took Zoe's fear to a new level.

Chapter Thirty-Four

After the police combed the apartment for clues of Nicholas's whereabouts, they deemed she was safe to return home. All Zoe wanted to do was lie down and cry herself to sleep, but her apartment was a mess.

Nicholas had indeed been here, rummaging through her filing cabinet and dresser drawers. Papers and undergarments were scattered all over her room. He'd written a message on her wall with black spray paint.

Die bitch!

Renji stayed with her. He cleaned the apartment and covered the message with a coat of paint. He was hesitant to leave her alone, but Zoe insisted he go home to Drema.

Fred had ordered a squad car to sit right outside her door. After she promised Renji she'd call if she needed him, didn't matter what for, he finally left.

After locking all the doors and double-checking bedroom windows, she ate her nightly bowl of fudge-ripple ice cream. It was the only food she could eat that never came back up. With a few shakes of shredded cheddar and a dill pickle on the side, the dessert was heavenly.

She got in the shower. She breathed deeply, closing her eyes, letting her mind wander through the roses in Ben's backyard.

It was a daydream she'd carried for months. It comforted her and usually made her happy. This time Nicholas stood by the fence line, roses trampled beneath his black-booted feet.

She opened her eyes and twisted the valve. A chill crawled over her skin as she stepped out of the shower. She wrapped the towel around her plump body and then went to the mirror.

A ragged, frightened woman stared back. Wet hair hung to her midsection. Colorless lips curved downward. Mascara blended with the dark circles below her tired eyes.

How did she become so miserable in just a few months' time?

She drew in a deep breath. *Concentrate on something else*. Nicholas couldn't hurt her now. Surely he wouldn't be stupid enough to waltz up to her apartment with a cop sitting outside and every uniform in Kansas on a statewide manhunt for the creep.

Zoe palmed her huge stomach. It was time for a change.

She got the hair scissors out of the drawer below the bathroom sink. For a good minute she searched her hair for the right spot to cut. Deciding on just below her shoulder, she held her wet locks in her hand, opened the scissors wide, and then squeezed.

Her hand trembled on the first snip. Six years of blonde hair landed inside the sink. It didn't take long to work around to the other side, clipping a good several inches off the length. She pulled her long bangs forward. Five more inches of blonde dropped onto the pile.

With her bangs cut below her brow, she felt lighter.

Not so ragged. The stoop she'd been in all day melted. The world became brighter. After a good face wash, her cheeks turned pink. The dark circles stayed, but there was nothing she could do about that. She slipped on her black sleeveless gown and made her way to bed.

When she climbed in, she gently squeezed the teddy bear Ben had sent last week. The lights glowed, pastel colors changing before her eyes. Soon, her baby—her and Ben's baby—would be mesmerized by it too.

She clutched the bear in her hands and curled up beneath the covers. It was ten fifteen. She closed her eyes. Ben's house was so inviting. She envisioned the room across from his painted a light shade of blue. A mobile made with little guitars and picks hung from the ceiling, entertaining the baby lying beneath it in a wooden crib.

****

Ben drove fast down the interstate, determined to get to Zoe. Careful not to swerve off the road, he glanced at his phone.

Dammit. He'd missed a message from her. It'd chimed earlier, but he couldn't check to see who it was from. He'd had to quickly retrieve his bag from the carousel at the Wichita airport and then hurry to his rental car waiting outside.

A picture popped up in the message field.

The photo was of Zoe, lying in bed on her side, arms around her pillow. The teddy bear he'd sent lay beside her with a greenish glow. With no blankets over her, her rounded stomach was prominent, and her gown bunched up to her thighs.

Beautiful. His eyes blurred as he glanced at the

photo again. Smooth, pale skin. Blonde locks fanned out in slight curls on the pillow beneath her head. She'd cut her hair to her shoulders and her bangs just below the inner corners of her brows.

He tossed his phone on the seat. He couldn't wait to get to her. To see her long, dark eyelashes flutter. To see his sleeping beauty stir. He longed to hear her soft moan resonate from her throat as her faded pink lips curved into a smile. Then her eyes would open, stopping his heart.

He stepped on the accelerator. Right now, he didn't want Zoe to feel scared or panicked. Nicholas was out there somewhere plotting his revenge, and Ben had to do everything in his power to stop him.

Chapter Thirty-Five

It'd been a long while since she'd dreamed about anything but holding her baby in her arms. Rocking him to sleep, singing a song of stars in the sky. Maybe it was the fudge-ripple ice cream that made the nightmare come.

Nicholas's face floated before her on a cloud. His skin was red. Demonic. Horns protruded on each side of his head. He opened his mouth. Baby rattles spilled out with his wicked laughter. A gun flew across the sky. The blast exploded in her ears.

Zoe woke with a jolt.

Tears crept into her eyes, but she blinked them back. Had she screamed out loud?

Zoe's stomach roiled. She'd eaten too much ice cream. The baby kicked like crazy. Probably on a sugar rush. Poor little guy was a party animal. He wanted out. She wanted him out.

Zoe rose to her aching feet. Rubbing her rounded belly, she shuffled down the hall to the kitchen. She must've been so out of it that she'd left the light on.

She drew in a deep breath and strode quietly to the window in the living room. She peeked out the curtains. The squad car was still parked outside. The street lamp was out, so she couldn't see the policeman inside. The only light came from the neighbor's Christmas lights still hanging from the window in her apartment.

A frigid draft brushed her skin. The brown curtains waved, sending an awful chill across her spine.

The window was open.

Spooked, Zoe folded her arms over her chest and rested them against her stomach. A thud from her bedroom sent a chill over her skin. Her legs wouldn't move. Another thud and the slide of her dresser drawers brought tears to her eyes.

The police was right outside. All she had to do was scale the steps, undo all the noisy locks on her door, and run.

Drawing a deep breath into her lungs, she headed for the stairs. She crept downward, trying not to make a sound. Her eyes blurred as she looked behind her to the kitchen, the dining room. Pitch black enveloped her as she clicked the first lock on the door.

She glanced back. Nobody was there. Hair rose on her body as she continued with the next two locks. Panic set in as she slid the chain to the side. In a hurry, she swiped the latch, twisted the knob, and then turned the handle.

As she stepped back to open the door, something hard touched her back. A breath tore from her lips and that chill from earlier spread through to her bones.

"I wouldn't go out there, if I were you." Nicholas's deep voice was loud in her ears. "It's too dark and scary."

Zoe cringed. She swayed slightly, turning to see her intruder.

Nicholas held a small black pistol in his trembling hand. Tequila was strong on his breath. He tossed the hood of his black sweatshirt to the back of his head and motioned with his gun to get back inside.

Her legs shook as she slowly made her way inside the apartment. The knot in her stomach tightened. The baby kicked hard, and she lost her breath.

She stopped in the doorway. "Why are you doing this?"

"You left me no choice but to come get you."

Fluid gushed down her legs to the floor. "Oh my God," she said, holding her aching stomach. *Not now. Please...don't let this happen now.*

"Disgusting." He waved the gun again. "Move your ass to the bathroom and clean yourself up."

"My water just broke, Nicholas. I need to get to the hospital."

"So you can call the cops?" He laughed. "I don't think so. We'll have the baby in the bathroom. Just...tell me what to do."

"I don't know what to do. That's why I need to go to the hospital."

"Not going to happen."

Sharp pain resonated through her as she stepped up the stairs. "At least call Renji."

"Ha." He grabbed her arm and jerked her up the last stair. She cried out in pain. "The idiot clings to you like a fucking magnet." With his free hand around her throat, he shoved her back against the hallway wall. "He interferes and he's dead. Understand?"

Unable to breathe or speak, she nodded.

"Good." He let go. She gasped for breath as he paced the room, hands on top of his head. "After you're done having the baby, we're leaving."

She massaged her neck. "Where are we going?"

"Mexico or something," he muttered. He pointed the gun at her stomach. "It's my baby. No way am I going to let some other prick raise him. Now get in the bathroom." He scanned her legs. "Fucking hurry it up. You're dripping all over the place."

Zoe used the wall as a crutch to get to the bathroom. She flipped the switch to the side. The globe bulbs on the wall above the mirror fluttered on.

Nicholas stood in the doorway with his gun aimed. She pulled the hand towel off the towel ring. She soaked the cloth in hot water and then leaned down as far as she could.

"You don't have to point the gun at me," she said, back turned to him. She wiped her legs with the warm towel. "I'm not going anywhere."

He paused for a moment and then lowered the gun to his side. "Whatever."

"If you love me, Nick, you won't shoot me."

"I don't love you." He snorted a laugh. "Not anymore."

Chills clawed her spine. "Then why are you doing this?"

"Two years of my life, Zoe. Shot to hell. My parents disowned me." He growled. "I lost my job…my career. When I got out, nobody would hire me. If it wasn't for my pansy-ass brother, I don't know how I would've survived. Everyone else said I was a bad guy. Now you're trying to hand my child over to some asshole."

Her gaze stayed on the gun as he wandered into the room. He turned down the toilet lid and sat. He leaned back against the tank, knees parted, gun dangling between his legs. His right knee bounced vigorously.

"I saw Renji in the back room of Holetzer's doing the nasty with the blonde from the bar. Man, the guy needs a good beating."

Pain crawled across her abdomen again. Zoe buckled over and gave a long moan and a few deep breaths. She dropped the towel to the floor then sat on the edge of the tub.

"Can I feel my baby kick?"

"He's not your baby." Zoe hummed from the pain.

He fisted the knees of his pants. The barrel of the gun turned toward her. His knee kept bouncing. The gun moved back and forth.

"It's his kid, isn't it?" He gritted his teeth as he stood, eyes shut tight. "You cheated on me. Slut. You're ruined."

"I can still go with you." She reached out to touch him, but he slapped her hand away.

"Cheating bitch."

If only the pain in her stomach would cease, she could fight him. God, why'd the baby have to be on his way now? It was too early.

Tears welled in her eyes. As soon as the last contraction stopped, another one began. Her lips trembled as she cried out. His arm swung around his front. He struck her cheek with the back of his hand. Pain shot down her face and neck. Zoe shrieked. She kept screaming in hopes someone would hear her.

"Shut the fuck up." Nicholas struck the top of her head with the butt of the gun.

The crunch of her skull silenced her scream. Vision bobbing in and out of focus, she slid to the floor. This was just a nightmare. Nicholas wasn't here. The baby wasn't coming.

He pressed the barrel against her temple and then exhaled a slow sigh. "You're nothing to me now. Just another bitch that deserves to die."

"Please." She slouched against the wall of the tub, arms protecting her aching stomach. "My baby…"

"I wish it didn't have to end this way. I really believed you were the one. Once. A long time ago. All the suffering you've caused me. I just want to ruin your life like you ruined mine." He wiped tears from his face. "Look at you now. Pathetic little Zoe's about to die."

Movement caught the corner of her eye. Zoe turned her head toward the figure standing in the bathroom doorway.

"Ben."

He bounded into the room. His hands wrapped around Nicholas's arm, forcing his aim away from her head. The gun went off. Zoe covered her ringing ears as he took Nicholas down to the floor.

The contractions held nothing on the pain shooting through her head and down her shoulder. He'd shot her. Nicholas had actually shot her. This couldn't be happening. She'd fallen asleep and was having a horrifying, vivid nightmare.

Tears blinded her. *Breathe. Don't let panic win over reason. Endure the pain. Stay conscious.*

She grabbed the hand towel beside her and pressed it against her shoulder. Blood quickly spread down her chest. The metal taste in her mouth nauseated her. Sticky warmth stung her eyes.

The room spun. Her vision blurred. She couldn't focus on the struggle in front of her. Being helpless to aid the man she loved was the worst feeling in the world.

The gun went off again. She screamed and covered

her ears. Every fiber in her body burned as Ben scooted toward her. He lifted the towel from her shoulder and inspected the wound. "Fuck. *Fuck!*" He pulled his cell phone from his pocket.

"There's not enough time to wait for an ambulance. The baby's coming. I need to get to the hospital now."

"I don't want to risk moving you."

Searing pain hit below her navel. She fisted Ben's sleeve. She shut her eyes tight, trying to stifle the intense scream building in her throat, but she couldn't. It came out in a long cry. "Just get me to the hospital."

He pressed the towel against the wound on her shoulder. "Hold it tight."

He scooped her up in his arms and carried her down the hall.

She cried out again. "It hurts."

"I know, baby," he said as he carried her down the steps, teeth bared, jaw clenched. "Dammit."

Two policemen burst through the front door, arms stretched out, and guns in their hands. Ben maneuvered around them. "She's been shot and needs to get to the hospital," he said as he carried her outside. He set her in the passenger seat of a car and buckled her in.

In no time, they were driving through town at top speed, out onto the highway, heading toward Wichita. Zoe stared out the window. At least she was conscious enough to see the bright flashing police lights pull forward to the front.

She woozily turned and caught Ben's gaze. "I'm glad you're here."

"I'm so sorry, Zoe." He grasped her hand. "I should've been here sooner." Tears were in his eyes, but he quickly wiped them away to concentrate on the road.

She scooted back in the seat. Pain shot through her chest and arm and then down to her stomach. She cried out, drawing in deep breaths.

She closed her eyes. *Remember the Lamaze video at Millie's last week. One long inhale through the nose. Three short exhales out the mouth.*

She cleared her mind until the pain subsided. The wound in her shoulder didn't hurt so badly anymore. In fact, she couldn't feel much at all. That probably wasn't a good thing.

Ben drove fast down the highway, quietly concentrating on the traffic. He passed in the left lane every chance he got, following the police car ahead of them as close as possible.

"*Oh.*" She moaned. Another contraction was coming, but this one felt different. It was lower in the gut.

She pulled her knees together, fearing the baby would come out here and now. Her moan sounded like a song, a horrible off-key tune that oddly made her laugh and cry at the same time.

"We're almost there, honey," Ben said.

"I don't know how much longer I can…stand this." She cried out in pain. "Hurry up."

"I'm going as fast as I can."

He swerved quickly into the emergency lane at the hospital and parked. He jumped out. He ran around to the passenger side and opened the door. "Come on," he said, offering his hand.

"I can't." She panted for breath. "I'm too dizzy."

He carefully scooped her up in his arms. As he carried her into the crowded ER, people stared. She closed her eyes, but another contraction was coming. She tried her best not to scream and draw more attention, but the pain was too much.

"She's been shot," Ben said through her cries. "Her water broke, but I don't know how long ago. She's not due for another three weeks."

He lowered her body to a stretcher. As a group of nurses wheeled her back into the emergency room, Zoe held Ben's hand. She shut her eyes, breathing, trying to control her whimpers, trying not to pass out.

Two more nurses met them in a curtained-off room. They sliced her gown up the center and pulled it off. They put her in a hospital gown that opened up in back.

With her feet up in stirrups, Ben holding her hand on one side, and a nurse inspecting her shoulder on the other, the realization hit Zoe hard. In just a little while, she'd have her own baby to cradle in her arms. She'd be a mom. This was the most painful and amazing thing ever.

"Call Millie and Renji," she said through an intense contraction. "Tell them what's going on and where I am."

Ben swallowed nervously. "Right now?"

"Yes!" She screamed. "Text. Call. I don't really fucking care. Just let them know."

He pulled his cell phone from his jacket pocket. He tapped quickly against the screen, and then pocketed his phone. "I texted them."

"Thanks," she whispered.

Sitting with her legs spread apart made the pain in her lower back better. The contractions were barely there anymore, and the throb in her shoulder and head had begun to dull.

"She's slipping in and out of consciousness," the nurse said. "The baby's head is crowning."

"What can I do?" Ben's voice was muffled.

Zoe tried hard to stay awake, but her eyes wouldn't open. "I can't do this," she said, reaching out for Ben. "I don't know what I'm doing."

Her ears rang. Her eyes begged for sleep.

Someone's warm hand held hers. Ben's voice whispered in her ear. "You have to push now, Zoe."

"I can't," she whispered back.

"Yes, you can." His voice was soft in her ear, like an echo in a cavern. It was oddly soothing. "I know you want to sleep, but you have to do this one last thing. Push."

Zoe fought the darkness. She forced her eyes open and cried out. Sweat dripped into her eyes as she pushed hard.

The doctor poked her head up, goggles making her eyes look bigger than they were. "One more push, Zoe."

Holding her breath, she clenched her jaw and pushed until all her strength was gone.

Ben swept his palm across her temple, holding her bangs up away from her eyes. He laughed and cried, attention on the screaming, tiny purple body below her knees.

"We've got a baby boy here," the doctor said as she placed the baby on Zoe's stomach.

Too drained to look, Zoe gazed at Ben. He kissed her temple. Tears glimmered in his eyes. He was so beautiful. And now he was a dad.

"You did it, honey."

The doctor said a few incoherent words. Ben's smile faded as, over and over, he said her name. The bright lights of the hospital lowered as the sounds of beeping monitors and a dozen shouting voices hushed.

Chapter Thirty-Six

Zoe's lips were blue and face as pale as the pillow beneath her head. She'd lost too much blood.

"She's hemorrhaging," the doctor said. "Let's get her to the ER now."

Ben's heart raced as he ran behind the group of doctors and nurses rolling Zoe's stretcher down the hall toward a restricted area. A blonde woman in pink scrubs stopped him at the double doors.

"I'm sorry. You can't come in here. You need to go back to the lobby."

"She's my wife…soon-to-be wife," he said, out of breath, tears flooding his eyes. "I need to be with her."

"What's your name?"

"Ben Solmer."

"The doctors need space to work, Mr. Solmer." She gave a short nod and then pursed her lips. "I'll let you know how she's doing as soon as I can."

"Don't let her die," he pleaded as the nurse hurried through the doors. *"Please* Zoe…don't die."

He caught a glimpse of her on a table, lights shining down on her. Blood soaked the sheets beneath her. The monitors gave a high-pitched whine. Then the doors closed.

"Dammit."

He ran his fingers through his hair, desperately wanting to go in, to be next to her. He'd give anything to trade places with her now. To take away her pain.

Ben stepped backward. He shoved through the doors to the waiting area. Millie and Hank stood near the window. The big grin on Millie's face faded.

"Oh my goodness." Millie looked him up and down. "Did she have the baby?"

"Yeah. They rushed her into surgery." He swallowed back tears. "She's hemorrhaging."

"Oh God no." Millie gasped.

"Nicholas was in her apartment with a gun. He shot her. I had to stop him. I had to…" Ben couldn't catch his breath. Tears flooded his eyes. This was all so surreal. Zoe was in there fighting for her life. "If only I'd been there sooner. I should've been there."

"Don't beat yourself up," Hank said as he placed his hand on Ben's shoulder. "Have faith, man. Zoe's one tough lady. She'll be all right."

"Quite a mess at your apartment." A tall, burly cop waiting near the doorway stepped forward. He took off his dark brown hat and massaged his stubble scalp. "Sergeant Wilkins. I escorted you and the victim here. I'll need a statement of what happened tonight."

"Why now?" Millie said, in tears. "Can't you get one later? Where's Fred?"

"If everything checks out, you can come in tomorrow to give an official report." The policeman nodded. "But right now, I need you to explain why there's a dead body in your bathroom."

Ben blinked away the tears and then sniffled. "Yeah. Okay."

Hank grabbed Ben's elbow. "Dead body?"

Ben shook his head. "The bastard had a gun to her head."

"Don't say another word until you get a lawyer," Millie said.

"It's fine. I have nothing to hide."

The nurse in pink scrubs leaned out the door. "Mr. Solmer?"

"Yeah, I'm here." Ben met her at the door with Millie and Hank. "How is she?"

"Between the gunshot wound on her shoulder and hemorrhaging during birth, Ms. Kearny's lost a lot of blood." Her palm slid over his arm. "Once the doctor's finished, he'll be out to discuss everything with you. In the meantime, send her prayers."

"What about my son?" he asked, barely able to speak.

The nurse smiled. "The baby is doing just fine. He's in NICU due to patches of peeling skin, which is to be expected at his gestation. Once he passes his heart and respiratory assessment, he'll be ready for visitors. I promise I'll come and get you the moment they're done."

Ben sat down in a chair along the wall. Head in his hands, he cried. This was all a nightmare he wished he could wake up from.

Millie sat beside him. As much as he wanted to be alone, her gentle hand on his back was comforting. For a long while he stayed in this position, ignoring everyone around him, listening for his name to be called.

Familiar voices filled the waiting room. "Where is she? Where's Zoe?"

Renji and Drema and Deputy Fred stood near the desk. There were three others he didn't recognize, but he was sure they were friends of Zoe's.

He stood, catching Renji's worried gaze. Other anxious eyes followed as he met them near the small coffee stand beside the nurse's station.

Drema stared, eyes wide. In all the chaos and worry, Ben had forgotten about the blood staining his shirt and body. His hands were covered in it.

"How's my girl?" Renji asked.

"She's still in surgery." Ben turned his tired gaze on Renji. "She's lost a lot of blood."

Renji's eyes watered. "I heard what happened."

"I wasn't there to protect her from him. I wasn't fucking there." Ben ground his teeth. Not wanting them to see him cry, he lowered his gaze to the floor and concentrated on controlling his emotions. "I failed her again, Renji."

"No way. You saved her life, man," Renji said. "The bastard's been stalking her for a long time. I should've done something about it the moment I found out he was released from prison."

Ben didn't deserve anyone's gratitude. If Zoe died, he'd never forgive himself.

Sergeant Wilkins stood patiently near the window. Ben wiped his eyes and then glanced at Fred. "Mind coming with me to give a statement?"

"Sure thing," Fred said with a nod.

He followed Fred and Wilkins into the hall. It was the first time he got a good look at the blood on his clothes. Zoe's blood. Nicholas's. Red splatters stretched down the lengths of his arms to his stained hands.

"All right, son," Wilkins said. "Tell me exactly what happened."

Ben pinched the crease between his eyes. "When I arrived at Zoe's apartment, I noticed the police car outside. I stopped to tell the officer I was there to see Zoe but found him unconscious. I dialed 911 and told them there was an intruder in Zoe's apartment."

Wilkins glanced at his notebook. "You went inside then."

"Yes."

"You knew the attacker?"

"Her ex-boyfriend. Nicholas." Ben clenched his jaw. "I couldn't let him hurt her again."

"There was a history of physical abuse?"

"Yes." Ben palmed his forehead. He glanced at Fred, who gave him a short nod. "He'd also raped her."

"Recently?"

"About three years ago. He went to prison because of it. When he got out, he wouldn't leave her alone."

"He stalked her."

"Yeah."

Wilkins jotted down more in his notebook and then lowered his arms to his sides. "So you went inside the apartment, had a struggle with the assailant, and then you shot him in the head?"

"It was his gun. He was about to kill her. I had to do something."

Ben's muscles tensed. The sick feeling in his gut intensified. The way the cop spoke made Ben sound like he'd purposely shot Nicholas.

Ben leaned back against the wall and folded his arms across his chest. The struggle with Nicholas replayed in his mind. Ben had beat the guy down, but the bastard wouldn't lose consciousness.

If Ben had thought of any other way to end the fight, he'd have taken it. Now he was torn between guilt and worry. But, deep down was immense relief Zoe would never have to deal with Nicholas again.

"The door was unlocked. I heard voices coming from the bathroom. When I got there, I found Nicholas pointing the gun at her head. He told her she had to die."

Ben switched his stance to the other foot. Seeing the woman he loved on the floor with the gun to her head, he'd never been more frightened in his life. He hadn't cared what happened to him or if he'd died to save her, as long as she and his son was safe.

"Go on, son," Wilkins said in a reassuring voice.

Ben cleared his throat. "I lunged for him. Grabbed his arms and shoved. The gun went off as I wrestled him to the floor. I fought to get the gun away from him, but he just kept pointing it at her. He was going to kill her. The only thing I could do to stop him was redirect his aim to his chin and help him pull the trigger."

Wilkins stuffed his notebook in the pocket of his brown slacks. "We'll need to bag your clothes for evidence."

"I've got a change of clothes in the car," Ben replied.

"I'll get one of the nurses to let you use a room for a shower. Just come into the station in the morning and give a formal, detailed statement."

Ben nodded. "Yes, sir."

"My prayers to your wife and son for a full recovery."

Ben shook his hand. "Thanks."

As Wilkins left, Fred stepped into his spot. "You know, I was Nicholas's arresting officer. Several of the girls he'd dated before Zoe had suffered fractures and broken bones. The guy was a vicious son of a bitch."

"Then why'd he only get two years?"

"Zoe was the only one who'd press charges. The other girls were too scared to testify." Fred lowered his voice. "Zoe called me right after the rape. When I found her, she was huddled in the corner of her room. Her gown was ripped and bloodstained. She had bruises on her back and face. Scratch marks on her legs and sides." Fred shook his head. "I'll tell you, if I hadn't been a cop back then, I'd have put a bullet in his head myself."

Ben clenched his jaw and tightened his fists. To hear this version, the reality of what she'd gone through, tore him up inside.

"Sorry," Fred continued. "Detailed story is a bit rough to hear. But I wanted you to understand, what you did tonight was a good thing. You saved her life."

"I didn't have a choice."

"Maybe not. But you also helped all those other women he'd hurt, and probably saved lives he may have ruined in the future."

Ben ground his teeth so hard it almost hurt. "I know this sounds bad, Fred, but I'd do it again. I'd make the guy suffer before putting him out of his fucking misery."

"Come on. Let's go find you a room."

After Ben washed up and changed into a black T-shirt and jeans, the door to the emergency room opened. Ben turned his tired eyes to the doctor stepping across the floor beside the nurse who'd kept Ben up to date on what was happening.

Everyone in the room stood as Ben darted from the chair.

The doctor shook Ben's hand. "Dr. Prius," he said in a gentle tone. "I performed surgery on Ms. Kearny."

"Ben Solmer." Ben folded his arms over his chest. "How is she?"

"Ms. Kearny made it through surgery, but not without complications."

"Complications?" Millie asked.

"I had a difficult time stopping the hemorrhaging. Her heart stopped twice during the blood transfusion. But once I found the tear and stitched her up, the bleeding stopped, and she stabilized. She's one heck of a fighter."

"Oh gosh," Millie said in tears.

Hank put his arm around her and held her close. "Is she going to be all right?"

"Unfortunately, Ms. Kearny suffered trauma to the head. She has swelling of the brain. We've put her in a medically induced coma until the swelling subsides."

"Coma?" Ben's heart dived. Whispers went around the group.

Renji blew a short breath. "How long will that take?"

"I really can't say," Dr. Prius replied. "It's too soon to detect how much brain damage there is, if there is any. Since this is injury related, the only thing we can do is monitor her closely and keep her medicated until the swelling goes down. Whether the coma is temporary or permanent is completely up to how well her body recovers."

"What are you saying?" Millie asked. "She might never wake up?"

"It's possible. It could be days. Weeks. If there's permanent damage, she could remain on life support indefinitely."

Ben strode to the window. Hands over his face, he

sat in a chair. Dr. Prius sat beside him.

"You're the father of the child?"

Unable to find his voice, Ben whispered, "Yeah."

"I hear he's passed his tests with flying colors," he said in a gentle tone. "If you're ready, I'll have Ingrid escort you back to NICU."

"That'd be great." Finally, a little light in all this darkness.

"If it's any consolation, Ms. Kearny pulled through the tough part. She's a fighter, Mr. Solmer. Have faith."

"Thanks, Dr. Prius."

Ben followed the nurse out the double doors and into the hall. She led him into another wing of the hospital to another set of doors. The sign hanging on the wall read NEONATAL INTENSIVE CARE UNIT. The surreal sensation washed over him again as he walked into a small room.

After he slid a gown over his clothes and washed his hands, the nurse took him into another, larger room. He strode past dozens of incubators. Monitors chimed. Babies so tiny he could fit them in the palm of his hand were in each enclosed crib. It was sad and yet reassuring. If these children could survive at such a minuscule weight, his baby would be just fine.

"Here's the adorable little guy," the nurse said, stopping at the first incubator in the last row.

Ben peered through the glass at the pale-skinned body. Black tufts of hair stuck up on top of his head. He waved his tiny arms and legs as he yawned wide.

"He looks just like you," the nurse whispered. She wrapped the baby up in a white-and-blue blanket. Ben's heart pounded as she carefully placed his son in his arms.

Tears welled in his eyes. This was the proudest moment of his life. Nothing would ever compare. Absolutely nothing.

"Have you decided on a name yet?"

"Not yet." Ben pressed his lips to the baby's temple. "Until Mom wakes, I'll just call him my wee one." He smiled at his son then whispered, "Score one for the humans."

Chapter Thirty-Seven

Everyone told him to have faith. Ben hoped when Zoe woke, she'd realize she wanted to be with him. He'd whisk her away to Denver. He'd ask her to marry him and she'd accept. Then they'd live happily ever after.

He'd spent two weeks sitting beside her in her room listening to the monitor's continuous beep. The doctor had taken her off the medication keeping her asleep. That was five days ago. She still hadn't woken up.

He'd prayed she'd open her beautiful eyes. He'd told her to squeeze his hand to let him know she could hear him, but there was always nothing.

Just like now.

"Our little guy's staying with Millie right now," he said in a low voice. "I'm comfortable with him. Getting in as much practice as I can before you come home. I get to feed him his bottle. I'm even changing diapers, if you can believe that."

He drew in a breath. The nurse had said Zoe would hear him, but it just felt weird. Frustrating. It hurt to want her response and not get it. If only her eyes would open. If only she'd squeeze his hand.

"I splurged last week and bought you and the baby a new MINI Clubman for your birthday." He blinked back tears. "I know how much you loved the old car, but the Clubman's a better, bigger version of it. It's blue. The gray seats match our baby's car seat. God, Zoe. I don't even know his name."

He sighed. "So…Sheron got him a new mobile. It's pretty cool. Has all these colorful hot rods dangling from a gear. Not sure he likes it, though. The music's a little loud."

He shook his head, trying to find something else to say. He'd already told her everything he could think of.

"I wrote a song." He blurted out the words he'd said yesterday. "I'll play it for you when you get home. So, come on, pumpkin. I know you can hear me. Just open your eyes so I can take you home. Squeeze my hand and let me know you're coming back." Ben pressed his lips to her wrist. "Please, Zoe. Come back to me."

He bowed his head, temple against her hand, concentrating on her movement. Nothing. This was ridiculous. Sitting here talking to her was useless. Maybe if he grabbed her shoulders and shook her, she'd wake. Maybe if he shouted her name in her face, it'd scare her into opening her eyes.

"I love you, Zoe." He stood, gritting his teeth. "Do you hear me? Wake up." He leaned close. "Open your eyes. Please."

He backed to the recliner along the wall. Frustrated, angry, he sat on the soft blue cushion. He shrugged off his jacket. The footrest wouldn't come out, so he tossed his legs over the armrest, covered his chest with his jacket, and then leaned back.

He stared at Zoe lying still, almost lifeless on the bed. Her monitors sang the usual song, recording her heartbeat. Heartbroken, Ben closed his tearing eyes and listened until he fell asleep.

****

Little voices called her name. "*Zoe. Wake up.*"

Children laughed and played chanting games—*the ABCs*. They sang a song about a boat and another about stars in the sky. As she opened her eyes and light rushed in, the voices faded into the sound of a steady beep.

It was hard to focus on anything with this blinding light. Vision blurred, body immobile, she opened her mouth to call for help. Nothing came out but a puff of air.

She drew in a deeper breath. Her chest hurt. The steady beep picked up into a series of chimes. The sound was loud in her ears. The light dimmed enough to see her surroundings.

"Hello," she managed to say. It was a slow, muffled call but oddly made her feel a little stronger.

She focused on the lump in the chair. Ben was here. He looked better than the last time she saw him. Much better. He'd changed his clothes. Cleaned himself up. Probably for the baby.

She gasped. *The baby*. She'd given birth to him earlier and had passed out before she could see him.

She held on to the rails of the bed and pulled. Her muscles were too weak. She couldn't sit up. What the heck was wrong?

"Ben." The sound of her scratchy voice deafened her.

He stirred. He didn't look very comfortable with his legs dangling over the armrest. Feet up and jacket covering his arms and chest, he was probably freezing. She shuddered. It was rather cold in here.

His head tilted to the side and then slowly slid down the vinyl material of the chair until it fell too far. His eyes opened then closed again.

"Ben," she called to him again. "I can't sit up."

He opened his eyes wide. "Zoe." He leaped from the chair. His jacket fell to the floor as he stumbled toward the bed. "You're awake." He repeatedly pressed the nurse's Call button on the side bar. He brushed her hair back with his palm and repeatedly kissed her temple.

"Wow," she said, her speech slow and slurred. "Happy to see me?"

"Oh, baby, you have no idea." He laughed as he sat beside her, hands holding hers. Eyes glittering with tears, he lifted her fingers to his lips. "I thought I'd lost you."

"Lost me?"

A short, stout woman in scrubs hurried through the door. Three more nurses rushed in after her with ear-to-ear smiles on their rounded faces. They hovered over her, playing with wires, checking the beeping box, and her IV.

"We are so glad to see you awake," the first woman said as she pressed two fingers against Zoe's wrist.

Zoe read the name on her badge. "Keila," she said groggily. "What's going on?"

"You're in ICU, dear."

"ICU?"

"I called for the doctor," Keila said as she rolled a thermometer across Zoe's forehead. "He'll be in here soon."

Zoe shuddered as she closed her eyes. *So tired.* A

memory flashed in her mind. Ben had lunged into the room right before the gun went off. She cried out. "Ben. Where are you?"

"I'm right here, baby."

She followed his voice to the foot of her bed. There he was, looking as if he hadn't seen her in weeks. Desperate to feel his arms around her, she pulled at the IV in her vein.

"Get me out of here."

"Ms. Kearny." The nurse grasped her arms above her elbows. "I'll have to restrain you if you try to remove your IV. I'll be right back with the doctor."

The room spun. The heavy weight on her chest when she breathed heightened as Ben walked around to her side.

She ran her hand over her flattened stomach. "The baby?"

He sat on the edge of the bed. "He's with Millie. He's doing great."

"I want to see him."

"You will. As soon as the doctor comes in to check on you."

Her eyes widened. "I don't know what's going on."

"Honey." He tucked a lock of her hair behind her ear. "You've been in here for a little while."

"What's a little while?"

He sighed. "Almost three weeks."

Three weeks? She closed her eyes. That was way too long to be asleep. Last thing she remembered, she was on the table. Ben had told her to push. The baby cried. Blood was everywhere. All over her. All over Ben. Nicholas pulled the trigger on his gun. Red streamed the walls in the bathroom and filled the garden tub at his house.

A gunshot exploded in her ears. A scream broke from her lips. She opened her eyes to find Ben holding her in his arms.

She cried against his chest. "I thought we were going to die."

"*Shhh*," he said softly. "It's over now. He can't hurt you anymore." He leaned back, eyes glistening in the low light of the room. "Nobody will ever hurt you again. I promise."

She shivered as he pulled a tissue from the box on the tray beside the bed. "What happened?"

"Don't worry about it right now." He dabbed her wet cheeks with the soft cloth. "Let's just get you well enough so I can take you home."

"Did they put him in jail?" She leaned back on the pillow. "He'll just get out and come after me again."

Ben inspected her bandaged shoulder. "He's dead, Zoe. I killed him."

The second gunshot. Ben had shielded her from seeing Nicholas's body. There must have been a lot of blood.

"Oh, Ben. I'm so sorry. You should never have—"

"—I did what I had to do, and I'd do it again. No apologies."

Thank God. Her nightmare was over. A wave of relief rushed over her. She breathed easier, as if the heavy weight had lifted. Now if only the pounding in her head would stop.

"My head hurts."

"You suffered a pretty bag gash." Ben swept his palm across her cheek. "You also feel a little warm."

He disappeared behind the bathroom door. The

faucet ran for a few seconds.

He returned with a wash cloth. His grease-stained hand brushed her hair back from her face. She closed her eyes as he pressed the cool cloth against her temple.

"Ben," she whispered.

"Yeah, Zoe."

She gazed up into his eyes. "You came to visit a day early."

A short grin spread across his shadowed face. "I wanted to surprise you with some good news. I meant to fly out the next day, but then, Renji called. So I caught the first flight out."

"He called about Nicholas?"

"Yeah." He sat on the edge of the bed.

"I'm glad he did. Otherwise, the baby and I might not be here." A chill shimmied up her spine. She didn't want to think about Nicholas right now. Or ever again. He was gone. She only hoped the nightmares would leave with him. "What's your good news?"

"I offered my share of the shop to Doogen. I also put my house up for sale."

She drew a quick breath. "You mean—"

"Yeah." He grinned. "Nothing's more important to me than you and our son. So, I've decided to move here."

Goosebumps spread over her skin. She'd prayed for so long he'd decide to take this step. But now...after what happened at the apartment, after all the bad that'd happened in this town, she didn't want to be here anymore.

"I never got to see the trees bloom behind your house."

"We can plant a tree behind our new place."

She shook her head. "I've had vivid nightmares lately. Nicholas is chasing me. I'm running toward your house in Denver. I can see the trees' blossoms falling to the ground like pink snowflakes. And I know if I can reach them, I'll be safe. No one can hurt me. *He* can't hurt me. Sometimes I make it. Sometimes I don't. But when I get there, I'm safe and…happy."

He set the washcloth on the stand beside the bed. "Your nightmares will go away in time."

"I don't want to live here anymore." She took hold of his hand. "I want to be with you in Denver."

He gazed into her eyes. "Honey. You just went through a traumatizing ordeal. Maybe you need more time to think about this."

"I've given this months of thought." She shivered. "Unless you've sold the house."

"No." He grinned as he palmed her cheek. "I was going back next week to sign the shop over to Doogen and start packing."

"Call Doogen and cancel. Let's be together in Denver."

"Are you sure? I mean, if there's any doubt in your mind—"

"Not a shred of doubt. So, just say yes, Ben."

"Yes, Ben." He kissed her lips. "So, love of my life, I have something for you." He reached into his jeans pocket and pulled out a tiny gray box. He fumbled the box in his hand, and then placed it on her chest.

The hairs on her arms stood. "What's this?"

"Open it."

As he held the bottom of the box, she pulled the top open. Tears blurred her vision of the most beautiful diamond ring she'd ever seen.

"When I saw you lying on the bathroom floor, it scared the hell out of me, put everything in perspective. I've been miserable without you permanently in my life. All I care about is you. Zoe, I can't imagine my life without you."

"Ben," she said as he lifted the ring from the box.

He gathered her hands in his. "Zoe Kearny. Will you marry me?"

"Yes." Tears streamed her cheeks. "More than ever, yes, I will marry you."

A grin crept across his face as he slid the ring on her finger. "I love you, Mrs. Solmer."

"And I love you too."

Chapter Thirty-Eight

Zoe stood in the middle of the driveway she'd parked the packed Jeep in. After two more weeks of getting poked and prodded in the hospital, she'd finally made it to Denver.

Ben stepped out of the house and hurried down the driveway. Zoe's heart leaped to her throat. He was handsome in khakis and a black shirt under his navy-blue jacket. He'd shaved his face smooth. His hair, trimmed perfectly around his ears, those dark bangs stylishly sticking up, reminded her of their first meeting.

He caught her in his arms and held her tight before setting her on her feet again. "Zoe." He gazed into her eyes as he lifted his hands to her face. "Promise me you're really here to stay."

Butterflies danced in her stomach. "I'm here for as long as you'll have me."

"Forever, Zoe Solmer." He leaned his temple against hers. "It's about time."

Her body shuddered with excitement at the sound of her soon-to-be name. He parted his mouth over hers. His cool hands cupped her face as his tongue swept against hers.

"I so missed you," he whispered against her lips. "I'm sorry you had to drive yourself up here."

"You needed to take care of the shop." She smiled,

loving the way he caressed her face. "I'm really happy to hear Doogen and Sheron ran off to get married."

"They're good for each other. Like us." White snowflakes caught in his dark brows and dusted his midnight hair. He was so handsome. "So, are you ready to go in, Missus?"

"Indeed, I am, Husband."

"Good." A grin crept across his face. "I can't wait to see our wee one. It's been too long."

A whirlwind of excitement rushed over her. She opened the back door. She picked up the baby and cradled him in her arms.

Ben gazed down at his son. "I have missed my little guy."

Zoe smiled. "You're going to be such a great dad."

"So much faith in me," he said, wiping tears with the back of his hand. "I still can't believe this is happening."

"Want to hold him?"

"Yes."

She carefully placed the baby in his arms and then stepped back. The bond between father and son warmed her heart.

"Hey, my little wee one." Ben kissed his forehead. "Benjamin Chase Solmer."

Zoe placed her palm on Ben's arm and straightened the blanket over the baby. "Just don't call him Junior."

He laid his son in the car seat and faced her. "Okay, my beautiful wife. I've been waiting for you to get here to do this."

He stomped out into the snow. With a quick jerk of his arms, he pulled the FOR SALE sign up, and then tossed it across the yard. It immediately sank into the white fluff.

He brushed his hands on his pant legs and returned to her side. He draped his arm around her shoulders, turned her toward the house, and then flashed his amazing smile she loved. "Welcome home, Mrs. Solmer."

Epilogue

Sonya stood near the entrance of the lighthouse with her baby in her arms. As the mothership appeared on the horizon, the child wailed. The vessel's dark gray hull stretched across the sky and turned the day to dusk. Hundreds of tiny ships emerged from its belly and swooped down over the ocean. Long gangling purple limbs protruded from each one as they took positions in small groups along the beach and turned in circles, taunting them to attack.

Of all places in the world, the evil aliens had made their last stand on her beach next to her lighthouse. It didn't make one lick of sense why they'd chosen this spot unless they knew how many of them they'd defeated. Maybe Soljer had become such a threat they'd sought out to destroy him.

Whatever the case, this was it—the final fight. This could be the beginning of a new age without the aliens. Or it could be the end of everything they'd built together. The lighthouse. The extended room on the side of the building they'd added for the baby. They'd even reconstructed the ice cream shop in the nearby parking lot and had planned on taking their wee one there when he was old enough to eat.

But no. The darned aliens had to invade her home, *again*, and on the day after she'd had her son. Sonya swallowed apprehension. This was such a disaster.

"It'll be okay," Soljer said, his deep tone sending a chill through her. Those deep green eyes made her fears melt away. He stood beside her, gun in one hand, sword in the other. His long dark hair waved in the breeze as he readied his stance for battle. "We'll do this together."

"I know." Goosebumps spread over her skin. She tightened her hold on her wee one who'd hushed as if he too knew evil threatened their world. She placed him in the carrier on her back, straightened her new dark green robe, and then conjured a fireball in her hands. "No way are the bad guys going to take my family down. Not today. Not ever."

"We'll all make sure of that," a familiar voice said behind her.

As Sonya turned to greet her friend, a message popped up in front of her. *Brenji would like to couple.*

She groaned. "Seriously?" Aliens threatened their very existence and Brenji cracked jokes. The man was relentless. Ever since he'd reached the level to gain Coupling mode, he'd sent her offers, but only when they played together which didn't happen often due to time sync.

Dreamer walked beside Brenji up the beach. A beautiful white glow surrounded her voluptuous body. Her yellow dress barely contained her huge breasts that bounced with every step she took until they reached the lighthouse.

Brenji's outfit didn't match at all. In lime green pants and a purple shirt, he looked a little like a clown. The bright red bandana around his head didn't quite work either, but Brenji didn't care. He was overflowing with muscle. And, as a tank, was quite able to take on four or five aliens at a time.

Sonya declined Brenji's offer as she always did. "I'm glad you two made it. This is going to be one heck of a fight. We definitely need a healer and tank for this."

"Wouldn't miss the opportunity to kick alien ass for anything." Brenji stepped in beside Soljer. "Hey man. How's it going?"

"Couldn't be better." Soljer gave Sonya a quick wink then turned his attention on Brenji. "How about yourself?"

"Tired. Baby Cassie doesn't sleep very well at night."

"I feel your pain." Soljer gave a short nod. "Little Ben didn't start sleeping all night until he turned six months old."

"Great." Brenji sighed. "That means I have four more months of falling asleep at my office desk."

"You own a coffee shop."

"Ha. All the caffeine in the world won't help. I need sleep. Just one night of uninterrupted Z's. You know, a few hours' nap would be fine too." Brenji unsheathed his giant axe. He sighed as he easily propped the weapon up on his shoulder. "But…I wouldn't give up being a dad for anything. My girls are my world. If I have to lose sleep for a while, then so be it."

Soljer turned toward Sonya. "I know exactly how you feel."

Sonya blew him a kiss. She'd ask him to couple if nobody was around and if aliens hadn't taken over the beach. But here they were, about to jump into one of the toughest fights they'd ever had to face.

"Everyone ready?" Brenji asked as he stepped toward the first group of aliens.

Sonya conjured another fireball between her palms. "Ready."

Soljer took aim. "Let's do this."

Dreamer's glow intensified. "I'll keep everyone healed."

Brenji gave a short nod. "All right then. Here we go."

Sonya's muscles tensed. Adrenaline pumped through her veins. Whether she lived or died and had to run a million miles from the graveyard back to her body, didn't matter as long as they were together. They were family, and nothing could take that away. Not even these evil little aliens who had no idea what they were in store for.

A word about the author…

Kira Hillins found inspiration to write when she moved to a small town located on the coast of Oregon. She now resides in the eastern U.S. with her husband, two daughters, and a spoiled Siberian Husky.

She continues to write to entertain her readers and find a sense of success within herself.

https://www.kirahillins.com

Thank you for purchasing
this publication of The Wild Rose Press, Inc.

For questions or more information
contact us at
info@thewildrosepress.com.

The Wild Rose Press, Inc.
www.thewildrosepress.com

To visit with authors of
The Wild Rose Press, Inc.
join our yahoo loop at
http://groups.yahoo.com/group/thewildrosepress/